LANDING BY
MOONLIGHT

A NOVEL OF WW II

NEW YORK TIMES & *USA TODAY* BESTSELLING AUTHOR

CIJI WARE

Cover design 2019 by BespokeBookCovers.com
Cover designer: Peter O'Connor
Formatting: Author E.M.S.
Proofreader: Emilee Bowling, Perfect Pages Final Proofing Services

Print edition ISBN: 978-0-9990773-2-0
e-Book edition ISBN: 978-0-9990773-1-3

Additional Library of Congress Cataloging-in-Publication Data available upon request.

1. Fiction, 2. World War 2—Fiction, 3. American women secret agents—Fiction, 4. Women spies in WW 2—Fiction, 5.British spies—Fiction, 6. American spies—Fiction, 7. OSS, SOE, CIA, MI6 intelligence agencies—Fiction, 8. Female secret agent—Fiction, 9. Spy schools and spy-craft training in WW 2, 10. 20th century fiction, 11. Washington D.C. in WW 2, 12. French Riviera in WW 2, 13. 20th c. OSS, SOE, CIA, MI6 intelligence agencies, 14. Female spies in WW 2, 15. Churchill's Secret Agents, 16. Operation Dragoon, 17. Spies in WW2, 18. France in WW2, 19. French Resistance

e-Book Edition © October 2019; Print Edition © October 2019

Published by Lion's Paw Publishing, a division of Life Events Media LLC, 1001 Bridgeway, Ste. J-224, Sausalito, CA 94965.

Life Events Library and the Lion's Paw Publishing colophon are registered trademarks of Life Events Media LLC. All rights reserved.

For information contact: www.cijiware.com

PRAISE FOR CIJI WARE'S FICTION

"Ware once again proves she can weave fact and fiction to create an entertaining and harmonious whole." – *Publishers Weekly*

"Vibrant and exciting…" – *Literary Times*

"A story so fascinating it should come with a warning—do not start unless you want to be up all night." – *Romantic Times*

"A mesmerizing blend of sizzling romance, love, and honor…Ciji Ware has written an unforgettable tale." – *The Burton Report*

"A romantic tale of intrigue…A compelling storyline and fascinating characters." – *The Natchez Democrat*

"Ingenious, entertaining, and utterly romantic…A terrific read." – Jane Heller, *New York Times & USA Today* bestselling author

"Oozes magic and romance…I loved it!" – Barbara Freethy, *#1 New York Times bestselling author*

"Fiction at its finest. Beautifully written." – *Libby's Library News*

"Thoroughly engaging." – *Booklist*

ALSO BY CIJI WARE

Historical Novels
Island of the Swans
Wicked Company
A Race to Splendor

"Time-Slip" Historical Novels
A Cottage by the Sea
Midnight on Julia Street
A Light on the Veranda

Contemporary Novels
That Summer in Cornwall
That Autumn in Edinburgh
That Winter in Venice
That Spring in Paris

Contemporary Novellas
Ring of Truth: *The Ring of Kerry Hannigan*

Nonfiction
Rightsizing Your Life
Joint Custody After Divorce

Find all of Ciji's books at www.cijiware.com.

DEDICATION

Dedicated to the heroic American women secret agents who joined British and French intelligence agencies—some prior to the United States entering World War II—and most especially:

Josephine Baker
Virginia Hall
Amy Elizabeth "Betty" Thorpe Pack
Elizabeth Devereaux Rochester Reynolds

FRANCE UNDER GERMAN OCCUPATION

D-Day - June 6, 1944 invasion: Normandy Beaches

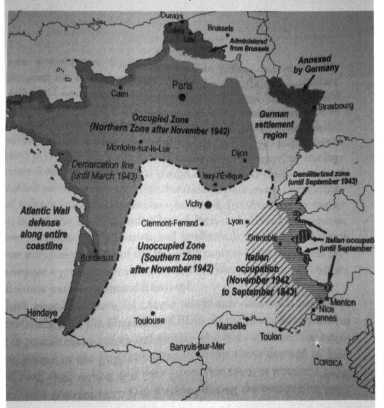

Dunkirk

Brussels

Calais
Lille

Administered from Brussels

Annexed by Germany

Paris

Caen

Brest

Strasbourg

German settlement region

Occupied Zone
(Northern Zone after November 1942)

Montoire-sur-le-Loir

Dijon

Demarcation line (until March 1943)

Issy-l'Évêque

Demilitarized zone (until September 1943)

Vichy

Atlantic Wall defense along entire coastline

Clermont-Ferrand

Lyon

Grenoble

Italian occupation (until September

Bordeaux

Unoccupied Zone
(Southern Zone after November 1942)

Italian occupation (November 1942 to September 1943)

Menton
Nice
Cannes

Hendaye

Toulouse

Marseille

Toulon

Banyuls-sur-Mer

CORSICA

D-Day/2 - August 15, 1944 invasion: Toulon - Nice

LIST OF CHARACTERS

Note: Check out the author's research photos on Pinterest at http://www.pinterest.com/cijiware/landing-by-moonlight-research-photos/

FICTIONAL CHARACTERS

Catherine Farnsworth Cahill Thornton/"Colette Durand" – American secret agent with the OSS and SOE wartime intelligence agencies

Henri Leblanc / "Claude Foret" – French diplomat; later SOE secret agent

Alice Leblanc – his wife; an American lumber heiress

Sean Eisenhower / "Guy de Bruyn" – American secret agent with SOE; later OSS/CIA

Gladys Farnsworth Cahill – Catherine's mother; American mining heiress

Colonel Amory Cahill – Catherine's late father, U.S. Marine embassy security officer

Annabelle Arlington – Woman's Page editor & society columnist, Washington D.C.

Lieutenant Peter Farley – U.S. Navy intelligence officer

Admiral Enzo Moretti – Italian envoy to the United States

André Didereaux – French national, guard at the (Vichy) French embassy, Wash. D.C.

Constance "Viv" Vivier Clarke / "Elizabeth" – American ambulance driver in Paris; later SOE secret agent

Remy Poché – Restaurant owner; French Resistance in Villefranche-sur-Mer

Jules and Eve Menton – French Resistance; olive farmers above Villefranche-sur-Mer

Tamara Polakov – a Jewish child in the South of France

Lucien Barteau / "Gilbert" – French circus stunt pilot; later SOE's Air Operations Officer

Alphonse Moreau – French Resistance member; chief pressman, Leblanc Printing, Paris

Alain Chapelle – French Resistance member; nephew of Alphonse Moreau

Gaston Peppard – Leblanc Printing, Paris; Moreau's assistant

Commandant Erik Heinrich – German SS Officer in Paris, Second Arrondissement

Captain Gunter Wintermuden – German SS officer in Nice, France

Guard Enoch Helgard – German SS officer in Nice, France

Josef Gumbel – SS officer in charge of *résistants* incarcerated in Nice, France

Shirley Newton-Elkington – records secretary for missing agents, SOE

HISTORICAL FIGURES (DEPICTED FICTIONALLY)

William J. "Wild Bill" Donovan – Director of the OSS (Office of Strategic Services)

William S. Stephenson – Canadian, Director, BSC (British Security Coordination)

J. Edgar Hoover – Director of the Federal Bureau of Investigation

Major John Pepper – BSC working with Stephenson in the U.S.

Colonel Maurice Buckmaster – French Section, SOE (Special Operations Executive)

Vera Atkins – Buckmaster's deputy, SOE in London

André Marsac – French Resistance member, Paris

Peter Churchill / "Raoul"– British SOE network leader, S. France & *Haute Savoie*

Odette Samson / "Lise" – French SOE secret agent

Francis Cammaerts / "Roger" – British SOE secret agent; network leader

Hans Josef Kieffer – Gestapo, Head of Counterintelligence, 84 Avenue Foch, Paris

Franklin D. Roosevelt – President of the United States

Winston Churchill – Prime Minister of Great Britain

Charles de Gaulle – led Free French Resistance against Nazi Germany, WW II

General Dwight D. Eisenhower – Supreme Allied Commander, WW II

PART I
CHAPTER 1

June 1942

"Is the dog drugged yet?" she whispered.

"Yes," he whispered back in English, although half the time he spoke to his accomplice in his native French. "Out cold, under the desk downstairs."

"We won't have killed him, will we?"

"Shouldn't have," came the reply.

"André's conked out too, then?"

Henri Leblanc could hear the excitement threading through Catherine's low-pitched, breathy voice, a soft, soothing sound that had so attracted him from the first time they'd met in this very building in the heart of the district known as Washington D.C.'s Embassy Row.

"We won't hear anything out of the guard—at least until dawn breaks," he assured her.

With a gesture, Catherine indicated they should advance from the public reception area of the French embassy, deep in shadow at 2:00 a.m., toward their next destination, down a long corridor in the converted mansion.

Never far from Henri's thoughts was the memory of the incredible day he'd first encountered Catherine Farnsworth Cahill Thornton, the Farnsworth part of her name having particular resonance given the legendary influence of her Minnesota mining family in the halls of Congress. Observing her slim figure in the embassy's dark hallway, it struck Henri that meeting Catherine nine months before the Japanese attack on Pearl Harbor was one of those moments that had changed his life. America was in the war now, a leading member of the Allies, rendering Leblanc's world even more chaotic, as it was for all French citizens wherever they might be marooned.

The embassy in the United States capital where Henri had worked as press attaché for six years had been turned upside down when Germany invaded France in June of 1940 and the French Vichy contingent took over. The new ambassador, sympathetic with his Nazi overlords, had asserted firm control at this overseas outpost. Worse yet, the country's leaders had committed their future to an elderly authoritarian, the French General Philippe Pétain.

On this late sultry night in June, the halls and offices of the French chancery were absent the normal daytime bustle. In fact, the entire building was deserted except for three humans and a guard dog whose water bowl had been secretly laced with Nembutal.

Following behind Catherine, Henri moved steadily down the corridor near the press office where he routinely spent his working hours and considered what it had been like this past year to toil there every day. He felt a surge of anger each time he faced the reality that the defeated French government had given up its sovereignty in the wake of the murderous German assault.

Catherine's whisper startled Henri out of his gloomy reverie.

"The safe is in that last room on the right, yes?"

Henri peered down the dim hallway in the direction of the locked code room. The spacious, former private home with its pillared, wrap-around front porch was set back from Wyoming Avenue, a thoroughfare with many grand houses, all silent at this late hour.

"Yes. The room at the right at the end of the hall."

Henri marveled at the surprising ease with which he and the American woman posing as a newspaper reporter for a right-wing D.C. daily had rendered the embassy's night watchman unconscious.

Their bold action this night had been preceded by a month of jovial byplay when the pair posed as clandestine lovers in search of a discreet trysting place where they could meet a few times a week. The friendly—but now insensible—André currently was slumped in his chair, mouth slightly open, snoring peacefully in his basement lair. To their relief, the guard had turned out to be only too happy to accept nightly bribes of champagne, chocolates, or cartons of American cigarettes and had eagerly quaffed numerous glasses of bubbly earlier that evening, passing out with gratifying rapidity.

Henri had a sudden, disturbing thought. Was *he*—a former French military officer and previously loyal French diplomat—accepting a bribe, just like André? Even more shocking, he was helping to steal copies of highly secret French naval ciphers, codes that were a crucial part of the Vichy government's encrypted system of communication with their German masters. On some base level was he, a French patriot to his bones, doing this in return for enjoying the alluring charms of his American partner in crime?

The thought was repugnant to a man who'd flown numerous risky sorties for France in the Great War. But was it true, nonetheless?

Pushing such unpleasant notions aside, Henri touched Catherine's sleeve, declaring softly as if checking off a list, "Step one accomplished: getting after-hours access to the embassy and ensuring that the champagne would do its job."

"*D'accord*," Catherine murmured, flashing him her lovely smile.

He was amazed that the calculated persona he'd agreed to assume as Catherine's supposed lover had so swiftly transitioned into reality. Catherine Thornton was unlike any woman he'd ever known. He considered himself a worldly man of wide experience and was wise enough to know that his life had taken a highly dangerous turn both personally and professionally.

Interrupting his jumbled musings, Catherine whispered, "The champagne had its effect, for sure." Her eyes alight with mischief, she added, "But don't you agree that the Nembutal I slipped into André's glass and the dog's bowl certainly helped?"

The trace of a grin, along with her delicate features, startlingly green eyes, and a halo of amber-blonde hair softened the message that she was actually the brains of this operation tonight. After all, hadn't *she* recruited *him* to switch allegiances? Or was it all just a matter of serendipity? Fate? Had their coupling merely been magnetic forces in the disordered world of war that had drawn them inexorably together?

Catherine halted near the door to the ambassador's empty office and inclined her head in the direction of the stairwell that led to the basement.

"Now that those two downstairs are neutralized," she murmured, "I hope to God we'll have enough time to do the job."

Henri stared down at her slender figure, distracted, as always, by the sultry sound of her voice in a distinctive register even Greta Garbo would envy. Her speech was warm, inviting, full of empathy and understanding for a man in an unsatisfactory marriage, tortured by desperate circumstances over which he had no control.

Catherine was looking at him expectantly, forcing his thoughts back to the task at hand in this pre-dawn hour in June.

"Conservatively, I imagine that we have no more than two and a half hours."

"Good grief!" Catherine exclaimed, glancing at her wristwatch encrusted with tiny diamonds around its face. She swiftly lowered her voice. "I thought that dose would give us at least four hours."

"Yes, but the nightly cleaning crew comes in anytime between four and five, so we dare not take that long. We have to move fast, just in case they show up early."

She cast him a measured look. "Well, then, we'd better get cracking," she replied, her Minnesota roots seeping through her East Coast polish.

"*Cracking*," Henri replied, deadpan, "would seem to be the operative word tonight—given that antique safe in the code room."

Catherine led them a few more steps down the hallway before she abruptly halted for a second time and turned around, rewarding him with a sudden, broad smile. For the operation this night, she was dressed smartly in cat burglar attire: black, pleated gabardine trousers and a turtleneck sweater. She took a step toward him, rose on tiptoe, and cupped her gloved hands on either side of his face. She hesitated only a moment before kissing him full on the lips.

Vintage Catherine, he thought distractedly. A secret agent willing to take outrageous risks, daring fate in her craving for physical stimulation in the face of high-stakes danger. It was a character trait he'd observed before and wondered at its origins.

"*Bonne chance* to us both, then, *mon amour.*" Her bilingual words were laced with the heavenly taste of the very pricey bottle of *Veuve Clicquot* they'd shared earlier with the hapless André, although after the first glass of champagne, the guard's portion had had that extra *something* slipped into it. "The sooner we're done with this assignment tonight, the sooner…"

She failed to complete her sentence, but rather pushed her trim pelvis suggestively against his mid-section and was rewarded with evidence of an immediate arousal. She could do that to him any time she pleased, Henri thought, with a stab of worry. He'd never known anyone like her. She was utterly irresistible. His feeble protest was more a groan than an admonishment.

"Now, none of *that*," he protested in hushed tones. "You said it yourself: We've got to get cracking."

"None of what?" she teased as he shifted his weight against her smaller frame to take full advantage of the friction mounting between them.

"Playing Agent Fifi at a time like this," he replied, making an oblique spy-craft reference to the practice of using women agents to prompt men to reveal secrets they shouldn't.

She pulled away, gazing deeply into his eyes. "A honeytrap, am I?"

Was she offended by his remark? He'd never found it easy to read her thoughts. There was so much about her past he did not know nor understand. What had drawn her to this perilous life? What had triggered her decision not to remain with her English husband posted to Chile? Why didn't she exhibit the conventional female desires to be a mother and loyal wife to her distinguished spouse? Who was Catherine Thornton *really*?

"*Ah, cher* Henri,*"* she said, switching to French, her voice resonating in the low tone she had of speaking that was as much an aphrodisiac as a plate full of oysters. Her confident, seductive manner reflected the fearless, privileged thirty-two-year-old American she was, a young woman who spoke three languages without the trace of an accent in any of them. "*Mon ange, ce soir je suis 'Mademoiselle Colette Durand.'"*

"And for this assignment, my angel," he said, parroting her words back to her in English, "your code name, Colette Durand, suits you perfectly."

"*Oui*," she shot back, flashing him a pleased expression. She took his gloved hand in hers and squeezed it firmly, guiding him the last steps to the threshold of a locked door on their right. They would leave no fingerprints—that is, if they didn't get caught mid break-in. If they did, Catherine's American government would probably step in to save her. His, on the other hand, would order him in front of a firing squad for being a traitor to, and enemy of, Vichy France and the German occupiers that were crushing his country.

"*Alors…Monsieur Attaché?*" she teased, gently mocking his title of French press representative. "Are you ready?"

"Yes," he answered, with a brief nod toward the code room. "And are you certain you can actually pick the lock on this door?"

He hadn't dared to try to steal the solitary key from the ambassador.

She pulled him close again. Sometimes he wondered if she didn't use sex as her preferred weapon of war. "Oh, yes," she sighed into his ear. "I've been well taught."

"*Mon Dieu,* let us pray you have."

He watched as she dug into her pocket and retrieved an implement given to her by their British handler, the mysterious Mr. Pepper, an army major from the British Security Coordination Office in New York, who had been guiding this adventure. Using the small tool, she swiftly and easily opened the door to the room where copies of the naval codes were kept.

"Step two…" Henri muttered admiringly, the enormity of their next task ahead sinking to the pit of his stomach. "But now to get past the locked closet door inside *this* room and then open the damn safe."

"Not a problem," she assured him, her soft laughter giving him a welcome dose of Dutch courage. "With any luck at all, right below that window over there awaits our friend, the Georgia Cracker—late of the State Penitentiary in Atlanta—who will break into this safe for us. It is Step three that will be awfully tricky, my darling Henri."

"Copying the codes and putting them back without anyone detecting the theft?"

"*Mais oui, mon amour…c'est ça.* But—"

She shot him an almost impish expression, as if filled with delight by the treachery they were about to commit.

"If we can just get those codes into Mr. Churchill's hands," she pronounced, barely above a whisper, "we'll help him *win* this blasted war!"

CHAPTER 2

Catherine had been confident that she not only could pick the lock on the outer door to the code room—which she certainly had done in good order—but that the second door to the closet where the safe stood in the corner, solid and seemingly impregnable, would pose no problem either. After all, she thought as she strode across the room that had probably once been a bedroom in the mansion on Wyoming Avenue, NW, she had practiced this part of the operation often enough under her handler's cool, assessing gaze.

She knelt on the carpeted floor, inserted her special implement into the lock, bit her lip, and gave the pick a delicate twist.

"Ha!" she chortled under her breath when the lock's tumblers made a satisfying *click*, and she swiftly turned the handle and pushed open the closet door. "*Voila!*" she declared, gesturing toward the large iron box in the corner that sported a bulbous knob imbedded at its center. "Behold the safe! I hope you're impressed."

She glanced over her shoulder where Henri stood, his tall figure looming behind her. From the moment they'd approached the entrance to the embassy, she'd sensed how nervous he was. She wagered that the French diplomat had summoned every bit of fortitude he possessed to mask his worry that one of them might botch this impossible assignment and end up on their way to prison—or worse.

"I am very impressed," he whispered, as she felt his hand lightly stroke her shoulder.

Henri Leblanc's physical affection for her, along with his sophistication, love of France, and his world-weary ways were attributes that had attracted her from the first moment they'd met. Like her, even if he were apprehensive of the consequences of their bold and daring commitment to obtaining the secret naval codes, he had proceeded with the plans anyway. Not once had he raised a single protest against any of the dangerous requirements of the task at hand. These qualities, and his handsome physique at age forty-three, had drawn her to him in a fashion she'd never before experienced with the many men who had wooed her.

Only her dashing father had shown the kind of courage and steadiness Henri Leblanc had exhibited. That, too, had been part of Henri's attraction. Of course, she couldn't deny that her late father's attentions to his only child had been painfully sporadic since Colonel Cahill's career had caused him to be physically absent most of her life. Henri, on the other hand, had been by her side from the day they'd met—so much so, she was amazed his American wife, Alice, had never seemed the wiser.

Catherine slipped the lock pick into her pocket, rose to her feet, and gazed at her accomplice. For a split second, she had a vision of how outraged the formidable Gladys Farnsworth Cahill would be if she knew the secret life her grown daughter had been living since returning to Washington after abandoning her husband at his current posting.

Catherine knew that somewhere in her file with the Brits were notes listing her specialty: "Mrs. Thornton, an American of means and a British diplomat's wife, is highly skilled at obtaining information from powerful, important men by means of her marked intelligence, physical attractiveness, linguistic skills, and prodigious feminine wiles."

Feminine wiles, my Aunt Fanny! Those handlers know exactly what I can do, and they're damn glad someone on our side is willing to do it!

Abruptly, Catherine dismissed thoughts about the annoying characters bedeviling her life. She looked up, favored Henri with another smile, and pointed to the window where a slender shape had just appeared, silhouetted in its frame.

"Tell the Georgia Cracker out there on the ladder that he'd better get in here and be awfully quick about figuring out the combination to this safe!"

Henri reacted swiftly. Striding to the opposite wall, he unlocked the catch on the window and slid its sash upwards toward the high ceiling overhead. A thin, unshaven slip of a man climbed through the opening. His pallid complexion bore witness to the years he'd been incarcerated…that is, until he was temporarily "liberated" by some covert means, due to his special talents.

With a brief nod, the safecracker headed in the direction Catherine indicated, entered the closet, and knelt before the mammoth iron box that the three of them had been assured contained the naval codebooks. He tenderly fingered the large, black dial as if it were a long-denied pleasure. Then, with an ear pressed to the lock's tumblers, he began the painstakingly slow process of wheedling the combination from the safe.

After what seemed like hours twirling the dial back and forth, he began muttering numerous curses during repeated failed attempts. At last, he announced in a hoarse whisper the first three sequences of numbers that, in turn, Catherine recorded in a small notebook she'd retrieved from her pocket.

"Y'all know that the last numbers are always the hardest," he mumbled under his breath.

Catherine merely nodded, while Henri stood quietly beyond the door to the code closet. Both held their breath.

After continued unsuccessful tries, the fourth sequence of numbers finally clicked into place. When the Georgia Cracker swung open the metal door to the safe, all three witnesses winced at the startling sound of the rusty hinges' high-pitched squeaks.

"Thank you, Jesus!" croaked the triumphant safecracker. He looked over his shoulder at Catherine and added with a snort, "Well, *this* should shave a few years off my sentence, dontcha think? Be sure that Brit boss of yours tells the Yanks how well I did this job, will ya?" he added in his slow, southern drawl.

"Absolutely!" Catherine said with delight. "You already came highly recommended, and you've done splendid work. I'm sure there will be other assignments that will earn you even more time served."

"All's I ken say is they'd betta keep their word," he growled.

Catherine could see that the prison warden's warning was accurate. Clearly, this diminutive man could be vicious if crossed by an adversary.

Without further commentary, the convict rose to his boot-clad feet and turned to go. Just then, the three froze in place at the sounds of clanking buckets and voices chattering in the hallway only a few yards outside their door.

The cleaning crew had arrived!

Without a word of farewell, the safecracker bolted for the window.

"Wait!" hissed Catherine, running after him. "What were the *last* numbers of the safe's combination?"

"Two clockwise turns to number fourteen and a half turn back to lucky number seven!" he hissed back, and before either Catherine or Henri could say another word, he disappeared through the open window.

Catherine leaned her head outside to watch the safecracker climb down the ladder. Another agent waited for him on the last rung, handcuffs at the ready, to return him to the Atlanta Penitentiary.

"*Merde!*" Henri exclaimed under his breath. "Now what? We won't be able to get the codebooks copied!"

"But at least we can now open the safe," she whispered back, jotting down in her notebook the last numbers of the combination. "We'll just come back another night."

Henri pointed toward the sound of the noisy cleaning crew. "What the hell do we do now?"

"Nothing," she replied calmly, although she could feel her heart thumping in her chest. "Only the ambassador has the key to this room, remember?"

Henri darted a gaze around the chamber. "Well, that's what the bastard told everyone, so I hope that's the case."

Outside, the clanging of buckets and the babbling cleaning crew entered a room across the hall. Catherine dashed to turn off the code room's overhead light while stuffing her notebook containing the precious combination to the safe into the pocket of her trousers. She signaled that the two of them should shut themselves in the closet where the safe stood, its door still open, and in seconds they were sheltered inside.

"We'll wait here until the coast is clear," she said, *sotte voce*. "Once they start cleaning the ambassador's office, we can sneak past the door and tackle this mission on another night."

"Major Pepper won't be pleased," Henri whispered in the dark.

"Major Pepper is damn lucky we got *this* far!"

"Maybe we should follow the safecracker out the window?" he suggested.

"The ladder and the other agents are long gone by now," she murmured.

To her, this was just one more challenge to be met, and meet it she would. It was exciting—highly stimulating, in fact, she thought, a familiar tingling fanning downward toward her thighs.

Henri reached for her hand, and Catherine was startled how comforting his touch felt. If she had allowed herself to truly think about their perilous situation, she might be as unsettled as he obviously was. One of her skills, she knew, was in not allowing her mind to move in dicey directions.

Without warning, Henri pulled her against his chest, and his lips sought hers.

"Oh, fearless, brave Catherine," he whispered in French. "You are a wonder. Do you know that?"

For a few seconds, she returned and even deepened their kiss. Then, for some reason she didn't understand, she broke their embrace and tucked the top of her head under Henri's chin, leaning against him while she wrapped her arms around his waist. The two waited in reassuring silence for a chance to escape the embassy undetected. His broad chest and pleasant, manly scent calmed her racing heart. Fifteen minutes later, she realized not a sound could be heard outside the code room door, and she dutifully called a halt to the comfort of their embrace. At length, she gave his hand another squeeze while listening intently to the silence that now filled the hallway.

"They must be cleaning the ambassador's office by now," Catherine declared softly. "Let's make a run for it."

Her gloves on, she cast a final glance at the codebooks stacked inside the safe and carefully closed its heavy door, wincing a second time at the creaking hinges. She returned the dial to the position she'd recorded in her notebook at the outset and then, after the two of them had stepped outside the closet, relocked that door as well.

Glancing around the code room to be sure all was exactly as they'd found it when they first entered the inner sanctum, she relocked the closed window, leading the way out of the room. A moment later, the pair quietly entered the hallway and shut the outer door that locked automatically. Single file, they tiptoed down the lengthy carpet, past the hardworking crew preoccupied with the task of tidying up the ambassador's private bathroom. Fortunately, the trio of cleaners remained oblivious to the presence of two secret agents gliding out the embassy's front door and disappearing into the sultry morning mist that was rising in thick waves off the Potomac River.

It was the dawn of June eighteenth, realized Catherine. The hammer of summer heat would soon descend once more, turning the coming day into another scorcher. There was no denying it: The Founding Fathers had built Washington, D.C. in a swamp.

She glanced up at Henri's classic Gallic profile as they continued to stroll casually down the sidewalk. She'd long admired the slight curvature of his nose and his full head of salt-and-pepper hair.

"*Vive la France*," she sighed on a long breath.

She wondered if the mission chief would entrust the two of them with a second attempt to copy the codebooks—an assignment that would be just as fraught with danger as the one they'd almost completed.

"Lafayette, I am here," Henri answered with the trace of a smile.

Catherine felt a soothing and totally unexpected wave of relief fill her chest. Despite Henri's understandable trepidation, he still considered himself her comrade in arms.

They'd try again to complete their nigh-impossible task, if only the enigmatic Mr. Pepper would trust them to complete the mission on another night.

———◇———

Catherine and Henri were silent on the walk to Catherine's car that was parked on an adjacent street. Once sitting in the passenger seat, Henri leaned back on the headrest and wondered at the turn his life had taken. Catherine started the car while he closed his eyes, his thoughts drifting back to the last fifteen months of his life as press attaché for the despised Vichy French in Washington.

He had responded dutifully to the newswoman Catherine Thornton's request for an interview with the current, loathsome

French Ambassador to the U.S. Henri had been prepared to find the stunning Mrs. Thornton thoroughly repugnant after she'd said on the telephone that she planned to write a magazine article *"laying out the Vichy side of the conflict"* for her American readers. Many of those readers had fought in World War I and wished America to remain neutral in the mushrooming conflict in Europe. That ruse, of course, turned out to be Catherine's cover story, a fact he discovered soon enough.

Henri had risen from his office chair that momentous day to greet her for the first time, her elegant, gloved hand outstretched. Of course, he'd recognized the name Farnsworth, which she employed as part of her byline, but he'd been startled by her patrician good looks and lithe, alluring figure cloaked in a chic green wool suit the color of her eyes. But the biggest shocker had occurred *after* that bogus interview. She'd smiled up at him as she prepared to leave the embassy, and the only mad thought in his head had been, *"I don't want this woman to walk out the door and never see her again..."*

That day, escorting Catherine down the embassy's hallway toward the front entrance to bid her farewell, he was incapable of stopping himself from inviting her to lunch at one of Washington's most expensive restaurants.

They'd lingered long over their mid-day meal and some excellent wine, which had undoubtedly led to his letting slip a few comments that indicated in what little regard he held his Nazi-sympathizing superior, the ambassador. When he'd offered to drive Catherine home to her fashionable townhouse in Georgetown, she'd invited him in for a cup of tea, of all things. Before he could begin to consider the ramifications, they'd fallen into bed just shy of five o'clock that afternoon.

He remembered that she'd never taken off the luminescent pearls nestled in the hollow of her slender neck. Just before they'd made love, she acknowledged to him that the beautiful string had been a wedding gift from her wealthy grandmother and namesake, Catherine Farnsworth, *the* original Minnesota mining heiress.

"I actually have dual citizenship," Catherine had disclosed to him that first day, handing him a lit cigarette as both leaned against the plush velvet headboard in her beautifully appointed bedroom on O Street. "British as well as American. Quite handy to have, as it's turned out, and all thanks to my own rather miserable marriage—when I was practically a child, mind you," she added with a sly wink.

"And where is *Monsieur* Thornton at this moment?" Henri had asked, attempting to mask his alarm, for she'd worn no wedding band.

"Currently and conveniently stationed at the British embassy in Chile," she'd replied forthrightly. "Jeremy and I are legally separated, by the way. No chance of him barging in or anything, so not to worry."

Then, shocking him to his core, she'd added casually that day, mere months before Pearl Harbor, "Actually, you probably ought to know that I'm working for the British secret services, given that the U.S. is stupidly refusing to join the fight in Europe. We are such head-in-the-sand Americans here in D.C.," she'd stated flatly, describing her years as a U.S. military brat studying in Paris and at exclusive schools in Switzerland, Germany, and Italy. Her late father, a Marine colonel, had been assigned throughout her youth as a security attaché overseas. "Anyone could see clear as day that we were all going to be fighting Hitler before long."

She'd cast him a sidewise glance across crisp ivory sheets and declared that it had been immediately obvious to her that Henri Leblanc was no enthusiast for the Vichy regime that now ruled life at his embassy.

"Having sensed your feelings at lunch, I've decided to risk telling you the truth about me," she'd said, maintaining her steady gaze across the small space that had separated them in bed. She'd sighed, her brow furrowed, and blurted a sentiment that endeared her to him then and there. "I so love France, Henri. I just can't *bear* to see what is happening over there."

He remembered, then, her staring at him with a look he'd never forget.

"Besides the mission I've accepted," she'd said softly, "I cannot deny that I found myself very drawn to you, *Monsieur* Leblanc. It's as plain and simple as that." With a slight shrug of her smooth, satiny shoulders glistening under the lamplight beaming from her bedside table, she'd leaned toward him and added with a throaty laugh, "Why pretend otherwise? And why not combine business with pleasure?"

Within a day or two, as well as several unforgettable nights, Catherine had set about to convince Henri that helping her obtain copies of the French naval codes from his embassy for the British government was an act of pure patriotism toward *La France.*

"Stealing the cyphers?" he'd replied. The mere thought was preposterous. "What an utterly mad idea, Catherine. And besides, they're locked inside an enormous safe in our code room, to which only the ambassador has the key."

As if she hadn't heard a word he'd said, Catherine continued with an earnestness he'd found rather touching. "Knowing where those French ships are—and their movements—will go a long way in preventing Germany from taking control of what's left of your poor Navy, to say nothing of your colonies in Africa."

Hearing her say that, Henri knew only too well that the United Kingdom needed to win at sea as well as in North Africa in order eventually to launch successful landings in the South of France and across the English Channel. With Catherine's unique form of persuasion, he came to see that forgiveness of Winston Churchill and the UK for the debacle at Dunkirk was his only option to help free France.

Adding to this surmise, Catherine had insisted that first day, "Now that the Nazis have taken control over most of France, the most loyal service you could possibly render your beleaguered country is to help me pass on the secret communication codes to the London War Office!"

How to achieve that virtually unattainable goal had been months in the planning. During it all, he had felt his fate and Catherine's inextricably were drawn closer and closer to the point where, now, he couldn't imagine his life without her.

The car rolled to a stop, jolting Henri back to reality.

"Well, here we are," Catherine said, parking the vehicle at the back of the Wardman Park Hotel. She cast him a sideways glance. "Mission halfway accomplished."

CHAPTER 3

John Pepper was waiting for them in Catherine's newly secured second-floor hotel apartment only a few minutes from Embassy Row. Clad in civilian clothes—and only addressed in public as "Mr." while in America, the high-placed functionary based in the New York City office of British Security Coordination sported a pencil-thin mustache and military bearing. It was precisely the look one might expect of a bureaucrat fighting his war-time intelligence mission from a desk.

"Problems, I understand?" Pepper said in his usual clipped fashion. He indicated they should each take a seat around Catherine's coffee table in the hotel sitting room that was decorated in heavy, pale-blue satin drapes and a matching blue brocaded settee.

Catherine pulled out her little notebook from her trouser pocket and waved it.

"The safe was hard to crack, even by a professional," she noted with a glance in Henri's direction, "but the man from Georgia did his job well, and now we have the combination. Hopefully, we'll make quick work of it next time."

"Excellent," Pepper declared with a nod of approval. "And by the way, 'next time' will be tonight."

"*Mon Dieu!*" Henri sought Catherine's gaze. "Need I remind you, Major Pepper, that we drugged the guard *and* the dog! Lord only knows what André will say to me if the dog died or he deduces the champagne we gave him was laced with—"

"I imagine he'll just think he's hung over," Catherine interjected, attempting to calm Henri's concerns. For her part, she was glad they'd get this business over with. Better to plunge right back into the thick of things rather than think about it and start to worry. "Henri, we both know that the guard has come to work in a hungover condition countless times before."

"And the dog...?"

Catherine felt her own short intake of breath at Henri's pointed question. She hated the idea of possibly harming an innocent animal, especially a dog.

For a moment, she thought of sweet Ensign Aubrey, her ginger-and-white Cavalier King Charles Spaniel, given her on her twelfth birthday by her father when they were living in Paris. Her mother claimed the animal had become ill and died while Catherine was away at university in Geneva. Catherine had always wondered if Gladys found feeding and walking the dog too troublesome and simply gave him away—or had him put down and lied about it to her husband and daughter.

Major Pepper interrupted her morose thoughts with an audible sigh.

"Hopefully, the furry beast at the embassy will have survived the little trick you two played on him. Mister Leblanc will undoubtedly hear what happened to the dog when he returns to work later this morning, but our experts have assured us the canine will survive on the limited dosage you gave him." He turned to address Henri. "To avoid any suspicion by your colleagues, it is imperative that you arrive at your office this morning at the usual time." He glanced at his watch, "That will be approximately three hours from now. It's also crucial that you go about your business there in your usual manner."

"But—"

Pepper continued as if Henri hadn't interrupted. "You left everything at the embassy in good order, am I correct? No one saw you, other than the guard?" Both nodded. "Good work. I need not remind you that your mission getting us those communication codes is of the *highest* priority, and you must do everything in your powers to succeed tonight."

Henri addressed Pepper in a weary, dejected voice. "Surely, you've heard that, any day now, the Americans are going to order the Vichy delegation to an internment camp like Manzanar, or to leave the country. I suppose that's why we have to turn right around and go back tonight?"

Catherine could see Henri was exhausted as well as dispirited. She realized that he was wondering what would happen to him at work if their break-in to the code room had been detected. And even if it hadn't, what would be his fate after tonight? Had they left any evidence that might render poor Henri under suspicion? Was the Vichy envoy suddenly going to be banished or put under house arrest the second he walked through the embassy door today?

And what about the rest of the embassy staff housed in Washington? Would tonight be the last time she ever saw Henri? Or would *Madame et Monsieur* Leblanc—whose apartment was conveniently five floors above hers here in this very hotel, thanks to Pepper's clever arrangements—be whisked back to France on some Vichy military transport to face the chaos now reigning in their country?

Pepper spoke quietly. "As of tomorrow, the Vichy contingent will be given notice that they're being interned at the Hotel Hershey in Hershey, Pennsylvania, for the duration."

"What?" exclaimed Henri, a look of horror invading his handsome features.

Catherine knew full well that the sharp-tongued, disagreeable Mrs. Leblanc was American born. What would the banishment of the Vichy staff mean for her? For her French husband? The complications were many.

Henri said to Pepper, "After what I've done for the Allies, you expect me to spend the next who-knows-how-many years locked up in backwoods of America with—"

Their usually expressionless handler cast the French press attaché what could nearly be described as a look of sympathy.

"My dear boy, not to worry." He hastened to assure him, "We have further assignments for you and Mrs. Thornton…*if* you can complete your mission tonight."

———◇———

Twenty hours later, as midnight approached, Catherine shivered slightly despite the prevailing June humidity. She parked her car on

Belmont Road, a few blocks away from the embassy. Then she and Henri trod the familiar sidewalk, eventually turning the corner onto Wyoming Avenue. Out of the corner of her eye, she noticed that a solitary automobile was parked beside the curb some fifty feet ahead of them. Two gentlemen, fedoras slouched over their foreheads, appeared to be sound asleep, one with his mouth slightly open and his head tilted back against the front seat. The other, however, slid to an upright position as they passed by on the opposite sidewalk fronting the embassy.

Catherine grabbed Henri's arm and pulled him close to her, resting her head on his shoulder, the epitome of a loving couple returning from a late evening as they continued walking toward their destination. Henri's response was to kiss the top of her head. Her pulse quickening, she said nothing to him about what she had just observed.

The feds were tailing her.

Pepper had warned her that FBI Director J. Edgar Hoover routinely ordered surveillance on Americans with dual citizenship, along with other "suspicious characters" he believed might be scheming with foreigners—even if they were supposed Allies of the United States. Hoover was resentful that America had lost its isolationist fervor now that the country was at war.

Pepper had even quipped a few days earlier, "Your Mr. Hoover has let it be known he thinks FDR deliberately encouraged the attack in Hawaii to bring America into the conflict."

Whatever the reasons for the unmarked car parked near the French embassy this night, Catherine knew she dare not tell Henri. Her co-conspirator was anxious enough about their complicated tasks this night.

"So, no one questioned you at all today at work?" she asked quietly as they drew near the front steps that led to the porch.

"No," replied Henri, "although everyone is clearly on edge. I'm sure the ambassador has gotten word by now from someone here or in Paris that the axe, as you say, is about to fall on our staff."

Catherine halted in her tracks, gripped by a horrifying thought.

"I just hope that wretched man hasn't already removed the naval codebooks from the safe!"

"I doubt it," Henri replied. "But the moment the order to leave the embassy arrives, the codes go into his personal diplomatic pouch, immune from any search."

"Hence Pepper's urgent directives to us to try again tonight."

As was their usual practice, the couple casually ambled up the wide front stairs to the wrap-around veranda at the front the former grand house. And, adhering to their routine, they shared a long, lingering kiss in plain view of any passersby before Henri withdrew his key to the entrance and turned the lock.

A voice from the shadowy front foyer greeted them, "*Bon soir, Monsieur Leblanc et Madame…*"

"Why, André!" Catherine exclaimed in French, her heart turning over in her chest. She forced a friendly smile. "I can see they've elevated your post to the foyer. A far more comfortable place than the basement, I imagine. Congratulations!"

This unexpected development put Catherine on high alert. Any change of this kind could only mean that something was afoot. Had André warned the ambassador that he suspected the champagne he'd been given had been drugged? But then why had he greeted them in his usual cheery manner and made no other moves? She glanced down and saw the large guard dog curled up, deeply asleep. She bent and gave the cream-colored Alsatian a friendly scratch behind his ears.

"Snoozing on the job, are you?" she teased, gauging André's reaction.

"He's been a bit off his feed today," André disclosed, adding, "and so am I, if the truth be told. I think I drank more than my share of that champagne last evening."

There was no doubt about it, thought Catherine: The guard held no grudge against them, but he was clearly nervous for some reason.

"I brought you some cigarettes," she offered, pulling two packs of Lucky Strikes from her jacket pocket.

André glanced around as if he suspected they might be being watched. Then he slid his hand across the desk and quickly shoved his bounty into a duffle bag beneath his chair, mumbling his thanks.

Catherine looked over at Henri, who spoke to fill the silence that had bloomed among the trio.

"Well, I want to thank you for your discretion all these months, my dear André," declared Henri, as per their latest plan. "Tonight, I fear, is the last time I shall bring this lovely young lady here. It seems my wife has grown a bit suspicious of my late hours, so we must sort out a new time and place to rendezvous. You understand, of course?"

"Ah, but of course," André said with a knowing shrug. "Good luck to you both, then. I will miss our evening chats."

Catherine almost laughed aloud, thinking, *And no doubt you'll miss those tasty bribes we've handed you, courtesy of the British intelligence services.*

Major Pepper had told them to inform the guard if they saw him that this would be their last night. This made Catherine even more apprehensive than before, for André had a look of relief pass over his features when he'd heard the news that they would no longer be using the embassy for their supposed trysts. However, she merely cast him one of her warmest smiles, seized Henri's hand, and sauntered down the hallway, turning left into the ambassador's office where the guard knew full well there was a lovely, comfortable, silk-covered *chaise longue.*

"Why are you going in here?" protested Henri under his breath. "We have no time to lose. The code room—"

"Because I want you to strip off your clothes...*now!*" she blurted, swiftly closing the door behind them. She began frantically shedding her jacket and then pulling her black turtleneck over her head.

"What in the world are you doing? We have only an hour to—"

"Do what I say! Strip!" she commanded. "That's an *order!*"

By this time, Catherine had disrobed down to all but her underclothing and was swiftly unhooking her garters, peeling off her silk stockings and black lace panties in one, swift action. Then she unhooked her brassiere.

"Forget about your trousers," she instructed hoarsely, relieved Henri was now shirtless. "Lie down on the chaise. *Now!*"

Footsteps were thundering down the hallway by the time she knelt on the floor, pushed Henri flat on his back against the length of the chaise, unzipped his trousers, and slipped her hand inside.

This is just the part of my job, she told herself as she heard the door to the ambassador's office flung wide and bang against the wall. But at least with a man like Henri, her very deliberate lovemaking had always proved to be an appealing assignment.

"*Mon Dieu!*" she heard André exclaim. In broken English, the French guard said to the two men in trench coats and fedoras standing a few feet inside the ambassador's office, "I *told* you these two were here merely for *l'amour*."

Catherine, clad only in a strand of snowy white pearls, slowly rose to her feet and turned to face the federal agents, making an attempt to hide her nakedness with a hand covering her crotch and an arm plastered against the nipples on her chest.

"Oh God," she cried, the deliberately heightened pitch of her voice signaling, she hoped, her shock and embarrassment. Then she gazed down at her bare feet as if stricken with mortification.

When she finally looked up, André briefly caught her eye. Their exchange of glances telegraphed to the guard that Catherine had deduced André had been harassed earlier by the Federal investigators. He'd probably been forced at gunpoint to grant them admittance into the embassy when they returned to nab their quarry.

With remarkable aplomb, Henri struggled to sit up.

"Gentlemen?" he said in English, his French accent pronounced, "is there any reason for this rude and unfortunate intrusion? As I am sure you are well aware, this is technically French soil. I have diplomatic immunity. What are you men doing here? André?" he demanded of the guard, "why did you grant these two admittance?"

Before he could answer, one of the G-men interrupted. "Uh… we…ah…are just doing our job," he said gruffly. "We wanted to be sure nothing that could be harming our country was going on at this embassy in the middle of the night."

Catherine snatched her black sweater and held it to cover her upper body.

"I see," she said. She lifted her chin, making a show that she was beginning to simmer with righteous anger at the agents' invasion. "And, since I am a newspaper woman myself, I'm just curious: What will your report say were the reasons that agents of the United States Government have broken into a *sovereign* embassy in the middle of the night? I hope, sir, written accounts of your deeds tonight won't do anything to embarrass you professionally, or our country, by describing what you saw or did."

Gulping, the other spoke up. "Oh, no…ma'am. We'll be sure of that. We'll just say we…uh…saw nothing that breeched national security. But just so you know, this place is going to be shut down soon. You and your…uh…"

He glanced at Henri, still seated on the chaise, bare-chested, his fly undone. Everyone in the room except Catherine appeared stunned by these lightning-fast developments.

The second G-man added, "Your fella here will have to find some other place to take you to…meet and…ah…"

"We appreciate your discretion on all fronts," Catherine interrupted in clipped tones. "Now, if you'll just allow us to dress and—"

"Sure, ma'am. So sorry, ma'am."

The taller of the two agents grumbled, "Jesus H. Christ, Joe, let's get outta here."

The pair swiftly exited the room, along with the shamefaced André. The taller FBI agent could again be heard muttering to his partner, "What a wild goose chase! Where do our guys get their supposed information about this shit?"

Once the door had shut behind the trio, Henri rose to his feet beside the chaise, zipping closed the fly on his trousers. Catherine dressed quickly and then pressed her ear against the door, hearing only silence in the hallway. She opened the panel a crack and saw that André was no longer at the front desk, having retreated with the dog back down to the basement.

"Come, quickly!" she urged Henri. "Let's get to the code room and pray the feds don't run into the British agent who's supposed to be here soon to take the cipher books out through the window and have them copied at the hotel."

Fortunately, Catherine had no trouble picking the locks to either of the two doors to access the safe. Even so, with her nerves still jangling from their run-in with the feds, it took her a couple of attempts to twirl the knob in such a way that the combination recorded in her notebook clicked properly at every stop. After what seemed eons, the last tumbler fell into place, and she and Henri together pulled open the heavy steel door.

"Brilliant," he said, expelling a long breath.

Much to the pair's relief, by this time Pepper's emissary was standing on the top rung of a ladder leaned against the back wall of the embassy, waiting for them to open the window and give their precious cargo to him, which Catherine duly placed in his hands.

"Give us two hours," the man whispered, storing the naval codebooks under his arm. "We'll be back so you can replace these and get away as quickly as you can. We've been told that the Capitol police will be here at nine to close down this place."

"What about the cleaning crew?" Catherine demanded, deciding she would reveal their recent interaction with the feds directly to Pepper when they saw him.

The agent replied, "The Vichy ambassador has been informed that the lease on the building has been cancelled. Apparently, he's ordered the cleaners to return only after everyone has moved out."

"Are you sure that's true?" Henri asked, sounding worried.

With a shrug the agent replied, "That's what I was advised," and within moments, he and his ladder vanished. Meanwhile, Catherine locked glances with her collaborator standing in the shadows.

"We did it!" she whispered, profoundly relieved that Hoover's federal agents hadn't sabotaged the entire enterprise. She took a step toward Henri and pressed the length of her body against his. "You performed wonderfully on the chaise," she teased.

"Well, our mission isn't accomplished *yet*," he murmured into her hair. "We still have two more hours of this agony waiting for the codebooks to come back."

She nuzzled his neck, her body beginning to hum with exhilaration for what they'd managed to accomplish by passing the valuable ciphers on to be copied. Adding to the aphrodisiac of this elation was the recollection of the danger they'd been in when the FBI crashed into the ambassador's office.

"I know something that might relieve the tension around here," she whispered, her voice low and inviting. After all, she thought, what if this turned out to be their last night together? Or what if the Feds decided to make another unannounced visit tonight?

Henri's glance swept the code room, taking in the code master's highly polished desk, leather chair, and the two upholstered, straight-back chairs situated across the room.

"Here?" he asked, his meaning clear.

"Why not here?" she smiled up at him. "We certainly could pass the time on top of this very lovely desk," she suggested, placing a few office items onto a chair. "After all, we were so rudely interrupted on the chaise in the ambassador's office."

In the two hours they had to kill, she thought, perhaps sex was the one sure way to take their minds off their treacherous situation.

"You are quite insane, you know," he growled, and then took her in his arms and demonstrated his state of full arousal by pressing his pelvis tightly against hers. At length, he stepped away, as breathless as Catherine had become. She could feel that her face was flushed with an animal desire as fierce as she imagined his was. She allowed herself to be led over to the desk, but it was she who pushed him against its edge.

"Now," she said in a low, husky voice she knew stirred him to distraction, "where, exactly, did I leave off?"

It's my job, she told herself once again in a portion of her brain that she never seemed able to shut down. With slow deliberation, she sank to her knees upon the carpet in front of Henri, just as she'd done when turning the tumblers on the safe. Gently, she pushed his knees apart to nearly the edge of the code master's broad desk. Smiling at him, she unzipped his fly for the second time that night and continued with the ministrations she had only just commenced when the FBI agents had so rudely burst upon them when *in flagrante delecto.*

CHAPTER 4

A good twenty minutes later, Catherine struggled to repress a laugh. Henri had received rather a pleasant bonus in the embassy's code room, which helped to calm his anxiety while Pepper's experts were photographing the codebooks in the privacy of her apartment at the Wardman Park Hotel. While Henri straightened out his clothing, she made sure the inkwell and desk papers were put back on the highly polished surface exactly as they'd been placed earlier.

Catherine chuckled aloud. "I can only surmise that the code master is responsible for dusting his own quarters, given that the cleaners aren't allowed to enter this room."

Henri made no response and merely continued to adjust his tie. As for Catherine, she understood that their desktop intimacy had served a dual purpose, both as a fulfillment of their mutual physical desires and as a security precaution. It was quite a sensible move in case the G-men decided to return unexpectedly and break the door down while she and Henri were marooned, waiting for the codebooks to return.

Catherine glanced at her watch and realized with a start that her nerves were just as frayed as Henri's. They absolutely *had* to get out of the embassy before dawn, with no one seeing them on the premises and the ciphers returned to the safe just as they'd found them. She glanced at the window but could only see the dark sky beyond the glass.

Hurry. Hurry up*, God dammit!*

———◇———

The sound of a sharp thump outside the window startled both Catherine and Henri awake. They had been sitting side by side on the floor, their backs against one wall, her head on his shoulder, fitfully dozing on and off while the hours ticked by.

"Thank God! They're back!" Henri said in a hushed whisper, struggling to his feet and offering Catherine a hand.

She glanced at her watch. It was nearly four o'clock, a half hour later than their planned timetable. She dashed to the window and pushed up the sash.

Without speaking, she gathered the heavy codebooks into her arms and ran to the safe in the closet, its door still standing open. Carefully placing the priceless cargo in the precise position where the books had been when they'd originally cracked the safe, she pushed the heavy door closed, reset the knob, and wiped all surfaces clean of fingerprints. Closing the closet door with her shoulder, she turned to face Henri.

"Can't we go out the window this time?" he almost begged.

Catherine shook her head and waved off Pepper's courier, sliding the window shut and locking it, just as it had been when they'd entered the room. She again surveyed the chamber, making sure to leave everything as it had been when the code master had departed his post nearly twelve hours earlier.

"It's safer to leave the way we entered," she cautioned Henri, "because this window must be closed and locked from the inside."

Henri, who looked bone tired, merely offered a shrug. Catherine smiled her thanks, pleased he wouldn't argue with her. It was one of his most endearing traits.

"Yes, we'll just leave the way we came in," she repeated. "And to hell with the feds if they're still on a stakeout in their car out front."

Henri stared at her and then accused, "You saw them when we first walked toward the embassy, didn't you?"

"I noticed the car."

"Why didn't you say anything?" he demanded.

"I only suspected…"

"You *more* than suspected, didn't you? And I never gave that car a thought!"

"I'd heard rumors that Americans with dual passports were put on a watch list by that odious Mr. Hoover, who thinks everyone who talks to a foreigner might be a pro-Nazi operative."

Henri paused, holding her gaze. "You saved my life tonight with that quick thinking, you know…making us strip off our clothing."

"No, I probably just saved your embassy job."

"I hate my job here."

"I know," Catherine replied, genuinely sympathetic, "but our Mr. Pepper sounded as if he might have another one for you that you'll like much better."

And with that, she seized his hand and led him across the threshold of the code room, its door automatically locking behind them as they left. They proceeded through the darkened embassy to the foyer and out the front entrance.

Catherine stood for a moment on the summit of the wooden stairs that led to a path merging with the city sidewalk. The FBI agents' car was nowhere to be seen. She inhaled deeply and then exhaled, the pent-up fear that she'd managed to repress all evening dissipating into the humid, early-morning air.

She was strangely gratified when Henri swung his arm around her shoulder and escorted her down the deserted street.

"Now we can say *mission accomplished*!" she whispered with a throaty laugh.

———◇———

The elegant marble lobby of the Wardman Park Hotel was deserted of even a bellman when the pair entered the elevator and got off on the second floor. For more than a month now, the British Security Coordinator had leased Apartment 215B in the name of The Honorable Mr. and Mrs. Jeremy Thornton. Major Pepper had told Catherine privately that the logistics of *les amorettes* would be vastly simplified if she moved from her rented townhouse on O Street to a suite only several floors below the flat inhabited by Henri and his wife of eleven years.

Catherine tapped on the door, identified herself and her cohort, and the pair were admitted into Catherine's latest abode. The hotel suite had been turned into a safe house for their mission, and it certainly looked like one. The room was filled to overflowing with photo equipment; two cameramen; their handler, Mr. Pepper, in the flesh; and—to Catherine's relief—scores of photographs of the French naval codebook pages that had been hung on clotheslines stretching across the well-appointed rooms. Other images that had been developed in the hotel bathtub were spread to dry on every flat surface, including Catherine's silk duvet-clad double bed, now covered with bathroom towels.

As soon as they walked into the suite's sitting room, Henri glanced at his watch and resolutely took his sham suitcase from Catherine's hall closet.

"Just getting home from your business trip, are you?" she teased.

Major Pepper stepped forward to congratulate them both.

"As soon as these photos are dry, they will be given to the American OSS here in D.C., and the second set of copies will be flown directly to London to guide the Allies during the planned assaults on North Africa." His glance moved from Catherine to Henri. "I don't need to tell you that, without pushing German forces out of North Africa, any future invasion of the Riviera or one from the English Channel would be impossible. Now knowing where the French navy ships *are,* as well as being able to listen and understand communications between Vichy forces and the Germans, make winning this war a much greater possibility." He placed a hand on each of their shoulders. "So, thank you. We are well aware of the risks you both took these last days and months."

Although gratified by Pepper's high praise, Catherine truly thought that if she didn't go to bed soon, she would drop from fatigue. The major appeared to understand the situation and conferred with a young woman whom Catherine assumed had been serving as a secretary or girl Friday on this project.

"Catherine, why don't you have a little lie-down in the bedroom in there while Miss Zinman here packs a bag for you at your direction. Jason?" he ordered one of the cameramen, "and Mildred," he addressed the assistant, "those images on the bed should be dry by now. Gather them up in proper order, and let's allow our heroine here to get some much-needed rest."

"Pack my bag?" Catherine asked, longing for sleep. "Where am I going?"

"New York City."

"Why?"

"You'll be told once you board the ten-forty train this morning."

Catherine knew better than to ask for more information, and yet she heard herself saying to Pepper, "And what about Henri? Does he dare return to the embassy?"

"Oh, he *must*," Pepper replied with a nod. "Absolutely, or he'll blow his cover."

Henri, a look of alarm invading his features, protested, "But we've been told the U.S. Government is going to close the embassy at nine o'clock this morning. What if those FBI agents write up a damning report about finding us last night?"

"They didn't," Pepper disclosed with a faint smile. Catherine marveled at the tentacles the Brits seemed to have with some of their counterparts in D.C. "So be prepared, my dear Henri," he continued, "for the Americans to send you to an undisclosed location where you will be questioned, along with your colleagues, and find yourself under house arrest for conduct deleterious to American national security."

"What? Why, that's—"

Pepper's smile broadened. "That's just the indignation I hope you'll display in front of your Vichy compatriots. At some point, you will be taken away from the Hershey Hotel for further questioning by U.S. military officers, and the word will come back to your ambassador that you are to be forthwith expelled from America, along with His Excellency himself," he added with a wink.

"And then what?" Catherine demanded, amazed that this plan riled her so at its unfairness to Henri, who had risked his life that very evening and whose Vichy colleagues could arrest him any second if they suspected something untoward.

"Ah, Mrs. Thornton," Pepper said with relish even his British reserve couldn't mask, "I am afraid I cannot divulge anything other than what I've told you."

"I think I have a right to know what happens once I'm in New York," she exclaimed, unable to suppress her frustration at the abruptness of Pepper's orders.

By this time, the usually taciturn Major Pepper was smiling broadly. Catherine could plainly see that their success tonight had put him in a very expansive mood.

"I'm afraid you will have to wait until you meet with my superior in New York, but I can tell you this; everyone on both sides of the pond is very pleased with your and Henri's work tonight."

So, she was going to meet with Pepper's boss. Obviously, she had probably earned a new assignment. And maybe there *were* plans for Henri and her as a team.

Catherine's fatigue and annoyance were dissipating at this thought.

"Well, whatever is being proposed for us," she told Pepper, "we accept, don't we, Henri?"

Before Henri could reply, Pepper clapped a hand on her partner's shoulder. "Excellent! Now, off you go, both of you. Good luck and Godspeed."

Catherine stared past the man with the thin mustache who had masterminded her latest adventure and felt a surprising amount of relief that tonight apparently did not necessarily mean a final parting of the ways for Henri and her. There was a war on. They were both married to other people, but they had formed an excellent collaboration which Pepper had just acknowledged. In the not-too-distant future, as the major had obliquely hinted, perhaps the fates would once again conspire to reunite Henri and her on British soil or, perhaps, even in France.

Catherine was surprised by how glad she felt at that possibility. Seducing and 'turning' French press attaché Henri Leblanc had merely been her original assignment, and she had done it willingly, with no shame as to her methods and no regrets for the enjoyment it had unexpectedly produced. It was a task that needed to be done, and she did it, just as any paratrooper would jump out of a plane or any soldier would drive a tank into battle.

Henri extended his hand to her to bid farewell. With a brief glance at Pepper, she accepted it and felt Henri's eyes bore into hers signaling—what? Fear for his future? Regret their time together had so abruptly come to an end? A plea they would one day meet again and work together to free France? His grip lingered, and she found herself unable to pull away either.

Finally he said simply, "*Au revoir,*" then, in a lower voice, "*chérie, a bientôt.*"

"Yes, goodbye for now," she answered in English, for Pepper's benefit.

She could tell Henri yearned for assurances they would somehow stay in touch, and she was shocked to realize she wanted that too. However, life and events made even discussing that impossible.

This assignment is over, she told herself sternly. The French press attaché was just another man in a long line of important male figures that she had bent to her will in the name of a greater cause. Or was she just telling herself something she knew was a myth and, instead, was employing her usual methods to keep safe emotional distances from men, including her latest conquest?

She gave Henri's hand a soft squeeze, wondering if the Allies for whom he'd risked his life would protect the poor man. Would Pepper's implied promises to Henri be kept? At least she could take heart that her own actions in the last eighteen months hadn't resulted in any harm to the stalwart *Monsieur* Leblanc.

At least, not so far.

Interrupting these thoughts, she watched Henri slowly turn toward Major Pepper, offer a brief nod, and then depart the hotel suite. Catherine stared at the door that had closed behind him, refusing to allow herself any further speculation as to whether they'd ever meet again. Instead, she determinedly conjured a sense of excitement and anticipation for what lay ahead.

———◇———

Later that same day, after two hours' rest, a steaming hot bath, and donning one of her Chanel suits, Catherine squeezed a light spray of Chanel No. 5 perfume under each ear and was escorted by a man she'd never seen before to D.C.'s Union Station. This taciturn companion led the way across the echoing marble grand hall to the platform for trains bound for New York City. Once on board, he ushered her into a private compartment devoid of passengers except for a handsome man in his late fifties with a sturdy soldier's build but clad in a well-cut Savile Row suit.

The gentleman rose and extended his hand.

"Good afternoon, Mrs. Thornton, and may I congratulate you and Mr. Leblanc for your amazing success in what I know must have been difficult circumstances."

Catherine warily eyed the gentleman clad in British-cut clothing but who was speaking with an American accent.

"And you are…?" she inquired.

"Major General William Donovan, chief of the U.S. Office of Strategic Services."

The American OSS!

Catherine could only stare. Major Pepper had informed her as she was leaving her hotel that President Roosevelt, mere days earlier, had authorized the establishment of the country's own intelligence-gathering agency. Beaming, Pepper had revealed, "It's an organization that will operate secretly behind enemy lines—in coordination with us Brits."

Catherine realized with a shock, the man in her train compartment was not William Stephenson, the head of the British Security Coordination based in New York with whom she would apparently meet later. Here was another William—a Yank, despite his English duds—the legendary "Wild Bill" Donovan, the most decorated soldier in the history of the United States, now tasked with rapidly expanding the American Office of Strategic Services.

Catherine hoped that the major general didn't hear her swift intake of breath. "Ah, the new OSS," she replied in a tone she hoped sounded calm and collected. "So, you'll be running the American side of all things cloak-and-dagger, am I right?"

Donovan nodded, chuckling. "Major Pepper and his boss, William Stephenson of BSC—whom I'm aware you already know of—were kind enough to allow me to broach a subject to you of mutual interest to both our intelligence services. Yes, it involves our spanking-new OSS, as well as our British counterparts at the SOE."

Catherine's pulse quickened. The Special Operations Executive, she knew, used civilian as well as military agents and was a recent offshoot of the overall British intelligence establishment. Pepper had described to her the early and full cooperation that had existed between the highly experienced British intelligence organizations, overseen by the War Office and MI6 in London, and the recently formed American OSS. Given this unexpected rendezvous with America's Donovan in person, Catherine now suspected that the mission she and Henri had just performed had been, from its inception, jointly run by the two new secret agencies.

"Please," Donovan gestured toward the upholstered bench seat opposite him in the first-class train compartment, "do sit down, Mrs. Thornton. Luncheon will be brought to us in just a few minutes, but first, let me explain why I wanted to meet you in person."

During the initial hour of their journey to New York City, Donovan disclosed that the entire Vichy embassy staff, including Henri Leblanc, was that very day being dispatched to the Hershey Hotel, a plush hostelry in the Pennsylvania town of the same name that was famous for chocolate.

Oh, Lord. Henri's not going to like this...

Donovan offered a wry smile. "Apparently, the American Cocoa King is a very loyal friend of our government and has offered to put up the French diplomats—for a bargain price to the U.S., I understand."

"Well," Catherine replied, wondering how Henri would fare in such confined, fragrant quarters with his wife, Alice, "I've heard one finds the constant scent of cacao that permeates the town quite tiresome after a while, but at least the accommodations will be far more pleasant than those at Manzanar."

Donovan merely raised an eyebrow at her allusion to the controversial detention camps out West. Even U.S. citizens of

Japanese ancestry who had lived in America for many generations had been ordered confined for an indeterminate time, along with numerous visiting Japanese and migrant workers that had the bad luck to be in the United States in the aftermath of the attack on Pearl Harbor.

The OSS chief pulled out a sheet of paper and then a second one that, from a distance across the train compartment, looked to Catherine like legal documents with room for signatures on the bottom.

"What I am here to propose to you is that, given your dual American-British citizenship and your facility with languages, you accept the official role of joint agent assigned both to the OSS and the British Special Operations Executive, the SOE for short, on an as-needed basis in the active European theater of war." He paused and then asked, "Does that have any appeal?"

Catherine's heart gave a lurch, signaling her unconstrained excitement at such a bold proposal, especially one offered to a woman.

"Yes, sir," she replied promptly. "It has great appeal."

"It would mean you'd need more training—"

"Would that be in Britain or America?" she interrupted.

"The United Kingdom," he replied. "We think it's best if you leave the country post haste, given the interest the FBI has shown in your activities."

Catherine raised an eyebrow. Wild Bill undoubtedly knew every nuance of the efforts that had been made to secure the codebooks.

He smiled at her again and continued. "Mr. Hoover remains highly suspicious of any American with links to diplomatic circles in Washington."

"Would this mean that I would eventually be sent into France?"

"That is certainly a likely assignment, given your French-speaking skills."

Before she realized what she was asking she blurted, "And what about Henri Leblanc? Would he and I continue to work as partners as we have so well in the past?'

Donovan cast her a steady gaze.

"Well…" he drawled, and Catherine could almost see the wheels revolving in his head, "Mr. Leblanc's future is still to be determined.

The man has surely proven his worth on this latest mission with you, but there are other factors at play, as I'm sure you can appreciate. When Germany invaded his country, many of his colleagues promptly resigned their posts rather than work under General Pétain—but Leblanc did not. He remained at his post here in Washington with that Nazi sympathizer ambassador of his, and as far as we can ascertain, he made no overt protests or objections about the Vichy regime taking over. Before we consider any official association with the man, we need to be certain of his loyalty to the Allies' effort to rid Europe of Nazi forces."

Catherine felt her face flush with indignation as Henri's many daring exploits the last few months flashed in her mind's eye. Had Donovan not been told of Henri's bravery, spiriting crucial cables sent between the French embassy in Washington and the Vichy French government that the press attaché had put into her hands in the months prior to their cracking the safe? Major Pepper had been the ultimate happy recipient. Surely, Donovan knew that?

"Of course he's loyal to our side!" she retorted, unable to suppress her frustration. "Henri has an American wife. Obviously, his position in the French diplomatic corps in Washington was rather...ah...complicated, but it didn't take much to persuade him that his help stealing the codes was the most patriotic act he could perform for the Allies."

"So I understand," Donovan said with a nod. "And I'm sure *you* deserve quite a bit of credit for...uh...convincing him to help you in that endeavor and with forwarding those cables."

There's that belittling honeytrap 'compliment' again...

Catherine stared at Donovan across the train compartment in silent fury. His remark about "convincing" Henri was nothing but an outright insult. That he would denigrate her for using sex to woo and convince certain men to collaborate with plans made by the two intelligence agencies! Employing a female operative as a so-called "Agent Fifi" was the only viable way the powers that be, like Donovan and Stephenson, *had* to obtain the information they so desperately needed. And they were judging Henri and her? What hypocrites!

Catherine narrowed her eyes. "Have you considered the possibility that *Monsieur* Leblanc was motivated, as am I, by a love of freedom and the rule of law, now absent in his country, sir?" she asked in a low voice. "And if that is not well understood by the OSS or the SOE, then I, too, will need some time to determine whether this assignment you propose is something with which I wish to align myself—or perhaps reconsider my prior enthusiasm."

CHAPTER 5

Catherine stared in silence across the first-class compartment at OSS chief William Donovan as the train speeding them from Washington to New York swayed gently on the tracks. She felt some satisfaction that the newly minted spy chief appeared startled by the frigid turn their conversation had taken on the specific nature of the assignments she had accepted on behalf of her government handlers.

"Please, Mrs. Thornton," he hastened to say, "do not misunderstand me. Both agencies greatly appreciate the amazing feats you have accomplished for us. And I assure you that all of Henri Leblanc's performance and service this last year will be taken into consideration, once he arrives in Pennsylvania."

Catherine felt her blood pressure lower a notch as Donovan continued. "Surely you can see that the safest way to thank him for the risks he took helping our cause is for him to continue to *appear* to be part of the ranks of the Vichy embassy and be declared, along with his colleagues, a U.S. national security risk by order of FDR. Otherwise, the Vichy ambassador will sniff betrayal, and the very worst outcome might result."

Upon reflection, Catherine was forced to agree that the American spy chief was probably right. If Henri's ambassador had the slightest notion that his press attaché had played any role in the theft and duplication of the secret naval codes, Henri would be summarily executed for high treason.

Meanwhile, Donovan glanced toward the closed glass door of their compartment, where a Pullman porter doubling as a waiter stood outside with a linen-clad tray that apparently held their lunch.

"And, now, let us move on from the matter of Henri Leblanc. If you're still interested, I'd like to tell you what plans we have where you could be of service to your country—and to the Allied cause."

The porter, in his starched white cotton jacket, gave a brief knock and opened the door to their private train compartment. He deposited the tray beside Donovan, then swiftly retreated with a polite bow and a promise to bring coffee at the end of their meal. As soon as the door closed, Donovan made it clear that, should Catherine agree to the proposed plan of becoming a joint OSS-SOE agent, she would be given only two weeks to prepare before leaving for Europe.

"The first week in New York will be devoted to briefings by members of the British Security Coordination on the details for your training and service in the UK and…" Donovan hesitated a second then added, "…and perhaps in France." He passed her a small cup of steaming *consommé* and took a sip from his own. "As a secret agent of both the OSS and the SOE, you would then undergo instruction on the various aspects of spy craft at a variety of training camps in Britain."

Catherine felt a sudden shiver of excitement. As a citizen of both the United Kingdom and the United States, she would now be working for *both* intelligence agencies fighting Hitler. Catherine briefly considered how ready to battle this foe her father would have been, had he survived the hideous cancer that killed him when she was seventeen.

"What sort of training is involved?" Catherine asked, aware of the hollow space that bloomed in her chest whenever she thought about her father's final year of agony, a year when her mother guarded his sickroom as if he were in prison and his only child an unwanted intruder.

Donovan replied, "You'll be taught subjects like coding and de-coding messages, wireless transmission, use of small weapons, silent killing, the best ways to blow up a bridge…things like that. Oh, and parachute training," he added. "Mustn't forget that. All our agents must be willing and able to throw themselves out of the belly of various types of aircraft. Do you have any qualms on that score?"

"None whatsoever." Catherine had thrown herself and her skis off many an alpine cornice on Mont Blanc and various other mountain resorts in the Swiss Alps.

"Excellent!"

Catherine asked, with a hint of skepticism that she couldn't disguise, "How many women have been recruited for this operation? We ladies won't just end up behind desks in the War Department over there, will we?"

Donovan took another sip of his soup and then set it aside.

"In your case, not likely. Both high commands, and especially Mr. Churchill, recognize that women working undercover beneath the noses of the Third Reich can often move about enemy territory with far less chance of their activities being detected than their male counterparts who should, by the Nazis' way of thinking, all be conscripted into the German army."

"You mean, we can carry hand grenades in our shopping bags more easily than young men can in the back of a truck?"

"Precisely! And your disguises can be more convincing," Donovan said with a short laugh. "Pillows around your waist under your clothing—"

"So we look—ah, yes!" Catherine chortled. "What a good idea! I must remember that disguise."

"I'm told Churchill himself, advanced that suggestion." Then Donovan's expression grew stern. "As Mr. Churchill has said, the men and women recruited are being hired—not to put too fine a point on it—'to set Europe ablaze' by getting arms and know-how into war zones to prepare the French resisters for the ultimate invasions of France. There may even be occasions when the assignment will be to spirit downed Allied pilots out of enemy territory to safety. Your being able to speak French, German, and Italian without an accent, along with the bravery and skills you've just shown in the operation at the Vichy embassy, make you eminently qualified for this highly dangerous work, Mrs. Thornton."

Catherine leaned back against her seat as the train swayed and the city of Philadelphia passed by her window.

"Why thank you, General. Your words are very inspiring."

"Well," he said, his expression now deadly serious, "I hope you also heard my underscoring the highly dangerous nature of the work.

The women will mostly be trained as couriers and wireless operators in the field, and incidentally, the wireless operators have thus far served an average of six weeks in France before they are either caught or killed." He paused as if deliberately allowing that startling piece of information to sink in, then he reached for two sheets of paper resting on the seat next to him. "Now, have a look at these."

Catherine scanned the documents he handed her.

"Before we go any further, I must ask you to sign this non-disclosure agreement and also one for the SOE, which Major Pepper has provided."

"The Official Secrets Act?" she confirmed.

"Yes. Each country has its own version, but their meaning is similar. If you sign both, you must not reveal your association with either agency to anyone, including members of your family, your closest friends, and certainly not any acquaintances." He cast her a steady gaze. "Not even any details of your specific assignments to other agents whom you may meet along the way."

Catherine glanced at the top of the two documents. One sported the British royal crest in one corner. Donovan's American document contained similar language with the official seal of the United States. Without a moment's hesitation, she seized the pen the major general offered her and signed the Secrets Act.

Accepting back the first of the two papers, her host noted, "A room has been reserved for you at the New York Ritz Carlton Hotel this week."

Catherine was about to sign her name on the OSS document when Donovan held up a hand to halt the process.

"I nearly forgot," he said. "I must ask you, Mrs. Thornton, how your husband would view—if he knew, which he must not—these activities of your becoming a joint agent in war-time Europe? Mr. Thornton is still assigned to a post in Chile, I believe?"

Catherine speculated that Donovan knew just about everything there was to know about Mr. and Mrs. Jeremy Thornton.

"As you may well be aware," she replied coolly, "I have been legally separated from my husband for more than a year and a half. He is twenty-two years my senior, by the way," she added, as if that fact alone would explain their estrangement. "He is Catholic, so he says divorce is out of the question. As I made clear to him when last we spoke, he—as a loyal British citizen and one of His Majesty's diplomats—will fight the war his way. I, with my dual citizenship status and language skills, will fight it mine, so his opinion really doesn't factor here." Catherine knew that her estranged husband and his pompous fellow diplomates in Chile would continue to sit on their asses, drink brandy, and wag their chins about the state of the world, never really doing anything to fight the fiend who had taken over Europe.

Donovan merely nodded, politely waiting for Catherine's next words. "And I can assure you, sir, I am more certain than ever that I wish to accept the offers you have extended to me today." Then, for good measure, she added, "And I trust that the OSS and the SOE will soon conclude the value of Henri Leblanc's services as a secret agent."

Donovan hesitated a moment then handed over the non-disclosure document for his organization, which she signed with a flourish.

Just then, the porter from the train's dining car returned holding a gleaming silver pot of coffee and matching cream and sugar bowls, along with two white porcelain cups. Catherine pointed to a small side table bolted into the carriage wall, indicating that the porter could leave the tray on it and remove their luncheon things. Without asking, she did the honors pouring cups for Donovan and herself, keeping her hand steady against the swaying of the car.

"Lovely. Thank you," he said, accepting the coffee she proffered him. "And might I suggest that, once you are back in Washington, you could consider holding a farewell cocktail party, explaining to all your friends and acquaintances that you've been hired by the *Chicago Tribune* as a foreign correspondent, based in London."

"What a perfect cover!" she exclaimed, thinking how jealous her classmates on her old secondary school newspaper would be to hear she scored a position on a major city daily as a war correspondent for American readers. "So, I reckon you know I had a similar cover story in Washington, thanks to Major Pepper."

"I did."

"And that I also edited the expat newsletter at the University of Geneva and had several travel articles published in English language magazines when Jeremy and I were posted in Spain."

Donovan nodded. "Another talent that has been noted. It's all been arranged with the publisher of the *Tribune*, who happens to be a friend of mine."

The old boys' network at work, she thought, but this time it was in service to hiring a woman in the prestigious role of foreign correspondent, even if it was as a cover for her true job as a secret agent.

Then a disconcerting thought struck Catherine. What of poor Henri's future, stuck in Hershey, Pennsylvania with those Vichy colleagues he abhorred?

What if Wild Bill doesn't keep his implied promise to evaluate Henri's service fairly?

Would Henri be offered as worthy a role as she was being given, along with a speedy escape from the clutches of Alice Clay Leblanc—to say nothing of evading the threat to his life posed by his Nazi-loving ambassador?

———◇———

Henri, sham suitcase in hand, opened the door to his suite on the seventh floor of the Wardman Park Hotel as quietly as he could. He might as well have slammed it against the wall.

There, in the middle of the sitting room, stood Alice, her coiffure already coiled into a large sausage above her forehead, with matching rolls of dark brown hair curling around her neck in a style that seemed to Henri was unaccountably fashionable these days. He thought of Catherine's halo of auburn hair and realized he missed her already.

Even though it was still an early hour, Alice had applied her full makeup: bold red lipstick and heavily arched eyebrows that reminded him of the American actress Joan Crawford. Henri's wife of eleven years was still in her dressing gown and fuzzy slippers. Suitcases and hatboxes were scattered around the room, along with a large steamer trunk pushed into the corner and overflowing with clothes and shoes.

Alice gestured toward Henri's own suitcase and said, "No point unpacking that. The U.S. Marshalls were here late last night. We have to be out of the hotel by noon today," she declared with indignation, "along with everything we own." She frowned and added, "By the way, we're being *interned*,' the man said, but then,

I'm sure you already know this and didn't have the courtesy to warn me before the officious brute pounded on my door at eleven o'clock last night!"

"It does seem a bit like the rug has been pulled out from under us," he acknowledged. He carefully closed the front door to the hallway and set his suitcase behind one of the two upholstered chairs which matched a pair in Catherine's hotel suite downstairs. "There had been rumors," he said. "But, no, I had not received the official word of this."

"Really?" Alice said, arching a skeptical eyebrow.

"Really. I've been traveling, remember?"

When was the last time that he and Alice had been able to have an honest exchange, he wondered? Not since he'd found out about the tennis pro at the Chevy Chase country club, he supposed. When was that? Less than two years into their marriage?

He watched silently as Alice threw a winter coat over the top of the trunk with an angry jerk, the heavy fox-fur collar thudding against the brass hinges.

"If I had wanted to live in the back-of-the-beyond, I'd have never left Wisconsin," she said, her voice oozing resentment. "I'm an American citizen, for God's sake. Can't you find a way to have me exempt from all this?"

"Sadly, no. No one attached to the embassy is exempt. Since the Pearl Harbor attack, we're all considered enemy aliens."

"It's outrageous! That beast, J. Edgar Hoover! I hate the man!"

Henri felt a twinge of sympathy for her. If there were any way he could pull strings on her behalf, he would—if only to distance himself from her. But he knew it was impossible, given his instructions from Pepper not to call attention to himself.

"Look, Alice," he said, attempting to offer some sort of truce, "I'm truly sorry you've been caught up in all this. I'll see if there's anything I can do."

"Fat chance you can—or will—do anything for me," she replied, her lips pursed in a familiar pout. "I know you."

No, you don't. You know virtually nothing about me these days.

Their lives had spun in utterly separate orbits for years now. Each conversation with Alice routinely became a battleground.

He gazed across the room at a woman who had once been very

pretty and quite slender. He'd first encountered Alice Clay one weekend, playing in the tennis doubles tournament at the country club in Chevy Chase. The great, great grandniece of the American senator and later Secretary of State, Henry Clay, had been attractive and gregarious at first blush. As their relationship developed, she seemed to enjoy playing the part of hostess when they held cocktail and dinner parties together. She was from a wealthy Midwest lumber family that had come to Washington when her father served in Herbert Hoover's Commerce Department. Alice and he appeared to be a good match, especially for a diplomatic life where they would be routinely thrust into exotic foreign surroundings. The job required them to constantly meet and greet a variety of people, including members of the press. It was part of Henri's assignment representing France in the United States.

And then everything changed.

Henri had been humiliated by Alice's "meaningless fling" (as she described it afterward) with the tennis pro. It had been one of those minor dramas where every one of their friends and acquaintances had known what had been going on—but not him. Alice had justified her behavior with the rationale that he was probably doing the same thing, given the late hours at the embassy and his frequent travels with the previous ambassador from France before the Vichy regime took over.

The ironic truth was he *wasn't* having any affairs. He was merely trying to cope with the tumultuous political situation in France during the rise of Hitler in Germany.

He'd freely admit to any critic of their ongoing estrangement that divorce after such a short marriage would have been complicated and bad for his career. But her betrayal signaled the unofficial end of their union. In his mind, he was then free to behave discreetly in whatever fashion he wished when it came to the opposite sex, and so he had. But, despite the truth of what had transpired between them, Alice had made him the villain within their circle of friends. In the end, he realized that neither of them liked the other one very much.

In fact, in recent years he had grown rather doubtful about trusting women in general. That was, until he had met Catherine Thornton.

Catherine was physically beautiful, of course, and her sultry manner of speaking had captured him from that first day. And then there was a spirit about her as fine and true as any patriot he had met when he'd been a young flyer in the last war. She recognized evil in an instant and fought for good. She faced danger with a cool head and a kind of bravery that put him to shame.

And as a lover...

Henri pulled his thoughts back to the situation at hand. He had only hours to pack. What would his future turn out to be? What if the ambassador somehow discovered that the secret naval codebooks had been copied and delivered to the Allies; that his press attaché was most likely the only staff member who could have accomplished the theft?

Henri glanced around the cluttered front chamber of the rooms he shared with Alice, a feeling of dread mingling with overwhelming fatigue, especially recalling his recent actions and their possible life-threatening consequences. Adding to the bolt of apprehension was the thought that he and his incompatible wife would be 'interned' in rooms much smaller and less accommodating than these for who-knew-how-long at the Hershey Hotel in "back-of-the-beyond" Pennsylvania.

Worse still, as a full-blooded Frenchman, he was no fan of America's Hershey chocolate.

CHAPTER 6

July 1942

A crystal vase of salmon-colored and blush-pink roses had replaced the drying photographed copies of the French naval codes on Catherine's stylish glass coffee table. In fact, there were no signs whatsoever of the earlier "safe house" appearance of Apartment 215B at the Wardman Park Hotel. The drinks cabinet, now replete with all manner of spirits and wine, stood stoically against one wall in the large sitting room of Catherine's government-supplied accommodations. Five stories above her, Henri and his wife Alice's former flat was now empty, its tenants gone.

In one area of Catherine's hotel sitting room, a long, narrow sofa table served as a makeshift bar. It was stocked with glasses lined up like soldiers heading to board the American ships soon to take them to the battlefields of Europe.

A butler-cum-barman, clad in a starched white coat and gleaming black trousers, had been hired for the occasion. He stood at the ready near the front door to receive the coats of the arriving guests. He had also been instructed to offer cocktails to the diplomats, government functionaries, and Catherine's mother, Gladys, along with several of her friends that the older woman insisted on bringing to her daughter's farewell soiree.

"If this is to be your *au revoir* to all and sundry, then I am inviting a few people that Annabelle Arlington will find worthy of mentioning in her society column," Gladys pronounced loftily. Her mother appeared genuinely stunned when Catherine sprung the news that she'd gotten a job as a foreign correspondent with the *Chicago Tribune* and would soon be leaving the country for London. "Annabelle was as amazed as I was about all this and tells me you're considered by her colleagues to be strictly an amateur," Gladys responded to her daughter's announcement, adding. "Well, at least your farewell party might serve to rescue your damaged reputation to some degree because I've run out of excuses why you're not living with your husband. It pains me to hear rumors about the kinds of people you've been consorting with."

"Really? Who?" Catherine had asked archly, although her heart skipped at the thought someone might have caught wind of her clandestine work with Henri.

"Oh, that Argentine polo player someone saw you with and that...I forget the name of the passport officer at the Spanish embassy. And there was some U.S. Navy lieutenant you were seen with at the officers club when you first came back from Chile."

"Oh, for goodness sake, Mother! I'm a thirty-two-year-old woman!"

"And a married one, might I add!"

"Who is legally separated, might I add," she'd retorted.

Catherine tried to push these recent exchanges with her mother aside to concentrate on preparing for the evening and the guests who would be attending. For the last half hour, she'd been sitting at the silk-skirted dressing table in her bedroom, staring at her reflection, her face scrupulously clean. She began her careful practice of applying makeup so skillfully that it appeared she wore little of it. Her thoughts began to drift back to the chain of events that had brought her to this day, a day which, henceforth, would mean living a life of secrets.

But, then, hadn't she been living that way for a very long time? Catherine was well aware that her mother had been scandalized to learn, after the "wedding of the season" ten years earlier, that her daughter's marriage had turned out so disastrously. But only Catherine knew the reasons the British diplomat, Jeremy Thornton, barely spoke to his new wife—or even saw much of the former debutante, except for formal occasions at the various embassies where Jeremy had been assigned in Spain and Latin America.

By year eight of their union, Catherine had abandoned her husband at his post in Chile and abruptly returned to Washington just prior to the attack on Pearl Harbor in December 1941. In the intervening months, it seemed clear to the haughty Mrs. Cahill that her daughter and Jeremy Thornton, whose rupture was still a mystery to her, were no closer to reconciliation than when Catherine had suddenly appeared on her doorstep, announcing their de facto separation.

"I came back to D.C. to get a job as a newspaperwoman," Catherine had told her mother the morning after her arrival.

"That can't have sat well with Jeremy. I'm sure the poor man is absolutely furious with you!" her mother exclaimed.

"Not really," Catherine had answered, maintaining the cool demeanor she knew irritated Gladys to no end. "Surely, you've heard that we've been living separate lives for years, now, Mother. He hardly noticed when I was away on an assignment for my travel pieces."

"Why would he?" she demanded. "You've only had one or two articles published! That silly newsletter for expats you wrote for in Geneva surely doesn't count," her mother had scoffed. "Who would hire you in Washington, for pity's sake?"

"I've sold numerous travel pieces," Catherine retorted. "And have you conveniently forgotten that, since I've been home, I've done those stories about groups opposed to America joining the war?"

"Your father would have been ashamed that you'd write anything positive about those dreadful Vichy collaborators or the neutralists," Gladys had declared. "I could hardly hold my head up at the club afterward each time an article of yours appeared."

But how would her mother know that Catherine's former cover story masked activities of which the late Colonel Cahill would be justly proud? Yet all Gladys could do was harp on how disgraceful it was to have a daughter who had run out on a "perfectly respectable husband of sterling character."

Tarnished brass is a more accurate description of the man.

There were many times, during the past two years in D.C., when Catherine had come close to shouting at her mother, "Well, if you like and miss Jeremy so much, why didn't you marry him, then? You were a widow, and you two were nearly the same age!"

But, no. If Catherine were truly honest with herself, in a remote part of her conscience where she sometimes acknowledged the truth, she had latched on to Jeremy like a drowning swimmer clinging to a piece of driftwood in a turbulent sea.

Her father had just died, she remembered, staring blankly into her dressing table mirror, slowly rubbing moisturizer onto her cheeks. No one except a certain "family friend" knew the real reasons she had latched on to the aloof, proper diplomat so desperately that summer when she'd just turned eighteen.

From age fourteen onwards, Catherine had been terrified that the identity of the man who had sexually attacked her would become public, an unthinkable disaster that could not only blowup her young life back then, but her entire family's as well. From the night she'd been raped as a boarding school sophomore, she'd been trapped into silence by an ongoing sexual relationship with one of her father's closest associates, a powerful man who threatened dire consequences for them both if she told anyone. In her youthful ignorance of human biology and an ever-present fear of exposure and humiliation, the predator's serial molestation predictably ended in pregnancy.

The one thing the younger Catherine had known only too well was that, if she'd told her mother what had happened the year that she'd returned to the States to go to boarding school, Gladys would have blamed *her* for disgracing the family names of Farnsworth and Cahill. From puberty onwards, Catherine knew that the Eleanor Roosevelt look-alike resented her daughter's good looks and the attention it inevitably drew to her only offspring.

Catherine, panicked by the fear she might truly be pregnant, dove into denial, keeping up the whirl of her debutante year and telling herself that her period was merely late. During those stress-filled weeks, she was introduced to the rather remote, dispassionate aide to the British ambassador in Washington at a typically boring D.C. drinks party. After a martini each that night more than a decade earlier, Jeremy Thornton had mentioned as part of the usual meaningless chitchat that he'd be attending a house party in Chevy Chase, to which he understood that she'd also been invited.

Catherine had merely nodded politely. Having been feeling under the weather for a number of weeks, she'd almost decided not to attend. But then, seven days later, on the broad lawn in front of their hosts' rambling brick mansion, there was Jeremy, whacking his wooden croquet ball just before she took a turn.

"Well, hello again," he'd said, with a courteous nod of his head. "How very nice to see you."

She'd barely recalled meeting the rather-stuffy-but-sought-after bachelor who, she learned that weekend, had just turned forty. She was still reeling from the morning's shock at the doctor's office confirming she was indeed pregnant. Suddenly, Jeremy Thornton looked surprisingly attractive—more so than she recalled from their previous encounter, attired for the match from head to toe in regulation dress whites. He also appeared fit and confident, and it occurred to her he just might be someone who could save her from the calamity overtaking her. As play on the field progressed, she'd shamelessly engaged in a flurry of flattery about his mastery of the game of croquet.

"It's really lovely you came," she whispered conspiratorially as they stood on the sidelines waiting for their next turns. "I was a bit worried that you might be called out to some important diplomatic duty this weekend and I wouldn't…well…get to see you."

Color had seeped up Jeremy's throat, and Catherine knew then that he was a man that could easily be guided by fawning admiration—at least she'd thought that, early in their acquaintance.

That afternoon, as the house party got underway, he had begun to shower her with attention each time he indicated it was her shot on the croquet green, a sign that her spontaneous crusade to capture his cool, assessing eye was succeeding.

Looking back on that fateful weekend, Catherine was ashamed to recall how she'd deliberately and expertly flirted with Jeremy at dinner and continued to do so when the guests retired to the library for coffee afterwards. After some dancing to phonograph records in the living room, she'd squeezed his hands, brushed her lips briefly against his cheek, and bid everyone goodnight, feeling his hungry eyes following her as she left the room. A wave of weariness had engulfed her suddenly, along with queasiness that had become her constant companion. She'd shut the door to her room, feeling a sense of conquest...until the reality of what was happening to her body caused her to begin to shake with pure terror.

What in the world will happen when everyone knows that I'm—

She pushed away the thought, replacing it with renewed determination to implement a desperate scheme to save herself. She opened the door to her bedroom just as the maid assigned to her wing of the house passed by. The servant happily accepted a five-dollar bill and directed her to Jeremy's room. In nightgown and silk robe, Catherine had skimmed across the main landing, down the empty corridor opposite the one she'd been assigned. Given the coast was clear, she boldly slipped inside a mahogany paneled chamber and slithered under the covers of his bed. She lay there, arms stiffly by her side, until he arrived after a few hours of drinking in the elegant pool table room shooting several boisterous rounds with a gaggle of other young men.

In his mildly alcoholic haze, Jeremy had been both startled and pleased to find a lovely-looking woman in his bed.

"Catherine?" he'd said with a hint of uncertainty, his tall stature looming above her prone figure. Recognizing it was truly her, he added with a note of trepidation, "Good God! Did anyone see you?"

She should have known right then that Jeremy cared very deeply about what other people thought, far more than his own views or desires or those of his nearest and dearest.

"Absolutely no one caught even a glimpse," she purred. "Truly, I didn't see a soul coming here. It's just that I wanted to see you again *so* much, Jeremy, so I decided to be daring and very naughty. Can you forgive me?" she asked.

Jeremy appeared to swallow hard and then nodded affirmatively.

Regaining her confidence, she smiled and pulled back the covers to reveal her long, lithe form, sans nightgown. "Aren't you going to come to bed?"

He did and, of course, made love to her. For her part, what may have appeared to Jeremy to be a woman madly taken by his charms was actually a frightened female summoning every sexual trick she'd been forced to learn from the sixty-year-old who had gotten her pregnant. In the days that followed, she'd encouraged the cautious British diplomat to enjoy more of the favors she had frantically dispensed that first weekend.

Within six weeks they were engaged.

Reflecting on the decade that had followed her impulsive act of self-preservation, Catherine realized it was the first instance she'd employed her so-called feminine wiles to solve a problem. Soon after the wedding, when she could no longer hide her pregnant condition, she'd announced with false joy to Jeremy they were going to have a child.

At first, her groom had been pleased and obviously proud they were to have a honeymoon baby, but unfortunately for Catherine, the man could count. By the time they were heading by ocean liner for his new posting in Venezuela, the child arrived, with the uncertain help of the ship's doctor, at eight pounds, seven ounces, a mere six and a half months after their nuptials in front of Washington's social elite.

"You slut!" Jeremy had shouted within the confines of their cabin after she'd gone into labor and produced a plump, lusty boy a good two and a half months before term. "This child can't be mine! Look at his dark hair and that olive skin! His eyes are black! You seduced me, you whore! You used me to save your reputation, and now you've wrecked mine!"

At first, she attempted to placate him with pleas of forgiveness and oaths swearing she loved him and that she "desperately wanted the child to be yours."

"Oh, come now," he said, fury and sarcasm dripping from every clipped English syllable. "All the chaps warned me about you. Oh, that you were charming and very pretty, all right, but that you're a tart through and through. That you played the tease toward all the boys during your debutante year. I was also told that there was some swarthy Italian you hung about with, old enough to be your father—"

Catherine had heard herself screaming, "Shut up, shut up, SHUT UP, you boring tiresome man! We're *married.* We have a child. And that's the end of it, unless you wish to make things even worse for yourself and your career!"

Jeremy had stood by her bed, arms stiff, fists clenched by his side. She wondered for a moment if he wouldn't use one hand to smash her face into the pillow. The baby had begun to whimper and then howled at the top of its newborn lungs.

"I can ruin you, you know," he shouted over the baby's cries. He was glaring down at her, his features distorted with an expression of searing hatred she had never thought possible, given his usual phlegmatic persona. His teeth were clenched, and his next words came out like a long hiss. "I can humiliate you so no one will want you, *ever.*"

A strange and unexpected courage surged through her, as she recognized his fury was based on terror that his colleagues at the embassy would dismiss him as a sucker and clueless sap if they knew of these circumstances. Emboldened by this insight, she sat up straight in bed.

"And I can ruin any chance for *your* advancement in the stodgy, old diplomatic corps if I breathe one word of what's happened to your ambassador or the fellows you work with," she retorted, knowing this was his most vulnerable spot. She cocked a raised eyebrow and affected a small shrug. "So why should either of us do something so stupid? I think it's best we simply call a truce, don't you?"

Jeremy again balled both hands into fists, and she thought this time he truly might attack her physically as she lay on the built-in bed in the ship's cabin. Silence bounced off the highly varnished walls that reflected her enraged husband's looming silhouette. Neither spoke, and the only sound was the Atlantic Ocean slapping the side of the ship.

At length, he replied, jaw clenched, seething with barely controlled wrath and indignation. "I'll find out who this bastard baby's father is, damn you! I'm sure your mother knew that you were tricking me into this marriage. I'll speak to that newspaper friend of hers at the newspaper! Or I'll—"

Taking in these very real threats of a man who'd clearly lost all control, Catherine had immediately lowered her voice and calmed her racing heart as best she could. Employing a totally new strategy, she composed her features and made a show of lowering her gaze to her hands resting above the bed linen, clasping and unclasping them to indicate remorse. Anything to avoid both her mother and Annabelle Arlington knowing the truth of what had transpired to create this nightmare.

"Jeremy, look. I am so very sorry to have deceived you like this, but I was scared, and I couldn't even admit it to myself. You must believe me that I do truly, *truly* care for you," she added with as much sincerity she thought might be effective. "I thought, perhaps, because I've come to love you, you could find it in your heart—"

"Oh, do be quiet!" he spat. "Once we arrive, I will pack you and this bastard child back to your mother in disgrace, and all of Washington will know why!"

Her sixth sense told her he was bluffing, for such a move would expose him to public ridicule as much as it would her. At this point in his emotional storm, she'd realized that she would have to surrender to whatever scheme would keep the disaster from destroying all of their lives, especially the life of her newborn son. She'd gazed at the innocent child in her arms with a fierce sense of protectiveness, positive that neither of the men in its life would safeguard the poor little thing.

And so, with as much dignity as was available to her eighteen-year-old self under the impossible circumstances in which she found herself, she agreed to abide by Jeremy's plan to place the infant for adoption. Even so, she'd held firm in her determination not to tell him or anyone else who had fathered the child, acutely aware of the explosive nature of the truth.

Two days before they were due to dock in Venezuela, Jeremy appeared in their stateroom and immediately closed the cabin door. He announced with grim determination, "I've located a childless couple I knew at another post. British expats who will meet the ship in Caracas."

She'd stared at him from a straight-backed chair, holding the baby to her breast.

"How in the world—?"

"There's a ship-to-shore radio on board," he interrupted, his staccato wording intimating that she was a stupid cow not to know this fact. "It's all been settled. A ship's steward will hand the child to them at the foot of the gangway the minute we dock—before you and I disembark," he added, in a warning tone that brooked no protest or interference. He shoved a paper in front of her that he'd written out on ship's stationery stating, *"Catherine Farnsworth Cahill Thornton releases her parental rights in perpetuity."* She'd stared at the holograph document until Jeremy clapped a pen in her hand.

"Sign!" he commanded.

"Who are these people?" she demanded, as no names were included in the document.

"Far more decent and trustworthy than you are!" he shot back. "They're about to depart for their next posting, so this entire disaster will soon come to an end. Sign, if you don't want me to put you on the next boat back to your bloody country!"

And sign she did, along with the birth certificate produced by the ship's doctor.

Catherine was never told the name of the couple adopting her son, nor was she allowed to leave her cabin until they'd sped away with the newborn swaddled in a large bath towel sporting the ship's monogram. Half an hour later, she and Jeremy were whisked into a waiting embassy limousine parked dockside next to their ship. As the car pulled away, diplomatic flags flying on the front fenders, and a window serving as a sound-proof barrier between the passengers and the chauffeur up front, she quietly proposed that they divorce with no fanfare after a decent interval.

Tight-lipped and staring straight ahead, he answered, "Any divorce within the first years of marriage would leave an indelible black mark on my record, from which, I can assure you, my career would not recover."

"And after three or four years?" she asked, dreading to hear his answer.

"For the foreseeable future," he said, shifting his gaze out the window on his side of the embassy car, "we shall continue as man and wife, or your mother will hear from me about exactly what her daughter has done."

Later, he informed her of the story he'd concocted for family and friends that their honeymoon infant had perished a few days before landing, due to a traumatic, premature birth at sea.

Once installed at their latest diplomatic post, Jeremy, seemingly unperturbed, went to work, returned home, and was content to exchange *please* and *thank you* as their main mode of conversation as their days together wore on.

She, on the other hand, had found herself awash in guilt and deep depression. Somehow, though, with the slow, painful passage of time that first year of her sham marriage, she'd finally succeeded in making an elusive peace with herself. Given her antipathy toward her own parent, she'd eventually concluded that, perhaps, she simply wasn't cut out to be a proper mother. At length, she summoned her remaining strength and managed to convince others around her that she had recovered from that early tragedy of losing a baby and was living a normal existence with her husband. Even so, there were many moments when she was filled with a burning hatred for him, salted with acrid remorse for her own behavior.

Advancing through her twenties in those early years in Venezuela, she eventually assumed an armor of bright smiles, performed as the perfect hostess, and managed, at length, to lull Jeremy into a sense that as long as they each played their part, the center would hold in their arrangement. The one benefit of their truce, she concluded with grim satisfaction, was that neither of them wanted to make love, for the feelings each had for the other were the exact opposite of human affection.

Then, there came the day when she and Jeremy moved on to a post in Chile. As the clouds of war were gathering in Europe and the Far East, she knew that if she'd stayed much longer with the man she had married in such desperation at eighteen years old, she might well murder him in his sleep.

On her thirtieth birthday, she'd booked a voyage home under the guise of visiting family. Once there, she hired a prominent D.C. attorney to secure a legal separation, and here she was, two years later, almost free from Jeremy's domination...and thirty-two years old.

As Catherine sat at her dressing table on this early summer's night, putting the finishing touches on her makeup and contemplating the previous decade, her unhappy reverie was suddenly interrupted by the ring of the doorbell.

Her farewell party as a secret agent was about to commence.

CHAPTER 7

From her bedroom, with the door slightly ajar, Catherine could hear the exchange between the butler/barman and the local delivery boy who'd brought extra ice. As the evening's hostess, she hurried to finish dressing in order to be ready by the time the first guest arrived.

She called out to the barman, "Thank you for seeing to that, Charlie! I'll be out in a minute."

Catherine seized a pale pink feather puff and dabbed it into the crystal jar containing an expensive brand of face powder. Sparingly applying it to her cheeks and forehead, she was perfectly aware that her even features, green eyes, and auburn hair had always aided her ability to attract men and persuade most of them—except Jeremy Thornton, of course—to do her bidding.

Yet, in reaction to her impossible marriage, she had sought a sense of satisfaction elsewhere by perfecting the art of persuading certain men to *tell* her things. Even as a young girl, if she heard something interesting, she passed it on to her father, Marine Colonel Amory Cahill, assigned to the security detail at a succession of embassies in Europe. She'd soon discovered it was an excellent way to get the busy man's full attention and receive, in return, a measure of the warmth and love she craved. Her father's sporadic expressions of fondness for her was her reward in those youthful days when no one thought a mere child in their midst was paying attention to unfolding events.

For her own diversion during those early, unhappy years in South America, Catherine had continued sharing certain items of information not only with the embassy's security officer but also with passport control specialists, the press attaché, and unspecified commercial operatives. Her talent for listening and remembering had been quietly observed by various British intelligence officials at Jeremy's several postings.

With a sigh, Catherine stood up from her dressing table, shaking off the gloom that descended whenever she thought about her current stalemated estrangement with Jeremy. She discarded her robe and slipped into her peach-colored, bias-cut silk evening gown. Resuming her seat in front of the mirror, she once again met her own gaze in the looking glass, silently confessing that the best antidote to fill the hole left in her heart by the theft of her baby was to collect and pass along the intelligence she gained from the powerful people in her circle and give it to the likes of the mysterious Major John Pepper.

Catherine felt the heat invade her rouged cheek at the thought of a certain Lieutenant Peter Farley, due to arrive at that evening's party. He'd certainly played a crucial role in connecting her to Major Pepper and set her on the current path she was following. It had all started on the first day she'd arrived back in the United States two years earlier, when the good-looking lieutenant had served as her courtesy escort, sent by the U.S. government to greet an arriving British diplomat's wife.

And now, everything that followed—painful as that relationship had turned out to be—had resulted in her getting a plum job working for both America's OSS and Britain's Special Operations Executive.

So, really, what could be more perfect? she reflected, lightly daubing her lips with color and brushing aside the familiar knot of regret that burrowed into her gut. Tonight she would greatly enjoy announcing to the elusive young naval intelligence officer that she was off to London as a war correspondent for a major American newspaper.

Catherine rose to her feet once more and slipped on a pair of satin mules that matched the silk gown clinging to her curves. It was an ensemble sure to catch the attention of Washington D.C.'s legendary social chronicler, Annabelle Arlington, to say nothing of

Lieutenant Farley's roving eye. She took one final look at herself in the long mirror on the back of her bedroom door.

The hostess with the most-est.

She almost laughed out loud at her reflection. Wasn't that phrase practically emblematic of the notorious Catherine Thornton?

———◇———

Catherine's mother sat on her daughter's blue silk loveseat alongside the Woman's Page editor, Annabelle Arlington, as if this were a cocktail party thrown in their honor. There was no doubt, however, that Gladys Farnsworth Cahill would faint if she knew Catherine had just enlisted in a clandestine agency completely at odds with J. Edgar Hoover and his ilk. In fact, Gladys would castigate her only daughter's latest career choice as a threat to *her* social standing as one of "the grand dames of the nation's capital." This was the cherished description once noted in print by Gladys's stalwart friend, the all-powerful Miss Arlington. Gladys had never hesitated to remind her daughter of the older woman's vaunted status in the eyes of Washington's elite.

Battle axes is a better description of those two, Catherine judged.

"Darling," her mother gushed as Catherine approached, "you remember Jayne and Stephen Gallagher? Stephen now works for the Wisconsin senatorial delegation and—"

"Of course, Mother," Catherine cut her short. Such was the small world of Washington D.C., she was fully aware that Jayne Gallagher was a sorority sister of Henri Leblanc's wife, Alice, who also hailed from Wisconsin.

The cocktail party was fast reaching critical mass, and now that it was well underway, Catherine wished only that people would have their fill of drinks and hors d'oeuvres and begin to depart. Aware of the familiar restlessness she often felt in crowds like this, she flashed her most winsome smile at Stephen Gallagher, an earnest young man widely known as Wisconsin Senator Robert LaFollette's right-hand man.

"I'm so delighted you both could come," Catherine said, beaming exclusively at Stephen. "And I'm especially delighted to shake the hand of a man with such a celebrated tennis serve. Pity we can't make up a doubles match before I leave for London."

"Well," chimed in Jayne, her critical gaze looking Catherine up and down, "we'd have to find you a partner, though, wouldn't we? Since your husband remains in Chile, that might be difficult."

"No, it wouldn't," corrected Catherine sweetly. "My husband and I have been officially separated for a year-and-a-half, so I'm free to play with anyone I like."

Again, she bestowed her warmest smile on Jayne's bewildered husband, who looked from one woman to the other as barely veiled hostility crackled between them.

Could Jayne and Alice Leblanc have discussed me over their many-martini lunches at the tennis club?

Well, if they had, it was probably because Alice Leblanc had seen Catherine in the hotel lobby, as part of her cover, in the company of scores of different "male friends."

Catherine swiftly turned away, pretending to be in search of someone. She had a sudden yearning to have Henri Leblanc there by her side. Both veterans of endless drinks parties for the embassy and politico crowd, she wanted nothing more than for this evening to be over and Henri lying beside her in her bed, dissecting the soiree and its attendees with his biting and highly amusing observations.

How was Henri faring, she wondered, locked in a Hershey hotel room with his unpleasant wife? She felt a startling tug of arousal at the memory of her final moments with Henri making love in the code room before it had been safe to depart the embassy.

For several minutes, she was only dimly aware of glasses clinking and the buzz of conversation surrounding her as she mentally shook herself and pushed such pointless musings aside. Henri was no different, was he? So why did her thoughts continually stray to him, now that their mission was completed?

Catherine breathed another weary sigh, concluding that the rush of sensation she felt was merely an itching for more adventure and certainly nothing more profound regarding Henri. The reality of war had relegated the future of her erstwhile collaborator to luck and fate.

Just then, a young man of about her age, with black hair slicked over his forehead and startling blue eyes, strode into the room in his full-dress whites, his naval lieutenant's hat tucked smartly under one arm.

Ah, Lieutenant Peter Farley arrives at last.

But, to her shock, standing directly behind him was her father's old friend, the Italian Admiral Enzo Moretti.

Catherine forced herself to take a deep breath and moved toward the new arrivals. Instead of greeting the handsome naval intelligence officer, she walked directly past Peter to extend her hand to the admiral, resplendent in his uniform and medals. The older man immediately inclined his head and pressed his lips against her skin.

"Good evening, sir," she welcomed Moretti in flawlessly accented Italian. "I wasn't certain you were still in America or I would have sent you an invitation."

The admiral blinked, a look of surprise invading his features. "Your mother extended my invitation," he replied in a low tone that indicated he didn't want anyone else to hear their conversation. "I hope, then, my coming here tonight hasn't upset you?"

Catherine *was* upset. Her mother had no right to invite people without running their names by her, and this was especially true when it came to Enzo Moretti. Even so, she merely murmured in Italian, "I would have thought that by now you'd be—"

Moretti interrupted, "Yes, as I am now declared an enemy alien, I will be leaving America next week. When Gladys told me you were off to England, I thought at least to come to say goodbye to you...and to your mother," he added hastily.

He again reached for her hand, but she was too quick for him and threaded her fingers behind her back. He sought her glance as an alternative.

"I'm glad I came, Catherine. It may be a very long time before we meet again."

"If we do meet again...ever," she replied. She knew her words were harsh and was glad of it. His country was at war with her own now, prompting his deportation to Italy. She need never see him again, and it felt like a victory.

"Catherine," he said, his voice full of regret. "Surely, you understand? I-I—"

"Don't even speak of it," she said with a carelessness she didn't feel. "My mother is right over there," she pointed. "She'll be so pleased to see you."

Wouldn't this be quite a scene if Mother only knew what her special pet, Enzo Moretti, did to young girls of fourteen.

Throughout this exchange, Lieutenant Farley had been waiting a few feet away. Catherine wondered how proficient he was in Italian.

As if on cue, Peter took a step forward. "Darling Kit-Cat, so good to see you. Do let me get the hostess a drink," he offered, ignoring the admiral.

Moretti had little choice but to cross the room to pay his respects to the widow of his longtime friend, the late Colonel Cahill. Peter regarded her intently.

"Well, that was certainly an interesting meet-and-greet," he said with a nod in the admiral's direction. "How awkward that he comes to bid you a fond farewell."

So, Peter did understand Italian.

"As you can imagine, whenever I run into that man it tends to be awkward."

Peter studied her again for a long moment then asked, "How the hell are you?"

"Lovely, now that you're here." She flashed him a smile, again making light of Moretti's presence at the party. "I see *you* got my last-minute invitation."

"Oh, I've known for quite some time that you're soon off to the UK."

Well, why wouldn't he have? she thought. After all, she'd known from the day they met that he was a naval intelligence officer.

Thinking back, it was the height of irony that her present official connection to the clandestine world was partially the result of her foolishly pouring out her troubles to the handsome Lieutenant Peter Farley after fleeing Chile to the United States to escape from her miserable marriage.

Lonely and unsure of her future once back in Washington two years ago, she'd been immediately drawn to the attractive escort assigned by his superiors to squire her around. And, oh, how attentive and empathetic he'd seemed, she thought, despising the bitterness she felt whenever she saw him now.

As her acquaintance with the friendly and amusing young lieutenant grew, she had reveled spending time with a man her own age. Within a few weeks of dinner dates, picnics on the Potomac, and coffees in local cafes, they fell into bed as a result of what Catherine had erroneously thought at the time was a genuine, loving relationship with someone who shared her generation, tastes, background, and sensibilities. In a moment of exchanging intimacies one night, she'd even revealed how she'd been serially molested by a family friend when she was a mere schoolgirl.

"Just to get away from him," she'd murmured, "I married Jeremy at eighteen."

"Good God, Catherine!" Peter had responded. "You were only fourteen when it started and the guy who attacked you was a pal of your *father's*?"

She'd shrugged. "I suppose, in Italy, bedding a teenager is no shocker. And when you're an admiral, it probably isn't even—"

"The guy was an admiral?" he'd exclaimed. "An Italian admiral?"

"Yes."

"When your dad was posted in Europe?"

"Oh, my father was posted overseas, but it happened when I spent a year in boarding school in the States."

"In America?" Peter had asked, incredulous. "This Italian guy was here then?"

"He's still in America."

"*Not* Admiral Moretti?"

Catherine had been astounded by the speed of Peter's deduction.

"He's more than twice your age!" he protested, shaking his head with disgust.

"Three times," she'd corrected him, furious with herself for her confession, and upset that Peter had figured out who it was. "*Please* don't repeat what I've told you to anyone. I was fourteen, for God's sake!" Catherine had abruptly sat up in bed, disquieted by the small world they inhabited in D.C. "*Merde!*" she swore, balling her fists on top of the sheets. "How do you know him? Admiral Moretti, I mean?"

"Can't tell you that," Peter had answered cryptically, his expression suddenly shuttered. "However, this particular man screwing a young teenager doesn't actually surprise me very much."

In that moment it had dawned on her that, all along, one of Peter's jobs was keeping track of all foreign naval personnel assigned to the Washington D.C. area, including enemy aliens like Moretti, as well as looking after top military progeny and diplomatic wives coming and going through the nation's capital.

Catherine then asked with an edge to her voice, "Well, does it surprise you that, once upon a time, Enzo Moretti was one of my father's *best* friends?" She felt anger all over again that the admiral's avuncular visit to her boarding school had ended in his hotel bedroom after taking a young schoolgirl out to dinner.

Insanely, she remembered feeling it would be impolite to march out of the admiral's hotel suite when the situation had begun to feel uncomfortable. And besides, how would she have gotten back to school before curfew?

"You're no wilting flower now," Peter had reminded her, "and I'm sure you weren't one even as a teenager. Didn't you ever tell anyone he'd sexually assaulted you?"

Catherine shook her head no, keeping mum about her pregnancy as well as Jeremy's reaction when the baby was born. And she'd certainly never told Moretti he'd fathered a son who'd been given away for adoption.

"What about your parents?" Peter had pressed. "You didn't even tell *them*?"

"At fourteen years old, I was certain my father would probably shoot Moretti if he knew, and my mother would say I must have done something to encourage him."

"Going up to his hotel room probably did encourage him a bit," Peter noted with a wry smile that immediately prompted in Catherine another surge of anger. Why did men just assume a girl or woman must have done something to merit sexual assault?

She'd looked away from Peter and affected another shrug. "I was fourteen," she repeated. "I'd known the admiral practically all my life. It never occurred to me, when I went up to his room to accept a book he'd said he wanted to give me, that he'd trap me in a bear hug and then push me onto his bed."

Peter had chucked her under his chin. "Well, Kit-Cat, no wonder he grabbed you, as I'm sure you were as pretty as a nubile teen as you are now."

What she hadn't told Peter was that the admiral's subtle threats of exposure continued until her emergency marriage to Jeremy. Once she'd become Mrs. Thornton and left Washington, she found a certain grim satisfaction in playing older men for the fools they sometimes were to glean information that she passed on to government authorities. In the end, hadn't Moretti launched her unique area of expertise?

Catherine bent forward to take a sip of her martini, musing how foolish it had been of her to think Peter's immediate rush of passion and their obvious compatibility had meant more than it apparently had to the handsome young naval officer. Proof of this was her surprise discovery two months into their relationship that she wasn't the only woman with whom Lieutenant Farley had been sleeping that spring.

Pushing his casual betrayal out of her mind, along with his ultimate indifference about the rape, Catherine took another generous sip of her martini. She continued to smile and nod as if nothing she and Peter had shared had been anything more than a pleasurable fling. She'd said at the time she broke it off that it was probably best that they both move on, and she pleasantly but firmly put a stop to sharing intimacies with him. Peter had accepted her decision with an ease that told her he'd never been in love with her to begin with, and their exchanges in the succeeding two years since became purely professional.

Catherine stole a glance at her gold and diamond wristwatch, a gift from an admirer upon her departure from Chile. It was nearly ten.

Glory, will Peter and these people please move on to dinner somewhere?

Peter had gone to fetch Catherine another drink from the busy bartender across the room. Soon, the lieutenant again appeared by her side, bearing a fresh set of frosted, conical glasses, each with an olive bobbing on the surface.

"Chin-chin, Kit-Cat," he said, handing hers over and then gently clinking their rims.

It had been Peter who had arranged the small dinner at which Catherine had been introduced to Major Pepper. Soon after, Pepper recruited her for her first mission for the Brits: to persuade the Vichy French ambassador or some higher-up in the D.C. embassy to provide her access to the French naval codes "by any means available, including feminine persuasion."

For Catherine's part, she'd ultimately concluded that certain sexual encounters could indeed be pleasurable, even useful, but such familiarities were definitely not to be trusted as a barometer of lasting happiness or fidelity.

And Henri...What category did he belong in, she wondered. Unlike Enzo Moretti or Peter Farley, Henri Leblanc had never failed to live up to any promises or commitments he had made to her.

But the whole world is at war, she reminded herself as the first guests had begun to take their leave. Normal lives didn't exist anymore. And who the hell knew where Henri was anyway...or where he was going?

She was startled when Peter leaned close to her ear and said in a low voice, "So, word is you're heading for the Brits' spy school. Are you?"

The bastard knew everything about her new life!

"Schools, plural," she shot back tersely, unnerved that he should know this, "and let's not discuss it here, shall we? Tell me instead where you imagine you'll be spending the next few years."

"Pacific theater," he replied, "but I'm only guessing, mind you. I speak some Japanese, having been based in Tokyo for a while. But knowing the U.S. Navy, I'll probably end up in North Africa or someplace equally alien."

She raised her glass. "Well, here's to us both jumping into the great unknown."

"How right you are, Kit-Cat" he said, with a sudden seriousness she'd never detected before. "How right you are."

Peter's glass was empty. She retrieved it from his hand, pleased that she would soon be ushering everyone, including him, out her front door for good.

"Thanks for fetching me the libations," she said. "I'd better attend to my other guests and before anymore leave, make my official announcement that I'm being sent to Britain on Monday as a full-fledged war correspondent for the *Chicago Tribune*."

Peter leaned forward and whispered, "Ah, yes, time to spread your cover story like Pepper's good little girl."

Before he pulled away, his tongue delivered a wet kiss to her ear. She felt no reaction whatsoever. She could tell by his face, flushed not only from the gin he'd consumed but also from memories of special favors she'd granted him in bed, that she'd hooked him good tonight.

Sorry, sailor boy, but my barman already has orders to see you to the door when this little nighttime farce concludes.

A strange coldness, as well as a faint sense of triumph, wrapped around her heart with the knowledge that none of the lieutenant's sexual expectations would be met this evening—or ever again.

CHAPTER 8

Henri Leblanc slouched across the aisle from the erstwhile Vichy ambassador, feeling more miserable by the minute as he heard the mammoth engines of the U.S. military plane engage and roar to life. After nearly three weeks of internment at the Hershey Hotel, he was now on his way back to France—via Lisbon—with his pro-German superior facing a future that could only be disastrous for body and soul.

He barely looked up when the military escort on this American transport ordered all passengers to fasten their seatbelts to prepare for takeoff. Henri, along with the sour-faced ambassador and the ambassador's personal secretary, would soon be hurtling across the Atlantic Ocean on a flight to Portugal, where the three would have to make their own way by ship or fishing boat back into France.

So far, no one appeared to suspect that, during the previous months, Henri Leblanc had secretly been working for the Allies. Even so, the former French press attaché still wondered if the Vichy diplomat he'd served in Washington was just biding time and would turn him in once they reached French soil.

Henri shifted his weight in the hard seat that had few of the comforts of a regular airplane. He'd had no word from Catherine in all this time, and his wife Alice's constant complaints had worn him to a nub. It had been a relief when the United States authorities declared he was being "expelled," but his wife, a U.S. citizen, chose to remain in the country. At this stage in his life, anything—even a long flight across an ocean where German Luftwaffe aircraft might shoot them down en route—would be preferable to the gloom he'd experienced living in close quarters with his estranged spouse. Equally wearying had been the total news blackout and separation from the beautiful, compelling Catherine Thornton, a woman he simply could not keep out of his thoughts.

Just then, a second uniformed officer boarded the plane and strode down the aisle, halting near the ambassador's party. He nodded politely at everyone seated nearby and then addressed Henri.

"Mr. Leblanc, I'm afraid I'll have to ask you to deplane with me. Your seat has been reassigned to a passenger with higher priority."

The ambassador roused himself, his chest puffing out with indignation. In heavily accented English he declared angrily, "How dare you! The *monsieur* is a very important member of my delegation! We both have diplomatic immunity! I demand to speak to—"

"More important than your wife, Your Excellency?" the officer inquired with steely politeness.

"W-what?"

"As a courtesy, your request to be accompanied back to France with your wife has been granted," said the officer. "The order just came through. Your press attaché will have to join the others of your delegation when transportation can be arranged for such a large group." He turned to Leblanc. "If you will come with me, sir."

Henri unbuckled the seatbelt and rose to his feet, wondering if he was doomed to be confined, again, with his surly wife? On the other hand, what if Catherine had somehow pulled some strings on his behalf or if Major Pepper—or even the Americans—had at last made other plans for him?

He gathered his carry-on belongings and inclined his head in farewell to his superior just as a flustered woman with her own escort made her way toward them, an expression of relief spreading across her lips at the sight of her husband.

Before the ambassador could rise from his seat to greet his wife, Leblanc said swiftly, "May I bid you *bon voyage* and a safe journey, Your Excellency?"

"Yes, fine," offered the ambassador absently. "Who knows where any of us shall be from here on out. I thank you for your service during these stressful times." Then, clearly dismissing his attaché from his thoughts—and his life—he said to his wife, "Ah, my dear, this is quite a delightful surprise."

If that old bastard only knew what service I have indeed performed...

It would seem, by this farewell, the ambassador apparently had no notion that his subordinate had copied the French naval codes under his very nose and returned them, intact, to the embassy's safe.

Henri allowed himself a moment to feel the pride of a patriot, as Catherine said he could be if he joined her in her daring mission to spirit the codes to the Allies, cyphers that were desperately needed in order to pursue the war in the Mediterranean.

Vive la France, indeed.

———◇———

Catherine hoisted the wide strap of her government-supplied khaki duffle bag over her shoulder and followed, single-file, down the aisle of the lumbering military plane that was scheduled to fly the third leg of her journey to Great Britain. The huge plane had departed on a steamy day in July day from New Jersey to Newfoundland, refueling there and then flying on to Iceland, where she'd deplaned into what felt like the dead of winter. Arctic air and gloomy skies had blanketed the airfield, and she shivered even in her wool pleated slacks and the warm turtleneck sweater she had fortunately brought with her.

After a cup of dreadful but hot coffee served in a frigid Quonset hut on the edge of a barren airfield, she and a few others had been instructed not to talk among themselves about their ultimate destinations or assignments. They were speedily ushered on board yet another aircraft where the passengers were due to land at some little-known airstrip in northern England and would variously be dispersed by land from there.

Halfway down the plane's aisle where the temperature seemed as chilly as it had been in the Quonset hut, Catherine halted in her tracks. There, on her left, by a window next to an empty seat, was Henri Leblanc.

For a long moment they simply stared at each other, mouths slightly ajar.

"*Incroyable!*" Henri exclaimed finally, and then lowered his voice. "I can't believe it!"

Catherine smiled broadly as she shook her head in equal wonder. Henri patted the seat next to him, indicating that apparently boarding passengers could sit wherever they liked. She stowed her bag under her seat, glanced around to see if they were being observed by anyone, and sat down.

Henri, clasping her hand, said under his breath in French, "So you didn't know I'd been released from Hershey by the Americans?" Catherine could only shake her head once more and squeezed his hand in return. She couldn't seem to stop smiling, taken aback by the rush of emotion she'd experienced when she'd caught sight of Henri.

Her new seatmate was smiling broadly as well. "No one told you that I'm to be interviewed by the SOE in London?" he asked. "I assume you are too?"

"I didn't know any of this," she responded in a whisper, her pulse beating a nervous tattoo. "And, yes, I'm due at SOE headquarters when I arrive in the UK."

Just then, a uniformed officer standing near the door to the cockpit addressed the group on board the plane in stentorian tones.

"Sorry, folks, but it's too icy to take off, and more bad weather is closing in."

A collective groan echoed throughout the cabin. Ignoring it, the officer directed, "Take your belongings and please deplane. You'll be issued blankets back in the Quonset hut and have your dinner there. We'll depart when we get the all-clear."

Henri grimaced. "I've already had two days of this. I'm amazed your plane even landed here today."

As the pair emerged onto the gangway, Catherine pointed to several other military aircraft and a few civilian planes parked on the tarmac. "Look over there. Those don't look as if they're going anywhere, either. C'mon, let's hustle to get in line for our rations." She flashed him a grin. "At least I've learned that much already."

"And let's fight for some decent blankets," Henri added. "The one I had earlier was about as thin as tissue paper."

Once back inside the Quonset hut, Catherine smiled prettily at the sergeant handing out the blankets, held up two fingers, and was rewarded with a pair that felt as if they weighed ten pounds each. Meanwhile Henri scored plates of something that looked suspiciously like chili beans but was minus any identifiable flavor. The pair found a spot on the floor not too far from the solitary heater that was tasked with warming a structure the size of a basketball court.

"I don't think we can actually call this *cozy*," Catherine joked, "but it's not too bad, is it?"

Henri reached for her hand under their blankets that overlapped at their waists. "*Chérie*, it's positively sublime."

By this time, the group of disparate passengers consuming their army rations had begun to socialize about the weather and the series of delays. This left Henri and Catherine free to exchange information about their previous few weeks, since neither was about to pay attention to the edict not to speak about past or future operations.

"Do you think that we've actually been approved by the powers that be to work together again as a team?" Catherine wondered under her breath.

Henri shook his head. "Who knows, but it's an encouraging sign, don't you think, that we've been scheduled on the same plane for the last leg of the journey to Britain?"

"Knowing the chaos around my own departure," Catherine replied, "it could also be pure happenstance."

Catherine paused and drank in the sight of him, attired in some sort of U.S. Army issue and looking quite dashing with lieutenant bars on his shoulders. She couldn't deny how her breath had caught when she first saw Henri on the plane. Now that they were sitting side by side on the cement floor, wrapped like sausages in their blankets, she suddenly had an overwhelming urge to press herself against his chest and blot out the time they had been apart. Such emotion, she thought with a start, was a ridiculous notion on about ten levels, not the least of which was the fact that some sixty other people surrounded them in the Quonset hut.

Catherine took a deep drink from her tin coffee cup, the contents of which, by this time, had grown as cool as the drafty building where they waited for the weather to clear.

"No one has told me a thing about any possible assignments," she said, thinking that her unguarded reaction to Henri's presence could land her in trouble. With a deliberate shrug, she added, "And they certainly didn't disclose to me your whereabouts or their specific plans for either of us. In fact," she said, "technically, we're not supposed to tell another agent anything about anything." At Henri's lowering of his eyes to focus on his own coffee cup, she added softly, "But I have to say I was never so glad to see anyone in my life as when I spotted you hunched next to that window."

Henri looked up and gazed at her steadily.

"*Bien sûr.* That's how I felt, too. And I missed you, Catherine. I feared I might never see you again. Now that you're here, tell me something. Did you truly miss me?"

Before she could reply, a loud voice suddenly boomed over a public address system,

"All right, passengers from the transport headed for England, please make ready to re-board your flight. The cloud cover has lifted enough to attempt takeoff. Hurry, now. You've got five minutes. Five minutes!"

Catherine tossed the edge of her blanket to one side and scrambled to her feet as Henri did likewise. She'd been spared having to respond to his pointed question whether she had missed him in these intervening weeks. The truth was she wasn't sure of the answer herself.

———◇———

A British military escort met Henri and Catherine at the foot of their army transport and drove them without delay from the airfield to a nearby railway station. They'd each been guided to a separate stateroom at opposite ends of an overnight train to London.

Catherine found herself in a restless state as she prepared for bed in a miniscule space with a narrow bunk that had been lowered from the train's wall by a harried-looking attendant. She seriously contemplated trying to locate Henri's quarters, and guessed he had the same lascivious notion, but then thought better of it. If observed, such indiscretions could result in being expelled from the organization before they'd even begun.

Their train had arrived in London just before 6:00 a.m. on an unseasonably chilly July morning. Another uniformed escort had spotted them as they emerged into the echoing station hall and had taken them to a waiting car. They were soon whisked through city streets that showed signs of the devastating blitz that had rained down on London for more than eight straight months beginning in June of 1940 through the spring of '41.

"We've had nearly thirty thousand killed and a good twenty-five thousand wounded," their driver disclosed with an expression so somber Catherine wondered if he had lost someone among his own family and friends. She turned her head to stare out the window of the car, stunned by the massive destruction she saw everywhere. Henri, too, remained silent as they passed roofless, multi-story office blocks without a single surviving windowpane and blackened hulks of individual buildings in the heart of the English capital. In one building with its front wall torn out, lamps still stood on sitting room tables and clothes spilled out of bedroom dressers.

"Some forty-one thousand tons of bombs have fallen on the city," their driver lamented, "scorching the city, courtesy of Hitler's *Luftwaffe*, and disrupting every aspect of life until our RAF began to ward the blighters off."

Catherine marveled at the resiliency of British morale in the face of such a brutal onslaught. *We are here,* she thought with pride, thinking suddenly of her father and the years abroad when he devoted his life in service to his country. *We will serve, too.*

A few minutes later, the car had pulled to a curb and stopped. The door to the back seat opened, and Catherine and Henri were directed to get out while their escort pulled their duffle bags from the boot, also known as the vehicle's trunk.

"Fortunately, the SOE headquarters on this street was spared serious damage," said their guide, "as was number twenty-two, of Sherlock Holmes fictional fame, fifty yards down there."

The military aide turned and gestured in the direction of the discreet plaque identifying the door at Number 64 Baker Street, the London headquarters of the SOE. This was where the famous—or infamous, according to rival agents at MI6—Colonel Maurice Buckmaster ran the F-for-French section, a daredevil group known as the Baker Street Irregulars.

"You won't be going in here," he advised them. Catherine and Henri both gazed at him, confused. "New recruits are never taken first to sixty-four Baker Street; they're interviewed as to their initial suitability around the corner at the Northumberland Hotel or at Hotel Victoria." He pointed farther down the street to their right. "As you've both already been accepted into the first phase by virtue of your previous service in Washington, you will please just carry on a bit beyond here to the building on your left, just off Baker Street, known as Orchard Court. Officers in F Section will be waiting to greet you. No one but seasoned staff is allowed at Number Sixty-Four," he added, indicating the nondescript door in front of them. "That's to avoid anyone hearing or seeing something they don't need to—or should not—know. I just wanted to help you get your bearings. Cheerio!"

And at that, their escort got back into the car and drove away.

As directed, the pair walked another block to their right and turned left into a quadrangle that made up the Orchard Court buildings where they were due to meet with F Section head, Colonel Buckmaster himself. They'd been previously informed that each of them would be individually assessed by their new leader but had every indication they'd both pass muster—at least as far as this first induction phase was concerned.

"Ready?" asked Catherine, glancing up at Henri's distinctive profile as they approached the building's beveled glass front door. Impulsively, she seized his hand and found its warmth comforting. "Here's hoping we both make it past the first hurdle."

"*Oui*," he agreed. Henri took a step toward an innocuous-looking doorway as the unseasonably damp London fog swirled over nearby rooftops. "Bloody cold country," he complained in English, and Catherine smiled at his attempt at the Briticism. "Isn't that the way they say it around here?" he demanded.

"You've said it exactly right, but to be fair, the weather in late July is usually better than this," she murmured, relieved she'd crammed one of her best wool suits into her canvas duffle. She'd pressed the garment back into its fashionable dimensions and was grateful to be wearing the chic outfit to ward off the chill. "We've had awfully rotten weather every step of the way so far, haven't we?"

"Hope it's not an omen," Henri said.

Once inside the building, a polite doorman who identified himself as Mr. Park greeted them in his dark suit and old-school tie. Oddly, he didn't even ask them their names, but seemed to be expecting their arrival as he ushered them directly into a lift fitted out with gilded gates. At the second floor, he guided them into a flat with an anteroom which, they soon realized, was the former apartment's bathroom, tiled in black and white.

Indicating the rim of the ink-black tub, Park bid them, "Do have a seat, won't you? We're rather short of space, I'm afraid, thus no waiting room or foyer."

Catherine barely repressed a laugh at this statement of the obvious. She was struck by the notion that she and Henri were like characters in *Alice In Wonderland*, about to fall down a rabbit hole whose darkest depths were unfathomable.

Less than five minutes later, the door opened halfway, and Mr. Park could be heard beckoning another arrival to enter and take a seat in the crowded bathroom.

"In there, sir," he said. "You'll be called right after these fine people."

A tall, well-built man in his early thirties with good bone structure and dark, wavy hair squeezed in beside Catherine and Henri, perched on the edge of the tub. The recent arrival's English was excellent, but clearly he was a French national.

"Captain Lucien Barteau," he said by way of introduction. "I formerly flew for Air Bleu before the war started. I'm hoping to do the same for Britain now."

Catherine wondered why he wasn't interviewing at Royal Air Force headquarters if he intended to fly for the RAF.

"Henri Leblanc," said Henri, turning to introduce Catherine.

"How do you do?" she said politely.

When Barteau turned to her with an appraising glance, she sensed he was one of those men that assessed women solely by their appearance and how impressed they might be by his obvious good looks and credentials.

"An American?" he said, focusing dark brown eyes on her as if she were a delectable morsel for his private consumption. "Ah, and to think your country claimed neutrality for such a long time. How amazing that you should be sampling the secret sauce here in London."

Catherine took an instant dislike to the man, who obviously felt he was God's gift to women. Even more distasteful, she was faintly alarmed that they should all be sharing their real names—that is, if Lucien Barteau was in fact the man's true identity. Much to

Catherine's annoyance, the two men began a conversation in French, but before she could put a restraining hand on Henri's arm, the bathroom door opened once again, and Mr. Park bid Catherine follow him.

Catherine rose to her feet in the crowded bathroom, leaving Henri and the pilot perched uncomfortably on the edge of the bathtub. And despite the butterflies in her stomach at the thought of her coming interview, her negative reaction to the swaggering monsieur was erased by the comical sight of the two men flanked by matching black porcelain toilet, bidet, and sink.

With a look at Henri, she bid both men farewell and followed her escort to the threshold of what had once been a bedroom, now an office. Seated at a desk across the short distance from the doorway, a tall, slender, rather athletic figure with angular features and hair both thinning and fair rose from his chair and extended his hand. Behind his welcoming smile she sensed he'd favorably appraised the chic cut of her forest-green suit that offset her amber hair and silk blouse to a certain advantage.

"Mrs. Thornton," he said, heartily shaking her hands. "How good of you to come all this way to help us. Do sit down."

CHAPTER 9

The colonel, in his crisp Army uniform, proceeded to sit on a corner of his desk, his long legs, clad in khaki trousers, swinging back and forth.

"Cigarette?" he offered.

"No, thank you," Catherine replied, and then waited expectantly, having been coached by Major Pepper not to ask any questions. The need for secrecy was stressed at all times, and inquisitive recruits were often given the boot from the get-go.

"Your accomplishments precede you, as I expect you know," he said genially, "but has anyone outlined the principle goals of the SOE and the jobs we need our new recruits to perform?"

"I'd be very interested to hear that description from you," she said.

"In the main, the job of an SOE agent is to gather as much information as possible about Nazi military positions in France and elsewhere, and to locate and organize the bands of anti-fascist resisters into fighting units. We need them ready when the time comes to sabotage the enemy's movements and fighting capabilities every way possible."

Catherine kept her gaze locked on his but remained silent, merely nodding to indicate that she was paying close attention.

"The overall plan of F Section, of course," Buckmaster continued, "is to infiltrate France with a sufficient number of crack agents to direct the partisans and, at the same time, disrupt the Nazi military machine any way we can until our Allied forces can invade the continent." He looked at Catherine steadily. "We also attempt to get downed pilots back to safety. Does any of this sound like you'd be a good fit?"

"Yes, sir," she replied. "I very much want to work in the covert field, the way I did in America with Henri Leblanc, as I'm sure you've heard." She paused and then plunged ahead. "And, sir," she added pointedly, "given what *Monsieur* Leblanc and I were able to accomplish in Washington, I certainly hope that, as a woman, I won't simply be assigned to a desk job, typing." She'd already heard that was the fate of many a female recruit. She composed her features and deadpanned, "I can write, news stories or propaganda, but I don't type worth a damn."

She sensed that Buckmaster was unable to detect if she was joking or deadly serious. She was a bit of both, she realized, glancing down at her hands in her lap.

After a pause, he said, "You'll no doubt be pleased to learn that Mr. Churchill has been a champion of women joining this service. In fact, we've found that female agents are often able to tackle problems only their gender can solve and also move about much more freely than men who normally would be serving in the military or as forced labor in German-occupied countries."

Catherine remembered Wild Bill Donovan saying something

similar and breathed a sigh of relief. "You probably read in my file," she volunteered, "that the OSS arranged my cover and credentials as an American war correspondent for the *Chicago Tribune.*"

The colonel smiled faintly. "There's always the chance you'll find that very useful at some point. Meanwhile, may I take you down the hall to introduce you to my deputy, Vera Atkins, who will fill you in about your courses of training and so forth?"

Buckmaster slid off the corner of his desk and extended his hand once more, which she accepted with a firm grasp.

"Thank you, sir," Catherine murmured with a brusque nod, trying to conceal her excitement. She felt she had cleared the first hurdle, that of being found fit for duty by the celebrated head of F Section. The question the colonel had yet to answer was the "and so forth" aspect of his plans for her.

What assignments would she and Henri be given? And where?

———◇———

"We'll be sending you to a remote country house for a rather intense period of student assessment," Vera Atkins declared within moments of Catherine taking her seat in another small chamber that might have also been a bedroom in this former flat on Orchard Court.

Assessment? Hadn't stealing and copying the naval codes proven to a fare-thee-well that she was right for intelligence work?

Catherine didn't respond, but merely observed the woman sitting opposite her. Atkins was attractive, of moderate height, perhaps in her late thirties or early forties, with dark, arched brows and fairer hair, lightly permed.

"Working in collaboration with other agents is not everyone's cup of tea," she continued pleasantly, "nor, for others, is working alone. We need to assess a candidate's strength and weaknesses as it relates to our current, specific needs in the field."

"I see," Catherine said, nodding, reassured somewhat that she wasn't starting at Square One within a new bureaucracy.

Unlike Buckmaster in his uniform, Vera Atkins was clad in a well-cut tweed suit and silk blouse not unlike Catherine's own, made in France before the war. A cloud of cigarette smoke enveloped the interviewer's head, an effect she produced by not inhaling deeply, but blowing extended tendrils through her pursed, red lips.

On the desktop, Atkins' varnished nails began to tap a folder that Catherine suspected was her own. The woman Mr. Park had addressed as Miss Atkins cocked her head to one side, her blue-gray eyes making a study of the latest recruit sitting before her in a straight-back wooden chair.

Finally, she spoke again. "I am aware, Mrs. Thornton, that you are proficient in three languages. I'm sure we will take advantage of that in due course. I also know that you're a credentialed journalist, but…"

Catherine felt a stab of alarm. *Why the* but*?* she wondered.

"We have great need of an agent with certain skills very few of our female recruits possess."

Catherine cast a questioning look at the woman who held her fate in her hands.

"As you know," Atkins said, "we expect our new recruits to pass any number of tests as to their physical, mental, psychological, and moral fitness before we dare send them into harm's way across the Channel. As it happens, we are in dire need of confirming certain facts concerning these volunteers who may have previously been anything from ale house owners to shopkeepers, bankers, research scientists, ditch diggers, and heaven knows what else before joining F Section. And…well, not to put too fine a point on it, we must determine if they can keep secret*s*."

The recruits Atkins was describing sounded to Catherine as if they were mostly of the male variety, but she merely commented politely, "I'm sure their being absolutely discreet is vital to the program." Meanwhile, she had become alert to the disappointing possibility she feared was about to be presented to her.

"Indeed, testing the recruits' ability to maintain security is vital to the program's very survival," Atkins emphasized. "We must know this before we send them off where they can get themselves or their fellow agents killed by committing the slightest indiscretion."

Testing the recruits before *the agents were sent abroad? Does this mean—?*

Vera Atkins continued earnestly, "We hope the newly-minted agents come out of their rigorous training with all the skills they'll need to stay alive, including an ethos of not disclosing a single thing that is not necessary for others to know. That, in short, they can keep their mouths shut under any and all circumstances about future planned operations—even to other agents—when they're in the field abroad."

"Including in pubs and brothels?" Catherine asked, certain what was coming next.

Squadron Leader Atkins' eyes brightened, and she offered the first unpracticed smile of their acquaintance. "All your fitness reports said you were one of the brightest, most accomplished, most capable women agents seen to date."

Catherine acknowledged the compliment with a slight nod. "I'd been given the distinct impression that, because of the languages I speak and my record of service in Washington, D.C., I was to be deployed as a secret agent in France or Italy." She paused, her stomach clenching. "Have these plans changed?"

Vera Atkins arched a penciled eyebrow, signaling that Catherine had breached the unwritten rule not to question her superiors about anything.

"In time, that may certainly be the case," Atkins said smoothly, and Catherine sensed that her value was being weighed against the impertinent faux pas she'd just committed. "We do have urgent need for the skills you've exhibited so brilliantly in the work you just referenced in Washington. Even so," she added, her voice steady, "you should only take this assignment vetting our latest graduates of the SOE training program if you can do it willingly and with a conviction as to its importance."

"Vetting recently-trained recruits in places of...shall we call them...*recreation,* here in the U.K., you mean?" Catherine inquired, her own voice as modulated and controlled as that of the woman sitting across from her.

Vera Atkins arched her eyebrow once more.

"Well put. Yes, in pubs, hotel lounges, train waiting rooms, dancehalls, or wherever you think you could discover if these men can keep confidential the crucial details of our pending operations."

Catherine remained silent. She knew in that instant that Henri was sure to be parachuted back into France after his training. He would be a full-fledged secret agent deputized to help his country drive out the hated Germans. And she? She would be expected to lie on her back and do her duty for God and two countries.

Henri will be in covert operations in the field, and I'll be sitting in some smoky dive in Britain, chatting up wet-behind-the-ears recruits who haven't had sex in months.

Henri and she could spend the entire war working for the SOE and never see each other again.

She could practically taste the bitterness at the impersonal injustice of it all. She'd be completely on her own during this assignment, without Henri backing her up with his solid judgment and his willingness to dare whatever she was also willing to risk.

Catherine was lost in the labyrinth of these distressing thoughts as Miss Atkins rose from her leather chair and, like Buckmaster, sat on the corner of the desk, leaning forward as if to show some empathy.

"I fully recognize what a valuable agent you could be for us in the theatre of war itself," she began, "and I promise to write a strong recommendation on that score. But for now, we are in dire need of making sure we're not sending some of these new recruits, who may be lacking in personal discipline, to certain death themselves while risking the lives of our other secret agents." She leaned back and reached for the pack of cigarettes on her desk. Clutching them rather firmly, Atkins added pleasantly, "Take a day or so to think about this assignment and then ring me, if you will. Mr. Park will give you my direct number."

Catherine bit her lip and inhaled a long breath. Then she said, "I accept."

Atkins angled her head to gaze sharply at her visitor.

"Just like that?"

Catherine nodded with a glance at the folder on the desk. "I judge you to be a woman of your word." She narrowed her gaze and added, "As the saying goes, I'll do this for God and the Allies until you can find a replacement, and I'll count on you to put a strong recommendation in my file, soon, for a future assignment across the Channel."

Miss Atkins pointed to the folder. "Done," she declared, and eased off her desk. She stood a mere foot away with a smile Catherine reckoned could only be one of relief. "And I thank you, Mrs. Thornton, as does the entire leadership of F Section, for accepting this rather, ah, challenging but extremely necessary assignment."

Catherine could tell that Atkins was thinking, *"Mission accomplished."* Buckmaster's deputy had successfully set emergency honeytraps for hapless male SOE recruits who might make it through the rigors of the various spy schools, only to fail another test that no one would warn them was part of their training.

With no small degree of resentment and jealousy Catherine thought, *What fine bargain has been struck with Henri?*

As it happened, she was never given a chance to find out, for when she again greeted Mr. Park in the lift on her way to the ground floor of the building, the doorman immediately informed her, "The man who accompanied you here asked me to apologize that he couldn't bid you farewell in person."

Shocked, she replied, "*Monsieur* Leblanc has already left?"

"Yes, madam. He has just departed as per his orders from Colonel Buckmaster. He also wished you to know he was frightfully sorry, but he'd been asked not to disclose where he was going."

Catherine realized that Henri was only obeying the strict rules of the organization. She had no standing to demand to know where he had been sent, so there was no cause to feel—what? Left in the lurch without a partner? Obviously, as far as the SOE or the OSS was concerned, the two of them were no longer a team.

CHAPTER 10

August 1942

"*Assez!*" Henri muttered under his breath on his second day at Wanborough Manor. *Enough!* The sprawling red brick country house near Guilford in Surrey had been the scene of the most rigorous physical assessment he'd ever experienced.

The major in charge of this Elizabethan pile turned into an SOE spy school was Roger de Wesselow. The Coldstream Guards officer's attitude toward his recruits was frigid as the water in the Spartan bathroom Henri shared with his fellow male recruits.

The supervising brigadier, on the other hand, Henri thought, seemed a decent sort of chap, as the Brits would say. He was tall and erect, with ribbons on his chest from the First World War and a pleasant, unruffled demeanor. He'd seemed to know that Henri had been a flyer for France in the Great War and showed him noticeable deference whenever they encountered each other.

Laid out in Henri's path on this day of drizzle and misery was a woven thatch of barbed wire set on stubby posts a mere foot off the muddy ground. Fledgling secret agents like he was were expected to crawl under the razored obstacle on their bellies for some thirty feet without shearing off their scalps.

A hundred yards farther on, in a soggy field where sheep had once been pastured, two gigantic elms beckoned with parallel steel cables strung between them, forty feet off the ground and five feet apart. Henri swallowed hard at the sight of this next test of his strength and endurance, to say nothing of sheer guts. Squinting, he could make out a fellow trainee tentatively sliding his booted feet along a high wire like an amateur circus performer. The poor sod held on for dear life to a matching length of wire stretched above his head suspended between the towering trees.

Henri groaned at the thought of an even tougher challenge: the wall. Everyone dreaded facing the sheer, ten-foot concrete barrier that he and his fellows were expected to scale up and over in less than ninety seconds.

"Hurry on, now!" barked the sergeant supervising this phase of their physical training, designed to test whether they were fit enough for overseas assignments behind enemy lines.

I'm a forty-three-year-old who's simply manned a desk since my flying days ended, Henri mused darkly. He sincerely doubted he could make it through the mud, let alone inch along the high wire at that terrifying height. As for the concrete wall...

But somehow the former French press attaché conquered all three assigned sections of the brutal obstacle course through sheer will. There were two women in his group, both of whom were struggling to keep up, a fact that only made him wonder how reed-thin Catherine would fare if faced with these same physical challenges.

———◇———

"Good work, Leblanc," the sergeant greeted him an hour later as Henri sprawled on the damp grass trying to recover his breath. "I had my doubts about you, but you managed bloody well."

High praise, Henri thought, closing his eyes and envisioning a straight shot of whiskey before bed after sitting down to an evening meal. Each night, he and the other agents assembled in the enormous dining room for fairly decent fare, considering the food in the rest of England. Mammoth, gilt-framed portraits of the manor's owner, Sir Algernon West, and his relatives stared down at them from the hallowed walls.

To his great surprise and personal gratification, Henri had excelled at all the tests for mechanical skills, such as pressing a key into wax and then manufacturing its duplicate from simple tools in record time. He wasn't bad at picking locks either, once he got the hang of it, inserting a device similar to the one Catherine had used to get into the code room at the Vichy embassy in Washington. As she had done, he learned to pull down and twist it simultaneously, relieved when the lock turned and he could pull open the door.

Henri wondered if Catherine had encountered the same sort of situational interview that had confronted him soon after his arrival. The no-nonsense major had wasted little time asking him a foreboding question during a one-on-one meeting in the manor's library. "Tell me, Leblanc. Do you think you could actually kill someone?"

Henri's answer was instantaneous.

"Absolutely, sir. My country's overrun with the scum of the earth. I would very much enjoy taking out as many of them as possible."

"Excellent." The stone-faced veteran soldier nodded brusquely, making a note on a page in his file. "But let's see how you are when you get to the paramilitary part of this dog-and-pony show. I see by your background you flew planes. But did you ever light a fuse and blow anything up?"

"No fuses, sir," he replied, his voice even. "We just dropped bombs from ten thousand feet."

"You weren't recruited for the RAF this time around?"

"Too old, they said."

And too French, Henri imagined the major thought, but he kept that observation to himself.

"Well," replied his superior officer, "we'll have to see if your prowess picking locks can transfer to putting *plastique* and timed pencil fuses on railroad tracks, without getting shot in the back while you're at it."

During the second week into the month-long assessment period, he and his fellow trainees were having their usual nightcap in the manor's elegant sitting room. Without warning, two uniformed men burst through the carved, mahogany doors, shooting off loud pistols while screaming epithets at each other. To the shock of the witnesses, they tore out the door to the flagstone terrace in another hail of ear-splitting gunfire and disappeared into the darkness.

Immediately, the major put down the whiskey he'd been drinking and jumped to his feet. He turned to a female recruit, an American named Constance Vivier Clarke, huddled in the corner of a sofa alongside a male trainee, shaken as they all were by the incident.

"What color were the men's hair?" the major demanded of her.

"I—I d-don't recall" she stuttered.

Henri guessed the young woman was in her early twenties, slender, her own hair the memorable color of a rich, dark cinnamon—henna, it would be dubbed in France. It was pulled back and fastened on each temple with tortoiseshell combs. She was a half a foot taller than the other female recruit, and her spare figure reminded him vaguely of Catherine, except for her mildly irritating New York lockjaw accent when they'd spoken French together during mealtime. Viv, as she'd been nicknamed, had proven to be a tough cookie during their physical training, and Henri could tell she was furious with herself for having been rattled by this latest test.

The major looked at her companion on the couch. "The chaps had *what* color hair?" he repeated.

"I-I don't recall either," admitted the young man who'd been a chartered accountant before joining the SOE.

To Henri, the major asked, "What *exact* words did one soldier say to the other?"

"They swore at each other, sir," Henri replied, searching his brain to remember what he'd just seen and heard.

"Exact words?" barked the Major.

Henri paused, and then replied, "The second one entering the room yelled, 'Halt!' and then disparaged the other's mother, as in 'You son of a whore!'"

The major allowed himself a faint smile. "Good translation there," he complimented. "Even in the midst of chaos, you must continue to listen and recall what's happening around you."

He then pointed to a recruit who was still cowering for cover under a mahogany library table littered with newspapers and magazines. "You saved yourself, certainly, son, but tell me, which soldier had his jacket open with a second pistol in his belt?"

Henri's fellow recruit slowly got to his feet, offered the major a blank look and shook his head, unable to answer.

The trainee to Henri's left had leapt to his feet when the fracas had erupted and had stood frozen in shock, merely gaping at the scene. The major turned to address him, noting matter-of-factly, "By the way, Eggers, you're dead. Either man would have shot you in the chest if he'd seen you standing there like a statue."

The point of the fracas, Henri realized, was to assess how keenly the trainees observed a situation under battle conditions. Could they have later described the assailants and the weapons they used? Even more important, did they instantly react to save their own lives and the lives of their fellow agents? If Catherine were undergoing similar training somewhere in this country of rain and fog, Leblanc hoped to hell she'd passed this test with more skill than Viv Clarke.

———◇———

God in heaven, Catherine marveled as she squinted across the smoke-filled pub toward the glass-fronted door of one of Manchester's dingiest neighborhood watering holes. Outside on the rain-washed street swathed in damp and fog, she thought that this northern city had to be one of the most depressing outposts any SOE agent could be assigned to, including the theater of war.

She tapped a varnished nail on the wooden bar and re-crossed her legs prettily as she perched on a worn leather stool. The air was thick with the scent of both cigarettes and cigars, as was the nearby lobby inside the adjacent hotel that was popular with a certain set of military volunteers. Since war had been declared, the proprietor had been more than happy to welcome those who were completing their training at a nearby manor house prior to being sent across the English Channel to fight the German war machine.

Catherine glanced at her watch. The two men in military uniforms that she had been told to be on the lookout for were due any minute. She could only imagine how they were set to enjoy themselves this night. Her contact had informed her that her prey had passed all their training courses conducted at a facility outside town and were soon to be deployed somewhere in France, Belgium, or Poland.

A burst of raucous laughter gave Catherine ample warning that her latest assignment was about to begin. Which man entering the pub would bite this night? Would he be easy to get inebriated or to be persuaded to join her upstairs in her hotel room? Would he eagerly partake of her charms or become dangerously aggressive with a need to relieve weeks of pent-up sexual tension?

Most significantly, would this duo of fledgling agents divulge any secrets about upcoming missions? Details that they'd been sternly advised to tell no one, not even a fellow agent and certainly not the attractive, warm-hearted woman with a halo of amber hair waiting in a darkened pub to welcome either one—or both—into her bed, per the implied orders from her superiors.

Fortunately, Catherine's duties thus far had not included actual intercourse. After a few weeks of playing bait in the SOE honeytrap, she had certainly witnessed just about everything imaginable. In several cases, she had most likely saved a few lives of other agents by enticing her quarry to reveal their weaknesses. She was quick to detect the men with a need to look important and full of daring-do by bragging about their prowess as newly minted operatives, unthinkingly revealing crucial details of their missions prior to their deployment abroad.

Her co-conspirator, a decoy agent named Michael Denney, would appear to his fellows to be taking the same course of instructions that they were. By this hour, he had already guided suspected weak links to another bar, where they tossed back a few beers or maybe a whiskey or two.

This particular night, Michael walked into the Eagle's Arms between the two trainees, with his own arms slung in almost comical fashion around their shoulders. On his right staggered a reedy slip of a man whose uniform appeared two sizes too large. Towering over both was a tall, burly gentleman who Catherine guessed was once a hod-carrier or ironworker in some factory before the war.

"What'll you have, chaps?" slurred Catherine's colleague, whom, she knew, was sober as a judge. Michael Denney never cast even a glance in Catherine's direction, but pounded a friendly fist on the bar and demanded jovially, "A Guinness for me and…"

The smaller of the two agents hesitated, deferring to his larger companion to order first.

"Same as Michael, here," the giant grunted.

"Same, then, for me," nodded the skinny one.

Catherine nursed her glass of dreadfully inferior red wine and smiled occasionally at the barman who had been part of the trium-virate playing this SOE game since her first night of duty. Barely two glasses of Guinness later, the man Michael had addressed as Kevin cocked his head in her direction and said loudly, "I bet that lovely young lady at the end of the bar wouldn't say no to another glass of wine if we bought her one."

"You're paying, then," Michael announced. "I'm tapped out, I'm afraid. It's been a long night."

Catherine pretended as if she hadn't heard any of the remarks and dug in her handbag to retrieve her lipstick, apply it, and shift her weight as if she were preparing to leave.

The barman had speedily provided Kevin with a fresh glass of plonk.

"Oh, no you don't, beautiful lady," Kevin said, sliding the glass down the bar and oozing his muscled bulk onto the empty stool next to her. "We can't have you leaving our little party so early, can we? After all, we three are celebrating, aren't we lads?"

Catherine slowly swiveled her head and bestowed upon him a hint of a come-hither smile, casting him a mildly curious look. He peered back at her, making a concerted effort to focus on her face, and she could see the sudden flare of hunger light up his eyes.

"Ooh, you are a pretty one, aren't you, darling?"

His breath was heavily laced with alcohol, and she would wager a new pair of silk stockings that he'd fall asleep on her bed, passed out as so many of them did, before he spilled any state secrets.

What a waste of everyone's time tonight.

In moments like these during the past weeks, she'd repeatedly asked herself why in the world she had agreed to take on this assignment when her language skills and other abilities could be put to far better use.

Meanwhile, Kevin what's-his-name reached out two fat fingers and caught a lock of her hair between them.

"Careful now," she cautioned him pleasantly in a low, breathy tone.

"So silky," he murmured, fingering her hair with surprising gentleness. They exchanged glances, and she could see that all the tension and stress built up by his efforts to master spy craft in the wilds of Northern England was writ large in his expression of longing for female company—and more.

Michael punched the khaki-clad arm of the third man in their group.

"Can't you see we're not wanted, here, Archie? We'd better make ourselves scarce, don't you think?"

Archie, forlorn in his baggy uniform and pale countenance, looked relieved. He nodded and dug into his pocket to pay his bill. "To tell you the truth," he said with a sheepish grin, "I'm totally knackered." Turning to leave, he called down the bar, "'Night, Kevin. See you at breakfast." To Michael he asked, "You staying or going?"

Michael Denney shrugged. "Going, I guess. We can share the fare back to the manor." He offered a noncommittal glance in the direction of Catherine and Kevin while he reached into his jacket for money to pay for his drink. "Don't be too late, old bean," he cautioned. "Our train leaves at zero eight hundred sharp tomorrow morning."

During the hour she and Kevin chatted at the bar, Kevin had revealed that he had been studying to acquire some important skills for the war effort.

"Really? How wonderful! We so need men of your talent to stop those dirty Jerries! What will you be doing over there?"

"Ah…top secret," he replied, touching his index finger to her lips. Before he could withdraw his hand, she flicked her tongue against his flesh in a movement she calculated would drive him to distraction.

After what seemed like hours to Catherine, Kevin quaffed his last whiskey and whispered into her ear that he'd be more than happy if they could "have a little cuddle" and would make it worth her while if she knew a place they could go.

She nodded, as if the idea was as tempting to her as it was to him. Catherine gestured to the corridor that led from the pub into the hotel lobby with its flowered, well-worn carpet and ancient lift that would take them to her room on the third floor.

CHAPTER 11

Without exchanging another word, Catherine led Kevin down a short hallway where they entered the lift and avoided each other's eyes as it rumbled upward. The doors opened with a slight screech just as she felt the large palm of Kevin's hand cup her bottom. She allowed him to follow her a few meters down the hall before turning abruptly and putting her arms around his neck, pulling him close. His telltale erection told her she'd better move fast; he'd either pass out or she wouldn't be able to fight him off if he got rough.

"It makes me quite sad to think you'll be leaving soon," she said in a deliberately throaty whisper.

"Now that I've met you, love," he replied, "it makes me very sad as well."

"I know you claimed what you are doing is top secret, but were you just saying that to get me to find you more interesting and to…well, you know?"

"No-o-o," he protested, his voice slurring. "I like you, but I do very much want to…well, you know."

She framed his face with her hands, stood on tiptoe, and kissed him with practiced slowness, inserting her tongue past his lips.

"Even if you're not some sort of super spy," she said, sounding plaintive, "I wish I'd be seeing you more than just one night." She kissed him again and whispered, "I like you, too…whatever it is you claim you're doing to fight this war."

"Oh, love…" he mumbled into her neck, his weight oppressive against her own. "Believe me, I'm more than doing my bit."

She'd left her door unlocked, and within seconds they were inside. As she expected, Kevin pinned her back to the wall while his pelvis began grinding against the front of her dress.

"Wouldn't we be more comfortable if we moved to my bed?" she murmured, wondering if the man would even be able to walk the ten steps before passing out.

"Yeesh…let's. I want…I want…"

By the time he'd struggled out of his trousers and flopped onto the bedcovers, the strength of his erection had flagged to mortifying flaccidity.

"Oh, bugger all!" he groaned, staring down at his groin with chagrin. "Can you…do you suppose you could…?"

"Do you think it would actually help?" she asked, deliberately sounding doubtful and keeping her hands to herself. "It looks like it's pretty much lights out for you, Kevin, I'm sorry to say."

To her surprise, a large tear appeared in the outward corners of both his eyes.

"Isn't it always the way? I'm leaving in the morning and may get blasted to hell where I'm going, and I can't even—"

Catherine felt an unexpected rush of sympathy for this hulking stranger lying prone on her bed, his erection having gone from half-mast to spent worm lolling against his upper thigh.

"It's upsetting to think you'll be in danger," she said, lowering herself to sit on the edge of the mattress, still fully clothed.

"Truth is, as of tomorrow, I'll be in danger every second," he said with a gulp.

"Truly? Oh, that's awful. How so?"

By now, tears were streaming down his face, and he was blubbering like a baby.

"I-I never thought I'd have to do the kind of things they taught us at the manor, and I—"

Catherine couldn't make out the rest of what he was saying, as he'd turned his face into the pillow, muffling his words. With a sigh, she pulled his head into her lap, cradling it while sobs wracked his chest and burst forth in strangled puffs of breath.

"Ah, Kevin. Are you frightened of what's ahead? What will you be doing over there that's got you in such a state?"

"Ex-explosives…" he stuttered, his shoulders heaving. "Slitting throats. Guiding in parachute drops. I'm a second-rate school soccer coach! I have a wife and a new baby. They want me to blow up railway bridges and munitions factories in central France. Lord knows, I want to do my part, but God almighty, I'll probably be *dead* in a month!"

The truth was, he was probably correct. Catherine suddenly felt pity for the giant of a man whose abject terror had surfaced after a couple of drinks. She'd already been warned several times that explosives experts, guerilla fighters, and wireless operators all had very short lifespans once they landed in Nazi territory.

She removed her shoes and stretched out beside him, gathering him in her arms and rocking him to and fro as if he were a frightened child. Within minutes, the shuddering sobs ceased. The secret agent who had apparently succeeded at all his tests of strength, endurance, and spy craft—except for one final exam in a pub to assess his ability to keep secrets about future assignments—had passed out.

As dawn broke and the sound of Kevin's noisy snoring awoke her, Catherine slipped from bed still fully dressed. She tiptoed out of the room with her shoes in hand, making herself scarce before he woke up. At a café down the street, she met her mission partner, Michael Denney, who waited, sipping coffee, while she wrote up her latest report. Once finished with the task, she handed it to him with a look of resignation. Returning the gesture, he rose from their table.

"Well, it's off to the Scottish Highlands for this poor bloke," he declared.

Catherine and Michael Denney both knew what would happen next: the erstwhile secret agent would be told that he would not be taking the train south with his fellow recruits at 0800 that morning. Instead, the poor sod would be transferred by lorry to the infamous Cooler, in some drafty castle in a remote part of northern Scotland, to remain quarantined there with other failed agents until the secrets he'd absorbed in spy school were no longer germane to the war effort.

"The washouts know too much about British spy craft and now we also know they can't keep their mouths shut…especially after a pint or two," Michael said with a look of disgust, and then headed out the door to return to the hotel to pick up his charge.

For a second time, Catherine felt a wave of sympathy for the unfortunate Kevin, brave enough to volunteer for dangerous duty yet not quite courageous enough to withstand the rigors of what would be asked of him behind enemy lines.

In the grand scheme of things, Catherine reflected, Kevin's banishment wasn't out of order. Even so, her own plight in back-of-the-beyond Manchester, England had become an assignment she really couldn't stomach for much longer.

———◇———

By the end of week three, Henri and his fellow recruits were practically crippled with fatigue before they fell into bed each evening. Henri was sure he'd lost considerable weight due to the rigors of the fitness regime. Strangely enough, despite his utter exhaustion, he felt physically better than he had in years. But through it all, he worried about Catherine's fate.

Where was she? Had she been sent to the women's version of assessment hell? Was she undergoing the same physical tests of strength he had been? Would he ever find out what had happened to her before the damnable war was over?

Would it ever be over? he wondered with a gloom that overtook him whenever he thought of the way their British superiors had so coldly separated them without warning.

Would either of them survive a world in such disarray?

Henri pushed his dire thoughts to the back of his mind this summer's morning as he dressed for yet another day of testing and hardship. The rainy weather at Wanborough Manor had, at last, turned fair, but now his scratchy wool uniform and the equipment he was required to carry in the training exercises were as miserable to bear as the mud.

To divert himself from all these complaints, he concentrated on his hunger pangs and his craving for a decent cup of coffee. He'd never ceased to marvel at the dregs the Brits served that were falsely labeled as his favorite beverage.

After the morning meal, near the end of the assessment period, his squad was divided into two groups and separated for the purposes of testing their ability to work as a team. While the first group was led from the room, Henri's section was told to select a leader. To his astonishment, he was chosen. Then he was ordered to guide his group to the edge of what had once been an ornamental pond on the estate but whose banks had been allowed to grow wild.

"Your task is to build a raft and paddle this cache of ammunition to the small island you see there in the middle, while keeping it dry," their trainer instructed, pointing to a heavy wooden box with rope handles. Scattered on the grass near the water's edge lay a half a dozen pieces of lumber, two wooden barrels, and several long lengths of stout rope. The training officer glanced at his watch. "You have twenty minutes to build a raft and get to the island starting…now!"

Henri stared at the scant resources he'd been given, noting that the barrels had several round holes in them that were likely to fill with water. He scanned the circumference of the lake in an effort to assess where would be the best entry point. With a start, he pointed to some reeds about forty feet away.

"Slattery!" he yelled at the man who appeared to be the physically strongest in the group. "You come with me. The rest of you, line up that lumber in the shape of a raft!"

Buried in the underbrush, with only a corner visible, was an abandoned, battered wooden platform that would provide much more stability than the flimsy frame the team was attempting to build from the random-sized boards. Together, he and John Slattery upended the platform and carried it back to the group.

"Put the two barrels under the wooden frame and lash everything together with those ropes," Henri directed. Within ten minutes, the makeshift raft was launched.

Later, the group was told in their debrief that the opposing team hadn't completed the mission. Their leaky barrels soon filled with water, swamping the entire enterprise.

"Unlike your group," the trainer in charge of the exercise announced, "the others never thought to check around the staging area."

The major, who had been standing to one side of the grassy verge that ringed the pond, stepped forward to drive home a point. "An agent must always make the most of whatever might be available," he underscored. "When it comes to executing a mission, assume nothing. Look around! Think beyond what might be within your immediate range of vision. Fortunately for your team, your leader, Henri, took time to examine his surroundings."

Henri could only wonder what Catherine would have done in such a situation. He imagined she would have spotted the barrel holes and stuffed them with turf!

After dinner, Henri was called into the brigadier's office where he was told that, the following day, he would be sent on to another of SOE's training camps.

"We've judged that you and a few others in this group are ready to proceed to the next phase of preparation."

Henri nodded and looked at his superior expectantly.

"On your docket next are explosives handling and paramilitary and guerilla exercises, including hand-to-hand combat and silent killing. That sound alright?"

"Yes, sir. Thank you, sir."

And I used to have a desk job shuffling papers from the inbox to the outbox!

The interview over, Henri rose, surmising that he'd survived here because he had somehow managed to get through the basic physical training and used his brain to figure out the rest. Despite these successes, he wondered for the hundredth time if he hadn't grown too old for this game. Every muscle ached, and he felt a complete alien among the much younger Brits that were his fellow trainees. Having lived in America for a decade, he had a longing to hear a Yank accent other than that of Viv Clarke's New York twang, and that brought him once again to the question of what had happened to the smoky-voiced Catherine after her meetings in London with Colonel Buckmaster.

Given that Henri had signed the Official Secrets Act, he knew full well he could never ask the brigadier where the hell she was.

His superior officer rose from his seat to shake his hand.

"Goodbye, then," said the brigadier. "You've done well so far. Best of luck, my boy."

I'm no boy, thought Henri glumly, *and as for luck...la chance?* Luck was the name of the game, and he wondered how long his would hold out.

———◇———

After Catherine's colleague Michael Denney had left the café with her damning report on Agent Kevin under his arm, she pulled out another sheet of paper from her handbag and began to write a second report—this one to Vera Atkins—obliquely describing various aspects of her service since the two women had last conferred and reminding Buckmaster's deputy of her solemn promise to recommend Catherine Thornton for duty across the Channel.

Sipping from her cup of tepid coffee, Catherine penned her plea.

As you surely recall, Miss Atkins, I speak three languages fluently and have already proven myself in the field of spy craft. Surely, I can be of more use to the SOE than in my current position, which I have no doubt many another female lacking my linguistic skills could fulfill. Therefore, I urgently request that Colette Durand be reassigned to the theater of war.

The air outside the café was heavy with moisture from the steady rain the night before. Catherine sloshed through the puddled sidewalk on her way to post her letter, wondering if it would be heavily redacted before it ever landed on Vera Atkins' desk.

———◇———

Henri fingered the army pistol in his hand, the first one he'd held since his flying days. He had turned to diplomacy when that brutal conflict was over, never wanting the world to see a clash of its like again. And now, here he was, two months after his arrival in Britain, assigned to Arisaig House. This spy school had turned out to be a lonely estate outside Inverness and to the west of Fort William in the remote Scottish Highlands where he was being schooled as a trained killer in paramilitary and guerilla hand-to-hand combat. He'd been taught that a swift knee to the balls or a bash with a thick stick to the brain would quickly dispatch an adversary.

What a world we humans have created...

"Leblanc! You're next!"

The instructor turned to Henri's group of recruits clustered around the human-shaped cardboard targets nearby, reminding them of the number-one safety rule that had proven counterintuitive to most of Henri's fellow trainees.

"Keep your finger off the trigger until you see something to shoot at! Then either take the crouch position and shoot from the hip if the target is close by, or stand upright and shoot, arm straight out, if you're aiming at a distance. And remember—get off two shots in quick succession. In SOE, we call that the double tap."

Later that day he was teamed up with one of the rare female American SOE recruits like Catherine. Viv—Vivier Clarke—had been the woman back at Wanborough Manor who had not been able to recall the hair color of the two gun-toting pretend enemy soldiers when they had burst into the manor's sitting room. Fortunately, and rather surprisingly, Henri thought, Viv had since proven herself a suitable agent in many other important ways during their training courses. And, like Catherine, she had an uncanny ability to pick French locks and had shown her instructors she could take down her opponents in a flash, thanks to her hobby of jujitsu.

The exercise Henri and Viv were assigned to do together today required that they shoot off blanks at paper targets moving on wires strung between trees, while in pursuit of one another through a thickly wooded forest on the estate.

Viv was a tall, athletic young woman. She frankly acknowledged to being a crack skier, thanks to attending school in Austria as well as England. Blessed with a perfectly straight nose set in porcelain skin, along with chocolate brown eyes framed by her distinctive, shoulder-length burgundy hair, she was a girl who turned heads.

"My German is excellent," she revealed on another evening when she and Henri were speculating on where each SOE candidate in their group might end up in this war. "Trust me, though, my French sounds pretty awful. My New York accent bleeds through, you know? It should be interesting where I'll ultimately be sent. That is, if I make it through all this."

During their weeks in training, Henri had grown fond of Viv and admired her spunk since the moment they'd been assigned to work together in an exercise crawling over rock and stream to get to their appointed rendezvous and pretend to be an enemy outpost in the woods. Strangely, her presence caused him to miss Catherine all the more. Besides, he was just old enough to be Viv's father, and that type of liaison had no appeal for him at all.

"Well, here's to us both making it through commando training and being sent on to finishing school," he said, tilting his glass of whiskey in Viv's direction.

"To say nothing of dreaded parachute school. Cheers," she said with a nod, then cocked her head as they both heard the sound of a vehicle's tires crunching across the gravel driveway in the gloom outside Arisaig House. "I wonder who this could be, arriving so late?"

Viv rose from the sofa, marched across the sapphire-blue Persian carpet, and pulled back the blackout drape a few inches. Leaning forward, she peered out the mullioned windows with Henri at her shoulder. The passenger door nearest them opened, and out stepped a slender woman who made even the FANY uniform, which most female SOE agents were assigned to wear, look fashionable.

"Catherine!" Henri murmured on a long breath.

"You know her?" Viv asked, with a startled glance over her shoulder.

"An acquaintance," he replied, his mind on red alert to avoid destroying Catherine's cover the instant she arrived at Arisaig House. "I remember meeting her during my days in Washington—and I shouldn't have even told you that. Cone of silence, all right, Viv?" he asked sharply. "She's come a long way to get here, and I don't want to make life any tougher for her than it's probably already been, OK?"

"Cone of silence," Viv repeated with a solemn nod.

And although the mantra that had been drilled into the heads of all SOE recruits since their first day of training was "trust no one," Henri prayed to a God he only half believed in that young Vivier Clarke would keep her word.

CHAPTER 12

It was after nine in the pitch-black night enveloping the Scottish Highlands when Catherine and her military escort entered the massive, bleak stone building perched on a rise in the wilds of a deep-sided glen. For the second time since she had left Washington, she was stunned by the sight of Henri Leblanc, who was standing among a group of curious trainees greeting her in the front foyer of the imposing hunting lodge. Mounted on the surrounding high walls were the stuffed and very dead heads of numerous animals, many with horns.

It had been raining steadily for most of Catherine's journey to the north, but it had let up just as the car passed through wrought-iron gates set alongside a brooding loch, its dark water rimmed by granite boulders. Thick woods stood on either side of the long, winding driveway, and through the car's back window she had just been able to discern the outlines of rocky terrain that undulated into foreboding peaks ringing the isolated property. The faint bray of sheep in the far distance added to the feeling she was far away from anything even as familiar as the moon.

The foyer where she, Henri, and the other housemates now stood was dimly lit by brass sconces on the wall, and heavy blackout curtains hung from every window. Dusty, gold-framed family portraits marched along a paneled corridor that led to some larger rooms that she glimpsed through several open doors. She offered friendly smiles as Colonel Rogers, apparently overseeing the operation, began to make introductions. She immediately perceived that both Henri and she were doing their utmost to conceal their shock at seeing each other again.

Arisaig House, she'd been told during the long car trip from the train station in Inverness, was an erstwhile country estate requisitioned by the government and transformed into a military installation. There she would be taught commando training that included map-reading, the use of both explosives and a sawed-off weapon known as the Sten gun, as well as various techniques for committing a silent killing. Her month-long marathon of physical conditioning and training in the use of handguns and lock picking at Wanborough outside London had been relatively easy. But silent killing? Learning to throw hand grenades or blow up a bridge without maiming herself? That had certainly given her pause as she contemplated the next phase of becoming a bona fide SOE agent.

"Good evening, everyone," she managed to say while still absorbing the startling sight of Henri standing not ten feet from her.

She felt a surge of relief that his being at the same training facility might mean they'd be deployed behind enemy lines together, too. After all, they'd been a successful team in D.C. Perhaps the powers that be finally had the good sense to team them together again.

The colonel stepped forward, extending his hand. "Welcome, welcome," he greeted her heartily. "I am Colonel Rogers. This is Major Hyatt, Captain Duran, and, of course, Sergeant Devere, who came up from London with you. Sorry about the rain." Rogers turned to the knot of agents-in-training, introducing them to Catherine by their code names. "And this is Agent Claude," he finished with a nod in Henri's direction. Colonel Roger's next words, however, dashed any expectation that her meeting Henri in the middle of nowhere was planned. "He'll be heading back south in two days for his next phase of training, but I expect we can all share a nightcap in the library before we retire."

Catherine did her best to nod politely at this news. She'd barely just arrived, and already Henri was due to leave shortly. And although the colonel's tone was light, his expression grew sober as he added, "Everyone knows the rules, newcomers included. No sharing secrets of where you've been and what you've been up to. And by the way, that's standard procedure whenever you encounter anyone you know from your previous lives or training elsewhere," he cautioned with a glance in Catherine's direction. He waved the group toward the library, lined floor to ceiling with shelves of dusty leather tomes. "Follow me, everyone. Whiskey's on the King!"

———◇———

"It would seem that I'm about a month ahead of you in this traveling training circus," Henri said in a low voice. He gazed at Catherine over the rim of his glass of Glenlivet, its amber hue nearly matching the shade of her hair, which seemed to glow in the light from the fireplace nearby. Perched above the carved mantel, flanked by bookshelves on either side, an enormous, twelve-point stag's head gazed down somberly at the assembled group clustered in groups of twos and threes in leather chairs and a ten-foot burgundy velvet tufted sofa. "I assume your arrival and my leaving are not coincidental."

"In fact, they actually might be," Catherine countered, quietly pretending that Henri and she were merely getting acquainted. "It took a bit of time and some persuasion for Miss Atkins and Buckmaster to get permission from the higher-ups to spring me from my prior post and get the required training for another assignment, wherever it is they decide to send me."

She definitely wouldn't tell Henri about her recent duties as a honeytrap seductress, as she knew it would likely upset him. She glanced around, but none of their superiors seemed to be paying them any attention. In fact, with the convivial but subdued conversations surrounding them, Henri and Catherine could have been at a typical country house party before the war, enjoying a fine example of Scottish malt whisky after a day's shooting.

"I expect you've done brilliantly at all your training to date?" Henri asked.

"In fact, I did quite brilliantly," she replied, with the confident grin she knew he'd appreciate, in contrast to the sour expressions of his estranged wife he'd described to her often enough in the past. "I was sent here after only two weeks of so-called assessment." She cast a casual glance in the direction of the colonel, who appeared deep in conversation with the major. "I take it I'm not allowed to ask where you've been since they whisked you away in London, but of course I'm dying to know."

Just then, the aforementioned colonel shifted his gaze in their direction. Catherine affected a laugh she didn't feel and continued in a louder voice, "I learned French and German as well as Italian when my father was in the military in Europe."

Picking up her cue, Henri nodded. "After flying in the last war, I thought I might wish to be a commercial pilot, and English was required, of course."

The colonel returned to his conversation with his fellow officer. Catherine continued quietly, "My mother recently forwarded a letter to me through Vera Atkins from my husband. Jeremy."

She sensed that Henri felt a jolt of—what? Jealousy aimed at a man he'd never met? But all he replied was, "Oh? Yes? What news from Chile?"

"A request that I rejoin him at his post because his ambassador thinks our living apart is 'bad form,'" she answered under her breath. "I wrote back that I am now a bona fide war correspondent for the *Chicago Tribune*, reporting on the blitz in London and the effects of war in other parts of Britain. Fortunately, he never reads that paper."

"And his reaction?"

Catherine threw her head back and laughed as if they were having a light, inconsequential discussion, and murmured, "No answer, of course. Atkins reminded me that having signed the Official Secrets Act, I cannot give even a hint of what I'm truly doing in the UK or elsewhere. I just said that I am nowhere near the front line—which is true as of my writing him." She met Henri's gaze, adding, "I told him that if my actions displeased him, he was free to arrange for our divorce whenever he felt the urge."

Henri's expression told her this was welcome news.

"I was allowed to tell Alice something similar," he confided.

"About where you are?"

Henri shook his head. "Didn't do that, of course. I was informed by Buckmaster she'd been released from the Hershey Hotel and has moved to New York City.

"And did the subject of divorce come up in your exchange?"

"No. I just wrote that we each must deal with the impact of this war in our own way and that the authorities insist I'm not permitted to tell her anything about where I am or what I'm doing. The SOE said they'd somehow have my letter posted from France, so she'll probably conclude I was repatriated and that I'm still working for the Vichy."

"That was clever," murmured Catherine.

"Her thinking that might actually prompt her to divorce me as a public show of allegiance to America," he said, adding "although at this juncture, the paperwork involved would be a nightmare."

Just then, the colonel's voice boomed over the murmuring conversations filling the library.

"Well, ladies and gentlemen, I must bid you goodnight, and I suggest you soon all do the same." He nodded in Catherine's direction, adding, "Our newest arrival here is bound to have a very full day getting her bearings tomorrow. Reveille's at six, after which there'll be physical exercises, followed by a mile run up the road to the loch for a quick swim to get the cobwebs off your eyelashes, and then a run back for breakfast. The first part of commando training begins after that." He turned to Major Hyatt. "Silent killing for the ladies on the docket tomorrow, eh, Major?" He turned to Catherine with a nod in the direction of the tall, friendly-looking woman sitting on the other side of the room, "Your American colleague, here, will show you to your quarters."

He addressed Henri with a swift nod. "And if I don't see you before you leave on Wednesday, I wish you the best of luck at your next assignment. Sleep well, everyone."

As the group stood up in deference to their commanding officer taking his leave, Henri turned and introduced Catherine to Vivier Clarke.

"What a wonderful name," Catherine said with a smile, extending her hand.

"My mother's a Brit," Viv disclosed with the ease of someone accustomed to explaining the evolution of her unusual moniker. "My birth father—whose middle name was Vivier—was Franco-American. He fought in France and died in the Great War, which is why I've taken a liking to the ace flyboy, the *monsieur* here," she added with a grin. "My mother remarried a man whom I didn't like much, so I renamed myself 'Vivier Clarke' and pretty much dropped the 'Constance.' My code name is totally boring—Elizabeth!"

"And now, here we all are," Catherine said, "in deepest, darkest Scotland, heading for who-knows-where."

Viv shrugged and said, "I'll go anywhere, as long as I don't have to jump out of an airplane to get there."

Henri looked at her with surprise. "A fearless girl like you...afraid of airplanes? You said you were a skier."

Viv leaned forward and lowered her voice. "I focus on my ski tips. Deathly afraid of heights. I barely managed to do that crazy tightrope exercise forty feet off *terra firma*. But jumping out of a plane? No, thank you. They'll just have to get me into France—or wherever—some other way."

Catherine shook her head, her doubt obvious. "What other way would there be?"

"Submarine," Viv suggested. "Or a fishing boat from Portugal. I'll go anywhere by land or water, just not jumping through the air," she added with a shudder. Then, like the sun coming from behind a cloud, her expression brightened. "But let's not dwell on such atrocities. Catherine—or should I call you Colette?" Grinning, she admitted, "We're not supposed to know each other's real names, but I can't keep all the codes straight. But c'mon, let me show you your bunk. Women's quarters are set apart from the lodge here. Our little stone building probably once housed the beaters who flushed out the prey for the local lairds during the shooting season. At least we've got a fireplace, decent blankets, and our secret stash of malt whisky, so you and I will do just fine."

Henri nodded. "Thanks, Viv. I suspected you two would get along famously if you ever met."

Viv cast a look of sly amusement from Henri to Catherine. "Just an acquaintance, huh?" she said to him. "Sure." She winked. "Never fear, your secret's safe with me."

Catherine looked at the plush carpet with mild embarrassment. Then she rose from the couch and stood for one last moment, with her back to the library's fire, the embers glowing orange and red. As she watched the other trainees file obediently out of the library, she could only marvel that Henri and she had crossed paths a second time since leaving Washington. Meanwhile, Viv rested a light hand on Henri's shoulder.

"Hope I see you before you go, but if not..." Her tone was no longer jovial, and the younger woman was gazing at him somberly in a manner that Catherine could see revealed they'd become fast friends. "Keep safe, *monsieur*. I learned a lot from you these last weeks, so thanks."

"You keep safe yourself," Henri replied.

To Catherine Viv said, "C'mon, sister spy. Follow me down the bramble path." She took a step toward the door that led to the hallway, looked back, and tossed them both a mischievous smile, adding "Whatever you do *after* that is totally up to you."

———◇———

Despite her inclination to try to find Henri's room in the main house, Catherine's good sense told her to follow Viv out the back door and down the path to her new sleeping quarters—and stay there. This proved to be an excellent decision. Just before slipping into her bunk, she'd pulled back the black-out drape covering the deep-set window in the stone wall for a last glance at her new surroundings. She reared back and let the curtain fall back into place at the sight of a uniformed member of the colonel's staff walking close by on patrol, a rifle resting on his shoulder.

Had Colonel Rogers ordered this watchdog based on gleaning from her personnel file that she and Henri had known each other intimately? Or was the guard there just in case they still doubted Henri's loyalties to the Allied effort? Maybe, she thought sourly, the colonel worried that, as an agent fresh from kiss-and-tell duties, she was a woman not to be trusted.

———◇———

By morning's light, Catherine was grateful she'd gotten a full night's sleep. As Colonel Rogers predicted, arduous was a mild description of her first day at Arisaig House. Fortunately, even at thirty-two years old, she could still claim athletic prowess as a runner, expert skier, and swimmer, although her arms ached the rest of the day from the thirty push-ups demanded of her that morning.

"Hey there," Viv called to Catherine, catching up with her as they entered the formal dining room that served as their mess hall. "How did you survive our plunge into the loch at six-thirty in the morning?"

"You mean getting the cobwebs out of our eyelashes?" she joked. "Wasn't bad."

"You looked pretty fit, I must say."

Catherine nodded. "Running and swimming were the easy parts. How'd you like it when they showed us how to place a swift knee to a man's crotch or bang the back of one's head into an attacker's nose before rabbit-punching them with an elbow to the ribs?"

"Might come in useful one of these days," Viv deadpanned. "Are you hungry?"

"Famished. Hope there's some food left."

"It won't taste like a New York sirloin, but at least we get plenty of it."

Catherine sensed the moment that Henri realized she had entered the room. She spotted him across the large dining hall, surrounded by a group of men, many of whom had been his training partners. She had barely cut into the piece of leather masquerading as their evening meal when Henri and a fellow recruit walked by. Viv, with a twinkle in her eye hailed them both.

"You still here, Henri?" she joked.

"Leaving at the crack of dawn tomorrow."

"At least let's have a goodbye hug." She stood up from the table and addressed his female companion. "We Americans like hugging, don't we Catherine?" She swiftly introduced their newest arrival to Henri's dinner companions.

Catherine also pushed away from the dining table to say hello, and in the next instant, she felt Henri slip a folded piece of paper into her left hand.

A second later, Viv turned and threw her arms around him. "I wish you all the best, kiddo. Take care, now, you hear me?"

Henri exchanged glances with Catherine over Viv's shoulder. "I'll try my damnedest, kiddo." To Catherine, the word sounded comical, given Henri's French accent.

When Henri straightened up, Catherine saw an intensity in his eyes that she knew was intended only for her.

"All the best with your training here," he offered by way of a formal farewell.

"And the same to you," Catherine said, wondering how long she would have to wait before she read Henri's missive. She almost laughed aloud at the thought that he'd delivered it with the *savoir-faire* of a secret agent's message drop to one of their own.

———◇———

"No one saw you leave?" Henri asked the second he opened the wooden door to allow her to enter the deserted stone cottage high on a wind-swept hill to the north of the lodge.

"Only Viv, who seemed pleased to be playing cupid and gave me directions how to get here without getting lost on the moor."

"We used this bothy in one of our field exercises," he confirmed. "I trust Viv."

"I do, too," Catherine replied, "although without as much evidence as I assume you have." For some reason, Henri's friendship with Viv seemed no threat at all.

And why would that even be an issue? We're all free in this life.

But Catherine felt unsettled even having these thoughts. Determinedly ignoring them, she peered past his shoulder at the blaze crackling in small fireplace built into the corner of a tiny stone shed where once a shepherd had sheltered from the sleet and storms of Scottish winters. She could just make out the braying of sheep that apparently still grazed on the vast tracks of land stretching beyond Arisaig House.

Henri stepped aside, allowing her to pass across the threshold onto a dirt floor. In the center of the hut, a planked table that had to be a century or two old held a lantern and two stoneware mugs. Wedged in one corner was a wooden frame covered with rough linen. Catherine judged it was a piece of furniture in stark contrast to her bed in D.C., with its gray velvet headboard that had once been their love nest in Georgetown.

"Viv gave me a flask of malt whisky," Catherine said, holding it out to Henri to cover a moment of awkwardness now that, suddenly, they were alone after so many weeks' separation.

Henri reached into his back pocket. "I brought one as well."

They both laughed as Catherine set hers on the wooden table with a thump. Henri did likewise.

"Well," she drawled, "I guess we can either get roaring drunk"— she pointed to the corner—"or make love on that bed over there, if we dare."

Henri seized her almost roughly and pulled her close, the buttons on his uniform pressing into her breasts. Murmuring in her ear in French, he whispered, "Ah, *chérie*, let's get a little drunk so we can ignore the rough accommodations but not so drunk that we won't remember this night during the many long days ahead."

CHAPTER 13

Henri awoke to the insistent sound of knuckles rapping on the small, grimy window at the end of the stone hut, sheltered by clusters of brush and a windswept tree.

"*Merde*," he muttered, sleepily pulling Catherine's deliciously fragrant form closer to him. A whiff of her Chanel Number 5 mingled with vestiges of their night of lovemaking.

In the next instant, however, he sat straight up in bed. His watch said 5:00 a.m. The knuckle tapping grew even louder, and he heard a voice. "Catherine! Hey, Thornton, move your ass!"

It was Viv, come to make sure Catherine got to the morning assembly and Henri departed for his next destination on time.

Henri whispered fiercely in his lover's ear, "*Chérie. Chérie*, wake up! Viv's come to fetch you, bless her."

"No…" Catherine moaned.

"Yes, you must. If the colonel learns you're here, we both could find ourselves headed for the Cooler." He kissed her shoulder until she turned to face him, and then he framed her dewy-eyed face in his hands and planted a lingering kiss on her mouth.

"Oh, Henri," Catherine whispered. "I don't want to leave."

He was stunned to hear these words. The one thing that had been constant about Catherine was that she rarely revealed her feelings or ever gave him the sense that she cared deeply for him. Liked him, yes. Respected him, certainly, and she clearly enjoyed him in bed. But her voice almost sounded like a small child this morning, sad and vulnerable. And last night…well, last night was something he would never forget, and he hoped that merely recalling each delicious moment would get him through the war.

"Come on, now, darling. You've got to wake up."

She was still barely conscious, which might explain the reason her guard was down, but it also made him hope that she was finally expressing to him something of how she truly felt. That he was as important to her as she had become to him. That she longed for his company in the same way he did hers at times like these, especially when they were about to part.

"I don't want you to leave either, my darling, but come, I'll help you dress. Viv and I know a way around the moor that's completely obscured by a forest until you reach the back of Arisaig House, so hopefully you'll return without notice. We've taken major chances as it is." To the door he called, "She'll be there in a minute!"

Henri rolled out of the uncomfortable bed and pulled Catherine to her feet. They stood, arms wrapped around their bare waists, and remained stationary, as if imprinting their bodies on each other.

Then she stooped to pick up the underwear she had discarded in such a hurry the previous night and, without embarrassment, began to dress, as did he.

As they turned to face the hut's wooden door, Henri halted abruptly, turned around once again, and put his two hands on her shoulders, forcing her to meet his gaze.

"Remember what I say to you now, will you?" he asked, leaning within inches of her lips. "I will find a way to see you again before this damnable war is over."

"Promise?" she demanded quietly.

"The odds are quite bad, of course…"

Neither of them would allude to the increasing devastation from bombs dropped over England, the disturbing loss of SOE agents sent into the war zones of France, or the dislocation and deaths of civilians everywhere in Europe.

"Don't you dare bring up the odds against us," she said, reading his mind.

"Catherine, the cat with nine lives, are you? I like that."

She stood on tiptoes and kissed him long and hard.

"Please remain the diplomat who can talk his way out of any dicey situation," she said, her voice barely above a whisper. "Promise me you will do that." He looked at her quizzically. "Stay alive for the duration, will you please?"

"I expect we'll both do our best on that score. *Au revoir, ma chérie. Je t'adore.* I'll try to say goodbye if I can before I leave today."

Before Catherine could reply, Viv yanked open the door, hands on her hips in frustration.

"I don't want to get court-martialed—or whatever they do to us SOEs for disobeying the rules—just because you two refuse to get out of the sack!" She took in the sight of the pair, arms still entwined. "Well, at least you finally have your clothes on. C'mon, Thornton. Chop, chop. We've got fifteen minutes to make it back before reveille."

———◇———

By midmorning, before Catherine and Viv had finished their daily calisthenics, Henri Leblanc had been whisked away en route to the south of England and his next assignment. His train crossed back into England by the time the two women had run the mile to and from the freezing waters of the loch, consumed their salted porridge for breakfast in the paneled dining room, and completed a rather harrowing second lesson in the art of silent killing. With nary a moment left for any goodbyes, Henri had departed, leaving no hint as to his ultimate destination.

As she had in London when the SOE so abruptly separated them, she felt a stab of worry that made her breath catch. Given their roles as SOE agents behind enemy lines, what were the odds they would both survive this brutal war?

At the end of the first of many exhausting and stressful days she imagined were to come, Catherine flopped down on her iron cot in the beaters' cottage and sought slumber. Instead, she stared vacantly at the ancient wooden joists that supported the thatched ceiling above her head. Would the man whose scent was still on her skin recall the night they'd just shared in a week or a month or a year? Would his private thoughts recapture the pure heat and light between them, despite a lumpy straw mattress covered by rough linen bedding that prickled and scratched their naked bodies?

And, in spite of all that, she wondered if Henri had been deeply moved—as she had—by the emotions they'd shared, startling sensations that hadn't existed when the two of them were originally on assignment in Washington.

Or at least, those emotions were ones that Catherine had to admit to herself *she* had never before felt...a longing to bond with him on some mysterious plane beyond the physical. The world of war was a constant battle between safety and danger. With Henri, she felt safe and more confident than ever in her ability to ward off the dangers they would face in the future. She knew his thoughts and believed he had known hers. And, oddly, it was this new experience that frightened her most of all.

Catherine squeezed her eyes shut and balled her fists against the rough army blanket covering her cot.

Good God, girl, get a grip, she told herself. The only reasonable thing to do during wartime was to live in the moment, wasn't it? That's what she and Henri had done last night, nothing more, nothing less. For her own sanity's sake, she thought, *Jettison the hearts and flowers.*

———◇———

A young lieutenant with a fledgling mustache, designed to make him appear older than his twenty-some years, entered the cheerful sunroom off the foyer at Beaulieu, the SOE so-called finishing school located south of London where newly minted agents got their final orders and equipment.

"Maurice Buckmaster is here to see our Frenchman," he said, pointing with a faintly sardonic sneer at Henri, who was sitting in a row of desks in the windowed chamber now used as a classroom. Leblanc had been outfitted in the latest French clothing and given Gauloise cigarettes to keep in his pocket along with all manner of items only available in France, in preparation for his scheduled parachute jump back into his home country.

In a small sitting room in the country house, Buckmaster greeted him with a cheery smile and extended his hand.

"We've been discussing your situation," he disclosed as the pair took seats in the leather chairs drawn up near an empty fireplace.

"Yes, sir?" Henri inquired politely.

"And we've decided that you will have to be dispatched to a remote outpost somewhere in France, given that someone from your diplomatic days might recognize you and betray your mission. We thought to drop you at a location where you can organize supplies for cadres of French resisters in an isolated part of the country."

"Excuse me, if I may," Henri intervened. "I've also been giving my assignment a great deal of thought. I think the fact I'm known as a former Vichy diplomat is absolutely to the SOE's advantage."

"Really? And how is that?" Buckmaster asked, skeptically.

"I was severely injured in a plane crash in the last war. I have scars on my body. It could explain why I could now be working as a salesman in the paper and printing industry that my father and grandfather owned in Paris before the war."

"Hmmm," mused Buckmaster. "That would allow you mobility."

"Exactly!" Henri nodded, encouraged to continue. "I could set up an office in Paris, perhaps even in the building where my family's business once was headquartered. That would allow me to serve as a traveling representative of printing supplies in and around Paris and Northern France."

Buckmaster looked noncommittal. "Our intelligence tells us that the Nazis are systematically shutting down newspapers and bookshops. Except, of course, for the ones that champion their anti-Semitic brand of fascism."

"The Nazis shut down our family's chain of centrist newspapers as well," Henri disclosed, "but our company also used to sell to art and stationery shops and any business that required paper or printing tasks, such as posters or advertisements."

Buckmaster suddenly looked intrigued.

"It would be dangerous," Buckmaster acknowledged, "but what a boon it would be if you could help the clandestine press, barely holding on in France, to obtain the supplies they need to continue publishing their work."

Henri gazed across the desk at the leader of French Section and slowly nodded.

"I might be able to do these things we've been talking about, provided it was obvious to the authorities that I was ineligible to serve in the military because of my injury and age. With the proper documents that I'd been released honorably from the diplomatic corps, I might be relatively free to go wherever I'm needed."

"Hmmm...." Buckmaster murmured again, his chin cradled in his hand, his thumb stroking his chin. "You know, Leblanc, if you could somehow requisition some actual printing equipment, you could even try to get contracts with the occupying Nazis, publishing their broadsides and propaganda rags. Then you'd really know what plans they were making."

Henri cocked his head in thought and then replied, "There is printing equipment housed in one building my family owned in Paris where I worked for my father as a boy. I know all the old-timers—assuming any of them are still alive."

"Maybe you could even manage to salt in a few subversive messages to the resisters embedded in the Nazi propaganda they're publishing in French, given how poorly many in the Gestapo speak and write your language."

Henri leaned forward, a feeling of excitement taking hold.

"*Absolument!* I could visit potential customers in and around Paris while assessing how strong the Resistance is in the places I visit. That would also give me a plausible way to interact with the enemy and learn more of their future plans."

Buckmaster's eyes were alight with enthusiasm.

"And, in your travels, couldn't you also try to set up networks of resisters to prepare for our eventual invasion? Paris is swarming with Nazis, and it's been very difficult for non-French SOE agents to avoid capture. The truth is, they've arrested or deported a lot more of our agents than I'd like to admit."

"So I've heard," Henri replied somberly. "But this cover story would allow me the freedom I'd need for such an enterprise. And if I ever encountered former diplomatic colleagues or the authorities, I can prove that I'm just trying to keep my family's old business alive. I was working in Washington when our chain of small newspapers was shut down after the Germans invaded. As they say, sir," Henri added, hoping he didn't sound too eager, "a good cover story like this usually works best if it's fairly close to the truth."

Buckmaster leaned back in his chair. "I must warn you, however, that even this kind of setup will be fraught with danger at every turn. You might encounter that rabid Nazi sympathizer who served as your ambassador in Washington, D.C. He would certainly know you were not formally discharged from the diplomatic corps but had unaccountably disappeared. Perhaps he'd think you've gone A.W.O.L."

"I could just say that I was interrogated in the U.S. over a period of weeks and finally released and flown to Portugal, just as he was, to make my way over the Pyrenees and back into France." Despite this invented excuse, Henri did have to admit that running into his previous superior could easily spell a speedy death by firing squad if he had any inkling that copies of the French naval codebooks had been obtained, surreptitiously copied, and given to the Allies, thanks to him. To convince both himself and Buckmaster the plan was still workable, he added, "The Ambassador is probably in Vichy with General Pétain and Pierre Laval, supporting that farce of a government there. Naturally, I'll avoid that area like the plague."

"It's still a risk, Leblanc..." Buckmaster said slowly, continuing to mull over Henri's bold proposal. "You would be, in essence, a double agent, consorting with the Nazis occupying your country while working for the Allies."

"Yes, I suppose one could view it that way." Henri met Buckmaster's gaze and held it. "But, sir, you need to know this: I'd have one loyalty, to the true France and the Allies trying to liberate her. And I'm willing to risk my life for that cause."

The head of the French Section division of the SOE sat quietly for a long moment. Henri could almost see that the spy-chief was weighing whether it was worth his risk to trust a Frog. At length, the SOE chief slapped both palms on the desk.

"Excellent, then. It's settled. I'll have the boys here set you up with all the credentials you'll need and drill you on all aspects of your cover story until you believe every detail of it yourself!"

Buckmaster rose from his chair, and Henri immediately followed.

"Sir, it might help you and your staff to know that I broke both legs when I landed in the English Channel during the Great War. A boat saw me pitch out of the sky and brought me to Britain to recuperate. Somewhere, there are X-rays on file to prove it."

"That's right!" Buckmaster exclaimed. "You were a bit of a daredevil, if I remember your file correctly."

Henri nodded, certain that the man had reread every single line of his dossier before he arrived at Beaulieu House that morning. Buckmaster chuckled.

"If we can't locate the films, I'll make sure we take some new X-rays that you'll have with you that show the leg breaks. You can keep the pictures in reserve in case you are ever asked why you were in the diplomatic corps rather than the army when the war began."

"That—and my age—were the reasons I became a diplomat before the Vichy took over. Even though my legs healed remarkably well, no military corps would have me."

"Well, your report says you held your own in the physical training in Scotland."

"I did, actually," Henri replied, thinking also of the hours he'd spent with Catherine in the stone hut perched on top of the moor. "Still," he admitted with a rueful smile, "the joints in my leg, knees, and hips warn me when the weather is going to change."

Buckmaster threw back his head with a hearty laugh. "So do mine!" Then he sobered. "Do your legs show any outward scars?"

"Big ones, sir. Left and right. Shins and thighs."

"Capital!" exclaimed Buckmaster. "I'm glad I made the trip down here and spoke to you in person. Nothing like hearing the facts from the horse's mouth. You've shown remarkable courage, both in that hat trick you pulled off in Washington with Mrs. Thornton and in all your training."

Ah...Catherine. What amazing things we could do together in France.

Henri was wise enough not to ask why he and Catherine had not been assigned to work as a team any longer. Instead, he merely nodded as Buckmaster declared, "I think you and I have devised a bloody brilliant mission for you and an excellent cover story. It has the double value of helping us secure the intelligence information about the Nazi operations in Paris and elsewhere around the country, as well as re-establishing new networks of agents to support the underground Resistance." He seized Henri's hand and pumped it with great vigor. "Believe me, Leblanc, I wish you all good luck in future."

They both knew what the odds most likely were. Given this treacherous assignment based close to Nazi headquarters in France, it would be a miracle if Henri survived this war.

CHAPTER 14

Much to Catherine's and Viv's surprise, another rare American recruit of about their age suddenly arrived at the SOE's Scottish training outpost. The morning fitness exercises at Arisaig House had just concluded when a lanky, bespectacled redhead in khaki shorts, sweating profusely in a tee-shirt declaring "U.S. Army" on his chest, hastened to catch up with the women as they entered the back door to the hunting lodge.

For a carrot-top, his features, tall stature, and porcelain-pink complexion were a combination that rendered the young man surprisingly handsome. Thrusting out a damp hand, he said confidently, "Hello, I'm Sean Eisenhower. I heard two other Americans were here, and I really wanted to meet you."

"Your name is Eisenhower?" Viv blurted. "Any relation to our general?"

"Sort of. He and my father are distantly related. His cousin and my cousin are cousins," he added with a grin.

"Not so distant," Catherine opined. She remembered only too well that in Washington, D.C., hostesses like her mother and society columnist Annabelle Arlington would hound a good-looking young man with a last name like Sean's to come to their tea dances and soirees.

Sean smiled. He pointed to his army tee shirt and then to his coke-bottle glasses, behind which his bright-blue eyes glinted with infectious humor. "We tended to have lots of boys in our family, but I was born with double myopia and came up 4F." He laughed with no hint of embarrassment. "My brother went to West Point like the rest of our tribe. He gave me this shirt as a going-away present, advising me to fake it till I make it."

"How come your poor eyesight didn't keep you out of Special Ops?" Catherine asked, curiosity getting the best of her manners.

"Turns out it was an asset!" Sean replied cheerfully. "The brass thought it would explain to the Jerries why I'm not in military service if I get sent behind enemy lines," he added with a shrug. "I'll probably be cast as an absentminded professor or something."

"Well, good for you for joining up," Viv complimented him.

"We Yanks have to stick together" he said with a smile that included both women.

Much to their astonishment, despite his visual impairment, Sean Eisenhower turned out to be a crack shot, a truth that Catherine and Viv learned when they spent the next day at small arms target practice.

During small arms training, Catherine stared at a moving paper target in the shape of a soldier with six bullet holes piercing the area of the heart.

"How in the world can you, of all people, do that?" she demanded. She had only managed to pierce the paper target twice—once in the shoulder and once in the neck.

"Why, ma'am, I am highly offended by such incredulity. We handicapped chaps have all sorts of unique talents."

"No, really," Viv insisted. "That was amazing!"

"Well," Sean said with a shrug, "despite my bad eyesight, my parents sent me to a military school in upper New York State where you cannot graduate unless you can officially shoot a salvo of bullets into that little circle on the target. Once I got the right set of specs my junior year, I was highly motivated to get out of that place. Up until then, no one seemed to notice that I was blind as a bat."

"Even so, I take it you didn't get into West Point," Viv commented.

"Nope. They wouldn't have me, and I didn't want to go, so everything worked out just fine. As soon as I saluted the sadistic commandant at my military school for the last time, I headed straight for *L'Ecole des Beaux Arts* in Paris."

"Wow, that was certainly an about-face." Catherine was as intrigued as Viv obviously was by the newcomer. "What made you gravitate there, for pity's sake?"

"*L'Ecole* taught architecture," he replied matter-of-factly. "Or at least, back then, I thought I would be an architect, but I soon discovered I liked drawing buildings much more than trying to figure out how to safely construct them." He shrugged. "My dad was stationed in France, then. The good news was that I learned to speak excellent French at *L'Ecole*, and I somehow managed to earn my certificate in architecture to satisfy the parents." Sean gave them both a sideways glance. "But guess what?"

"What?" the women asked in unison.

"Once I had my degree in hand, I got a job as a magazine and fashion illustrator for a bunch of publications in France and the U.S."

"You're making my head spin!" Viv exclaimed.

"It was great!" Sean enthused. "In those days, before the Nazis invaded, I had a fabulous apartment on the Ile St. Louis and had morphed once again from an illustrator into a painter, as in fine art. Landscapes, especially."

"I bet all those career changes threw your family for a loop," Catherine noted with no attempt at tact. "Did you actually make a living, or were you a starving *artiste*?"

"Yes, I made a living." Sean met her gaze. "A good living. In fact, I probably should stop kidding around about that."

"Well, then," she said with admiration, "if you could make a living as a painter, you must be damn good." She extended her hand. "Delighted to meet you."

"Me too," Viv exclaimed. She turned to Catherine, "But let's not just stand here yakking. Aren't you starving? Let's teach our new pal how to cut into the chow line so expertly no one ever gets mad at us."

"The Brits are too polite to complain, Viv," Catherine admonished with a laugh.

"And besides," said Sean, his cheeks growing a telltale pink, "you gals are both stunners, so I bet nobody minds standing aside for you two."

Catherine grinned back. "Let's go, flatterer. You showed us how to shoot today, so we'll show you the ropes around here."

Viv linked both their arms. "Three Yank musketeers are we!"

———◇———

For the rest of September 1942, Catherine, Viv, Sean, and the rest of the recruits buckled down to the serious business of learning how to handle high explosives safely. Their instructor demonstrated techniques for turning a common plastic material into a deadly bomb using wires, timing pencils, and fuses that could blow up in one's face without proper care.

As the days flew by, Catherine and Sean discovered they had a lot more in common than merely enjoying the company of a friend their own age. Sean's father, like Catherine's, was a U.S. military officer assigned overseas throughout the 1930s. One night after dinner, the young secret-agent-in-training disclosed how he came to hate the Nazis with the same fervor as Catherine and Viv. Sent as a youngster to grammar school in Germany, his father continued to serve at various posts in Europe during most of the same years Catherine's father had been posted abroad and Viv's stepfather made repeated business trips to Hitler's enclaves.

"Even in the mid-1930s, any observer living in Europe could guess how extreme the political climate was becoming," Sean noted with uncharacteristic seriousness. "After I was back in the States at military school, I would visit Germany during holidays and summers, and I witnessed the massive parades with Hitler screaming at thousands of cheering Germans during endless rallies."

"I hated all that, too," Catherine murmured. "I was wondering, Sean, after all that education in Europe and military school, how upset were your parents when you rebelled against, uh…"

"Going into the Army?" he interrupted. "They always assumed that my bad eyes would probably make me a washout in any of the military services. Even my family's name couldn't make up for my having to wear these," he added, pointing to the specs perched on his nose. "Actually, Mom and Dad were great when I said I wanted to be an architect instead."

"But when you switched from architecture to art?" Catherine asked, thinking of how her mother objected to her daughter's announcement that she wanted to be a working journalist. "Was that okay with them too?"

"Being a landscape painter? Not so much," he admitted, "but our whole family is pretty tight, you know? And my brothers kept saying one of us had to be the oddball, so better me than them. The parents eventually came around. Especially when the General bought one of my pictures."

"I bet they're pretty proud of you now that you enlisted in the SOE," Viv said staunchly.

Joining in with this crowd?" Sean grinned. "With FDR's sons and all those movie stars like Jimmy Stewart and Kirk Douglas joining the Air Force and the Navy, I'm small potatoes." He offered a small shrug, admitting, "But I think my parents are proud I signed up, although they don't really know what the hell I'm doing." Sean paused. "Well, maybe my dad has some inkling."

Catherine glanced at the wedding ring on his hand. "And your wife?"

Sean reddened slightly at Catherine's query. "She thinks I'm working for *Stars and Stripes* as a civilian illustrator. And besides, she's pretty busy with the twins. That was a big score in my favor after I got married—two boys, right off the bat. Now our home is close to her parents in Arlington, Virginia."

"Let me guess," Catherine said, laughing. "She's a military brat like you and me, am I right? You met her during high school and kept in touch when you went back and forth to Europe."

Sean raised his right hand as if holding the pistol he'd shot so well at target practice and pretended to pull the trigger. "You got that right, sister. Marilyn's U.S.A. all the way."

"Is that why you eventually came home from Paris? True love?" Viv pressed.

Sean hesitated just long enough for Catherine to surmise the probable reason that the charming Sean Eisenhower had married his first girlfriend.

"Well, ah, let's just say there were pressing circumstances that prompted my decision to come back to the States." He looked serious. "And, besides, virtually every American who could left Paris when it was clear the Nazi's would soon be goose-stepping down the Champs-Élysees."

Just then, the Colonel appeared in the sitting room doorway. "Just a reminder, everyone," he announced in a loud voice, and they all sprang to their feet, at attention. "I understand from your instructor that tomorrow you will be shown how to blow up bridges and rail stations. Trust me, you'll need to be particularly on your toes, so I'd suggest you all get some beauty sleep. There's a five-mile trek to get to the explosives area where there are some old railway tracks and structures built over a fast-flowing burn, high up on the moor."

Sean groaned. "Five miles, sir? Uphill? And what's a burn? A bomb?"

The colonel, who always appeared to be mildly amused by this American artist-turned-marksman, smiled indulgently.

"A burn in Scotland, young man, is a wee river. And yes, your journey tomorrow is straight up. Have to train you chaps and ladies to handle explosives in remote spots, don't you know? Can't have our Scottish neighbors complaining about the noise.

———◇———

The next morning dawned frigid, with a high wind blowing off the steep-sided terrain that rose to fifteen hundred feet above Arisaig House. Viv was assigned to the team whose mission it was to blow up a bridge. The span, flung across a fiercely flowing stream, was repeatedly reconstructed after each team's session aimed at destroying it.

Three hundred meters further uphill on a rocky plateau, Sean and Catherine were given instructions on laying handmade bomb *materiel* along some railroad tracks already blackened in various spots—some sections even bent—from previous explosions.

For Catherine, the work required even more concentration than twirling the dials on an ancient, cranky safe in order to secure the cipher books at the Vichy embassy. This time, if she made a mistake, she could unwittingly detonate herself and everyone else.

"The pencil fuse!" exclaimed Sean under his breath. "I think you missed one."

"Oh, hell. You're right," she replied, relieved they were out of earshot of their hard-nosed instructor. With fingers numb from the frigid temperatures, she managed to attach the wayward wire just as Sargent Mallory arrived at their backs and leaned over their shoulders.

"Not bad," he grunted, "for a *gel*," he added, his Scottish accent giving away his place of origin. He put a paw on Sean's shoulder. "Okay, lad. Your turn. Let's see you do an even better job. Uphold the males of the species, canna you please?"

Sean understood the mechanisms of the explosives far better than Catherine, but by this time, his fingers were even stiffer from the cold than hers. His progress proved slower than the other two teams working further down the makeshift tracks.

"All right, chaps and ladies," barked Mallory. "Two more minutes! Two more minutes, now!"

Catherine watched the sergeant turn his back to inspect a team thirty meters away from their position on the track and swiftly grabbed the wires from Sean. She inserted them properly into the pencil fuses, tightened the screws, and poked them into the plastic just as Mallory shouted, "Time's up!"

"You're an angel," Sean whispered to Catherine under his breath. "I never would have made it."

Her thoughts careened back to Henri on the night they'd worked in perfect harmony, pulling off the heist of the French codebooks. An ache invaded her gut, and she was stunned to realize how much she missed him. Having a partner one trusted made all the difference, she thought, glancing sideways at Sean.

"All right, everyone," shouted Mallory. "Get back fifty meters from the tracks." He pointed to an outcropping of rock. "Stand behind those boulders for protection. Quickly, now!"

The group huddled together as ordered, and several deafening explosions ripped along the tracks. Much to Catherine and Sean's relief, their bombs had detonated properly. Mallory offered them another grunt of grudging approval. Then he ordered the recruits under his charge, "Please pack up your equipment and prepare to head back."

"To a very stiff whiskey, I hope," whispered Sean. "My God, it's arctic up here!"

As the explosives squad did as directed, the sergeant approached with clipboard in hand and informed the pair that they had both officially passed the day's various tests.

Sean reached for Catherine's hand and gave it a surreptitious squeeze. She'd sensed for more than a day or two that he was attracted to her, despite having a wife and twin boys back in the States, which certainly served to distract her from any foolish thoughts of Henri and their chances for meeting again. She had found Sean's good looks, humor, and boyish enthusiasm quite refreshing, and this mutuality of purpose during training was certainly one way to fend off such unexpected and pointless longing for a man who was far beyond her reach and likely to remain so forever.

On their way down the moor, Viv strode up and excitedly announced, "Did you see how our end of the bridge blew sky high? Thank God I passed. How did you two do with the railroad tracks? I heard several big explosions."

"Thanks to some good teamwork, we both passed too, right, Catherine?

"Teamwork, plus attention to detail on your part and a bit of dexterity on mine," she teased.

Sean shared their secret of mutual assistance with a pleased grin. "I just hope I'm not ever solely on my own with this stuff. I think women have much better fine motor skills and—"

"And men have better brains?" Catherine shot back with mock indignation. "Not a chance. We all just have to help each other until we get the hang of everything—both physical and mental."

Sean turned his head and muttered under his breath in

Catherine's direction, "I could use some help with the physical. How 'bout you, sweetheart?"

Catherine reacted by giving him a sharp jab in the ribs.

Not hearing Sean's aside, Viv chimed in, "Amen to the teamwork." She hoisted her heavy rucksack higher on her shoulder and lowered her voice. "The guy I was working with was a scared rabbit about handling the fuses but a total ace when it came to figuring out where to position the explosives under the bridge to effect the biggest bang."

Viv disappeared into the stone storage shed to hand in her equipment. As soon as she was out of sight, Sean glanced around the vicinity and cupped Catherine's derriere with the palm of his hand. The wind had died down now that they were near the lodge, and Sean leaned forward to whisper into Catherine's right ear.

"I can think of another way to effect a big bang."

"Sean!" Catherine whispered. "Someone will hear you!"

"A guy in our barrack knows about a deserted stone shed not too far from here where—"

Just then, their instructor appeared in the doorway.

"C'mon, you two! Hand in your kit. The rest of us want to warm up and head for the mess."

Catherine turned abruptly and strode toward the equipment shed, shrugging off the rucksack with relief from its heavy weight. To her chagrin, a familiar tingling began to course through her. Sean's touch had awakened sensations she'd kept strictly in check. Even so, perhaps a discreet tryst with him was just the antidote she needed to put all thoughts of Henri out of her mind. But then a thought swept over her like icy water from a Highland stream. She would certainly not rendezvous with Sean Eisenhower or anyone else, for that matter, at a stone bothy deep in the Scottish woodlands near Arisaig House.

Any other place but there.

Catherine felt an odd sense of reprieve, knowing that there were no other places at the training camp that could provide the kind of privacy she'd shared with Henri that memorable night. Furthermore, she scolded herself, she and Henri had been incredibly lucky not to have been caught. She certainly didn't fancy being thrown out of the SOE for conduct unbecoming, should the fates fail her this time.

Meanwhile, Viv and Sean were already walking toward the stone lodge, its clocktower looming overhead. Trailing behind them a few paces, she was helpless to prevent her thoughts from straying to the memory of a singular night spent in a lumpy bed with a Frenchman who could by now have parachuted deep into his native country and was liable to be arrested or killed any day.

CHAPTER 15

Sean and Catherine were not teamed together in successive exercises. Catherine speculated that the sergeant in charge of the explosives course had sensed the pair might be getting, in British Army parlance, "a little too cozy for government work." She couldn't help but notice that they were put on different squads for the rest of their time at Arisaig House, although they encountered each other every evening in the book-lined library when the group shared a tipple before the exhausted recruits retired for the night.

Although Catherine recognized that, had Henri not been part of her life or had she and Sean met under different circumstances, the copper-headed lad and she would likely have formed some sort of romantic liaison. It was obvious that they had much in common in terms of family background, a droll outlook on life, and an obvious enjoyment of...what?

Physical closeness in times of stress.

Wasn't that the polite way of describing the sexual attraction she'd experienced whenever she had been in the company of the wry, witty, spectacle-wearing member of the celebrated Eisenhower clan?

Within the next week, and without even a day's warning, Viv was sent off to wireless school in southern England. Soon after, Sean was due to be shipped to a mysterious destination that, if he revealed where and what it was, "I'd have to kill you, Catherine, and I very much do not want to do that."

On the eve of his departure, they were standing in the paneled hallway outside the dining mess, with fellow recruits streaming by. Sean's canvas travel bag was on the floor beside their feet. Catherine could sense a familiar hollowed-out emotion enveloping her chest that was akin to the feeling she'd always had whenever her father had announced he'd be leaving her and her mother for a new assignment, with no set date when they could join him.

"Well, all good luck, then, Sean," she managed to say, keeping her tone light.

"And, of course, the same to you." He was less than a foot away, gazing down at her, his features uncharacteristically somber. "You're off to parachute school, I hear."

Catherine reared back. "How in the world do you know that?"

Sean cast her a smug smile. "I have my sources."

"You have your strings to pull, I expect," she retorted, thinking of the way her mother had inserted the name Farnsworth in certain power circles in D.C. "Special privileges come with a famous last name, am I right?"

"You betcha, and you never know when they might come in handy for both of us."

"Wha—?"

But before she could complete her sentence, Sean leaned down and kissed her firmly on the lips. Fortunately, by this time, the corridor was empty. Catherine relaxed in his arms and kissed him back.

"Mmmm," he said on a long breath, taking a step back. "Wish there'd be more where that came from."

"Me too," she admitted, and then for some reason, the thought of Henri popped into her head.

Damn it! She owed that Frenchman nothing! God knows what he'd been up to in the world of female charms since he'd left, she thought, irritated to no end that a vision of Henri Leblanc in her mind's eye had been her immediate response to someone else's arousing kiss. Sean pointed out one of the lodge's deep-set windows, its beveled glass panes obscured by blackout curtains.

"I do wish we could continue this conversation," he murmured, his lips still close to hers, "but much to my sorrow, sweets, gotta go.

My group is already in the transport out back. It's a full moon, so we can travel without headlights. Take the best of care, you hear?"

And then, just like Henri, Sean Eisenhower was gone.

————◇————

The second week of parachute school at Ringway Field, a secret air facility somewhere outside Manchester, Catherine got the surprise of her life when Viv Clarke suddenly turned up, entering the Quonset hut that was the women's sleeping quarters.

"I was a total washout at wireless," she announced, throwing her duffle bag on Catherine's cot with embarrassment that was palpable. "It was made very clear to me that doing decently in this course is the only chance I have of being sent into enemy territory."

"But aren't you the one who said you absolutely refuse to throw yourself out of an airplane?"

"I said exactly that to every big wig who's ever interviewed me!"

"But now?" Catherine pressed, worried that Viv truly might be on her way out.

"The colonel at wireless school told me, basically, to pull my socks up and get on with it so they can make me a courier for some SOE circuit leader or something."

"You'd be a great courier for a unit coordinating with local Resistance leaders, Viv. They don't want to lose you," Catherine insisted, wanting to bolster her friend's confidence.

"You're right," Viv said, her expression brightening. "They know damn well I speak excellent French *and* German, even with my New York twang. I guess they thought that's got to be worth something, don't you think?"

"Absolutely!"

Catherine had grown very fond of Viv when they were in the Scottish Highlands, and she hated the possibility that either of them might not make it through the coursework. Plenty of women they'd met along the way had been "sent down" for one reason or another.

Catherine put an arm around Viv's shoulder. "There are just a handful of American women in this corps," she reminded her. "No matter how hard it gets, we've got to show the flag, right?"

"Thanks for the pep talk," Viv said with a grateful smile.

Catherine clapped Viv on her shoulder for a second time.

"C'mon. Let me show you your bunk over there in the corner… where the walls leak."

"Gee, thanks," Viv replied.

"The last gal left a tarp you can sleep under," said Catherine. "And don't worry. I'm a week ahead of you in jump school, and I'll be your coach. Once you get the hang of jumping out of the plane's hole and mastering the land roll, it'll be a cinch."

"Says you," Viv replied grimly. "My stomach's in knots already. And what the heck is a land roll?"

"The way you rejoin *terra firma* once you've catapulted out of a plane."

"And that is?" demanded Viv.

"Tucking your head lower than your shoulders, putting your forearms over your face, and gluing your legs and feet together. We've been practicing this for hours, jumping off higher and higher parapets each time. If you don't go out stiff, you'll break your nose…or something even more important."

"Oh, God," Viv groaned. "I'll never live through this! When do we get taken up in a real plane?"

"Not before you learn how to fold your parachute."

"We pack our own chutes?" she demanded, her eyes wide.

"No, but they want you to know how it's done. Then they take us up in a real plane so we can lie on our stomachs looking through the hole in the fuselage where eventually we'll jump, just to get used to how it all feels."

"It *feels* like I'm in the middle of a nightmare."

———◇———

By the first week of October, Catherine and Viv were sitting side by side on a hard wooden bench that ran along inside the fuselage of a lumbering twin-engine bomber called the Whitley. The plane had been modified to carry parachute trainees, and the interior of its square-shaped tail had space for ten passengers in full jump gear.

"My back's killing me. Is yours?" Viv yelled over the roar of the engines. They were circling the flat, bleak drop zone over Ringway airfield. "These chutes strapped to our backs and legs must weigh a hundred pounds."

Catherine nodded, shouting back, "With our chutes, helmets, and canvas overalls, we looked like a bunch of hunch-backed crabs when we boarded the plane."

Interrupting this exchange, the dispatcher barked, "Standby! Move forward, move forward!" He waved on the seven trainees, each connected to a static line that would ultimately release when the jumper left the plane. "Don't let go of your ripcord—ever!"

"I think I'm going to be sick," gulped Viv.

"Not now, you aren't!" Catherine shouted. "Go, hurry. Go, scoot. Hurry!"

Catherine had no time to think about how Viv's first practice jump out of a real airplane would go. Next thing she knew, the light flashed green above the hole where she would lower herself. In an instant, she swung her feet down, felt the rush of the wind on her legs, and gripped the rim of the open fuselage.

Keep your head up. Never look down through the hole. Go out stiff. Shove off hard when the dispatcher's hand goes down and he says—"

"Go!" yelled the dispatcher.

And out she went with deafening noise roaring around her as the wind buffeted her sideways beneath the looming plane passing over her head. She was caught for a few seconds in the slipstream, dangling like an airborne puppet. The only thought in her head was, *"I could die today."*

Somehow, she remembered to count, as she'd been directed in all those practice jumps, and only then pulled the cord. Immediately she felt a painful jerk wrenching her shoulders as the chute pulled away from the packing strapped to her back and zoomed to the heavens above, safely clearing the plane's fuselage.

She glanced up and felt a rush of relief as the puffy canopy ballooned to its full extension above her. Suddenly, there was a wonderful silence. She reached up to grasp her rigging lines, drew them closer to her torso to steady the chute, and began to enjoy herself.

The Ringway runways outside of Manchester stretched to one side opposite the open fields where she was supposed to land. Suddenly, the flat stretch of ground was rushing toward her at an alarming speed. A voice from the ground shouted at her through a megaphone.

"Pull your rigging lines to the left! To the left! "

A stand of trees seemed far off, but fortunately the parachute instructor had warned her in time.

"Good! Good! You're coming down fine. Bend your legs. Forearms over your face! Head down. Hunch your shoulders! Now roll!"

And with a thump, she was down, being dragged along the field by her air-filled chute. A few of the other jumpers, including Viv, ran to help her, and soon the recruits were hugging each other and sharing their short-lived but exhilarating experience falling from the plane to the ground.

"That Jason fellow in our group broke his leg when he landed," Viv commented, soberly. "I got sick in the air, but still I made it," she added, "but I hope I *never* have to do this again." She leaned closer to Catherine's ear. "I've made friends with that pilot over there," she whispered, nodding in the direction of a tall, debonair young man with wavy dark hair who was smiling and heartily patting a recruit on the back. "He's French. Used to fly for Air Bleu, but now he's in the SOE ferrying agents like us across the Channel. He told me that now many of them are being dropped off and picked up on the ground in planes instead of parachuting into France. Isn't that aces?"

Catherine squinted to bring Viv's new friend into better focus. Sure enough, it was the self-assured Lothario that Henri and she met in the black-tiled bathroom waiting room before they each had their interview with Maurice Buckmaster at Orchard House.

"His name is Lucien Barteau, right?" asked Catherine. "I met him once, for about five minutes, the day I officially signed up for SOE."

Viv nodded. "Really? Wow. I guess they've given him the code name Gilbert. C'mon. Say hi to him. And, by the way: dibs!"

"He's all yours. I like parachuting. I can't wait to do it again."

Viv laughed. "You're nuts!" She leaned in conspiratorially. "After I landed, I batted my eyelashes at him and told him how much I hated jumping. He says he'll do his best to get me into France on one of those Lysanders that can operate from very short takeoff-and-landing strips."

Viv dragged Catherine across thirty feet of grassy field. "Gilbert!" she called. "I want you to say hello to someone you may already know!"

Lucien Barteau cast a glance in Catherine's direction. She hoped that, what with her flight suit and helmet on, he wouldn't recognize her. But she was wrong.

"Ah, another American. You're Catherine, aren't you?" he said, flashing a wide smile. "I never forget a pretty face." He turned to Viv. "Like this one!" He swung an arm around Viv's shoulders and gave an intimate squeeze.

"So, you're a parachute instructor now?" Catherine asked, pulling off her leather helmet, relishing the cool breeze blowing through her hair.

"Just helping out for another day or two. I've got a new mission coming up," he said, "so I'll be off soon." He squeezed Viv's shoulder again. "And this lovely lady is coming with me, if I can possibly manage it. Aren't you, *chérie*?"

Viv grinned and winked at Catherine. Clearly, Vivier Clarke was a gal who could take care of herself with the likes of Lucien Barteau. Dismissing the full-of-himself Frenchman as just another ship passing in the night, Catherine could only wonder if landing by Lysander was how the SOE powers that be had slipped Henri back by plane to his home country. She would like to think that he'd been able to avoid jumping from a Whitley or Halifax. She dreaded the idea of him floating to earth under a moonlit sky as some German marksmen used him for target practice.

The same could be said for her own descent into France, she thought suddenly, and shivered despite the protection of her canvas flight overalls.

CHAPTER 16

The parachutist qualification badge on SOE uniforms depicted an embroidered, open white chute, flanked by a pair of wings stitched in light blue and worn on the upper right sleeve of their jump suit.

On the same day that Viv and Catherine sewed theirs on, they found themselves ordered to finishing school.

They'd been advised that the English country house with the French name Beaulieu, tucked away in the New Forest outside London, was the final stop before being deployed to the Continent. There they received clothing with French labels and French cigarettes and equipment, while their documents established their new identities. For several days running, they were drilled repeatedly on their personal cover stories that they'd assume the minute they landed across the Channel.

Late afternoon on their third day, Viv ran up beside her just as Catherine was going into dinner.

"I'm off tonight. Just like that."

Catherine froze.

"Where?"

"Frenchie land." Then she added hastily, "Only guessing, of course."

"Oh, come on!"

Viv arched an eyebrow, replying, "You know the rules." She flashed a grin. "If I tell you, I'll have to kill you, etcetera, etcetera."

"Yeah, yeah, yeah," Catherine said peevishly, surprised by how bereft she felt that Vivier Clarke and she were to be suddenly parting ways.

Would they ever meet again? Would she ever meet any of the SOE agents she'd trained with?

"Let's have a drink," she proposed, remembering the same twist in her gut when saying goodbye to Henri and Sean. "There's some good scotch in the library."

"Can't," Viv replied, shaking her head. "I've been ordered to pack my gear, and then we're off in half an hour to some secret airfield hereabouts."

"Do you have to jump?" Catherine asked.

"Well, I can only tell you that we're flying out aboard a Wellington with a lot of equipment."

"And did your friendly Captain Barteau squeeze you in?"

Viv wagged her finger. "Naughty, naughty. But, yes, Lucien— a.k.a. *M'sieur* Gilbert—told me I'll have to wear my chute, but he said that I only have to jump if they can't put down on the intended field.

"Can you at least tell me what you'll be doing once you get there?"

Viv looked around to be sure no one was within earshot.

"As we thought, I'll be somebody's courier, but I haven't a clue whose or exactly where. They said they'd tell me once we're airborne."

Catherine impulsively threw her arms around the girl with the cinnamon hair who looked too tall to be French.

"Take care of yourself, dammit!" she said, giving Viv an awkward hug.

"I'll do my best." Viv hugged back, hard. "Do the same, will you, dammit?"

"Roger, that," Catherine answered with a bravado she didn't feel at all.

"Buckmaster's got my home address in New York on file."

"Ditto D.C.," Catherine said, the constriction in her throat making it hard to speak in a normal tone of voice.

"Well, maybe I'll see ya someday, kiddo, one place or another," Viv said with nonchalance that didn't ring true to Catherine. She spun on her heel and bolted up the stairs to fetch her newly issued belongings before disappearing into the night.

"See you," Catherine echoed, but she doubted Viv had heard her last words.

———◇———

"Thornton?"

"Yes, sir?"

Catherine stood alongside the rest of her graduating class inside the Beaulieu finishing school's book-lined study, a former masculine lair on the estate of its absent owner, Lord Montagu of Beaulieu.

"Come with me, please," directed the military aide.

This was the way each portion of spy school concluded. It was always a meeting with the commanding officer, who either told a recruit they'd washed out for a last-minute failure or revealed what would come next.

The colonel's aide led her to a small room nearby. Once inside, she stood at attention, facing her superior officer, who sat behind a desk. As he began to speak, she struggled to subdue her growing excitement at the prospect of at long last being given orders to deploy somewhere across the English Channel. Learning she was finally leaving England to help fight the war suddenly felt as if she were poised to leap off a cliff into the deep unknown, and yet she was exhilarated to finally be putting all her rigorous training to work.

"Your plane will depart at twenty-two hundred hours tonight for Gibraltar."

Gibraltar?

Catherine stared at the colonel in charge. She was going to be parachuted into Gibraltar. Had the Brits suddenly lost that pile of rock as well as the territory at Dunkirk?

The colonel observed her look of astonishment and added with a faint smile, "No skydiving for you, my dear. How are your sea legs?" Without waiting for an answer, he continued, "From Gibraltar, you will then be taken by *felucca*, which is a small fishing craft, to a point off the French Riviera near Marseilles, where you will contact the unnamed agent who is detailed in your orders." He leaned forward to hand her a manila envelope. "This person will take you on to Cannes to secure your assignment as a courier to one of our men operating in the hills above Nice and Villefranche-sur-Mer. You will be told of your duties from there."

Flashing before Catherine's eyes were visions of her arduous parachute jumps, flinging herself several perilous times from the belly of the modified Whitley into the piercing, cold autumn air above Manchester.

What a waste of time, effort, and His Majesty's money, she thought crossly. But then she realized she was being sent back to France to the so-called free zone, an area south of Burgundy that was, thus far, officially unoccupied by Nazi troops. She'd heard, however, that Axis agents came in and out of the southern area and had the French authorities singing their tune. Even so, the Côte d'Azur region was bound to be somewhat less hazardous, and the work they expected her to do sounded important.

"Can you ride a bicycle?" inquired her superior.

"Of course," she replied, adding a more respectful, "Yes, sir."

"Needed to check with you on that," he said, making a mark in her file. His eyes roamed her figure, from her head to her sturdy brogues. "Fortunately, you look to be trim and in good condition. Once you put your foot on French soil, my guess is that you'll cover as many miles on two wheels as a competitor in the Tour de France." He made these observations with no glint of humor, referring to the famous three-week, countrywide summer cycling competition, now cancelled due to the war.

"Shouldn't be any problem for me, sir. I've ridden both a bike and a horse since I was five, sir."

"Excellent. In the next hour or two, I suggest you eat a fine dinner in the mess hall, gather your kit, and prepare to leave here by nineteen hundred hours for the drive to the airfield. Best of luck. Dismissed."

Catherine saluted the colonel just as the next recruit entered the room. With a nod to the others, she sped out of the adjacent study and bolted up the manor house's wide, mahogany staircase. Filled with sense that she had drawn some lucky cards in terms of her new duties and their location, she wondered at the rather circuitous journey that would bring her to the Riviera.

Most of her clothing with the carefully curated French labels was already stowed in her canvas duffle, so all that she had to pack were her toiletries.

Then she paused. Among her personal items was a collection of pills: aspirin, of course, as well as other remedies that had been dispensed to her for typical ailments.

Then there was the L-tablet—L as in *lethal*.

"Should the need arise, and you feel there's no alternative," said the supply sergeant cryptically, placing it in her hand, "you crush it with your teeth, releasing potassium cyanide. It causes instant death."

Catherine paused as she held the small packet poised above her canvas duffle and then tucked it into an inside pocket. She quickly donned the specially tailored light wool suit that, with its skirt split like a pair of knee-length shorts, would be perfect for cycling.

The wardrobe orderly must have known.

Her authentic attire, along with her perfect French accent, would go far to disguise the fact she was an American. Putting aside thoughts of the L-pill, she lectured herself that her thorough preparations were bound to keep her out of harm's way.

At least she hoped so.

Catherine crossed to the bathroom mirror and combed her auburn hair. She set a chocolate-brown felt cloche at a jaunty angle on her head, a *chapeau* that was probably far too chic to wear on the fishing boat that would spirit her to an out-of-the-way drop-off spot. Once on the Côte d'Azur, however, it would be rather fine for wearing on some boulevard in Cannes.

For a long moment, she gazed at her reflection, wondering just where Henri Leblanc was now. Were her humble bicycle routes ever likely to cross his path? The chances of that ever happening, she speculated, were probably a million to one, and her initial excitement gave way to an automatic reflex that predictably lowered her expectations.

You're on your own, Mademoiselle Colette. Hasn't the SOE warned you enough times to trust no one and rely on no one but yourself?

And for Catherine Thornton, that felt like a very familiar state of affairs.

PART II
CHAPTER 17

Autumn 1942

The trees skirting the Seine were beginning to lose their leaves, and a chill wind ruffled the river's waters. Henri turned his back on the Eiffel Tower and walked toward his destination on the western edge of the city's 2nd Arrondissement. Twenty minutes later, he peered into the deserted below-ground basement of his family's abandoned newspaper office building. The empty space was located in a part of Paris famous for its red-light district, the old Stock Exchange, and other vacant offices that had once housed several of the city's shuttered daily and weekly newspapers, including *Le Figaro*, a few blocks away. On nearly every street were enormous black, white, and red banners flouting giant swastikas like carpets waiting to be beaten. Even the street signs in this district had been changed from French to German.

Henri walked down a short flight of concrete steps and soon was standing at the threshold of a large room below the ground level. Looming in the shadows a few feet from where he stood were several silent printing presses, including a black behemoth with giant metal cylinders that had once produced editions of the Leblanc newspaper. Henri recalled how several smaller presses nearby had been used for placards, posters, and other products of paper communication before the war. The dust-laden equipment brought back memories of his grandfather giving him his first lessons in how to set type and make the hulking machine, bolted to the cement floor near the narrow windows on the street level, do the pressmen's bidding.

Thus far, Henri thought to himself, his cover story had held. The local authorities had approved the returning diplomat's plan to re-activate his family's former printing and paper supply business on a small scale, "to give employment and help stimulate commerce hereabouts in any way I can," as he'd said to the local *Kommandant* who, fortunately, spoke enough French so the two men could understand each other.

"Good," the short, squat functionary named Erik Heinrich had replied in guttural tones. He'd looked at Henri steadily, his eyes cold and calculating. Glancing at a file on his desk that Henri assumed was about him, the German bureaucrat said, "Now that you have left the Vichy diplomatic service, you are not thinking of resurrecting your family newspaper? Just the printing enterprise?"

"Yes, just the printing operation."

The Leblanc family newspaper had been considered centrist, but Henri was only too aware that even such neutrality hadn't been acceptable to Hitler's emissaries who now occupied France. He glanced at a pile of ashes nearly as tall as a haystack heaped in a corner flanked by the concrete walls. Someone had incinerated the final editions of the Leblanc's daily and then doused the flames to prevent the building from burning down.

Henri had managed to keep his voice calm even as he'd made his case before Herr Heinrich the previous week.

"Now that I've returned home," he'd explained, "I'm just hoping to make a living printing whatever my customers need in the way of paper products, business cards, advertisements, and announcements. Perhaps even the occasional work of poetry or family reminiscence... that sort of thing. Whatever I can find to keep the presses running and my neighbors employed."

"In that case, I may ask you to print some broadsides for me from time to time...to be posted hereabouts, *ja*?" the *Kommandant* stated.

Henri knew such work would be done for no fee in exchange for the needed permission to reopen the printing works.

"Most certainly," Henri replied, nodding. "Happy to be of service."

It had been immediately obvious as the meeting progressed that the *Kommandant* glimpsed certain benefits in having the Nazi occupiers utilize the Leblanc printing presses for their own purposes.

Amazingly for Henri, the tete-a-tete at the German headquarters a few blocks away had turned out as favorably as he could have imagined, although he knew he would always be in spine-tingling danger in playing both sides.

What a game of chess Herr Heinrich and I will now embark upon.

With the necessary documents in hand, Henri had expressed his thanks and departed down the steps of a lovely stone home the Germans had stripped from a Jewish family Henri's parents had known for years. As he'd left the front parlor converted into Heinrich's office, he had pretended to limp slightly.

Heinrich called out, "I see your leg is bothering you?"

Henri turned around and gave a small shrug, assuming his inquisitor knew perfectly well his file contained a note about his service in the First War.

"Old injuries linger a bit, especially in this rainy autumn weather we've been having," he'd replied. "On a sunny day, I sometimes forget I have a problem."

He'd been glad to underscore for Heinrich the reason why, as a returning consular officer, he was not currently pressed into active military service. He could only hope the *Kommandant* was not aware that his year recovering from his wounds in the Great War had been in a British hospital.

With a slight bow, he'd left Heinrich's office, walked along the Seine until the bad taste from conversing with the pig had left his mouth, and had come directly to the building where he now stood.

In the dim basement, Henri heard a door opening behind him.

Alphonse Moreau, his father's retired pressman who had overseen printing operations for decades, appeared on the threshold, a slim, slightly bent silhouette, outlined by light filtering down from the floor above.

Abundant gray hair and eyebrows accentuated the old man's gaunt face. That, along with his emaciated appearance, was proof that food rationing had taken its toll in recent months. Henri remembered then that his family's employee had turned quite deaf from years of working near the incessant noise of the Leblanc printing presses; it was a job that had dominated the man's life for some forty years. Too old to be conscripted, Alphonse Moreau was clearly suffering the same deprivations as most civilians Henri had met since returning to Paris.

Advancing into the basement room, Moreau said in a gruff but fatigued voice, "I got your note. I couldn't believe it, actually. I figured the Leblancs were long gone from these parts, especially after the death of your father and…well, everything since."

"Hello, Alphonse," Henri greeted him, extending his hand.

Instead of shaking it, Moreau looked around at the room's interior, now empty except for the silent printing presses and the pile of ashes in the corner. His bleak expression hardened when his gaze returned to Henri.

"You were working with the Vichy, I heard, and—"

"I hated it," Henri interrupted, raising his voice for his visitor's benefit. "Pétain ordered the diplomatic corps in America to conform, as he did every other government department." Henri and Alphonse exchanged glances. "And you should know that I did a few things for the Free French when I was in Washington that nearly put me in front of a firing squad. Fortunately, my superiors never found out. I finally made it back to France and was released into civilian life— such as it is, now."

Alphonse merely cocked a bushy eyebrow.

In the past week, Henri had reached out to people like Alphonse that he and his family had employed over the years. He'd found very few reasonably able-bodied men who had not been ordered to work in Germany. Even worse, ever since the Nazis had occupied Paris, he'd learned that many in the neighborhood had disappeared, with no one having any idea what had happened to them. Thus far, Henri had a difficult time convincing those left behind, like Alphonse, that his former position as a diplomat, along with his family's once-privileged position, hadn't rendered him a Nazi collaborator.

"You were gone a decade," said Alphonse. "A lot has happened, *monsieur.*"

Henri raised his voice once more for his visitor's benefit. "You've known me since I was in knee pants. I—"

"No need to shout, *Monsieur* Leblanc," Alphonse interrupted. "If you'll face me, I've learned to read lips."

"Address me as Henri, please," Henri urged, relieved that he would not have to risk the entire neighborhood hearing their business here today. "To be frank, I can't quite believe I'm back either after all these years." He beckoned Alphonse to follow him into the small, interior office with a dirty window that looked out on the basement's expansive production area. "Come. Come in. I have no coffee, but at least I still have two chairs and a desk. Please sit down."

It had taken him more than a week to confirm in various clandestine ways that Alphonse Moreau had ties to a rather disorganized group of older men who ostensibly despised the local Nazis like Herr Heinrich, the officer Henri had dealt with who held sway over everyone's life in the vicinity. With any luck at all, this rebellious cadre might form the core of Henri's first unit of resisters. His hope was that his father's former employee could help him to re-establish a small printing enterprise as well as to assemble a cadre of Parisians working for the ultimate end to Nazi occupation of the country.

"I've managed to obtain permission to restart Leblanc Printers," he disclosed to Alphonse, "though on a vastly smaller scale than before. No newspapers. Just small printing jobs from local customers and selling paper to firms who need it."

"Paper is on the rations list," Alphonse replied, his skepticism about such an enterprise obvious.

"Yes, I know. The black market comes to mind," said Henri with a slight smile. "Meanwhile, I could use your help and skills—and those of a few men you trust. There are other things to be done besides printing restaurant menus, you know."

"You want a bunch of old men to come back to work here with a rusty press and little paper to be had?" Alphonse demanded, his words reflecting his suspicions.

"Who else is there to hire?"

"Just to get the printing presses going again...or to do *other* things, as well?"

Henri offered his visitor a steady gaze. "You are very perceptive, my friend. Yes, other things. I think you understand what I mean?"

"So, you intend to outfox the dirty Krauts at their own game?" Alphonse said with the first glimmer of enthusiasm in his tired eyes.

"Something like that," Henri replied.

Silence filled the space between them. Henri hadn't spoken to this man in years. He couldn't be sure he knew everything he should about Alphonse before revealing his specific plans for establishing a new network of resisters to be called Pinwheel. With each outreach to another person, everyone in the expanding group became more vulnerable to betrayal. Food and funds were scarce. Informing on one's neighbor for a reward had become a profession unto itself. On the other hand, Henri had performed as much due diligence as possible, given the circumstances, and now had no choice but to take a calculated risk and pray the older man wasn't a Nazi sympathizer in disguise. Simultaneously, Henri had to convince Alphonse and his friends that he himself wasn't still one of the Vichy scum. It was indeed a dangerous game.

Alphonse's next words riveted his attention. "How many do you need to…uh…get such an operation going?"

"How many do you think you could recruit?" he asked, his spirits lifting a notch as he thought, *He's willing to take a chance, just as I am.* He hastily proposed, "If you can get me a handful of men, we could get the presses humming, and I could begin to fan out throughout the region, posing as a traveling paper-and-printing rep to set up other Resistance networks."

And who knows? he thought, trying to gauge Moreau's reaction. *Maybe, in the course of this work, I could even catch news of where Catherine Thornton has been sent.*

Alphonse abruptly brought him back to the matters at hand. "A bunch of those *riseaus* in and around Paris have been all smashed to hell."

"More Resistance networks have been betrayed?" asked Henri, alarmed.

"Yes, but no one knows by whom. Everybody's been laying low for weeks."

"That's why I've been sent here," Henri said. "To start new ones, only this time, with strict security."

Alphonse paused, as if considering his next words carefully.

"At my brother's place in the country outside Paris, we've hidden a few Allied flyers we linked up with underground escape routes to Spain or Switzerland. We need money to continue to do this."

Henri felt a rush of relief that he had chosen well to reach out to Alphonse.

"Absolutely. I have been supplied with money. Our job," he

added, "would also be to locate farmers' fields outside Paris where RAF planes could drop needed supplies and whisk downed pilots and any stranded agents in dire straits back to England."

"That would definitely be better than an escape route by land," Alphonse grunted.

"Are you willing to help me take that on as well?"

A doubtful expression suddenly invaded Alphonse's thin face as Henri concluded his description of his overall plan.

"You never said who sent you here. How do I know this isn't a trap?"

Henri didn't blame the man for raising the issue. Hadn't "trust no one" been drilled into his brain often enough during his training in England?

"Brit and American intelligence agencies recruited me," he replied with no show of rancor. "I worked for them jointly in Washington before I came here after a few months of special operations training in England."

Alphonse leaned back in the dusty, straight-backed wooden chair, apparently satisfied with Henri's response.

"Did you ever meet de Gaulle?" he asked. "He's on the radio from London...that is, if we dare listen. People have been thrown into Fresnes Prison for less," he added, alluding to the enormous facility south of the city.

"No, I haven't met de Gaulle, but I met the head of the French Section of the British Special Operations Executive. A good man."

"Don't know if I like de Gaulle," Alphonse pronounced, shaking his head, "but at least he hates the Krauts."

Henri relaxed a bit. He even felt himself smiling.

"By the way, Alphonse, it's good to see you," he said, and he meant it. "So much of what we knew, so much of what we had, has been swept away." He felt a sudden wave of emotion. "My father...my father always said that Alphonse Moreau was a man he could depend upon. A man of honor."

"You father was a good boss," Alphonse said, his voice thick. "Leblanc Printing was fair to its workers and provided the glue that held our world together around here."

Henri looked down at the scarred wooden desk to hide the moisture rimming his eyes. He'd received word in Washington, shortly after Germany invaded Paris in June of 1940, that his father's weakening heart gave out under the pressure of the Nazi occupation of his beloved city. That same week his father died, the Vichy forces had arrived in D.C. to take over the French Embassy, and thus, Charles Leblanc had been buried without his eldest son in attendance. Now that Henri was back on his home soil, acting as an agent of the Allied forces, he didn't dare seek out his mother in Southern France to let her know his internment in Pennsylvania had ended and he was home.

To disguise the flood of emotion that had nearly overtaken Henri, he fumbled with a canvas pouch he'd strapped around his waist under his shirt. It was stuffed to the gills with franc notes that Buckmaster had handed him just before he boarded his plane in England. Slowly, in silence, he counted out a pile of money. Alphonse's thick eyebrows arched with surprise, hinting of his lingering suspicion and burning curiosity.

"Are those genuine?" the old man asked, nodding at the cash.

"Yes, and now let me tell you exactly what I'd like to do with this," Henri began.

"Are you offering me my old job back?" Alphonse wondered. Henri could sense the stooped man with permanently ink-stained hands was trying to hide his pride and pleasure.

"That I am, my dear Alphonse, plus I'm also suggesting a very important new one."

CHAPTER 18

Much to Catherine's relief, after her plane from England successfully dodged tracer fire from German aircraft based in North Africa, she landed in Gibraltar safe and sound. Stepping on the tarmac, she was greeted by a land of sunshine adjacent to Spain, where eighteen varieties of sherry were served at her hotel's bar, and monkeys chattered in the trees outside her window. A sea of khaki-clad British soldiers poured down the sharply angled streets that led to the sea, while RAF pilots landed in steady succession on a suicidal airstrip perched on a tiny plateau above the Straits of Gibraltar.

Soon after settling into her small hotel, she received word to prepare to head down to the docks. On an evening in late October, the forty-foot long sardine fishing craft named *Dewucca—Seawolf* in English—cast off and slid silently past the brooding submarines berthed in the harbor like bobbing gray whales tethered to long piers. With the boat's motor throbbing quietly and its solitary sail furled tightly to its mast, Catherine sat topside in the *felucca,* facing the stern, with her back to the galley that was housed in a minuscule hutch on the deck. From below, a paraffin stove released malodorous fumes into the freshening wind.

The captain of *Dewucca,* a Pole named Jan who had lost his family and home when the Nazis invaded his country, stood stone-faced at the helm. He was a young man in his twenties, slim and pale as a Norwegian—and he was scowling.

"I do not think it right to take young women such as you and Madam Samson to this…this business. A man, yes. A woman, no."

"But you *are* taking us," Catherine observed as the boat headed toward the open sea.

She was aware that Jan's superiors had threatened him with a court martial if he refused to transport not only Catherine, but a Frenchwoman named Odette Samson and two other male agents to a landing spot southeast of Marseilles. About Catherine's age, the dark-haired Samson was to be slipped back into her home country. She had married a Brit and joined the SOE in London, just as Catherine had. Catherine suspected that Odette and their other companions might already be feeling the action of the waves. As soon as they'd pushed off, the three took to their bunks and hadn't been seen since.

Jan, attired in a patchwork of navy uniforms from a variety of countries, continued his dour commentary. "To travel to France now is no good for you or the lady below. It's damn foolish." He paused, and his gaze held fast. "If, however, you live and return to Gibraltar someday, perhaps you will permit me to invite you for some dancing?"

Catherine could hardly keep from laughing at his outlandish invitation, but she managed merely to nod. "Oh, yes, I definitely would like that…if I live," she added with mock solemnity.

Jan nodded with equal gravity. "Do you fancy sherry or a whisky? You can bring one for each of us from the galley, yes?"

And so their voyage began.

———◇———

Eight days and some very rough autumn seas later, the *Dewucca* slipped into a deserted inlet near Cassis, identified on Jan's map as Port Miou, a coastal region about twenty-five kilometers southeast of Marseille on the Côte d'Azur.

Odette had reappeared on the last day of the voyage, a few pounds lighter, "but finally feeling more myself," as she said to Catherine. Her orders, like Catherine's, were to link up in Cannes with an SOE field officer named Peter Churchill, who she described as "possibly related to Winston Churchill," who'd been assigned to establish the Spindle network of *résistants*.

Catherine gave a small laugh at hearing this. "This Peter fellow is the second person I've encountered during this adventure of ours with a famous name."

"Really?" Odette replied. "What could be more celebrated than a Churchill?"

"How about a man named Eisenhower?" Catherine said with a smile, recalling the mischievous bespectacled crack-shot charmer she'd met during her training course. She thought about how physically drawn to him she'd been in that brief, sexually charged moment they'd shared after the explosives exercises. How odd it had been that the thought of her time with Henri in the stone bothy had prevented her from engaging in a night's diversion before he left.

Odette's next words riveted Catherine's attention to the here and now.

"I was told the Spindle network is the name given the replacement for another group of SOE agents that was recently discovered and crushed by the Nazis. *M'sieur* Peter Churchill has just returned from London with these new orders."

Catherine felt a stab of unease at the mention of an SOE led Resistance network decimated by the enemy, its Allied and French members alike probably shot or sent to prison. She followed Odette's gaze along the distant coastline, a few scattered palm trees barely visible in the bright moonlight glinting off the water.

"Landing by moonlight," Catherine murmured. "And I thought that would mean a parachute jump."

"Paddling in on an inflatable is not quite as romantic," Odette agreed.

After all, Catherine thought, they may now be in the sunny southern climes of France where vacationers once frolicked by the Mediterranean Sea, but she and Odette both knew the dangers that would lurk everywhere the minute they stepped on the beach, where the curving shore stretched out in the silvery light ahead.

"Well, let's hope that someone..." Odette said, her lips pursed, "...*anyone*...will be there to meet us when we land and show us to the train station. Once I rendezvous with this Mr. Churchill in Cannes, I've been ordered to go to north to Auxerre."

"In the Occupied Zone?" Catherine said, arching an eyebrow at a fellow agent revealing her mission. South of Lyon, the Germans had allowed their allies, the Italians, to keep an eye on the French using far fewer extreme tactics than the Nazi playbook dictated. But in the Occupied Zone things were grim, she'd been told. "You are brave. But then you're native French," she added. "You'll have a much better chance convincing the Nazis you are an ordinary citizen than would I."

Odette didn't smile at this. "You speak French like a native, but I think we all will have a difficult time avoiding the notice of the Nazis. I've heard the Germans don't trust the Italians one bit and are planning to take over the Free Zone *tout de suite*."

Catherine felt a frisson of apprehension. She reflected on her lessons in silent killing and deadly sabotage. As difficult as the training had been, it had felt more like a challenging competition, a grown-up game, not the lethal business Odette's comments had reminded her it was. She was about to plunge into the deadly unknown. Once she set foot on French soil, she could be called upon to kill—or be killed at any moment. She raised her eyes and followed the moon's pewter path on the water, which led toward a murky shoreline some three hundred yards ahead.

At the helm, Jan announced, "Ladies, we will not be tying up the boat to a dock." He pointed to the inflated dinghy now perched next to a depth charge and a few tommy guns that had been lashed to the deck during their voyage. "Please gather your belongings and prepare to row yourselves ashore."

The two other male passengers, also newly enlisted secret agents, had remained below deck with Odette during most of the trip, suffering various intensities of *mal de mer*. Within minutes, the pair had managed to lower the small craft over the side. The foursome, each with a small suitcase, gingerly stepped one by one into the inflatable bobbing on the water and waved goodbye to their captain. The moon hung low in the last silent vestiges of night. With only the sound of the oars slicing into the Mediterranean Sea, the men rowed toward a tiny stretch of beach shielded by a natural wall of high rocks. As the rubber raft approached the shore, Catherine caught whiffs of mimosa and thyme, pine trees and seaweed, and even a hint of garlic.

France! I'm back in France.

She inhaled the scents of the country she so loved and intended to help free from the Nazi stranglehold. And then another thought struck as she prepared to step ashore.

I wonder if I will survive whatever comes next.

The disciplined part of her brain told her to cease such reflections and pay attention to the scene unfolding before her. Their first problem was that the beach was bare. There was no one to meet them. In succession, each agent stepped out of the craft onto the sand.

Odette spoke first. "I can find the train station. I vacationed here long ago, when I was a child. We can proceed to Cannes on our own."

"But first," Catherine reminded the group, "we must deflate this dinghy and bury it in the sand so no one can see someone has landed."

"Right you are," said Geoffrey, one of the two male agents who'd come with them. He pulled out a knife and stabbed the boat's inflated side. Quickly the group squeezed all the air out and then pitched in to rapidly dig a hole with their hands. In minutes, they'd covered up evidence of their clandestine arrival.

Dusting the sand off her hands and clothing, Catherine advised, "Once we find the road, we should probably pair up and pretend we're couples on holiday." The others nodded, glancing back in unison at the motionless *felucca* coming about like a shadow on the now pellucid waters a few hundred yards from shore. Soon it would disappear over the dawn-dusted horizon. "Let's go!" she urged.

The four agents somehow managed to climb the rock wall with their belongings and locate the road that led to Marseille. The sun's rays were just beginning to bathe the countryside. Their path would take them to their next destination, now guarded by Mussolini's finest, whom they could only hope were lounging in a nearby café sipping cappuccino rather than lying in wait for them.

———◇———

Catherine barely heard the voice whispering in her ear. It was male and speaking in French above the clamor of train whistles and the bustle of luggage being wheeled along the platforms in the small station not far from the local Riviera beaches.

"Fancy meeting you here."

Her pulse sped up as she forced herself to turn slowly so as not to attract notice. There, not a foot from where she stood, was Sean Eisenhower, dressed in a tweed suit too warm for the balmy climate and sporting a black patch over one of his eyeglasses' thick lenses. Before she could even utter his name, he threw his arms around her and gave her an effusive hug, saying under his breath as he slipped her an envelope, "Just greet me as a French friend you are happy to see by chance. Code name: Guy de Bruyn."

Catherine, in a state of delighted amazement, did exactly as he'd commanded and introduced her three companions to their unexpected greeter.

Sean quickly said, also in French for the benefit of any eavesdropper, "I am Colette's old friend from our school days in Paris." He grinned with a glance at Catherine as he extended his hand to the men. "Guy de Bruyn, here. Originally from Belgium and now a professor of French at the Sorbonne." Sean paused and nodded at Odette and the two men. "Very happy to meet you all. I've been in the South of France recovering from my recent eye operations, although today I must travel to Cannes to see my surgeon for a follow-up."

Catherine assumed every sentence Sean had uttered was part of his assigned cover story. She imagined her companions thought the same thing but were adhering to their training by acting, for the benefit of any bystanders, as if they believed every word.

"What a lovely coincidence," Catherine exclaimed, while scanning her surroundings to see if there were any authorities in the vicinity. "We're also traveling to Cannes for a bit of a holiday."

Smiling at the group surrounding her, she dug into her pocket for the envelope Sean had just slipped to her, sure by its shape he'd secured their train tickets, as he had no doubt been directed from London by the wireless. She would also bet money that the machine was hidden inside the leather suitcase at his feet. She opened the envelope's flap.

"Here you are, everyone," Catherine announced with a happy laugh. "I did the best I could, but God only knows where each of us is sitting."

Sean linked his arm in hers as the others studied their tickets and soon headed off in several directions to find the coaches that would carry them away from Port Miou.

Continuing to speak in French, Sean said with a sly grin, "I'm in coach five. What car are you in?'

Catherine glanced down at the ticket in her gloved hand.

"Why…" she said on a long exhale, "what another amazing coincidence."

"What is that?" Sean asked innocently.

"I'm in coach five as well."

Her eyes swept the area before she took a step, noting two men in Italian army uniforms were headed their way. The area was supposedly free from Nazi authorities, although rumors abounded that, in the wake of the Allied attacks on North Africa three months earlier in August, Germany had been threatening to occupy all of France to guard against any Allied attack from the Mediterranean.

With a glance at the oncoming soldiers, Sean threw an arm around Catherine's shoulder and gave her cheek a long, loving kiss.

"Come, my darling," he said in a loud voice, waving his ticket in his hand, "we'll miss our train if we don't hurry along."

Catherine allowed Sean to pick up her suitcase as well as his own as her urged her forward. The Italian soldiers passed by within feet of the pair, never giving the amorous young couple a second glance.

And so it all begins, she thought.

She didn't dare wonder where it would end.

————◇————

"A beauty salon?" Catherine exclaimed quietly, staring at the gold lettering *Salon du Beauté* on a shop window on the rue du Canada in a fashionable section of Cannes. "Lord knows we bedraggled bunch could use the services, but..."

Her voice drifted off, and she knew the sorry band she'd traveled with was thinking: *What kind of safe house is this?*

Sean and their group had endured an uncomfortable all-night train journey with numerous stops and delays along the way. By ten-thirty on this morning of November 2, 1942, Catherine longed for a hot bath and some decent food, neither of which was likely in an establishment catering to providing coiffeurs and polished toenails to wealthy, post-invasion refugees from the north, not to mention the usual lay-abouts who frequented the Riviera's bathing beaches by day and the casinos by night. For these lucky few, Catherine imagined, the war must seem a far-off fantasy.

Led by Sean, the gaggle of red-eyed women and unshaven men filed into the establishment's plush lobby where the proprietress, Suzanne, who turned out to be an ardent Anglophile, hurried them past a solitary customer standing at a desk, who was absorbed in booking her next leg waxing appointment.

Suzanne raised a finger to her lips indicating her latest visitors should refrain from idle chatter and swiftly ushered them down a corridor flanked by curtained-off back rooms devoted to massage, facials, and all manner of beauty treatments for both sexes. Operating her clandestine activities in plain sight, the middle-aged owner was a woman obviously willing and eager to do everything in her power to assist the British officer—code name Raoul—to whom the new arrivals were to report.

As directed by their hostess, they entered what appeared to be a private dining room normally dedicated to Suzanne's most favored patrons.

"Please do sit down. I'll send tea in a minute."

The exhausted travelers took seats on well-worn reproductions of Louis XV upholstered chairs. Odette offered a faint nod in Catherine's direction when a slender, attractive man in his mid-thirties with dark brown hair but rather unmemorable features entered a doorway and stood before them. Catherine was amused to see that their apparent leader was attired in a loose linen shirt, cotton slacks, and black canvas espadrilles, as if he'd arrived from a luncheon served on a terrace overlooking the sea.

Catherine shot a glance at Odette and murmured, "Peter Churchill?"

Odette lowered her head, answering barely above a whisper, "I assume so."

The other famous-named leader in the room, Sean Eisenhower, had taken a seat in the far corner as they all waited intently for Raoul to speak.

"Good morning," Churchill greeted them cheerfully. "The amazing Suzanne has managed to secure some lovely sweet pastries for you all, though how she did it must of course remain a guarded mystery." His gaze rested on the two women. "Hot baths and a good afternoon's rest come first, and then—"

Odette, whom Catherine had quickly surmised in the course of their association didn't greatly suffer fools, interrupted with an edge to her voice.

"I must say, this is quite a change from the austerity of life in England these days," Odette spoke up. "However, my mission was to proceed directly to Auxerre, not to lounge around Cannes, watching the wives of collaborators get their hair done and their nails polished. Can someone please tell me how best to get to that city?"

The air in the room grew chilly despite the sunshine pouring down on the beach only a few blocks from where they sat.

Peter Churchill, who introduced himself simply as Raoul, replied with a look of mild amusement, "Shall we go into that a bit later? In the meantime, welcome to Cannes." He then addressed himself to the men. "You lot will be taken by Guy, here," pointing to Sean, "to the Villa Diana, quite close by, where the Baron de Carteret will give you your next instructions." To Sean he said, "When you return, I will detail your next assignment." To the other new arrivals, he added, "I'll supply you with the particulars of what happens next after you poor souls have had a hot bath and lunch that has been arranged at a nearby café. Separate bedrooms have been arranged for both of you here, so do have a rest. I have a busy afternoon before me, but I hope you will be comfortable until I return."

"But, sir," Odette persisted, "I'm not at all tired, and I should like to know why the orders from London are being disregarded?"

Churchill cocked his head and gazed at her for a long moment. In a tired, patient tone of voice he said, "Much has happened since you left London, Mrs. Samson. Auxerre lies in the Occupied Zone. On a lucky day, journeys across the demarcation line are complicated and difficult to arrange. Very soon, they may become impossible."

"Then it is all the more important that I cross now. I'm willing to take that risk."

"Ah, but I am not. Since August, General Montgomery's Eighth Army has been making excellent progress in North Africa. As you may have heard, Hitler worries there will ultimately be an Allied invasion from Africa across the Mediterranean to here on the Côte d'Azur. We have reliable intelligence that the Nazi High Command will soon take over the entire so-called Free Zone. This means any day now, the Germans will sweep down to occupy the rest of France, all the way to the Riviera. Until we know if or when that is going to happen, we cannot risk the lives of many to get just one agent into areas north of here." He paused, studying Odette intently. "So, Agent Lise," he continued, addressing Odette by her code name, "you will have to content yourself with a hot bath, a good lunch, and perhaps a nap, until I decide what to do with you." He offered a rakish grin. "From what I've observed, you need all three."

Odette pursed her lips but reluctantly nodded her acquiescence to superior authority. She pulled herself ramrod straight in her chair and then looked away as if she both accepted her de facto leader's lighthearted orders and dismissed him from her thoughts.

Catherine glanced at Sean, who was doing his best to keep a straight face. Lise and Raoul had tangled, and Catherine could only wonder what would come of it.

CHAPTER 19

December 1942

For Catherine, the previous weeks in November had been filled with numerous traveling assignments, carrying messages, delivered verbally for safety's sake, to a variety of *résistants* in and around Cannes. Adding to the normal tension such an enterprise entailed, the Italian occupiers had been joined as of November 11 by swarms of German troops. All of France, south of the city of Vichy, was now to be under their control.

No more Free Zone.

Catherine also picked up the news, on one of her bicycle forays, that a contact she'd met on her earlier mission had been seized by authorities, jailed, and tortured. Another, she'd learned on a different trip, had been arrested and simply hadn't been heard from since. Like Peter Churchill, who was obsessed with security issues and frequently complained about the lax approach to secrecy he'd found among his French counterparts, Catherine, too, began to wonder which supposed French resister with whom she exchanged information might be a friend or secret foe.

Following the Christmas holidays, which slipped by practically unnoticed, Peter Churchill dispatched her by bicycle on a journey to rendezvous in Marseille with one of his most important leaders. Once her courier duties were completed, Catherine rode like the wind back to Cannes to give a crucial warning to her network leader.

Barely catching her breath, she speedily made for the back room of the *Salon du Beauté*. Peter, whom she tried to remember to call Raoul whenever she saw him, was standing near the door, looking as if he were ready to depart.

"Can you spare some time for a short walk?" she asked him. "It's important."

Peter glanced at his watch and then studied her agitated expression.

"Certainly, if you are in need of some fresh air despite your recent trip. Let's have coffee at a café I know."

Churchill had established a number of places in Cannes and Nice where he determined it was relatively safe to meet in public. He led her to one of Cannes's lesser-trafficked back streets and across the threshold of an establishment he'd described as "a working man's café."

When the pair had been served, he asked quietly, "So tell me, how did you get on in Marseille this trip?"

"Not well," she told him bluntly. "I'm sure you're aware that Marseille is now teaming not only with Vichy police but now with a lot of German soldiers. I can confirm that even the Gestapo is now there. I wore my pillow under my clothes to appear pregnant, so I went undisturbed, but I saw a number of Jews hauled out of their shops and onto the streets, carted off to God knows where. As soon as I arrived at the appointed rendezvous, my contact informed me that one of the French resisters in his group left a list on a train of some two hundred names of people in the south associated with, ah, our activities," she added in a harsh whisper, grateful the café was empty except for the barman. "At least forty of them, I was told today, have already been rounded up."

"Do you think anyone followed you back to Cannes?" Peter inquired calmly, although Catherine detected a faint widening of his eyes.

She replaced her coffee cup in its saucer, her stomach tight. "I don't think I was being tailed, but do you suppose you and those of us in your network were included on that list? Because if we were—"

Peter set down his own cup of coffee with a thump and said, "Thank you, Catherine, for appreciating the urgency of this message, but I'm afraid I must leave you for another appointment." He rose from his chair while Catherine gazed at him, mouth agape. "Isn't this rather important information?" she demanded of him quizzically, but Peter merely said, "I want you and Sean to carry on per your previous instructions until you hear from me."

"But—"

Peter gave a sharp nod, telegraphing that he did not wish to discuss anything further. Upset by this, Catherine felt again the sense of fear she had experienced on the long ride back from Marseille. Had her name and those in Peter's Spindle network stupidly been put on the list by their French colleagues? The shuttered expression on Peter's face as he stood ready to depart warned her it would not be wise to speak on this subject any longer. Yet, for the first time, she quietly acknowledged how harrowing it felt to imagine the prospect of being arrested and tortured by the enemy. Until now, she'd successfully kept such thoughts buried. Today, they were very real.

She inhaled a long breath and began to lecture herself.

Absolutely nothing has happened to you, Catherine. Just do as Peter says: Carry on as before until you hear otherwise.

Winston Churchill's distant relative took a step forward and put a hand on her shoulder.

"Please understand. I'm extremely grateful for your fine efforts these last months, especially bringing me this intelligence so quickly. You'll hear from me soon."

Raoul could be a phantom at times, gone for days. If their Cannes network was under threat and needed to scatter to the winds, she knew Peter Churchill, with his high-level connections in London, would demand permission to abort all plans immediately and order a move somewhere else. She was startled to realize that a gnawing sense of panic had her in its grip, but it wasn't for herself. Peter was the only person she could think of that might know something as to Henri's whereabouts. She'd been waiting for the right moment to approach him, but given that their Spindle Resistance network might be dissolved, this could be her only chance.

"Before you go," she said hurriedly, "may I ask you something on another subject?"

She could tell he was anxious to be on his way, but he inhaled as if to maintain his patience and said, "Depends, but go on."

"I worked with an agent," she began, "A...a Frenchman who became a very valuable asset for our side in Washington D.C."

Peter retook his seat.

"Henri Leblanc?" he asked. Catherine could hardly mask her surprise that his reply had been so immediate. "I read about him in your file," Peter went on. "You were the one who turned him to work for the Allies, am I right?"

Catherine stared into her cup of cold coffee. *Turned* was such a nasty-sounding way to describe the danger and bravery involved in the kinds of services Henri ultimately provided to the Allies. It was practically a truism that the Brits never truly trusted the Frogs, as they so rudely dubbed their neighbors across the English Channel. Her ire raising a notch, she thought Churchill sounded like a pompous ass.

Keep your cool, she silently reminded herself. *Don't blow your only opportunity to find out what's become of him.*

"Well," she said in a neutral tone she hoped disguised her annoyance, "Henri Leblanc did some very brave things when we were both in Washington. He volunteered for the SOE when he got to England, and they gladly accepted him into the service. In fact, he and I ran into each other again during our training there. I...well, I just wondered if you've encountered him yourself or, by chance, heard where he was sent."

Peter tilted his head to one side and said somewhat sternly, "You know perfectly well agents are not supposed to share that kind of information."

Catherine felt duly chastised, but something within her made her persist.

"I saw him the night he flew out. I...I was just hoping to learn if he...well, if he made it all right."

Peter's expression softened somewhat, but his words were as unyielding as before.

"A bit of a warning, here, Catherine. As you are well aware, Leblanc worked for the Vichy for several years, so to my way of thinking, I'd have been a lot more careful about making him a member of SOE than Colonel Buckmaster was. However, to be fair, six months ago, old Buck was pretty desperate to enroll French speakers for the cause."

"So, you don't think French Section Leader Buckmaster is a good judge of character?" Catherine asked, unable to keep her tart tone from leaking into her question.

Peter fell silent for a long moment. Then he said, "As it happens, I can tell you that I heard Leblanc was flown by Lysander to a landing field outside Paris. He was told to make his own way from there to the city to establish a new Resistance circuit where so many others had been rooted out by the Nazis this year. No one yet knows what he did after that, as nothing has come back to London." Peter paused, and then added, "I must again warn you, Catherine, there are skeptics that speculate he may have simply rejoined the Vichy regime in some capacity."

"You've met the man?" Catherine demanded. "And you're one of the skeptics?"

"Yes, I am a bit skeptical. In fact, given that he tolerated working for the Vichy for some years, I'm tempted to wonder why we just didn't drop him in the middle of the English Chanel and make him swim back to France."

Catherine willed herself to remain silent, but a storm of thoughts whirled through her head.

One's personal loyalties aren't as simple as you make them sound, Peter.

The chief of Spindle narrowed his gaze and asked in a low voice, "Tell me, Catherine, why are you so interested in the welfare of Henri Leblanc?"

She looked across the table at her network leader, wondering who could be trusted in this three-dimensional chess game they all seemed to be playing.

"I can tell you this," she said. "Henri Leblanc was crucial to our pulling off an operation that may eventually prove to have made it possible to win this war. And if I revealed what it was, I'd have to kill you."

"I know what it was. Stealing the French Naval Codes, copying them, and returning them without anyone in the embassy suspecting."

Catherine stared, astounded. Finally, she said, "Well, then, dammit, Peter, given the service Henri Leblanc performed for the Allies, I hope to hell he survives!"

"I hope that for all of us,' he answered in a mild tone. "That's why I caution you, my dear Colette, to stay on alert, no matter what."

To Catherine, it was clear he'd used her code name with obvious intent. In the next instant, an unwelcome thought struck her: What if

Henri, due to dire circumstances or even his own natural inclinations, *had* become a double agent? What then?

Upset and more confused than she'd ever been, she rose from the table and, before Peter could do likewise, announced, "I won't keep you from that meeting you were going to before I asked to speak to you about what I learned in Marseille."

Peter gazed at her from his chair, his expression almost kindly.

"Catherine, please know that I'm seriously taking under advisement what you've just told me about the list of all those agents having gone missing. It was sheer stupidity on the part of whoever committed them all to paper," he added with undisguised disgust. "Meanwhile, you've done well. Carry on as before. I'll be in touch."

How often had she and Sean heard that phrase?

"Thank you, sir," she said stiffly. "Permission to leave now, sir?"

Peter breathed a small sigh before saying, "Granted."

Catherine felt her leader's eyes on her stiff back as she departed the café. So, Henri was posted to Paris or thereabouts. There couldn't be a more dangerous assignment in all of France. It would be the height of folly on her part to ever try to get in touch with him or send him a message somehow. In fact, any such action could put both their lives in danger.

She walked through the narrow back alleys in Cannes, wishing she could simply head for the beach, lie down to soak up the sun, and forget about everything having to do with the Special Operations Executive. What else did Peter Churchill know about Agent Claude, she wondered?

Was it truly possible that Henri could have switched sides, now that he's on home soil?

How well did she really know this man she could never quite banish from her thoughts? He'd been turned once. Why not twice? The many courses she'd taken in spy craft to become a member of the SOE flashed across her memory. First and foremost: Trust no one.

Peter Churchill had warned her, not once but twice just now, not to trust *Monsieur* Henri Leblanc.

———◇———

"C'mon, Colette, time to hop on your bicycle and off you go!"

Sean, as always, addressed her with her code name and spoke to her in French in case anyone should overhear their conversations when they were on the street. Several relatively uneventful weeks had gone by following her conversation about Henri with Peter Churchill. Their group continued to be headquartered in Cannes, so her daily routine of fetching and delivering messages by bicycle had remained the same. She had followed the rules and hadn't even told Sean about the list of two hundred Resistance agents that some fool had left on a train.

This day in early February was sunny but cool. Sean pointed to Catherine's assigned mode of transportation, leaning against the alley wall at the rear of the *Salon du Beauté*. Her requisitioned bike was on the small size—perhaps having once belonged to a young boy—rusty and equipped with only a battered straw basket attached to the handlebars. Catherine had found that her long legs made riding more than ten miles a difficult and ultimately painful exercise. Mounting this child's bike with a pillow under her clothes, once again to feign pregnancy, made things even more uncomfortable. Earlier that day, when Sean let it be known that, this time, she wasn't merely carrying messages, she had suggested that she should don this disguise.

"So, what *am* I carrying this time?" she'd demanded.

"Seven hand grenades under a pile of dirty, smelly rags in your bicycle basket, plus a baguette of stale bread in the shopping sack on top."

"*Live* grenades?" Catherine murmured. This would be the first time she'd transported actual weapons. Raoul must have deemed her worthy of his confidence, a development that pleased her no end.

"They're only live if you pull the pin," Sean reminded her with his cheeky grin.

Catherine glanced down at her bloated figure, suddenly overcome by a painful memory of what it had been like to carry a real baby inside her body. It had been fourteen years since that terrible voyage to Jeremy's new post with the British mission in Venezuela. She'd been too weak from childbirth to stop the bastard from grabbing her infant and then ordering a steward to spirit the baby down the gangway the moment the ship had docked in Caracas.

Rousing herself from the agonizing memory of that day, Catherine watched as Sean pulled the bike from its spot against the wall and pointed to its leather seat.

"Think of it this way, *madame*," Sean said, pointing a finger at her, "the sooner you're on your way, the sooner you'll be at your destination."

"What a brilliant observation," she said with a sour look. "Can't I ride your bike this time?"

"Ordinarily, I'd be gallant and say yes, but Raoul said this morning that he has other plans for me today and that I'll need my bigger bike."

He pulled out a map printed on silk and pointed. "You're to take the goods to a barn on this olive farm above Villefranche-sur-Mer belonging to a Jules Menton. Then ride down to *La Citadelle* in town and meet me there. We'll try to find a café open for a coffee that isn't made of ground acorns." He sought her eyes. "And be careful."

The pair had recently learned that more agents from the list of two hundred that had been left on the train had been captured that week at various locations in the South of France and sent to prison, some in Germany. Catherine figured it was only a matter of time before Raoul would order his group to leave Cannes and head for who-knew-where. If that happened, Catherine had no idea how poor Sean would surreptitiously deal with carting his bulky wireless set that was stashed in a battered leather suitcase, to say nothing of the antenna and yards of wire that he rarely allowed out of his sight.

In the mild winter sunshine, she cast him a long, penetrating stare. 1943 had dawned with their network chief having declared Sean and her a team, to be known forthwith as the Trenches Network, with Sean performing as both its named leader and wireless operator.

"And I've been meaning to ask you. Just how did you manage to get me assigned as your permanent courier and assistant recruiter of resisters?"

Sean cast her a smug smile. "I have my ways, *chérie*. I have my ways."

Catherine lowered her voice. "Oh, you Churchills and Eisenhowers! I just bet you have your methods."

Sean gestured toward the azure skies above their heads. "And you don't like this assignment?" he demanded. "You could have been parachuted into Lyon or Vichy and landed on a flagpole at the *gendarmerie,* like one of your spy school classmates!"

"No!" Catherine said, and burst out laughing, adding, "I hope it wasn't poor Viv."

Then her smile faded. As Peter Churchill had been constantly warning his agents, Axis uniformed men were everywhere along the Riviera. The two newly minted male agents with whom Catherine and Odette had traveled aboard the *Dewucca* and on the train from Port Miou to Cannes had been arrested after crossing into the old Occupied Zone near Dijon. Raoul had given his comrades in Cannes that unfortunate news, along with approval from London to install Odette/Lise as his official courier. Vichy France was a mere shadow now, and Cannes, with the Vichy police now taking orders from the Germans, had become a very dangerous place to be. More people were disappearing with no explanation—either on orders from Axis authorities or because they'd been arrested by the hated *milice,* France's own version of the brutal SS, made up mostly of former criminals, youthful hooligans, and extortionists.

That had been the toughest part so far of her experience in the SOE, thought Catherine, grasping her bicycle's handlebars, one foot on the pedals. One met people one grew to care about, and then *poof,* they were gone.

She shivered as an unwanted image of Henri Leblanc came to mind. She had ridden her bicycle hundreds of miles in the three months since arriving in France, the days blurring one into the other. She'd delivered messages and money, gathered missives sent back to Peter about local conditions, and helped to find out-of-the-way landing fields for the increasing RAF drops of supplies, cash, weapons and personnel. Since her conversation with her chief network leader about Henri, she hadn't gleaned an inkling of his current whereabouts or of anyone else's she'd known in training— except for Sean.

Despite Peter's warnings, and try as she might to forget all about Henri, she couldn't stop thinking about the dangers confronting him every moment since she'd last seen him. Even so, in the back of her mind, the same worry persisted. Could he possibly be turned again and start working for the Vichy—or worse?

Never for the Germans, she insisted to herself.

Yet, how could she know for sure? In their time together in Washington, she'd learned so little about Henri's family, except that his father had passed away in Paris while he was at the embassy in D.C. Henri's mother, Catherine vaguely recalled, had moved back somewhere at the western end of the Riviera. She remembered him mentioning it was a town that was within mere miles of the border with Spain. Far too distant for Catherine to travel by bicycle, even if she knew the town's name.

Sean wagged a finger at her, bringing her thoughts back to the present.

"Catherine! Stop your wool-gathering, will you please?" he demanded, his words pulling her abruptly back to the dangerous task ahead. "You've got miles to go before you sleep, my love."

Sean's calling her *my love*, even in jest, brought her up short.

"*My love*, my foot!" she retorted. "I just hope I don't fall off this midget bike and these damn things in my basket don't blow sky high."

Allowing her mind to wander as it just had could get her killed, she realized.

"I have every confidence that you will peddle those twenty-four miles to Villefranche just fine. The main thing to look out for today is that there might be new road checks along the way. Keep alert, will you please?"

He was right to remind her, but even so, his superior attitude irked her. She patted her belly, swollen with its plump pillow tucked beneath her cotton dress.

"Isn't that why you want *me* to deliver these lethal baby pineapples?"

Sean offered her a look of apology.

"Actually, given what's been going on around here these days, you're the only one who could pull this off." At her look of alarm, he wrapped one arm around her shoulders. "Just think of yourself as a woman practically ready to deliver twins. You shouldn't have a bit of trouble."

"Easy for you to say," she retorted. "Is this what your wife looked like before the boys were born?"

Sean paused and appeared as if the thought of his two little boys back home in Virginia had thrown him off balance. Instantly, Catherine regretted having referred to anything so personal. They were working as partners now, and they should both just stick to the business at hand.

She didn't wait for him to answer, saying by way of farewell, "Well, no one less than Wild Bill Donovan told me to try this little subterfuge." She hitched the pillow higher, wishing suddenly she and Sean would make this trek together. "Winston Churchill reportedly suggested the idea for the female agents to *him*!"

"And it's going to work like a charm," Sean assured her.

"Let us hope."

Despite their banter, they exchanged a look that silently acknowledged what a risky business they were engaged in this day. Moving about in the South of France had become more perilous with each passing week now that Germany put all of France under its boot.

As she readied to push off, Sean bestowed on Catherine his usual encouraging smile. He then gave a shove to the back fender of her vintage bicycle.

"*Bonne chance, chérie*. See you tonight."

CHAPTER 20

Even in wintery sunshine, the coastal scenery along the cliff-side road between Cannes and Nice via Antibes was spectacular. With each turn of Catherine's bicycle pedal, she wished once again that Sean and she were doing this mission together. Also wishing her current assignment was over and done with, she stepped up her pace around each turn, grateful at least that the stunning scenes unfolding before her made it seem for a moment that there wasn't a war going on.

The sea this day was a deep sapphire blue, with few boats bobbing on the water. Winter beaches were deserted, the colorful umbrellas folded and tucked away in rows of square, two-person wooden changing rooms that lined the waterfront. Most of the cafes, too, were shuttered, but occasionally she saw a child skipping down a narrow lane with a dog trailing behind or a line of women holding baskets, waiting patiently for the bakery to dispense what little bread might be available that week. She wheeled past a horse-drawn cart whose wooden sides sported the large, hand-painted image of a honeybee. The rear platform of the creaking conveyance was stacked high with a dozen boxes emitting distinct buzzing sounds.

A beekeeper, off to sell his wares, she thought, wishing she had time to stop and browse at the open-air farmer's market in a village square nearby.

As she passed into the outskirts of Nice, more horse-drawn carts, a truck or two, and numerous cyclists began to clog the road. The traffic suddenly slowed to a crawl and then stopped. Catherine leaned to her left, squinting in the anemic winter sun to peer ahead. Just as Sean had warned, a hundred yards distant, she spotted an ominous check point where uniformed agents—whether local policemen or Italian Army officers, she couldn't tell at this distance—were blocking each traveler's progress, demanding identification papers. One of the rare trucks traveling on the road had been forced to halt, its driver ordered out of the cab while his cargo was pulled out and tossed on the ground. A German Shepard suddenly appeared, sniffing the packages strewn across the gravel.

They're looking for black market goods or weapons! Oh, God! My basket!

Catherine's heart thudded at the realization that seven hand grenades were easy targets for any human or canine searcher. Her vision almost seemed to gray out except for her view of the sentries, rifling through the belongings of the hapless truck driver. One soldier suddenly banged the butt of his rifle into the man's shoulder, roughly pushing him against the side of his vehicle.

For several moments, Catherine remained frozen, straddling her bicycle, with her two feet on the ground and the pillow strapped to her waist under her cotton dress pushing against the handlebars. Behind her, an insistent buzzing sound rent the air as she quickly tried to form some sort of plan of defensive action. A bee zoomed by and landed on the dirty, smelly rags in her bicycle basket. The insect's rounded head poked at the cloth and then lit on the stale baguette like a tiny sniffer dog looking for contraband.

Catherine tried to steady her breathing; her hands were wet and clammy on the handlebar grips despite the cool temperatures this wintery day. She flinched as another bee flew by, also landing on the pile of rags, searching, no doubt, some scent of food or wine that still clung to the cloths. By then, the beekeeper's cart had pulled up beside her.

Catherine swiveled her head and exchanged looks with the hunched-over soul holding tight to the reins of the plow horse that pulled his ancient vehicle. No petrol to be had, so he'd obviously requisitioned an old cart, and here he was, facing a delay getting his honey to market—or worse.

Honey! Boxes and boxes of bees making honey!

Catherine sat up on the seat of her bicycle and bestowed a rueful smile on the man sitting high on his cart. Then she turned her bike around, as if to give up on her journey. She rode a few feet and then turned again, positioning herself and her bike directly behind the cart, out of view of its driver. She cast swift glances to the right and left, hoping that no one was behind her. Her heart sank. Another bicycle rider was approaching some one hundred yards distant, pulling a *velo-taxi*, a small wagon attached to his two-wheeler.

Realizing she had to assume the person behind her might betray her to the authorities, she swiftly pried open the top of one of the boxes containing a hive of bees busily making honeycomb, and gingerly slipped two of the grenades in, gently shutting the cover just as she felt a sharp sting.

"Owww, *merde*!" she hissed, but she barely paused before prying open another box, slipping three more grenades into the soft honeycomb. She forced grenade number six and seven into their new home in beehive box number three.

The cart lurched forward, leaving Catherine to suck the tip of her little finger, pulling out the stinger with her teeth. She only prayed that the soldiers, hearing the buzzing sound and not wishing to get stung, would be convinced the beekeeper was carrying legitimate goods to market.

Her hands sticky and her finger beginning to swell, Catherine glanced over her shoulder once more and nearly fell off her bicycle seat when she spotted Sean with a jumble of items stacked in the small wagon clipped to his bike, a contraption that probably once pulled toddlers behind their mother wheeling about town.

Oh, God! The list from the train! The Germans must finally be rounding up the names on it from Nice if Raoul ordered Sean to clear out less than an hour after I left.

Did Sean see the checkpoint up ahead? He was hauling all their possessions behind him.

But what if he packed the wireless beneath that pile of our stuff?

Sean drew ever closer, but as they were trained, he did not give her a moment's recognition, cycling on ahead. She barely refrained from calling out to him as he pushed steadily past her without a glance. For her part, Catherine remained in line where she was. Relief swept over her when, in quick succession, Sean's wagon and his person were inspected, his papers checked, and he was waved on, along with the beekeeper and his cargo. Catherine could only assume that someone else on another day would deliver that precious wireless set that was their lifeline back to London.

When it was her turn to approach the sentries, she handed over her papers while tamping down feelings of rising panic. Somehow, she remembered to massage her swollen belly and grimace as if she might have a baby at any moment. The guard was an Italian and his glance at her documents was perfunctory. His nose twitched as he looked down at the smelly rags in her basket.

"*Avanti!*" he barked, bidding her to move on.

Catherine put her foot on the bike's pedal and rode onwards, grateful that the appearance of her pregnancy had so effectively warded off unwanted male advances, a serious problem for women encountering foreign soldiers who typically felt they could do whatever they wanted.

On the other hand...she had outfoxed them!

A strange excitement unexpectedly engulfed her. The danger had been acute. As trained by her SOE instructors, she had automatically surveyed her surroundings to see what might be of use and had seized on the bee boxes to save herself. Yes, seven precious hand grenades were lost, and yes, she'd been lucky the bee cart had rolled by just then, but she'd proven to herself she was a worthy member of a very select group of undercover combatants willing to risk everything to outwit the terrible forces enslaving France.

But if anyone but Sean had seen me with a grenade in my hand...if that guard had—

Catherine forced herself to banish such thoughts and instead take notice of the cramping in her legs due to the ridiculously small-sized bicycle she rode. For the next six miles, she concentrated on peddling doggedly toward the seaside village of Villefranche-sur-Mer, only a short distance from the Principality of Monaco and less than twenty miles from the border with Italy. Without any grenades to deliver, there was no point now, riding up to the olive farm of *résistant* Jules Menton. With only a moment's hesitation, Catherine turned right, heading downhill.

Her spirits rose another notch when she spotted the first *La Citadelle* sign that had guided tourists before the war to this mighty stone landmark built in the sixteenth century by the Duke of Savoy. The harbor's waters lapped at its base, and a Nazi swastika had taken the place of the French flag, flying high above the fortress with its red, white, and black colors snapping in the wind.

Sean was waiting in the deserted stone-paved courtyard in front of a rounded entry that rose forty feet above their heads. Devoid of any stray visitors on such a windy winter's day, he stood beside his bicycle attached to the cart that was filled with the sum of their paltry possessions.

He pushed his bizarre glasses with the black eye patch to the crown of his head and spread his arms wide open.

"Come here, you," he shouted.

Catherine threw her bike to the ground and ran toward him. Without really thinking, she flung herself into his arms.

Sean buried his face in the hollow of her neck as he pressed the full length of his body against hers. "Every second waiting for you to show up just now was...horrible." He leaned back and met her eyes, still filled with barely disguised fear from her recent brush at the checkpoint and the overwhelming joy she felt at seeing Sean waiting for her. "How ever did you manage to get through?" he asked. "They pawed every single item in my wagon," he added, nodding in the direction of his pull-cart.

"I thought you saw."

"Saw what? All I could think about was that you were in line on your bicycle with a basketful of grenades behind that horse and cart, heading for the checkpoint."

Catherine nodded. "Well, here's the good-and-bad news: those seven hand grenades you gave me are now safely hidden inside those boxes of bees, also covered with honey and wax." She held up her swollen pinkie finger, its tip an angry red and puffed up like a cooked sausage. "I, however, was not so lucky."

Sean reached for her hand and gently kissed the swollen tip. "You sure *were* lucky and thank God for that." Then he pulled her close again. There was a long silence before he whispered into her ear, "Trust me, Catherine, you are worth far more to me and our operation than a bunch of hand grenades." He rested his cheek alongside hers and then nuzzled her neck again, inhaling deeply. "Mmm…you smell like honey."

"I see you've come to Villefranche with everything we own," she murmured, an electric sensation skimming down her spine when he playfully gave her earlobe a lick.

"The Spindle network is toast," he whispered, "Kaput. It has to be completely reorganized."

"I take it Raoul's told you about the list of agents' names that some jackass left on a train a while back?"

Sean leaned back. "You knew about that?" he demanded.

Catherine merely shrugged.

"Raoul's arranged a new safe house for us. It's in a boatyard somewhere, next to the harbor down there," he added, pointing toward the water on the other side of the citadel. "He's assigned someone to bring the wireless to us in the middle of the night soon. Everyone else has already left. Raoul, Lise, and their wireless man, Arnaud…they've all gone north to Lake Annecy in the *Savoie* region."

"Peter and Odette are now in the Alps?" Catherine confirmed.

"They will be soon, not far from the border with Geneva. The Carte network, like our own Spindle…they've all been blown. By whom, we don't know for sure and—"

"Well, I'm not surprised," she interrupted. "I was the one who told Raoul about some idiot Frenchman leaving the list of two hundred agents' names on a train out of Marseille. Our names must have been on it, too."

"So that explains what happened," Sean said, his arms still draped around her shoulders. "Raoul must have gotten word from somebody this morning right after you left and so he immediately pulled the plug."

"One betrayal has probably led to another."

"But one good thing…the name of our new Trenches network that Raoul just chose for us was apparently never written down anywhere."

The pair stared at one another; each thinking how lucky they'd been not to be arrested.

"God, Catherine," he groaned, tightly wrapping his arms around her again, his cheek against her hair. "That checkpoint could have been the end for you. Such a clever girl you are, getting the word back to Raoul in time and saving all of us, frankly. And the bee boxes! Brilliant!"

He gave her neck another gentle nuzzle, setting off a new wave of warm sensation. She was certain that next he would kiss her. Did she want this? Sean's affection was such a welcome relief from the spine-tingling fear of the last half hour, but should she give in to it? Everything was so complicated. Wouldn't it be pure insanity to allow a fellow agent to complicate her life even more?

But at least I have my life, thanks to those boxes of bees.

She might not be so lucky on another day. It had been so long since she'd felt a man's arms around her, warm and safe in a bed. For an instant, the thought of Henri intruded, and she mentally batted it away. Events at the checkpoint just now prompted the inevitable question: How many days could she could count on in the future?

In the space of time it took to lean a few inches away from Sean, Catherine made her decision. She framed his face with the palm of her hands.

"Look, Professor Four-Eyes," she teased, patting his cheeks and mildly stunned by the arousal the cockeyed Sean Eisenhower seemed to have summoned in her. She met his intent gaze with one of her own and whispered against his mouth.

"We didn't die today, so I think it's time we found our way to that boatyard, don't you?"

CHAPTER 21

Paris was crawling with more Gestapo officers than ever before. Even winter's stormy weather hadn't kept them from making their presence known on nearly every street corner.

This gloomy March afternoon, Henri had a bad feeling in his gut as he stared through the light drizzle coming down on rue du Croissant, a side street off rue Montmartre. He had no specific reason he felt this way, but still he couldn't shake his unease. He stood in the shadows of a doorway in the heart of the city's newspaper district in the 2nd Arrondissement, considering his options. Under his arm was a wrapped stack of newly printed menus and fifty thousand francs in a money belt strapped to his waist.

Gazing at the Café Le Croissant, an establishment that had been in business at this corner since 1850, he wondered if another of his father's old acquaintances, journalist Jacques Sauvette, could be trusted with such an important assignment as the one he had proposed at an earlier meeting. Had the two veteran newsmen's twenty years of casual camaraderie been enough to cement a new relationship with the erstwhile Vichy diplomat, Henri Leblanc, son of the late Georges Leblanc?

Henri's pressman, Alphonse Moreau, had minced no words. He avowed that he despised Sauvette for the yellow journalism he'd peddled before the newspapers had been shut down. Besides, he "hated snitches," which Alphonse considered gossip monger Sauvette to be.

But the plain truth was Henri was running out of options to fulfill the urgent request he'd received from London to locate hiding places for a big cache of grenades and Sten guns. During the next full moon, the weapons were due to be parachuted in oversized cigar-like metal containers from a British Whitley to a field outside the city.

Thus, the question of the day was: Would the sixty-four-year-old Jacques Sauvette be willing to take on the role of a reliable *résistant* and help him establish a network to receive and stockpile weapons in unlikely places around Paris?

Sauvette had once been a print reporter working for a paper that rivalled the Leblanc's weekly publication. In his salad days, he was known in the trade for being a tipster, whispering a tidbit of information picked up in his urban travels to his editor, which was usually written up by some other journalist. That way, the editors could keep Jacques's fingerprints off a published story so his sources would trust that he wasn't the tattletale he actually was.

Sauvette was one of those people who knew "everything about everybody who was anybody," a valuable commodity in both the newspaper and clandestine trades. Despite this, few journalists were employed these days, and the aging reporter had found needed work assisting the proprietor behind the bar, washing dishes and sweeping the floor. Henri was gambling that, in these tough times, the former scribe might, at the very least, be persuaded for a few francs—or perhaps even a sense of national patriotism—to host a kind of in-plain-sight safe house for other agents or airmen.

On the other hand, a few members of France's Fourth Estate, acting for a fee as Nazi intelligence operatives, had recently helped blow several Resistance networks to bits. Was Jacques Sauvette a loyal Frenchman or a *collaborateur*? Henri was about to find out.

And, after all, beggars can't be choosers.

The head of the Pinwheel network pulled his fedora down to ward off the rain beginning to fall in earnest as he entered the side street where he would find the café's entrance to the bar. On his left was a row of enormous garbage containers lined up on the brick wall opposite the series of restaurants, bistros, and cafes for which this business district was known.

What if we made some false bottoms for some of those refuse bins?

Henri judged that modified garbage containers like those in the alley could be excellent places to sequester a cache of weapons.

Eager to propose such a scheme, he strode into the café and waited for Jacques to take his order.

On the shelves behind the scrawny figure with a beak-like nose whom he'd known since he was a boy were spare rows of bottles, most only half full, as supplies of fine brandies and cordials were hard to come by, except for the black market. For some reason, Henri's mind strayed to the wonderful array of liquor Catherine always kept in a drinks cabinet at her place on O Street in Georgetown. He remembered the beautiful flowing negligee she often wore when pouring him a—

"Hello, Henri," Jacques called out from behind the bar. "What can I get you?"

Startled that Sauvette would identify him so publicly, he glanced at a solitary drinker sitting at a table pushed against the opposite wall.

"A cognac," he replied, "and don't stint this time!"

He was deliberately loud in his reply so as to make this exchange seem like normal bantering between barman and customer. He was relieved when the other patron rose from his seat, deposited some coins on the table, and wandered out into the rain-soaked street. Out of the corner of Henri's eye, he saw a door to the left of the bar open an inch but no farther.

He called out to Jacques, "Tell the boss that I brought the menus he ordered printed up—and the bill for printing them. I'd like to be paid today, please."

Jacques merely nodded from behind the bar without looking up as he poured amber liquor into a small glass. The door never opened wider, nor did anyone appear. Every bit of intelligence training Henri had acquired told him something was very wrong.

Before Jacques could bring his drink to the table, Henri stood from his chair, strode swiftly to the door, and gave it a hard push. A young German soldier, very blond and very plump in his ill-fitting gray-green uniform, was forced to leap back. Henri felt the blood pounding in his chest, but he managed to nod politely and indicated the package of menus he was carrying.

"Do you speak French?" he asked.

The soldier's stare was cold and calculating, but he nodded affirmatively.

"I've brought some menus the proprietor has ordered from my printing company. Have you seen him?" It was a stupid question, but it filled the silence. He placed the package on a shelf nearby in a room that stored items used in the business.

At that moment, Jacques appeared in the doorway to the storeroom.

"The boss isn't here this afternoon," he said, looking shaken. He peered down his long nose at the package on the shelf. "I-I'll tell him you delivered the menus. He'll pay you when you're here next."

Henri turned slightly and cast Jacques a steady, accusing gaze.

"The invoice is on the top." He glanced in the soldier's direction, adding, "Well, then, since the boss is out, I might as well be on my way. I guess I won't have a cognac today. I'll just slip out the back? Closer to the Metro."

Without waiting for the soldier or Jacques's permission, Henri walked past, hoping to reach the exit into an alleyway he'd used on his previous visit.

"Halt!" demanded the soldier. "Papers, please!"

The German's last word ended in a hiss. Henri turned around in time to see Jacques's scrawny figure backing out of the storeroom and shutting the door. Henri knew then exactly what trap he'd walked into. The journalist's latent rightwing sympathies—or perhaps merely his tendency to gossip or an urgent need for money—had prompted him to inform one of the café's Nazi patrons that a suspected member of the French Resistance was due to make a call that afternoon. Henri wondered what benefit Jacques would receive if the bastard had passed that information along to local Nazi headquarters. Perhaps merely a promise not to be arrested himself. All journalists were suspect, according to the occupying forces in France.

Henri dug into his pocket, confident that his documents were as convincing as any false papers could be. After all, one of his printing presses, plus the brilliant forger he'd recruited to work with him on a regular basis, had produced ration and local identity cards that Henri dispensed to whomever he encountered that needed them. He presented his personal versions, along with the original papers the SOE had provided which verified his retirement from the Vichy diplomatic corps.

Henri waited while the soldier scrutinized his documents, one by one. The man's uniform revealed he was not a member of the dreaded security forces, merely an ordinary foot soldier, a customer of Jacques. Perhaps the *Bosche* was simply trying to move up in the ranks by responding to a tip from Sauvette and scoring an arrest of a resister?

With a frown of disappointment, the German returned Henri's papers. Then he grabbed the package of menus off the shelf and ripped open the paper wrapper. After a brief examination flipping through them to see if anything had been hidden, he tossed the stack onto the floor in a fit of frustration. Henri affected a bored shrug and then pointed at the back exit.

"*Auf wiedersehen*," he said with a calm he didn't feel, and began walking past the scowling figure.

The soldier turned around and lunged toward him, wrapping his arms around Henri's shoulder and chest. Henri's own reactions were instantaneous. He tossed his head backwards as hard as he could, smashing the back of his fedora-covered skull into the soldier's face with the brute force he'd been taught in the SOE's silent killing school. He heard the crunch of the man's nose breaking and a deep-throated groan as blood filled his target's throat, cutting off any other possible sound.

Henri turned and knelt next to the crumpled, writhing figure and crashed the side of his palm into the man's Adam's apple, followed by a second chop, the kind of blows that guaranteed a quick death.

The soldier lay on the floor, blood streaming from his nose, his chest not even quivering. Arched over his body, Henri grew very still, relieved to hear the normal clinking of glasses through the closed door to the bar. Jacques called to the boy in the kitchen to hurry up and finish his dishwashing chores. Obviously, he had not heard the altercation in the storeroom.

Henri sprinted to the room's back door and opened it a crack. Across the alley was another of the huge refuse containers he'd seen earlier that held the garbage from the numerous cafés in the neighborhood. He returned to the body and pushed the soldier onto his back to stop his blood from staining the floor. Clutching a bunch of menus scattered nearby, Henri mopped up a small pool of crimson and dashed back to the bin in the mist-turned-to-steady rain that was now coming down in the empty alley. He pushed the blood-soaked papers deep into the pile of refuse and returned once again to the storeroom. It took some effort to heave the body onto his shoulders and haul it across the alley, where he pitched his victim into the metal box.

It was a smelly business covering him up, and Henri was reeking with the scent of decaying food by the time he returned to close the café's back door. Examining his sleeves for bloodstains, he crossed to a sink and sluiced his hands and rubbed a spot on his shoulder with cold water, drying himself with a barman's towel lying nearby. He gathered the remaining menus from the floor and stacked them in a neat pile, placing his invoice on the top. His clothes against his skin were wet and clammy, and he remembered then that his coat remained on his chair inside the café.

Taking a few breaths to steady himself, he opened the door that led back into the bar. Jacques Sauvette looked up with an astonished expression, offering more proof the former journalist was indeed the snitch Henri now figured him for.

"Just so you won't forget them, here are the menus," Henri said, slapping them on the bar in front of Jacques.

"Where is…?"

Jacques peered around Henri's shoulder at the closed door to the back room. Henri affected another shrug.

"My documents were fine. The bastard went out the back way." He paused, feeling Jacques's stare at his rain-spattered shirt. "The damn *Bosche* tore the wrapping paper on these menus to shreds. I got soaked putting the mess in the garbage bin outside in the alley. By the way, it's pretty full. When do they pick up around here?"

Jacques waved a hand as if this were the least of his problems. "Tonight, after midnight. At least, they're supposed to."

Henri nodded, masking the relief he felt. He tapped a forefinger on the bar.

"On second thought, I think I *will* have that cognac while you tell me just how that German soldier happened to be in your back storeroom when you and I had an appointment today."

Jacques, eyes lowered, reached below the bar and retrieved the drink he'd poured for Henri earlier.

"He stopped for a beer and had gone back to use the latrine." Then, accusingly, Jacques added, "There wasn't much I could do about that, right? His being here was just an unlucky coincidence."

Henri tossed back the cognac in one gulp and placed the glass on the bar with a thud.

"Coincidence, was it?" Henri repeated, heading for his chair to retrieve his jacket.

Jacques said, "I-I thought you wanted to talk to me about...ah... well, that perhaps I could help you with..."

Eyes narrowing, Henri walked back toward Jacques and leaned his chest against the lip of the bar that separated them.

Once a snitch, always a snitch.

"Now listen to me carefully, Jacques. This afternoon, I merely delivered the print job your boss wanted, you understand?"

"Yes, but—"

"And no soldier ever walked in here this afternoon, is that clear?"

Shrugging, Jacques replied, "I-I guess so..."

"And should German authorities make any inquiries on that subject, I will know instantly if you played your old tipster game with any *flics,*" he added, using the derogative slang for certain members of the local police who supported the occupation. Henri knew Jacques had a wife crippled with arthritis and an unmarried daughter who took care of her. "Trust me, if you say a word about anything today, life could become quite miserable for you and your entire family."

Jacques Sauvette's eyes widened with fear. Henri felt fairly certain that the bastard would now never dare disclose to anyone that a soldier that had gone missing had been inside the Café Le Croissant this day.

Without another word, Henri left the café as he had come in, his thoughts filled with the lesson he had learned this day. As he walked down pavement sheened by the recent downpour, he realized it had been sheer folly to try to recruit a man into his network whom he instinctively mistrusted, no matter how pressing the circumstances were. Believing in his instincts was exactly what he'd done the day he met Catherine and took her to the lunch that had changed his life. She had taught him so much, but especially about what risks were worth taking.

Today, the risk would have been in not taking the actions he did to kill the soldier. His current danger, of course, was that someone would find the body before the bin was removed and Jacques would then rat on him. But if his luck held, the body would disappear like so many others. Even if it was discovered near the cafe, there was an excellent chance Jacques Sauvette would plead ignorance out of fear of Henri's threats.

Henri suddenly felt light-headed. He paused and leaned against a rain-washed building. His clothes under his jacket were still damp, made more so by the sweat seeping under his arms. His entire body started to tremble. The back of his head was throbbing at the spot he'd smashed it into the soldier's face. He felt bile rise to his throat where the cognac still burned.

A young man from somewhere in Germany is dead, buried under stinking fish bones in a trash bin not a hundred yards from where I'm now standing.

Seeing an enemy die a foot in front of him was far different from dropping bombs on foes from thousands of feet as he had from his plane in the First World War.

Henri swallowed hard, took one step, then another, heading toward the Bourse Metro station. As he continued in the damp dusk of evening, he banished all other thoughts from his mind except considerations of where he could conceal the next drop of three hundred Sten guns, weapons that would one day wipe out many more soldiers just like the one he'd killed this day.

CHAPTER 22

"This is unreal!" Sean exclaimed as he pushed open the door to the loft above the former sailmaker's loft in Villefranche-sur-Mer. The village was situated on the Mediterranean, a few miles along the coast to the east of Nice and had been recommended as a refuge by Peter Churchill.

Catherine followed in his wake, gazing around their new lodgings, the latest safe house their circuit leader had arranged.

Each of them carried an armful of the belongings that Sean had pulled from Cannes in the cart behind his bicycle. They gazed at a room with a wide-planked wooden floor, whitewashed walls, and crisscrossed wooden beams arching high above their heads. The glass-paned windows flanking the door faced a large boatyard with all manner of dry-docked vessels perched in wooden cradles and in various stages of repair. Beyond them, on the other side of a stone jetty, lay Villefranche's harbor, glinting a deep sapphire that melded into turquoise in the bright sun of early spring.

Sean turned and made a sweeping gesture around their new quarters' large, open space that was nearly empty except for some folded sails piled along one wall. In a far corner was a small table with a kerosene hotplate, a kettle, and a frying pan sitting on its surface. In the opposite corner was a folding canvas screen, behind which stood another small table with a pitcher and basin for daily ablutions.

"No running water up here, right?" she said. "And the latrine is out back?"

"It does feel a bit like a budget holiday home, doesn't it?" he said with a laugh.

Catherine advanced a few more steps and turned in a circle.

"Could be a lot worse, but it doesn't seem very secure for a safe house."

"Raoul says we're to hide in plain sight until we get further orders. I'm a semi-invalid recovering from eye surgery, and you are my beloved spouse, looking after me during my recovery while we wait for our child to be born."

Catherine glanced down at her swollen mid-section, the pillow still strapped to her waist, rendering her hot and uncomfortable on such a sunny day.

"So, I'm to be your pregnant wife during all this, am I?"

Sean set down his burdens as she set down hers.

"Only when you venture outside," he said, reaching for her hands and holding her gaze. "You could be un-pregnant when it's just the two of us up here." He cast a glance at the pile of canvas sails and then pulled her into his arms, pillow and all. "We could make this into quite a little love nest, you know," he suggested, bending forward so his forehead touched hers. A roguish smile played at the corners of his mouth. "We'd just be following our orders to the nth degree."

Catherine didn't smile back. All she could think about was the close call they'd just had at the roadblock on their way down the hill to Villefranche. A wave of exhaustion took hold, and she momentarily closed her eyes. When she opened them, Sean was staring at her with a look of concern.

"You look as if you're about to drop."

"I am." When he pulled her against his chest, she allowed her head to rest on his shoulder. "All I want right now" she murmured, "is to make a bed on that pile of canvas over there and sleep for days."

"Is that all you want?" he whispered into her ear.

Is it all? she wondered. When she'd flung herself into his arms in the courtyard at *La Citadelle*, she knew she'd sent a signal that she longed for a safe haven and some physical comfort. But with whom?

She had barely escaped being arrested this day. And what of Henri? Had he managed, in all these months, to stay safe in Paris, the headquarters of Hitler's forces and currently the most dangerous part in all of France? Or had the bad luck she'd evaded this day already caught up with him?

Catherine raised her head to meet Sean's gaze. After a long moment, she spoke, surprising even herself with the honesty of her answer.

"What I really want, Sean, is a nap. Followed by something to eat. Followed by a walk along the jetty at sunset, and then..." Her tired voice trailed off. Finally, she said, "Let's decide later if what you're obviously proposing is such a good idea."

———◇———

A few hours later, Sean and Catherine located a café Peter Churchill had recommended to Sean. Fortunately, it was open for business and situated along the main waterfront on the other side of the mighty stone citadel. The enormous fortress separated the boatyard works adjacent to an oceanographic station now housed in an old rope factory and the main harbor that made up the town of Villefranche-sur-Mer proper.

The establishment they chose, whose awning declared it *La Mere Germaine,* was nearly deserted at this early evening hour. Its quay-side tables were as empty of humans as the deserted fishing boats bobbing in the bay a few feet away. Stretching beyond was the curving shoreline that led to the nearby principality of Monaco and, some 16 kilometers further east, the border with Italy.

Sean and Catherine took their seats away from the bay at a tiny table for two under the awning, a spot they deemed would avoid direct scrutiny from anyone walking along the waterfront. A moment later, a waiter who moved with a slight limp that had probably exempted him from military service hobbled toward them to take their order.

"We were just about to close," he informed them as he hastened to unfurl a cloth napkin for Catherine across her bulging lap, "but we still have the fish and some greens we can steam."

"*Bien d'accord*," murmured Catherine in her impeccable French. "And if you please, perhaps a glass of wine?"

The waiter smiled, offering another sympathetic glance in the direction of her swollen belly. "Yes, madam. A boisterous little red." His response told Catherine that the *vin* would be *très ordinaire*. The waiter added with a sheepish frown, "I'm sorry we don't have a white wine to go with the fish, but—"

"*Pas de tout*," she swiftly replied with a friendly wave of her hand. "Not at all. We're just grateful you still can serve us."

When the waiter departed to inform the kitchen of their order, Sean echoed her thoughts. "By boisterous, he probably means the wine was bottled in these hills yesterday."

Catherine laughed. "We're lucky even to get that. With the Germans swarming down here now, confiscating everything from local farmers they can lay their hands on, we're fortunate to get any meal served us at all."

She glanced up at the plaster-covered buildings, painted in a variety of now faded colors, that climbed the hill behind them. The two- and three-story houses faced narrow lanes twisting and turning their way nearly to the top of the surrounding heights, where a few impressive villas clung to the cliffs.

"Aren't you surprised Peter didn't send us to a safe house in that rabbit warren up there?"

Sean followed her gaze. "Didn't have time, I suspect. I think, though, I'll explore there tomorrow and see if we can find a back-up place." He nodded at a rectangular, five-story building that stood a hundred yards from the café and faced the broad expanse of the deep-water bay. "There's the Welcome Hotel. It's known to live up to its name when it comes to opening its doors to *résistants* in the region."

"Then, why aren't we staying there?" Catherine demanded, nearly swooning at the thought of a real mattress and crisp hotel linens.

"You know why," Sean scolded. "Hotels are the first place the Nazis look when searching for agents. No, I'm going to check out those streets higher up the hill. For a second safe house, just in case we ever need one here."

"Just be careful, though," Catherine urged. "We don't know anyone here except the farmer in the hills where I was supposed to deliver the grenades. I'll have to go up there tomorrow and let him know what happened."

"Perhaps he's acquainted with the beekeeper," Sean suggested. "If your savior hauling those bee boxes isn't a collaborator, he'd better be warned about what you hid in his hives."

Catherine nodded as their waiter approached with two steaming plates in his hands.

"Ah...how heavenly." Catherine breathed in the scent of olive oil, cracked pepper, and fresh herbs coating the fish. Looking up at him as he set their plates on the table, she said, "You are my hero."

The waiter blushed, completely under her spell and bathing in her smiling gaze.

"Ah, madam," he murmured. "Only too happy you're pleased." He waited while Catherine poked her fork into the delicate flesh. "No butter, I'm sad to say, but I did the best I could for you."

Catherine took a bite and sat back in her chair, savoring the taste and feel of real food. She looked up at him.

"It really is heavenly," she pronounced, chewing slowly. "You made this, didn't you?"

"Yes, madam," he admitted. "The Jerries conscripted my chef two weeks ago."

Catherine replied with genuine sympathy, "Well, we will come here as often as you are open."

The waiter-cum-chef's smile lit up his face.

"For you, *madame*," and then he cast an embarrassed look at Sean, "and you as well, *monsieur*, as often as we have food to cook, we will be here to welcome you." He glanced around and then whispered, "That is, if the filthy *Bosches* don't eat everything in my restaurant's pantry first."

By the time the waiter, whose named they learned was Remy Poché, removed their dinner plates and served them their coffee cut with chicory, Sean had invited him to take a seat and enjoy a cup with them. At meal's end it was clear to all three that they were *sympathetique* on matters political. Before they departed for the evening, Remy had brought out a treasured bottle of calvados, and the trio toasted *"Vive la France"* under their breath. Sean, thanks to Raoul's francs, left a generous gratuity for their new friend.

"*Monsieur* Remy will be of help, don't you think?" Sean said with a chuckle as he and Catherine walked along the waterfront in the direction of the looming fortress separating the town from the boatyard.

"A few more meals there and we can confirm you're right, although I suspect our Raoul had already made his acquaintance," Catherine said. "Even so, we've got to be cautious and not rely solely on first impressions."

They set off in the direction of their new lodgings, with a full moon streaming a path across the water to the base of the citadel's steep, stone sides. Catherine felt herself relaxing for the first time in weeks. Sean kept his arm loosely around her shoulders as they strolled along the narrow, cobbled route that circled the tall, rounded tower. Breathing in the air fragrant with mimosa and night-blooming jasmine, they meandered their way toward the boat slips and the adjacent area dotted with wooden frames that cradled vessels awaiting repair. Long shadows cast by the fortress soaring a hundred feet above them hid them from view while seawater quietly lapped against the bulwark of boulders stacked against the curving shoreline, ten feet below. Alone, with beauty and stillness on all sides, it was if they were suspended in time and space.

"We may be at war, but I think Villefranche-sur-Mer is one of the most wonderful places on earth right now," she declared in hushed tones, the calvados still warming her.

Sean halted their progress and turned toward her, wrapping both arms around her torso as he had when she'd first thrown herself into his arms earlier that day.

"Your damn pillow is driving me crazy," he whispered into her ear, his breath smelling of the heady liquor Remy had shared with them. "I want to feel you next to me, Catherine. All of you."

He kissed her, and his lips, too, tasted lushly of calvados. A new strain of languid warmth spread through her mid-section, and moisture seeped between her thighs.

Despite the dangers of this day, I'm still alive.

She had eaten well for the first time in months. She was in the arms of a man who was aroused and wanted her with an intensity she knew was heartfelt. Sean's ardent embrace also served to awaken her own sense of longing for closeness with another human being as she fought the sense of darkness closing in on all sides.

Also, she was slightly drunk.

Sean suddenly released her, grabbed her by one hand and, with a determined look, led her beyond the path that circled the citadel and into the eastern end of the boatyard. Catherine felt herself caught up in his urgency, and the pair quickly walked past the dry-docked sea craft and the old rope factory and then up a few steps to another large building, its three wooden sides constructed against a stone wall.

By the time they both reached the sail-maker's space on the top floor, they were breathing heavily. Once Sean had closed the door, each began to strip each other of their outer clothing. Catherine reached up and took off Sean's spectacles, tossing them on the pile of sails stacked on the floor.

"That means I get to remove that damn pillow," he murmured, his voice hoarse with desire.

He grabbed the loose dress she'd been wearing and slipped it up her arms and over her head. He easily found the belt buckle that kept the leather strap in place against the down puff that had bulged so convincingly against her stomach. The entire apparatus fell to the floor, and Catherine heard Sean's swift intake of breath as he took in the sight of her slender form clad only in her last pair of decent underwear.

"I knew you were beautiful, but, Jesus, Catherine…"

"How can you see without your glasses?"

"I see up close just fine," he murmured.

He began to tug at his own clothing. Catherine helped him pull his shirt from the waist of his trousers and then reached for the button above his fly. For no reason she could fathom, unwelcome thoughts of fumbling to disrobe Henri the night the FBI agents burst into the French embassy intruded on their romantic scene like party crashers.

Henri, goddamn it, why do I think of you at a moment like this?

All she yearned for was oblivion. She longed for the haze of pure pleasure that could blot out all reflections on the war, the dangers that surrounded them, even her memories of Henri himself and especially of their last night together, deep in a Scottish glen. As was the case when she'd last made love, she was filled with profound gratitude that she had just finished her period and could not complicate her life any further than it already was by becoming pregnant.

Rousing her from her jumbled thoughts, Sean brushed her hand away from his waist. He kicked off his shoes, undid his pants button himself, and skimmed his trousers, along with his underwear and socks, down his legs, sweeping everything aside with his right foot. Then he reached for Catherine's waist and slid his fingers inside the elastic of her panties, cupping her derriere and pulling the entire length of his body against hers as he slid the scrap of lingerie down her legs to join his own clothes on the floor.

The warmth and urgency she'd felt as their bodies touched limb to limb was the same as when they'd embraced beneath the citadel that afternoon, only this time, she experienced the fullness of his arousal. Delicious sensations flooded through her again, and all she could do was *feel*—feel the sacredness of being alive, feel the soft pile of clothing Sean had thrown on top of the sails before they'd left for dinner.

He drew her down with him when he sank to his knees and then stretched out on the canvas, pulling his coat over their two clinging bodies. Facing him, she threaded one hand through his tousled wine-red hair and, with her other, traced a finger down his nose to his lips, intending to speak to him one last time of his wife, of the twins, of the danger this moment would eventually hold for them. But before she could say a single syllable, Sean seized her wrist, pulled her hand away from his face, and stopped her words with a frenzied kiss, his tongue seeking hers, one palm drifting down to her thigh.

All she found herself capable of doing as a tide of longing swept through her was to bow to the potency of what was taking place between them. As she had so many times in her life, she simply surrendered to the intoxicating desire to absorb the overpowering sensation of a man entering her body, moving rhythmically inside of her, and relishing the moment when Sean's actions told her more than words ever could that, miraculously, they were both alive this night and would live at least one more day. Here was a man, however unsuitable for this time and place, that cared about her and would do everything in his power to keep her safe, as she would do the same for him.

To her great surprise, Catherine's last thoughts before she gave into the full force of a roaring tide of pleasure coursing through every cell of her body was a prayer for Henri's safety. In the exquisite moments of pure sensation produced by Sean's expert and passionate lovemaking, Catherine felt protected from a dangerous world whose existence, at least for the present, was banished to a remote corner of her conscious mind.

CHAPTER 23

"Good news. I've solved your problem."

Henri looked up from his desk at a customer who went by the name of Alain Chapelle. Sandy-haired and only a few years younger than himself, the visitor walked into his small inner office with an order for intake forms requested by a nearby hospital. In truth, the man was one of the fortunate few of Henri's acquaintances in the regional underground of *résistants* with access to a wireless. Alain and the operator of the transistor worked with yet another agent near Compiègnan, seventy-five kilometers north of Paris. Under the guise of placing an order for the nearby hospital, Alain had come to Leblanc Printers to deliver an important message.

He took a seat in Henri's office, which had a large window that overlooked the printing presses and production area.

"A hop farmer outside the village of Estrèes-St.-Denis is not only willing to provide a field for landing RAF planes," he announced, "but also has offered us an array of storage sheds where the metal canisters full of weapons can be hidden beneath tons of grain, as well as a goodly number stashed in a pit filled with pig shit."

Henri expelled a long breath that made obvious his relief at hearing this news.

"Well, there is certainly no possibility of hiding them within Paris city limits—at least not right now," he told Alain. "How long can the farmer keep them?"

"He understands that the weapons might have to remain on his farm until the Allies invade and it's time for action."

"Well, that's a blessing."

Henri made a wry but grateful sign of the cross as Alain continued with his news.

"I told him, though, that if we can, we would certainly want to transport them here to Paris, but…" Alain's words trailed off.

"But, right now, that is totally impossible," Henri finished the sentence. "The SS noose grows tighter each day."

Henri knew that British military planners in London's Whitehall were counting on arming partisans in Paris with these weapons so they could, on a signal, rise up to help drive out the enemy.

That is, if there are any of us left to fight.

The Germans had been putting enormous efforts into tracking down and stamping out pockets of resistance whenever they got wind of them. The way things stood at present, any invasion on French shores was likely to be far in the future, given that March had indeed come in like a lion. They'd be lucky if the planes could even land during the flight operations scheduled to take place near Compiègnan, let alone land undetected.

"There will be two birds," Henri's contact divulged with a sideways glance at the pressman, Alphonse, who was tending to the medium-sized printing press fifty feet from the office where Henri and his visitor conferred. "One will have the gifts you are expecting," he noted, obliquely referring to the six-foot-long, cigar-shaped metal canisters that would be dropped from the plane's bomb bays and filled with everything from weapons to cigarettes. "The second, a Lysander, will ferry a couple of Joes back to London for consultation, while dropping off a pair of new SOE agents to help replace those who've recently been arrested."

Henri stared thoughtfully out the window of his office at Alain's uncle, Alphonse, who had stopped the press. His grizzled head was bent over examining the color separation on a curfew poster the local German *Kommandant* had ordered them to print. Henri wondered what Alain's reaction was if he had seen the new billboard—*WARNING! NO CITIZEN SHALL BE ON PUBLIC STREETS AFTER 11 P.M.!*—when he walked through the production area.

Turning out five hundred copies to be distributed all over Paris by *Kommandant* Heinrich's minions was the price Henri and his network had to pay to keep Resistance efforts alive and secret. He had explained this to Alain on his last visit, but he'd been aware of the whispers among others in their circle that he, Henri, with his former Vichy connections, might indeed be a double agent.

Henri glanced over at the 1943 calendar on his wall that Leblanc Printing had produced and hawked to all likely clients at the start of the year. One specific square on the page for March declared that the full moon would be on the twenty-second, in three weeks' time. As leader of SOE's secret "Pinwheel" network, Henri still had to recruit a small army of *résistants* willing to risk all by meeting those planes sometime after 2:00 a.m.

Alain revealed, "One small problem. Not too far from the designated landing field is a group of Nazi-run camps."

"Not the best location for a drop area," Henri noted, unable to hide his frustration. "Who have the Krauts locked up there?"

"Captured resisters, enemy aliens—including some Americans stranded in Paris—along with undocumented refugees, POWs, and others the Germans deemed miscreants," Alain said with disgust. "But at least the garrison there has only a small contingent of guards."

Henri sighed. "It sounds risky, but our choices are nil. Storing the weapons outside of Paris is the only solution right now. The main reason I haven't been arrested is my company's printing those curfew posters that you probably saw as you came in."

Alain's speculative look expressed without words that he thought Henri might indeed be simultaneously working for the Resistance *and* the occupiers. Henri didn't blame the man for his doubts. How many times lately had he suspected other supposed *résistants* might be double dealers? There were times when "trust no one" would simply mean the end of French Resistance. Hence, he would have to trust the man appearing in his office today, and Alain would have to trust him. At least for now.

Elbows on his desk, Henri steepled his fingers and said, "Please tell the farmer that we're grateful to him and will do our best to move the goods on as soon as we can."

"*D'accord.*"

Henri cocked his head to one side as a disturbing notion struck him.

"Can you explain the choice of the landing zone so near those German installations, other than that the farmer is willing to host them on his property? Who chose the field?"

"The hop farmer's field is definitely a bold choice," Alain agreed, "but supposedly a good one, according to the agent that arranged all this. His thought is that it's the last place the *Bosches* would expect to be used for something like this."

"Do you agree with this thinking? Airplanes flying overhead at three hundred feet to parachute cargo give plenty of notice to the enemy, don't they?"

Alain shrugged again. "Like you, Gilbert said there's not much choice."

"Well," Henri said, "I have a bad feeling in my gut about this, but it's one of those situations where we're forced to accept the hand we've been dealt." He nodded final acquiescence to the plan, signaling that the agent was free to adjourn the meeting. "Thank you for coming," Henri added, confirming that he would join Alain at the field on the evening of March 22.

Alain stood, poised to depart, adding, "A cadre of men have already been recruited to create a flare path at the landing field. They'll be armed with pocket torches to guide in the planes and then haul the containers to their designated bolt holes."

"Another blessing," murmured Henri.

"Oh," the agent said, turning around, "and by the way, this Gilbert fellow's recently been made the Air Movement Officer for F Section, coordinating flights back and forth for SOE agents, along with his deputy, Andrè Marsac."

"So, Gilbert is the agent who picked this landing spot?" Henri asked.

"Yes," answered Alain with no further elaboration.

"Do others in our network know these two men?"

"I've worked with André Marsac, who coordinates a lot with Gilbert these days. Marsac seems fine. Gilbert supposedly is a close friend of the few leaders of the Prosper network who have managed to escape arrest. Someone said he once flew for Air Bleu and is a former circus stunt pilot."

"Not flying for the RAF, but coordinating from the ground?" Henri commented.

Alain merely nodded. Meanwhile, Henri's mind raced back to a black-tiled bathroom at Orchard House in London. Didn't that leering Frenchman that he and Catherine had met before their interviews with Maurice Buckmaster say he'd once flown for Air Bleu? The bastard's stare had practically stripped Catherine of her clothing that day when the three sat on the rim of that black tub in the bathroom waiting room. Leblanc couldn't for the life of him remember the man's last name, but he was instantly suspicious of anyone in the Prosper group who was still at large. No one knew who had betrayed scores of arrested SOE agents in that large Resistance network the previous year.

"I'd like to know a bit more about this Gilbert character."

"Well, he's tall, dark, and handsome, so all the ladies like him," noted Alain, with the first grin Henri had ever seen on his face. "The only other thing I heard is that he was a French air force test pilot in Syria before it was overrun by the Allies," Alain replied. "Somehow, he made his way from North Africa, through France, to Glasgow and volunteered in London for the SOE."

Ah. Henri suddenly knew exactly who Gilbert really was.

So, Lucien Barteau, the former pilot for Air Bleu, had been given the code name Gilbert and was now in charge of all air operations for SOE agents in France? In front of the departing Alain, Henri did his best to mask his growing sense of dismay. He wondered why a man like Lucien Barteau, with such a sketchy background, had passed muster with Buckmaster and the other higher-ups for such an important job that made him privy to the travel schedules of secret agents in and out of France.

To confirm what he'd just heard from Alain, Henri asked, "This Gilbert fellow went from Syria all the way to Scotland without getting caught?"

Henri paused a moment, reflecting the same suspicions of double-dealing that could be—and *were*—made about his own service with the Vichy diplomatic corps. Just because Lucien Gilbert's leering at Catherine rubbed Henri the wrong way, he shouldn't condemn the man out of hand until he had a chance to see him in action on March 22.

Meanwhile, he offered a wave to his departing visitor, saying by way of farewell, "Oh, well, you know Buckmaster's French Section. They grab who they can get, and this Gilbert fellow seems to know a lot about airplanes."

Alain Chapelle offered a noncommittal nod and turned to take his leave. After the door to the inner office closed, Henri sank back in his chair and closed his eyes. He was aware of the rhythmic thrum of the printing press that had started up once more, vibrating the very desk at which he sat.

Whoosh, whoosh, whoosh...

In rapid succession, the Nazi paper broadsides slid out of the mammoth machine outside his door. It felt to the exhausted leader of this covert, basement-based operation as if he were dancing on the edge of a knife. Whichever way he might fall, he feared grievous harm would result.

Was grievous harm the fate that had befallen Catherine, working somewhere in France as Colette Durand? Despite the discreet inquiries Henri had made through various channels, he had heard not a single word about one of the few female American agents that Britain had sent behind enemy lines.

Perhaps a man like Agent Gilbert who supervised the comings and goings of SOE operatives all over France had heard of her whereabouts?

That's just one of several questions I'd like to ask that man.

———◇———

"Sean, you've been on that wireless more than fifteen minutes!" Catherine declared, pointing to her watch. "Close it down, will you?" she added, her tone laced with concern. "Remy told me he'd seen the SS triangulation van cruising past his restaurant a few days ago. They could be trying to home in on you and—"

"Done!" Sean declared, turning several knobs sharply to his left before jumping from his chair situated by the window. He swiftly began to roll up the antenna draped along the roofline that overlooked the harbor. "Wait till you hear!"

"What?" she demanded, making a grab for the leather wireless case he handed her and preparing to stash it below a set of floorboards they had pried up to hide the set out of sight.

"We're getting a new big boss. His code name is Roger, and he's being put down by Lysander somewhere near Compiègne outside Paris the next full moon."

Catherine was well aware that the safest—and yet also most treacherous—time for RAF planes to operate in France was when the landing field was naturally illuminated. But a bright moon also made it easier for the enemy to spot infiltrators and especially parachutists descending from the heavens.

"March twenty-second and twenty-third is the total full moon," she murmured, "but even if he lands safely, how is he going to make his way down from Compiègne here to the South of France?"

"Trains are still running sporadically from Paris's Gare de Lyon to Marseille. The big news is that the RAF is landing Lysanders now instead of parachuting in all the new agents or paddling them ashore from fishing boats, like your arrival."

"Fewer broken bones or drownings that way," she noted with a wry smile. "How lucky is *that* for those new SOE agents?"

She thought back to Viv's horror of flinging herself out of an airplane, to say nothing of the rough eight days on the fishing boat she'd spent with Odette Samson, getting from Gibraltar to the Côte d'Azur.

"Not so lucky if the wrong people hear the plane's approach in time to greet them when they land," Sean noted.

"You are so right," she agreed.

She rose from having knelt on the floor to stow the wireless equipment and regarded Sean for a long moment without speaking. Now was the moment to bring up a subject that had been nagging at her even before the word had arrived that a new leader would be assigned for the two of them. She pointed to the small table where they had their meals when not dining at Remy's restaurant.

"Sit, won't you?" she directed Sean. "Given that things are about to change around here, I think we need to discuss something."

Sean took a seat opposite her, a wary expression having replaced his usual cheery demeanor.

"What?" He then shook his head as if to answer his own question. "I know, I know. You think we've made our cover story all too real posing as man and wife, and now we have a new boss to explain that to."

"You're as smart as I always thought you were," she replied.

"And you think, with Roger What's-it coming, we have to—"

"Yes, we do," she confirmed. "We have to return just to being two agents, working together and doing it according to SOE rules. And besides, Sean, you conveniently keep forgetting we are both married to other people. If we both manage, somehow, to survive this war, you know as well as I do that we will eventually each go our own way and return to whatever is supposed to be our normal lives."

Catherine wondered silently if there ever was, or ever would be, a normal life in her future. She truly cared for Sean, but their new leader's arrival was a clear sign that the physical liaison between the two of them should come to an end. As fond as she was of Sean, she'd already decided that she could never envision a long-term relationship with the charming Mr. Eisenhower. Truth be told, Sean often felt more like a brother to her than a lover, however skilled in that department he'd turned out to be.

She held no illusions. She might never see Henri Leblanc again, but all the while she'd been with Sean, the Frenchman who'd helped her steal and copy the Vichy naval codes had never left her thoughts—and that told her something she could no longer ignore. With Sean she felt...well, she admitted silently, having sex with Sean made her feel slightly tarnished. Like a person who was merely using another human being to blot out the world.

Sean's next words abruptly pulled her thoughts back to the sailmaker's loft. He seized her hand and held on to it tightly.

"I know what you're also thinking," he said, seeking her gaze. "That we've broken all the rules and we should—"

"Go back to the way we were in Cannes," she interrupted, her steady look brooking no argument. "Yes, that's exactly what I was thinking."

"But what if I've fallen in love?" he protested. "I mean, *really* fallen in love with you?"

"Well…" she replied quietly, realizing he meant every word of his confession, "I'm afraid you'll just have to fall *out* of love. We have to go back to just being two partners seeking landing fields above Villefranche for supplies and finding places to stockpile them with the farmers in these hills. We both know that neither of us should have been risking what we've been risking. We're just damned lucky we haven't tripped up yet."

And that I didn't get pregnant…

Raising their clasped fingers, she leaned forward and kissed his hand.

"No one else could ever understand what you and I have gone through since the day you met me at the train station and led our landing group to Cannes."

"Or the day you got bitten by the bees when you stowed the grenades in the hives?" he murmured.

They smiled at each other across the table. Then Catherine's expression grew somber once more. "We've had so many close calls, and it's only going to get worse. And now, here, working together, evading danger at every turn, we have to be extra vigilant not to get caught." She squeezed his hands between her own, willing him to understand the peril they were in. "The more we know about each other and care for each other, the easier it will be to torture one of us for information that could bring down our entire Trenches network, just like the Prosper and Peter Churchill's Spindle circuits were betrayed." She released his hands. "Continuing as lovers as we have been is simply not possible or prudent anymore, and we both know it."

"How about just being part-time lovers?" he said, his stricken look slowly morphing into a sly grin.

She reached up and ran her forefinger along the side of his stubbled cheek. "We are friends forever, Sean. But from now on, just friends. And it's absolutely crucial for both of us, and for everybody else's safety, that we hold true to that."

CHAPTER 24

On March 22, Henri Leblanc and Alain Chapelle arrived from Paris close to midnight. The full moon had risen high in the cold night sky above the farmer's field outside the village of Estrèes-St.-Denis. Headlights off, Alain nosed his dented black coal-converted Citroën off the dirt track and parked it on the other side of a hedge, where it almost appeared to be part of the landscape. The pair got out of the car, their boots sinking into the loamy soil of harvested hop field, and tramped past a large, flatbed wagon with a plow-horse harnessed to it. Two of the operation's "reception committee" stood in shadow under a cluster of trees off to one side from the designated landing area.

To the right, three unlit pocket torches mounted on tall sticks had been laid out in the shape of an *L* over a distance of 150 meters to guide the plane. A trio of men recruited from the local village appeared at the ready to turn on the torches as soon as the hum of a plane engine was detected. An additional two men stood off to one side, clad in street clothes, dressed for their return flight to London.

A tall, well-built man with dark, wavy hair emerged into the silvery moonlight, along with his deputy, André Marsac. Alain introduced Henri by his code name Claude to Gilbert. A moment after they'd shaken hands, Gilbert registered a startled look of recognition, followed by a simple nod of greeting. Henri felt his own sharp intake of breath as he silently confirmed that Air Operations Officer Gilbert, late of Air Bleu, was indeed the same Lucien Barteau whom Henri had met so briefly in the odd bath-chamber-cum-waiting room prior to their individual Special Operations Executive interviews in London.

Whatever my opinion of the man, I have to say he's done an excellent job tonight organizing the drop.

Marsac waved at the two men in civilian attire to come closer and declared, "A pair of new Joes will disembark the first plane, making room for you two gentlemen to grab your suitcases and quickly board the Lysander for the return trip to London."

Henri surmised that one of the two departing agents, addressed as Raoul, was clearly not a native Frenchman, but spoke French well enough. Before he could determine what seemed so familiar to Henri about this man, too, Alain disclosed to the departing agents that Henri was based in Paris but was assigned to the night's operation to stow parachuted supplies dropped from the second scheduled aircraft.

Henri informed the group, "The goods will have to be hidden locally until safe storage can be found within the city's limits. SS are on every corner in Paris these days."

Agent Raoul turned toward Henri and asked in terse tones, "Aren't you the man who parachuted into France with me on my last trip? You were formerly with the Vichy diplomatic corps in Washington, D.C., yes?" Before Henri could respond, Raoul added, "I met a lady friend of yours recently who seemed very interested to know if you'd made it safely to France." He cast Henri a steady gaze. "I told her yes."

Henri gave silent thanks that the night's gloom disguised his shock. It had been startling enough to encounter Barteau—known now as Gilbert—once again. But what an amazing coincidence to cross paths with a second agent he'd met before, Peter Churchill, code name Raoul. The fact that Churchill had crossed paths with Catherine recently was a blessing beyond belief.

He remembered only too well the harrowing flight with his fellow SOE agent across the Channel, their pilot dodging tracer fire nearly every mile of the trip. The name *P. Churchill* had been embroidered on the man's uniform when they'd first met in the canteen in Sussex before they'd donned their approved French attire worn under their flight suits and parachute packs. The Brit's attitude toward him that night had bordered on rude, as if a Frenchman of any stripe could not be trusted as an Allied secret agent, given the rout that the French army endured during Germany's initial invasion of their country.

In this moonlit field, Henri wanted nothing so much as to pepper Peter Churchill with a barrage of questions about Catherine, but he merely replied, "Who could forget bailing out of our plane with that wind dragging us off course?"

Fortunately, that night, he and Churchill had both landed safety and had been met on the ground by a dogged gaggle of local *résistants*. Their reception committee had quickly located them a half mile away from the target area and helped them bury their parachutes.

Churchill reminded Henri, "You were spirited away in a farm truck as I remember."

"To Paris, as it turned out," Henri said. "I had no idea where you were being escorted."

"That's as it should be," the Brit replied curtly.

The man's attitude was just as offensive as ever, Henri thought. Determined not to show he took umbrage, he summoned a pleasant tone of voice.

"And now, here you are, on your way back to Britain."

"For meetings," was Churchill's terse reply. "I'll be back in France soon."

The astonishing fact that Peter Churchill had encountered a woman who could only be Catherine Thornton continued to send Henri's mind reeling. To gain a moment to think, he extended his hand to Churchill's companion, a man by the name of Frager.

Turning to face Peter once again, he asked casually, "This woman you mentioned. I'm trying to place her. Was she an American? Slender? Auburn hair?"

"And absolutely beautiful?" cut in Churchill. "Yes. I suppose I shouldn't tell you this, but she appeared worried and concerned about you."

"Where did you meet her? In Britain or in France?"

"I shouldn't tell you that either, but it was in Cannes. She was one of my couriers before the Spindle network down there was betrayed."

Alain broke in, his voice laced with anger. "Some double-dealing swine left all those names on the train, right? Lucky you and Lise got out of there alive, Raoul."

Catherine had been part of Spindle? Oh God, what if...

Churchill nodded. "I took most of the surviving group to Lake Annecy in the Alps, but I dispatched the Americans—my former courier and a wireless operator—further east along the Côte d'Azur. They're doing good work there, organizing supply drops and greeting new agents, just like you're doing here."

Catherine is alive and operating in the South of France!

Henri had to look down at his boots to mask the flood of relief he was certain would be obvious to all, even in the dim moonlight bathing the hop field.

Just then, Agent Gilbert pointed skyward. "Shush! Do you hear that? That's a Lysander engine." He turned on his giant flashlight and signaled to his cohorts to turn on theirs to illuminate the landing area. "All right, everyone," said the self-assured Air Operations officer to the group that clustered more closely around him. "We have exactly two minutes, once the plane rolls to a stop, to unload the passengers and get you two men"—indicating with a toss of his head toward Churchill and his companion—"off, off and away. The second plane will be right behind, dropping fifteen cargo canisters by parachute." To Henri and Alain he said, "Marsac and the torch men will remain to help you load the canisters onto that farmer's wagon over there. Then you all are to go unload the supplies in the pit at the pig barn."

By this time, the engine's roar sounded positively deafening to Henri, its sounds filling him with gut-wrenching apprehension. He wondered exactly how far away the Germans were that Alain had mentioned were bivouacked at a camp nearby.

To Henri's relief, Gilbert's organization of the landing and reception went flawlessly. In less than two minutes, the arriving pair of men, along with their luggage, swiftly exited the thirty-foot-long Lysander. Its engines still running, Churchill and Frager jumped aboard, pulling their battered leather suitcases in behind them. In seconds, even as the plane's side door was being fastened shut, it rolled down the dirt runway and headed for the moonlit skies.

Amidst the roaring noise, Henri nodded welcome to the arriving passengers as Alain leaned near his ear and said, "Marsac tells me we'll be driving those Joes back to Paris with us. Let's ask them to help us load the gear."

Without waiting for Henri's reply, Alain approached the two men and shook hands. After a brief conversation, both newcomers indicated their willingness to help out with the arriving supplies that were already floating down from the heavens as the second plane slowly passed overhead. From Henri's vantage point on the ground, the fifteen parachutes looked like oversized white mushrooms, buffeted by the wind until they collapsed in heaps of white silk onto the mowed hop field.

The next twenty minutes were the longest of Henri's life. One by one, the heavy canisters full of weapons, ammunition, and some special requests for clothing, cigarettes, and food were dragged to a large, wheeled wooden flatbed cart. The horse harnessed to the wagon stood ready to pull the cargo to the local farmer's pig barn a half mile away. Once the goods were on board, Marsac's crew frantically buried piles of telltale parachutes in a pre-dug mass grave and smoothed out the topsoil as best they could to make it look like a normal part of the landscape.

Then, without warning, headlights at some distance down the valley blinked like earthbound twinkling stars. Sounds, both of automobiles and of motorcycles, rent the air as a caravan of unexpected visitors toiled at a fast pace from the hillside below.

It's the Germans from those nearby camps! They heard the planes' engines!

Henri felt his heart go cold and turned to see members of the reception committee stash the last of the shovels onto the cart and then scamper on top of hay bales now camouflaging the cargo.

"Go, go, go!" Henri shouted to the cart's driver.

"Yes," shouted Gilbert, running toward the wagon. He yelled over his shoulder, "Quickly! Into the car, everyone else! Marsac! Alain! Follow on as fast as you can," the Air Operations officer commanded, pointing at Henri and his group. "Try to make the turn into the farm behind the wagon before the blasted *Bosches* see you and catch up. Help the others unload. I'll head in the other direction on foot, down the back side of this plateau."

Henri, Alain, and the newly arrived agents made a dash for Alain's car parked beyond the trees near the road. Gilbert sprinted across the plowed field like an Olympian distance runner and disappeared over the ridge. Henri could only wonder if the Germans at the nearby installation were light sleepers and had awakened, en masse, when the planes flew overhead—or had been tipped off by someone to mobilize as soon as they heard the roaring sound of engines.

The two arriving agents from England piled into the backseat of Alain's ancient automobile—retrofitted with a coal-gas-powered apparatus mounted on the roof to work around the petrol shortage. With Henri's deputy Alain at the wheel and the agents' luggage stored beneath their feet, the vehicle chugged slowly in the wake of the horse-drawn wagon. Henri swiveled his head, catching a good view of headlights fast approaching the summit of the hill.

"Do not drive down the road to the farm," Henri shouted in Alain's ear, his jaw clenched. "Just continue straight on!"

"But the canisters—" protested Marsac, sitting to Henri's right in the front seat.

"That's an order!" Henri commanded.

He had been feeling the same sharp pangs of uneasiness that he'd experienced when walking into Café La Croissant the day he killed the German.

Alain's knuckles were white as he gripped the steering wheel, and the old Citroën slowly gathered speed. He shot a startled glance at Henri who was squeezed in the middle of the front seat next to Gilbert's deputy, Marsac. Much to Henri's relief, his driver did as he'd been charged and didn't make the turn.

"Gilbert won't like this," Marsac warned.

"*Tant pis,*" Henri said tersely. *Too bad for Gilbert, the swine*, he silently cursed. He made a grim calculation of what was about to descend on the poor pig farmer, along with anyone caught in the vicinity by the squadron of Germans roaring up the hill.

As directed, the driver of the vintage contraption sped past the narrow road on their right and continued straight on toward Paris.

———◇———

The skies over the City of Light were muted gray. Blackout curtains eliminated virtually all illumination on the ground. By the time Alain's aged Citroën lumbered through the gloomy outskirts of Neuilly-sur-Seine and approached the checkpoint guarding access to the Champs-Élysees, Henri had decided on a plan. He glanced out the front windshield at the vast wooded area of the Bois de Boulogne and directed Alain, "Pull into that side road over there."

Sitting next to Henri, Marsac—agent Gilbert's second-in-command—wasn't happy. He'd continued to protest loudly when Henri countermanded the order from the Air Operations Officer to follow the weapons drop to the farm. After hours squeezed in the car, Marsac grew more disgruntled.

"Oh, for God's sake! We've been up all night. And besides, Gilbert supplied me with a doctor's pass that'll get us through any checkpoint if we're stopped. I want to get to my bed."

"And beds in prison for the rest of us, is that it?" Henri shot back. "Your doctor's pass may be fine for *you*, Marsac, but how do you propose to explain the presence of these fellows?" he demanded, indicating the exhausted agents dozing in the back seat.

"By this hour, the Krauts will be wanting their breakfast and probably won't even be on duty. They're such lazy swine."

Henri countered sharply, "But if they *are* there, they'll demand to see all of our local ration cards and updated identification needed here in Paris, documents which these men don't yet have, and—"

"All right, all right!" groused Marsac. "Have it your way. We'll wait someplace till curfew lifts."

Ignoring the two men bickering next to him, Alain had pulled into a wooded area and parked out of sight of the main road. Henri spoke over his shoulder to the recent arrivals, awakened by the argument with Marsac.

"I don't know about you two back there, but I need a piss. Marsac, please open the door."

With a grunt, Marsac complied and stomped off into a stand of trees. Henri, beckoning to the agent whose code name he'd learned was Roger, said, "Let's walk this way," indicating they should head in a different direction.

While the two men relieved themselves against a tree some fifty yards from Marsac, who was doing likewise, Henri spoke in a low voice.

"I can put you two up for the night at my place and get your local papers organized. Marsac may offer you the same, but I suggest that perhaps my document forger is more expert than his."

What Henri didn't say was that Marsac's casual disregard for the safety of his passengers by trying to pass back into Paris before curfew was lifted struck him as beyond curious. Even more disturbing had been the appearance, as if on cue, of a troop of Germans at their landing field. Both events this night had all the signs that the entire situation had been set up as a trap. Marsac, with his doctor's pass, could well have passed muster at the checkpoint, leaving the rest of them to face arrest—or worse.

Roger zipped up his trouser fly and cast Henri a speculative look.

"So, is it true that you were part of the Vichy diplomatic corps in Washington before joining the SOE?"

Henri wondered if every SOE member had access to his private files in Buckmaster's office before they were sent to France.

"I was a diplomat long before the Vichy took over," was Henri's terse reply, "and I flew for France alongside of Britain in the last war. Was that mentioned in my dossier as well?"

Roger paused and then replied, "Even so, you worked a couple of years for the enemy. Why should I believe that you're looking out for my safety any better than Marsac?"

Heavy exhaustion, thick as cement, settled into Henri's bones. After dealing with Peter Churchill's unwarranted antipathy, he was feeling utterly drained by yet another Brit's assumed skepticism and annoying air of superiority. With his frayed temper barely in check, he answered Roger's question in even tones.

"Would you like to know why you should trust me? Because something wasn't right about those Germans suddenly storming up the hill last night." Henri knew he should remain unruffled, but Roger's insinuations had hit their mark. "You should trust me because Marsac's doctor's pass would protect him at the checkpoint when a curfew is still in place, but mine wouldn't, and your lack of current, locally issued documents could get you shot on the spot."

Roger looked away and remained silent.

Henri paused, his gaze narrowing. "And you should probably trust me because I helped the Allies in Washington in ways significant enough that they recruited me to join SOE. But, Roger, old bean," he said, switching to English with a phony, clipped accent, "do whatever you damn please!"

He turned on his heel and walked back toward the car, pulling from his pocket one of his preciously saved cigarettes and lit up. Marsac, standing twenty-five yards away, was also having a smoke.

After a few calming puffs, Henri leaned in the car window to speak to Alain.

"Are you good with leaving the car in Neuilly? We can walk to the Les Sablons metro and get into the city from there."

Alain nodded, as he and Henri had often thought that this was the safest procedure when they had to go in and out of Paris on various missions. By this time, Roger had caught up with Henri, his hand on the back door poised to get into the car.

Marsac was within earshot when Alain announced, "End of the line, boys."

"What?" protested Gilbert's deputy.

Henri said with a shrug, "You can use your doctor's pass to cross the checkpoint on foot. It's always safer for Alain to leave his car with some trusted people outside the city proper. He and I are happy to escort our new friends into Paris by metro to avoid risking a checkpoint without their proper papers."

"There might be soldiers in the metro," challenged Marsac, clearly annoyed by Henri's taking charge. "Gilbert told me to escort them to the train."

"But with the morning crowds, we'll have a better chance of not being stopped. You can meet them later and guide them to the station."

"But Gilbert said—"

"Change of plans," Henri cut in. To Roger he offered, "However, if you two prefer to go with Marsac, feel free. Curfew's almost ended."

Roger didn't even consult the other agent before replying, "No. It would seem best we come with you."

CHAPTER 25

Henri entered his inner office, patting his damp face with a small towel. He'd spent the last half hour having a shower and shaving in the owner's bathroom off the press room, a luxury that had once been reserved for his late father. He couldn't stop thinking about the local men at the makeshift airfield to whom he'd never even been introduced before the Lysander landed. Perhaps, by some miracle, those members of the reception committee had somehow been able to hide the cart loaded with the night's haul of weapons and disperse before the Germans arrived. All he could do was hope.

Huddled around Henri's desk, the two newest SOE agents were being handed their required ration cards and travel passes that Henri's expert forger, Jean-Paul Roland, had produced on short notice. Without the brilliance of Jean-Paul's handiwork creating papers that included the unusual quirks and variable shades of ink used by local authorities, Agent Roger and his cohort could very easily be apprehended at the first checkpoint they crossed.

Henri draped his face towel on the arm of his chair and said to his guests, "These papers should get you past the officials at the Gare de Lyon when you board the train for Annecy. With any luck, they'll also stand up to scrutiny when you cross into the former Free Zone, which, as you've undoubtedly heard, is now swarming with Germans."

Roger stored his documents in his inside jacket pocket, giving a nod of thanks both to the forger and his host. Henri turned to address the member of the Resistance in Paris whom he considered the best documents forger to be found in all of France.

"Jean-Paul, thank you once again," Henri said as Roland picked up his leather message bag filled with the tools of his trade and prepared to take his leave.

The forger merely inclined his head and exited the printing establishment through a door that led to a back alley. Henri motioned his visitors to take seats opposite his at his desk and sat in his chair. Alphonse and his co-workers weren't due to start up the presses for another hour, but Henri felt an urgency to speed the new agents safely on their way.

"Did Marsac say where you would meet today so he can guide you to the train station?" he asked.

"Lunchtime on the Pont Neuf, wherever that is," replied Roger.

Henri suppressed a sigh. It was only nine o'clock. "Well, I'd best take you where you can wait for him, hopefully out of harm's way."

From what Henri had witnessed, the security precautions of Gilbert and Marsac were shockingly lax. Marsac should never have been assigned the job of seeing these men safely to their train. Gilbert's deputy could have been apprehended at the checkpoint or even followed by the SS from the minute he entered Paris. Then where would these poor novice agents end up?

But all Henri said to the men was, "It's early. I can't let you stay here because my staff will be here soon, and customers come and go all day. We can try to find some decent coffee on the way and a place for you to wait where you won't attract attention."

"Will there be problems on the train now that the Germans have moved south to occupy the former Free Zone?" asked Roger.

"There are always problems traveling on the train," Henri replied, "especially at crossing points near various cities as you head toward the Riviera. Best thing you can do is each of you ignore the other from the moment you enter the train station."

Roger exchanged looks with the other agent and nodded in agreement. Henri considered his next words carefully.

"Roger, I have a concern that perhaps you can answer." He paused and then decided to risk it. "I've heard that Gilbert has told other agents that your assignment is to set up a new network south of Vichy, perhaps in the southeast region of the country. Jockey, I understand it's to be called. I would have thought there were good reasons not to spread around that sort of intelligence, given the disastrous demise of the Prosper, Carte, and Spindle One, Peter Churchill's old Cannes network."

Roger's expression grew stern. "Good God, you heard all that? Haven't agents here learned anything?" he demanded. "Too damn many people have been told about each other's operations."

"I couldn't agree more," Henri replied. "That's why I raised it."

And when one is caught, all are caught, he thought to himself.

Roger's lips had settled into a thin line, "Well, I fully intend to compartmentalize my work here. As one example, once I head south, I doubt you and I will meet again."

"That is how I operate as well," Henri replied coolly, "but by necessity, like today, occasionally there are circumstances when one has to coordinate." Henri glanced at his watch. "I think it's time we left."

Henri worried that Alphonse might take it upon himself to come to work early to proof yesterday's production run of the billboards due to be delivered to *Kommandant* Heinrich later that day. It was safer for all if no one but the forger knew what Henri had been engaged in these last eighteen hours.

Agent Roger and his fellow traveler donned their coats and picked up their suitcases. As they passed by a long table positioned near the printing press, Roger pointed to a stack of posters, each stamped with a swastika.

"You print broadsides for the Germans?" he asked, arching a brow.

"I do indeed," Henri replied, "and with the full knowledge and endorsement of Buckmaster," he added pointedly. "It's proved quite a good cover story so far, and I learn a lot I can pass on to London."

"Wheels-within-wheels," Roger murmured.

"And it's quite exhausting to keep them spinning, I assure you. We must go."

Within ten minutes, Henri and the two men had taken the metro at Opéra near the Louvre to a café known by Henri to be sympathetic to their cause. There, they sipped coffee made primarily from acorns, along with a thin slice of toasted bread—but no butter. The majority of the food in Paris went to the Germans or the black market.

Henri took a sip of the bitter brew. Out the window was the Pont Neuf, a low-lying bridge that connected the Right Bank with the Ile de la Cité. By the time they'd had their abbreviated breakfast, Roger seemingly had come to better appreciate the serious risks Henri had taken not only to provide his charges food, forged documents, and cash, but also to serve as escort in broad daylight for two young men that authorities might well consider draft dodgers.

By their second cup, Roger and Henri had established a rapport that allowed for quiet conversation in a secluded corner. After their waiter left them, Roger said in a low voice, "Have you heard? The Germans have begun a withdrawal from Tunisia."

Henri brightened. "Wonderful news! We rarely know about such things unless we dare listen to the BBC on the wireless—which is now against the law."

"Yes, it's very good news, because we're apparently bashing the hell out of the German Navy in the Mediterranean." Roger cracked a thin smile. "Next stop, an invasion of the Riviera, let us pray."

For a moment, Henri's mind whirled with memories of stealthily handing the book of Vichy naval codes out the window at the D.C. embassy, to be copied and returned to the safe with no one the wiser. The codes most probably had proved very useful in knowing where the German and Vichy French naval ships were operating in the Med. His spirits rose at the notion that his and Catherine's act of bravery might truly be helping the Allies win this war.

Roger's next words extinguished Henri's brief flirtation with optimism.

"You also may not have heard that, last week, twenty-seven merchant ships were sunk by German U-boats in the Atlantic."

"Good God, twenty-seven?"

"Terrible, isn't it?" Roger agreed. "So, let us also pray we kick the bastards out of North Africa so we can attack Italy and make our way to the South of France."

Before Henri's musings began to spiral down at the thought of what a full-on invasion meant to SOE agents on the Riviera, he checked his watch.

"I really should get back to the shop." Henri pointed out the window. "If, for some reason, Marsac doesn't show up at noon, wait inside here another half hour and then go out the back door of the café and walk to the Les Halles metro." He pulled out a small map from his pocket and pointed. "Take it to Gare de Lyon. They'll ask you for your documents when you purchase your tickets and also when you board the coach car," he advised, "so be ready with your papers and act as if you know the routine. With any luck, your train for Annecy leaves at three."

Henri swiftly folded the map, rose from his chair, and in a loud voice for the benefit of any eavesdroppers said, "Great to see you again, Roger. Let's try to meet here next week, yes? I can bring your printing job to you then, as the paper I ordered for it is due to be delivered to my shop tomorrow. At least let us hope so."

Roger nodded, as did his companion. "Many thanks, Claude," he said, waving his folded newspaper.

Henri murmured, "*Au revoir*, and best of luck to you both."

———◇———

It was the first of April, April Fools' Day as Sean noted wryly to Catherine. A wireless message was received that day that had instructed the two agents to ride separately into Cannes to rendezvous with their immediate superior, Pierre Berthone. The twenty-four kilometers from Villefranche seemed endless as Catherine pedaled against a stiff wind blowing off the sea. Her legs ached as she dismounted and secured her bicycle out of sight behind some oversized rubbish bins, before venturing into the train station.

She quickly spotted Pierre standing near a news kiosk a hundred paces from the entrance. Passengers scurried to and fro beneath a glass-and-iron ceiling that soared eighty feet above their heads. Only recently assigned to oversee their small Trenches network operating primarily in Nice and Villefranche, Pierre, in turn, was to report to the new leader of Jockey, the elusive Agent Roger of whom they'd heard but none had met. The Trenches group knew only that Roger had first gone to the lakeside town of Annecy, in the Alps, and then had come further south to select a base of operations in the eight departments of the southeastern section of France. Today, at long last, Roger was due to arrive in Cannes.

According to plan, Sean had left Villefranche for their shared destination ten minutes after Catherine had pushed off on her bike. Each minute that ticked by as she waited for him tied a bigger knot in her stomach. Then, suddenly, she felt a tap on her shoulder. When she turned around, Sean pulled her to him and kissed her soundly on the mouth, apparently relishing playing the role of besotted husband.

"So lovely you could meet me at the train, darling."

Catherine had kept to her determination that they live only as roommates, and thus Sean took advantage of a public display of affection whenever he thought he could get away with it.

Their plan had been for him to stow his bicycle at the back of a café whose owner they trusted and then for the two of them to play husband and wife once again as they sauntered in the direction of Pierre.

"Let's hope Roger's train isn't five hours late," Sean mused.

At the news kiosk, Pierre Berthone was pretending to be absorbed in a German-authorized French newspaper when the couple exclaimed loudly how surprised and pleased they were to see their "old friend from their school days" as they declaimed for anyone in the vicinity listening.

Under his breath, Pierre said, "The train will be here momentarily.

Thank God you've arrived. I've got to make myself scarce. I think I was followed, but I shook them off about four blocks ago. The authorities are really clamping down here in Cannes and Nice. Take Roger in hand when he gets here, will you? Tell him I'll meet you all in Villefranche in a day or two."

As Pierre turned to go, Catherine asked, keeping her voice low, "What does this Roger look like?"

"Tall. Sloping shoulders," Berthone whispered hurriedly. "Actually, he's a dead-ringer for de Gaulle," and in a flash, he disappeared into the crowd.

Catherine demanded crossly of Sean, "And just how are we supposed to take Roger in hand with no transportation *at hand*? Give him my bicycle so I can walk all the way back to Villefranche?"

Sean soothed, "I know. French planning sometimes leaves a lot to be desired."

Meanwhile, the passengers from the arriving train were surging down the platform in their direction. Catherine was first to notice a man over six feet tall, Nordic in appearance, his head above the rest of the crowd. She elbowed Sean at the sight of the man's sloping shoulders and a profile that did indeed resemble the looks of the Free French leader living safely in London.

"The Brit does look like de Gaulle," Sean whispered in Catherine's ear.

Nodding her agreement, she stepped forward, raising her arm to Agent Roger with a friendly wave as if she'd known him for ages.

"Hello! Hello!" she called gaily in French as fellow travelers passed them by. "So glad to see you again!"

Fortunately for Sean, Catherine, and their newly arrived superior, the German soldiers checking identity papers waved the trio through; the three were chatting and laughing with their arms linked as if they were enjoying a grand reunion.

Sean led them to the café in one of the back streets off Cannes's grand promenade where he'd parked his bike. It was the same establishment where Catherine had once had a serious conversation with Peter Churchill concerning Henri Leblanc's whereabouts.

The newly assigned leader of the nascent Jockey and smaller Trenches networks wasted no time in letting them know he would not be traveling with them to Villefranche.

Over a lunch of roasted potatoes and a precious poached egg each, Roger informed them briskly, "After paying a few calls on people here in Cannes, I'll then head north immediately to Montélimar, a much safer location than Nice or Cannes, to create a new network."

Sean agreed. "Our local leader couldn't even stay to meet you here because he thought he was being followed today."

"I'll catch up with Pierre later," Roger said. He reached for his wine glass and took a sip, gazing at them over its rim. "I wanted to meet you both in person to let you know officially that we'll be folding your Trenches network into our operation, but with new and stricter security rules."

Catherine was relieved to hear that, at long last, someone in overall charge was proposing sensible protocols.

Roger continued, "You aren't to know who the new *résistants* are that we'll be recruiting outside the Villefranche area, and *they* will know nothing about your operations. That way, if any of you get caught, you honestly can't betray your fellow resisters." He addressed Sean as he took another sip of wine. "You will continue as wireless operator but never broadcast or receive in the same location twice in a row. The Germans are getting too good at using triangulation technology from those white vans they drive everywhere."

Catherine shot Sean a look of *See? I told you that!*

To her, Roger said, "You will continue as courier between Villefranche and the *résistants* in your immediate area. You will also both carry on serving as the leaders of the reception committee for delivery of arms and supplies parachuted into that field above your village." He paused, shifting his glance from Catherine back to Sean. "In due course, you'll receive orders to blow up the odd bridge or power transformer."

Sean grinned and looked at Catherine. "Now, that sounds fun."

Roger let the remark pass, only adding, "With Allied successes in North Africa, there's been renewed hope for a Mediterranean-launched landing on the Riviera."

"How soon?" asked Catherine, thrilled to hear some encouraging news amidst so many reports of agents and Resistance members apprehended, tortured, and killed in prisons in France and Germany.

"Ah. When. That's the key question, isn't it?" Roger said. "The timing is up to Churchill and your FDR, I imagine."

He then changed the subject with a casualness directed at Catherine that immediately alerted her antenna. "When I landed earlier this month, a friend of yours, Colette, was part of the reception committee that greeted our Lysander. A Frenchman, code name Claude. Do you recall him?"

Catherine frowned, looking at Roger blankly.

"Claude? I…don't know anyone by that name."

"Really? He said you first encountered each other in Washington through the Vichy embassy, I was told."

Hearing this, Catherine fought to meet his steady gaze and remain cool.

"Oh. That must be the code name SOE gave a man I knew through my former job," she managed to reply, buoyed by news of Henri in France and the thought he must have been asking after her. "He was a press attaché when I was a reporter working in D.C. If…if this is the same guy we're talking about, I saw him again, briefly, when we were both in training in the U.K. He was sent behind enemy lines long before I was, and I haven't seen him since." She stared calmly at Roger. "Why do you ask? I thought we were never supposed to speak of other agents we've known or worked with."

"Well," replied Roger, his eyes fixed on her face as if gauging her every reaction to his next words, "I need to ask you a few more questions about Agent Claude Foret."

CHAPTER 26

Catherine and Sean's new network leader took a sip of his coffee, set down his cup, and addressed Catherine directly.

"After I landed," Roger began, "this Claude fellow got us off the mountain despite the sudden appearance of a platoon of Germans storming up a nearby hill. He and his driver made a quick decision and went down a different road, spiriting us directly toward Paris. Then Claude provided my necessary papers and guided me safely to the train that took me to Annecy." He sunk his fork into a small potato and used it to scrape up the last of the egg yolk napping his plate. "So, you say you've had no contact with him since the last time you met in England?"

This is starting to feel like an interrogation.

Catherine raised her chin and replied firmly, "None."

"There are those in London who think Claude Foret could be playing both sides."

Catherine felt her own swift intake of breath.

That again!

Sean was watching both of them with curiosity. Catherine ignored him and returned Roger's penetrating gaze.

"A double agent, you mean. And what did you think?" she asked.

Roger paused again. "Perhaps the more important question is what did *you* think?" He cocked his head to one side and asked, "When you knew Claude in Washington, did you find this fellow to be as dependable as I've just described?"

Catherine's mind was awash with memories of the brave, selfless acts Henri had performed when they worked together to secure the codebooks. Why, then, was he always dogged by these veiled accusations?

"I can only say, Roger," Catherine replied evenly, "that my experience with Claude Foret proved him to be a true and loyal French patriot of the first order. But *why* I have good reason to say that, I cannot reveal."

Catherine could sense Sean's brewing curiosity to know who this man was for whom Catherine had expressed such clear admiration but had never once mentioned to him. Ignoring him, she and Roger exchanged a look of complete understanding before her commanding officer offered a reply.

"That was my experience as well," declared Roger, "but in this three-dimensional chess game we're playing, one must be very careful."

"You mean the old 'trust no one?' Not even a man who saved your life?"

"The only answer, I suppose, is that one always must go by one's instincts."

During these exchanges, Sean's head was swiveling as if he was watching a tennis match. Breaking into the conversation, he blurted, "I had a wireless message yesterday that a cache of parachuted arms and supplies near Paris had been seized by the Krauts within minutes of their landing. Was that your landing, do you figure?"

Roger slowly nodded his head in the affirmative. "I just had word of this as well. Those poor bastards on the reception committee guiding in our plane that night went to hide the canisters that arrived after us," Roger explained. "Minutes later, the Germans at a nearby camp came after them and our men ran right into a trap."

Sean said, "I guess it's taken some time for word of their executions to get back to London and then forwarded to me via wireless. The message said all of the *résistants* that night were gunned down at some pig farm."

Roger nodded. "Those of us in the car were lucky to get out with our lives."

"Dear God," Catherine whispered.

Roger glanced around the café and lowered his voice to match Catherine's. "The Air Operations officer in overall charge that night also avoided the Nazi net by running across the field and down the ridge before the Germans made it up the hill." He offered a warning gaze to Catherine. "Either Claude or SOE's Air Operations officer is suspected of tipping off the *Bosches* who were bivouacked less than two miles away."

"No!" declared Catherine. "It couldn't be Hen—uh...Claude."

Sean, again, was closely observing Roger and Catherine's exchanges. He asked, "So, those who went to the farm with the new weapons were ambushed and killed?"

"That is the intelligence I received," replied Roger. "So, I'm afraid I must urge that, should either of you ever encounter the operations officer or Claude, do take care. It may be some time before we learn who among us is the traitor playing a double game."

———◇———

For the next few weeks, Catherine pushed from her mind any possibility that Henri had become a double agent—or was being scapegoated by someone who *was* a double agent. Her first priority, she kept telling herself, was to focus solely on the next assignment ordered by Roger—that of blowing up a small rail trestle leading to a depot that housed foodstuffs and ammunition the Germans had stored outside Nice.

As they'd been taught in training, they were to use the bodies of dead rats to disguise the thin pencil fuses and *plastique* so the explosives wouldn't be easily spotted where they lay in strategic positions on the tracks or under bridges. And even if they were noticed, the carcasses were considered repugnant and rarely disturbed by soldiers making track inspections.

Despite these clever subterfuges, Catherine knew that Sean was as nervous as she was about executing this assignment. The night of the mission was starless and the rail yard deserted when they cut through a fence near the spur of track they planned destroy.

"Sean!" she cautioned in a hoarse whisper. "You've got to dig a small *hole* in the gravel before you insert the explosives under that rail!"

"The rat is too fat," he whispered back, holding by the tail a rodent packed with the prescribed explosives. "I've already ignited—"

"Jesus, Sean!" she cried. "Drop it! Quick! Let's go! "

Sean grabbed his canvas bag he'd used to carry his equipment, and the pair scrambled through the hole they'd cut in the fence. They were barely twenty yards away when the explosion went off, rail ties flying through the air in all directions.

"Oww!" Sean cried as a length of wood about a foot long slammed into his back.

Catherine turned in time to see him fall to the ground as clouds of dust filled the air, choking her and making it hard to breathe. She helped him struggle to sit up.

"Can...barely...breathe." He gasped. "Wind...knocked...out..."

"Come on," she pleaded, grabbing him by one arm. "We've got to get out of here, fast!" A loud, wailing sound of an emergency alert split the air. Sean groaned as he pulled himself to his feet. "Have you broken anything? Can you ride your bike?"

"Ribs hurt," he said, still gasping for air, "but I-I think I'm okay."

The pair staggered the last few yards to the spot where they had hidden their bikes behind a hedge and mounted them, speeding off in the direction of Villefranche. Behind them, they could hear the sound of motorcycles roaring from the heart of Nice, obviously heading toward the railway depot. Catherine guessed that by now, the yard foreman had leapt out of his warm bed and, with his lantern casting beams in all directions, was searching for the area of track where their night's handiwork had blown a large section of the rail line to bits.

Fortunately, the saboteurs made it safely to the deserted boatyard before the authorities had time to sound the alarm in the villages east of Nice.

Catherine helped Sean up the outside wooden stairs and into the sailmaker's loft.

He staggered across the floor and immediately sank down onto the pile of sails that served as his bed. Catherine, out of breath herself, leaned against the door she'd just shut.

"Jesus, Mary, and Joseph," he murmured. "That was close." He rubbed the small of his back and winced.

"Are you really okay?" Catherine asked, crossing to him and kneeling beside his makeshift sleeping pallet. "You were lucky that flying projectile didn't conk you on the head!"

He pointed toward his midsection. With a smile he asked, "Want to rub my ribs?"

Catherine wagged her forefinger at him with exasperation. "No! Next time, dig a hole to bury the rat *before* you light the fuse under its tail!"

———◇———

Less than a month later, Catherine heard Sean's familiar footsteps hurrying up the stairs. She was sitting at the small table where they dined each day. She'd been in the process of carefully unwrapping the usual number of time pencils and detonators that came swathed in cotton and then laying them out in a neat row. Beside her was a mound of *plastique* she would later use to create more of the slender explosives stuffed in a few more dead rats that Sean had trapped in the boatyard. The innocent-looking carcasses would be left later that night under the girding of an electric transformer that fed power to several rows of barracks housing the region's Italian occupiers.

These audacious acts of sabotage were not without consequences, however. Immediately after their attack on the railway depot, several citizens in a village outside Nice had been plucked out at random and shot. The stains of dried blood on the walls Catherine passed in her travels made her question if what they were doing was right—or even worth it—unless the longed-for invasions were near. Still, each day, she prepared more explosive devices, and nearly each night, she and Sean set out for another target.

Sean threw open the door to the sail loft and leaned against the threshold, panting and completely out of breath.

"You will not believe…what I…just learned!" he said breathlessly.

Catherine looked up, alarmed by the urgency in his tone. "What is it? What's happened? Come inside! Where'd you leave the wireless?"

"It's still in Jules Menton's barn at the olive farm," he said, still breathing hard as he shut the door. "It's hidden well enough under bales of hay, but word's come through that something terrible's happened."

Sean had taken Roger's warning to heart and now routinely moved the location of the suitcase containing his wireless apparatus, along with the antenna that made broadcasting back to London possible.

"What's happened? Tell me!"

Reports had flown up and down the Riviera that, north of the coast, both the SS and the local French *milice* were ruthlessly deporting Jews and supposed terrorists to German labor camps. The latter was what the Nazis dubbed members of the French Resistance and their Allied accomplices, which had resulted in deportations tripling in recent months.

"Peter Churchill parachuted over the mountains above Lake Annecy the night of April Fifteenth, and before dawn the next day, he and Odette were immediately arrested at the hotel in St. Jorioz."

"Oh, God, no!" Catherine exclaimed. "Roger also traveled there at one point. Is he—"

"No, no, no. Roger's fine—at least for now. He told me on my last rendezvous with him in Cannes that he blamed Raoul and Lise," Sean said, using the code names for Peter Churchill and Odette Samson out of pure habit. "In his words, they were 'very careless about security matters,' particularly their habit of staying in hotels instead of safe houses. Roger himself had departed Annecy only the day before they were caught."

"Does London have any idea where they are now?"

"Taken to Paris," Sean said, glumly. "Word is Raoul's in Fresnes Prison, and Lise—God help her—was sent to Avenue Foch for interrogation by the Gestapo. The butchers, of course, want to pry out of them names of every agent they know."

"Including us," Catherine murmured.

During their training, each SOE agent had been apprised of the dreadful fate in store for any Allied secret agent that ended up at 84 Avenue Foch in the heart of a fashionable part of Paris. The Gestapo headquarters for counterespionage was housed in a beautiful *Beaux Arts* building. Word had gotten back to Britain from a few captives that were lucky enough to escape that harsh interrogations there inevitably ended in the physical torture of inmates. The goal, of course, was to get information about other agents so they, too, could be apprehended and often executed.

"Oh, God. Poor Odette," Catherine moaned. All she could think of was what a brave person the woman had been on the boat those eight awful days sailing from Gibraltar. It had been obvious to all of them in Cannes how quickly Odette and Peter had fallen for each other after their initial sparring. Their intimate relationship, recalled Catherine (with a twinge of guilt about her own behavior on that score), turned out to be another security risk for everyone concerned.

"So, what do we do now?" she demanded. "The Nazis might torture them to learn about our operations, even down here. Either one of them might be beaten to a bloody pulp or have their eyes put out with lighted cigarettes by the SS sadists."

Sean pointed to the fuses Catherine had laid out upon the table like soldiers on parade.

"We just can't think about that right now. London's message to us was to do the demolition job on the electric transformer near Nice tomorrow and then meet a munitions drop they've scheduled for our landing spot on Tuesday night."

"And after that?" Catherine felt a feeling of doom invading their sailmakers loft.

"Get the hell out of our boatyard safe house, at least for a while."

———◇———

Within two hours, Sean and Catherine packed up their belongings, along with the wireless, and hid everything they owned inside a decrepit, dry-docked boat not too far from the sailmaker's loft. The abandoned craft was raised fifteen feet off the ground on a cradle of sawhorses. The hulk had been left in a spot hidden from view under an enormous series of stone arches, which were the only remnants of a former aqueduct built by the Romans more than a thousand years earlier. The structure now supported a road constructed in the 19th century that ran above the harbor. Its sheer mass protected the thirty-foot vessel's peeling, battered hull from any curious eyes passing through the main section of the boatyard.

"No one has lifted a finger to repair this hulk the entire time we've been here," Sean said. "It's an inspired choice, even if I do say so myself."

Catherine nodded in agreement as she stuffed her pregnancy pillow on top of the pile of their possessions in the dusty cabin. "I won't miss wearing *this* anymore."

The story they'd told in Villefranche was that she'd tragically miscarried and that the couple was mourning their loss. But each time she'd donned her pillow, it only reminded her of another baby whose life and whereabouts she was likely never to know.

Once they'd stowed all their gear, the pair emerged cautiously onto the teak deck, its paint peeled and sun bleached. Sean battened down the battered hatch that was missing one of its two hinges. He said, "I stopped at Remy's restaurant before coming back to the loft, and he thought he could provide us a safe house further up the hill where we could stay for a few days."

"That'll do for a while, at least," agreed Catherine with relief.

She hoisted the strap of a canvas sail bag over her shoulder that was chock full of the fuses, detonators, and *plastique* assembled for their next assignment. Sean's bag contained several of the dead rats they routinely used to camouflage the explosives.

Catherine surveyed the shadowed area beneath the stone arches and saw there was still no one in sight. "Too many people have seen us in the boatyard, but on the other side of the citadel we know no one in the town itself except Remy."

"All right, then," Sean said, pointing to their pair of bicycles on the ground below, leaning against one of the cradling sawhorses supporting the dry-docked boat. "Let's blow this bucket."

Sean was the first to back down the wooden ladder they'd used to gain access to the interior of the abandoned vessel. Soon, they were both beside their bikes, stowing their canvas bags in the baskets attached to the handlebars.

Catherine began to push her bicycle up the hill. Without looking back she said, "Let's get this over with."

"Believe me," replied Sean, inclining his head toward his bicycle basket, "these rats stink to high heaven. The sooner we get rid of them, the happier we'll both be."

CHAPTER 27

The metal transformer that was Catherine and Sean's sabotage target on this balmy May evening fed electricity to the barracks where the occupying Italian soldiers ate and slept. Sean pulled out a set of wire cutters from his canvas bag and made fast work of creating a hole in its protective fence large enough for the two of them to crawl through.

"Now comes the hideous part," he said, grimacing while pulling out three rat carcasses by their tails from the same bag. "This was never in the SOE job description when we signed the Official Secrets Act."

"Oh, come on!" Catherine blurted. "Give them to me. I'll do it. And stop speaking English!" Kneeling, she swiftly inserted the slender explosive devices into the animals' posteriors and then wedged each plump rat beneath the metal equipment, where it would do the most harm. "The timers and pencil fuses are connected, so I'll let you do the honors and light 'em," she directed.

"How much time will we have?"

"Fifteen minutes to clear out."

Sean pulled out some matches and lit one. "You're my hero," he said, continuing to speak in English. "There are just some things I—"

"Shush! Listen!" She blew out his match.

The pair crouched in the dirt near the recumbent rats and flattened themselves against the metal sides of the transformer. Catherine felt the generator's vibrations against her backside and heard the motor's low hum while straining to listen to footsteps that could only be those of troops assigned to guard the perimeter.

Fifty feet away she saw a pinpoint of light suddenly flare. Then another. She relaxed a bit, realizing that the patrol was lighting cigarettes and chattering in Italian about women they knew back home.

In the darkness that surrounded them, Catherine felt Sean's hand seize hers and hold on tight.

"What are they saying?" he whispered, having no command of Italian.

"How horny they are."

"We can't just sit here," he hissed with a nod toward the timed explosions that were in position but whose fuses hadn't yet been lit.

She was just about to shake free of Sean's grasp and reach for her service revolver stuck between the back of her trousers and her belt when, mercifully, the two soldiers turned and ambled off in the opposite direction. She stared at their retreating backs as they headed for the barracks, whose outlines were just visible in the pre-dawn gloom.

The instant the two men disappeared around the corner of the building nearest them, Sean swiftly lit the fuses and then whispered, "Let's beat feet outta here!"

Sean and Catherine grabbed hold of their canvas sea bags and squeezed through the fence's cutout. They made a dash to retrieve their bicycles and within seconds were peddling furiously down the road that would lead them back to Villefranche. Before long, a series of explosions rent the air.

"Bingo!" exclaimed Sean over his shoulder.

"Just keep going!"

Catherine leaned over her bike handles, peddling even faster. They hadn't traveled another two hundred yards before loud Claxton horns could be heard behind them, soon joined by others blaring the alarm up and down the coastline. As fast as they could, the pair covered the few miles that would take them to the entrance of the upper village. As they drew closer, Catherine's heart began to pound from both exertion and icy fear. A hundred yards ahead of them, she could see the outlines of shrouded figures hurriedly assembling at the main city portal, long guns in hand.

A checkpoint has been set up already!

"Dump the bikes over the wall!" she ordered. "We can't enter town the usual way. They're sure to wonder why we're on the road at this hour with a pair of wire cutters and a gun."

Sean jumped off his two-wheeler and peered over the low stone barrier skirting the Nice-Villefranche road.

"Look!" he whispered, pointing. "See? Over there it's not quite so steep down to the outskirts of the upper village." He hoisted his bicycle over the barrier, then hers, and laid them flat against the sloping hillside. "There's even a faint path where villagers take a shortcut down to town."

"Right," she agreed, scrambling over the waist-high wall. "Let's pray our bikes will still be here tomorrow and that it'll be safe to come collect them."

Holding hands, they slipped and slid down the grass-covered descent until they reached a cobblestone lane that marked the beginning of dwellings that marched up the hill from the sea behind Remy's harborside restaurant. Moving swiftly, the two of them were relieved that all the two- and three-story buildings flanking them were shuttered and silent. When a cat suddenly darted from a dark alley, Catherine stifled a scream.

A block from the promenade that skirted the harbor, Sean halted at a shadowed doorway and felt in his pocket for a large metal key. "Courtesy of a friend of Remy's. It's not much to look at, he told me, but it's a roof over our heads, and we'll be safe."

Despite the warm evening air, Catherine stood beside him, shivering and longing for sleep. The thick wooden door hung on outsized iron hinges swung open with a loud creak, startling a live rat that scurried across the floor and scampered out an open window.

"Can we never be rid of these vermin?" Sean complained.

On the floor, fishing nets were stacked much the same way the sails had been in their other hideout, only here, the tangled piles were frayed, coated with dirt and seaweed, and sorely in need of mending.

Catherine surveyed their latest hideaway. "We seem to have come even more down-market in our vacation abodes," she joked grimly.

Sean, sweeping his torch in an arc around the whitewashed, low-ceiling hut, replied, "but at least no one is likely to look for us in here, right?"

Without answering, Catherine allowed her canvas sail bag to slip to the floor. The strain and intensity of the previous two hours had caught up with her, and the muscles of her entire body felt rigid with fatigue. Meanwhile, her stomach could be heard rumbling, since they'd had to forego their evening meal.

And tomorrow there's the weapons drop at the olive farm in the hills.

As if reading her thoughts, Sean said, "I'm starving! Let's hope those Brit packers included a few chocolate bars in those metal canisters we pick up tomorrow night."

"I think tonight I'll dream about biting into a nice piece of Cadbury," she said with a yawn.

Sean tossed his canvas bag next to a heap of nets. "By the way, speaking of the weapons drop," he said, peeling off his jacket, "I didn't have time to tell you, but I also got a message in the last batch from London that U.S. and British forces have linked up in North Africa. The German and Italian troops surrendered there.

"You're kidding! When?"

"Two days ago, May thirteenth. Next stop for our guys: Sicily."

"Whoa…" said Catherine, suddenly wide awake. She unbuttoned her own jacket and tossed it on the nets. "Don't you imagine that the Germans are starting to worry about an invasion here along the Riviera? How much longer will they let the Italians run the show in the southeast?"

Sean gave a shrug. "It's no secret that the Germans will probably make a move before long to occupy this last section of the country."

Catherine grimaced. "How terrible that'll be for all the Jews who fled from Eastern Europe to the Côte d'Azur for safety. The Italians are no angels, but…"

"No need to finish that sentence," Sean said, sinking down on a pile of nets. "Oh, and here's another by-the-way," he added, looking up at her. "In the last transmissions from London, SOE said Roger instructed me to refresh you in the rudiments of wireless transmission in case…well, you know why."

"In case something happens to you, you mean?" Catherine asked.

She struggled to keep her tone light although the import of Sean's words began to shoot frissons of anxiety straight through her. "I suppose that's not a bad idea," she added, attempting to sound nonchalant. "I did okay in that course at Bletchley. Not brilliantly, mind you, since obviously they slated me as a courier."

"It's just a precaution," Sean said. "You know how valuable SOE considers those wireless sets to be. They don't want any to go to waste."

Catherine summoned an I'll-be-a-good-sport-about-this smile, but the truth was, facing life in war-torn France without Sean's cheerful companionship, and with only a wireless set for company, was a state of affairs she really didn't want to think about.

She suddenly found herself battling the return of a crushing weariness that typically caught up with her after one of their operations. Like Sean, she sank down on one of the piles of abandoned fisherman's nets and punched her sail bag and jacket into the shape of a pillow. Within minutes, both she and Sean were fast asleep.

———◇———

The next evening, Catherine was the first of the reception committee crouched atop the olive farm on an open plateau to hear the drone of an airplane engine. She could only hope authorities along this stretch of the coast were fast asleep at this hour and wouldn't descend upon them while the operation was in progress.

"Flash your light to the others!" she called hoarsely to Sean.

As instructed, Sean blinked his battery pocket light and quickly ordered three more electric torches positioned into the shape of an *L* to illuminate the landing area. Within minutes, the plane, a Halifax, roared overhead. Heads tilted to the sky, the reception committee took in the awe-inspiring sight of cigar-shaped metal canisters, full of weapons and supplies, dangling from their open parachutes.

"There should be twelve chutes in all. You count them coming down," Catherine directed Sean, "while I spot where the majority of the canisters land."

"Right," he replied. "There's one...two...uh, three, but the chute's not opening on that one, damn it! Four...five..."

Having dispatched its cargo, scattered like silken mushrooms across the nighttime landscape, the plane arched in a northerly direction, heading back to England.

"Ten…eleven…twelve," called out Sean, adding, "thirteen! There's one more than what the manifest said."

Catherine barely heard him as she signaled with her own flashlight toward the other members of the reception committee, indicating they should begin working in teams of two to find each canister once it hit the ground. They knew to spring into action, hauling each container to the flatbed cart attached to a rusting tractor stationed at the edge of the makeshift landing area. Jules Menton, the farmer who owned the olive groves and the hectares surrounding them, was poised to drive the night's haul to its hiding place behind towering stacks of wooden boxes in the large shed where oil was pressed each autumn after the annual olive harvest.

Sean lifted his pair of binoculars to his eyes and whistled.

"Well, isn't this a surprise? Look up there! There's a new Joe floating down to us. Where in hell are we going to hide the guy?"

"The thirteenth chute is a new agent?" Catherine said, startled not to have been informed by wireless ahead of the drop. She seized Sean's field glasses to have a look herself, adjusting them drastically, given his poor eyesight. It took a few more moments to focus in on the figure, now a hundred feet off the ground. Her sharp intake of breath caught Sean's attention as the parachutist, in helmet and jumpsuit, drifted ever closer.

"What?" Sean demanded. "It's not Roger, is it?"

"Uh-uh" she murmured. "But it's someone I know."

Henri Leblanc was about to drop to earth ten yards from where she was standing.

——◇——

Henri watched as the dozen canisters were swiftly loaded, one by one, onto a flatbed on the side of the landing area. Waiting for Catherine to finish directing her team, he pulled off his helmet and stood rooted in the farmer's field like one of the ancient olive trees lining the hill behind him. He was just as shocked as she was when they came face to face in the moonlight.

At length, Catherine and the young man assisting the operation turned from the tractor and approached where Henri was standing beside his silk parachute that lay in a heap, its harness buried in the folds.

"Catherine!" Henri called out softly. Then he quickly amended, "Colette!" He cast a glance at the man of about her age with thick glasses and red hair walking beside her. He thrust out his hand to her, pretending to be merely an acquaintance. "How...utterly... amazing! Do you remember me? Claude Foret? From our training course?"

He could tell she almost laughed aloud at his use of his *nom de guerre*. Taking his hand, she replied, "That seems a lifetime ago." She turned to the carrot-headed gent beside her. "This is Guy de Bruyn, the fellow who first detected that we were getting more than just canisters on this drop."

The sound of her low, breathy voice instantly summoned the memory of her intimate whispers the last night they'd spent together in the Scottish Highlands.

She turned and admonished her fellow agent, "C'mon! We've got to move the tractor, pronto. And let's get this unexpected visitor off the mountain."

Henri knew that Catherine's urgent orders telegraphed the very real peril they all were in, given that the sound of a plane's rumbling engine often alerted local authorities who then swooped down to arrest everyone.

"But why wasn't the arrival of this agent on our manifest?" the colleague beside her demanded.

Henri offered a casual shrug, providing his listeners with the cover story he'd been given when leaving Ringway Airfield only hours earlier.

"I was supposed to bail out near Lyon, but the wind and overcast skies there forced a change of plans. So, here I am." To Catherine he asked, "Are there still trains running north-south from Cannes or Marseille?"

"A few," she replied, adding hurriedly, "but you'll need the right documents, so we'll have to sort that out later." To the others standing near the tractor, she declared firmly, "Look, we've got to get this show on the road. You men, get the canisters stowed away at the olive mill and bury the parachutes before you leave, but do it quickly!" She turned to her compatriot. "Let's you and I have a final word with Jules about storing the weapons behind those wooden boxes, which I want you to supervise. Then Claude and I will meet you back at our new safe house."

"New?" Henri queried before he could stop himself.

"There have been reprisals recently around here," responded Catherine. "We thought it best to, uh…vacate our former premises, right?" she said, turning to her comrade with whom she had obviously coordinated the night's activities.

"Bad ones," was his short reply, and then he pointed to the farmer. "Let's get the canisters hidden away."

Henri stood to one side as the pair walked swiftly toward the farmer sitting atop his tractor. After a brief conversation, Catherine patted her gloved hand on the boot of the older man as a sign of her appreciation. Two members of the reception committee were already digging holes to bury the chutes. Her fellow agent gestured to the others on their team to follow alongside the farm machine that, in the next few seconds, was traveling at full throttle with the canisters piled on the flatbed like stubby logs.

Henri drank in the sight of Catherine, trim as always in well-cut wool trousers and a smart tweed jacket as if she'd been riding to hounds. He found a spot under a nearby olive tree and sat down to rest, marveling at his last forty-eight hours.

When Henri had returned to London to deliver his damning, in-person report on Lucien Barteau—*nom-de-guerre*, Gilbert—he'd eagerly volunteered to take on the dangerous assignment of surveying the Axis coastal defenses in the south of France. He never figured he'd be so lucky as to have Catherine literally there to greet him on the landing field! At most, he'd hoped to confirm, through the *résistants* he'd meet during his work in this section of France, that she was still alive, and then perhaps he'd even gain some word of her whereabouts.

Yet here she was, trotting away from the tractor and jogging in his direction. He wasn't surprised she'd be running a complicated landing operation with her fellow agent and obviously doing it in her usual fearless and business-like manner.

Two bicycles were lying on the ground nearby. Catherine stopped beside them, righted one, and indicated they should start walking side by side. Even on this moonlit night, he could see that she was thinner and quite pale. If the Riviera was anything like Paris, a decent diet was almost impossible to maintain, as the occupiers confiscated most of the available food for themselves. Henri remembered the feasts of caviar and champagne they'd shared at her apartment in Georgetown, and, yes, how long ago that seemed.

As he looked at her now, her expression was both quizzical and welcoming, which warmed every cell in his exhausted body. As they trod down a well-worn path, an odd silence bloomed between them.

Finally, she said, "For the rest of my life, I'll never forget looking through those field glasses and seeing you floating out of the sky."

They both halted in the shadow of one of the hundreds of olive trees growing beside the dirt road.

"Believe me, darling Catherine, I am as stunned as you are."

"Stunned doesn't even come close to describing how I feel," she replied. "You'll never know how glad I am to see you, Henri, but your arrival complicates the heck out of everything."

A mere two feet separated them now. For a brief second, they simply gazed at each other, both fully aware they shouldn't embrace or make a gesture to indicate that they were anything more to than two agents who had met once during their training.

As for Henri, all he wanted at that moment was to pull her against his chest and hold her tight. Out of the corner of his eye he saw Catherine's cohort turn and stare at them over his shoulder while continuing to walk some hundred yards in the opposite direction, taking the canisters to their hiding place. Henri knew then it was safest for them both if no one else guessed how stirred he was to see her again.

"I promised you that night in the Highlands I would make a way to find you."

Catherine's eyes grew luminous and she murmured, "Yes you did."

"And here I am."

But before he could say another word, she pointed toward the distant, curving coastline and its expanse of silvery water lapping the harbor. In the breathy tone that he loved, she took charge of the situation.

"Welcome to Villefranche-on-the-Sea. Let's get you to the safe house," she urged. "I believe I've just thought of a very good idea."

CHAPTER 28

Henri was bone tired from the day's stress and exertions, but he kept up the fast pace Catherine had set as she walked her bicycle downhill alongside the olive groves toward the water. Once they were safely out of earshot he said, "You know, I want very much to kiss you."

"Extremely tempting, but not now," she declared. Her anxious tone expressed a disquiet he'd never sensed during all the operations they'd shared in and out of the Vichy embassy in Washington.

Henri gave a quick glance over his shoulder. Agent Guy de Bruyn and the reception committee had almost reached the large building Catherine had mentioned housed the olive mill and storehouse. He could see by her gaunt face and her worried manner that her clandestine work had taken its toll.

She, too, cast a glance behind her. "I've got to get you safely out of sight. I'm wondering, should we use the wireless later to inform London that you're with us now? And by the way," she added, "what were you doing in London?"

"Letting Buckmaster know that I think the man you and I met briefly in that bathroom the day we had our SOE interviews is a double agent."

"No! The Frenchman who said he'd flown for Air Bleu? You mean the bastard who openly raked me up and down with his eyes? *That* Frenchman?"

Henri nodded.

"Lucien Somebody, wasn't it?" Catherine asked without waiting for his answer. "Our boss came into France on one of his flights and said you saved his life driving straight into Paris instead of following Lucien's directives."

"So, you had word of that." Henry well remembered that close call with the newly arrived agent, Roger. It was one of the concerns he'd related to Buckmaster.

"Yes, Lucien Barteau, code name Gilbert," Henri confirmed. "He's now SOE's Air Operations officer, and people around him in the Occupied Zone have a way of being arrested right and left by the Gestapo."

She indicated they should go through a wooden gate and down a narrow path toward the main road into Villefranche.

"And did Buckmaster believe you?" she asked.

Henri wondered if Catherine had heard any of the rumors alleging that he, Agent Claude—another Frog, as the Brits like to call the Frenchies—might be "doing the double" just like Lucien. Henri certainly had taken a chance to appear, uninvited, in front of Maurice Buckmaster's desk at SOE headquarters.

"I'm not sure if he believed me or not," Henri told her, closing the gate behind them. "But I felt I had to tell him what I'd observed in and around Paris since I arrived."

"But how did you get permission to go to London?"

Henri laughed. "I didn't. I managed to talk Gilbert himself into putting me on a plane to London when I heard that one of his flights would do a fast turn-around outside Paris. I told him I thought I was having an appendicitis attack and needed emergency medical treatment which would attract the wrong kind of attention where I was. These days, the SS are even combing the Paris hospitals demanding patients' papers."

"A ruptured appendix?" Catherine said, appearing amused despite the seriousness of their subject. "How inventive of you."

Henry gave another short laugh. "Maybe because I was a fellow pilot once upon a time, this Lucien-Gilbert character decided to believe my lie—or perhaps it was the orders I had my forger, Jean-Paul, create that stated I'd been summoned back for medical treatment." Pushing himself to keep up with her hurried pace, Henri waved his helmet in one hand and added, "And speaking of my health, I'm still amazed that I managed the landing without breaking one of my legs again."

"That would have been bad," Catherine said with the first smile he'd seen from her. Then she murmured, "I remember those scars."

"Ah...yes, you would have seen them in Scotland," he said, smiling. "Well, anyway, the second my feet touched solid ground, there *you* were, alive and well."

"I'm alive," she acknowledged, staring straight ahead as they continued down the dirt track. "And that's about as far as I'll go on that subject. But what about London?" she insisted. "If you were being dropped in Lyon, then you don't have the right documents if the Jerries stop you anywhere along the Riviera."

"It's London that decided to send me directly here."

Catherine halted in her tracks. "What?"

"What I said before was just part of my cover. I've been ordered to inspect the enemy's coastal defenses along the Riviera and report back."

"Oh my God!" Catherine said, placing her hand on his arm, the first time he'd felt her touch. "Please tell me there'll be an Allied landing here sometime soon."

"Soon may be an exaggeration," he replied soberly.

"That's always the answer I hear," Catherine replied with a sigh of annoyance as she resumed walking on ahead with her bike.

Catching up to her, Henri said, "Well, the Americans think they'll subdue Italy in good order, and they're the ones who favor an assault here."

"So? When's it to be?" she asked, her bike rolling over the dirt bumps.

"Maybe never. The British are opposed to a coastal invasion in these parts. That's why the SOE wants someone to assess what the difficulties would be, probably to convince the other Allies it's foolhardy to land in France from the south."

Catherine turned toward him, unable to hide her displeasure with the higher-ups.

"So, you've been sent into the lion's den by Whitehall to prove how dangerous and risky it would be to launch such an operation— one they oppose to begin with? Why didn't they send a Brit to do their dirty work?"

"Because I jumped at the chance to volunteer," he answered. "I'd heard through your former network leader, Peter Churchill, that you were down here somewhere and thought, if I accepted this assignment, I might be able to find out where you were."

Catherine allowed her bike to fall to the ground, turned to face him, and threw her arms around him. "Oh, Henri," she murmured. "After Peter and Odette were arrested, I was so worried something horrible had happened to you in Paris. It's so dangerous there."

"It's dangerous everywhere."

Within seconds, he'd pulled her against his chest and was kissing her hard. Her mouth felt wonderful. He knew she must be aware of how aroused he was despite the canvas flight suit he still wore. Finally, she pulled away, laughter bubbling to her lips. She reached for his flight suit's front zipper that started at his neck and traveled down past his crotch.

"I can't wait to get you out of this," she said, tugging it down an inch or two.

He stayed her hand. "When I heard they were looking for someone to do the survey down here, I knew it was the only chance I'd have to try to find you. Frankly, I don't give a damn whether or not Buckmaster and the rest of them like the results I find."

Catherine framed his face between her hands. "I asked Peter Churchill if, by chance, he'd encountered someone of your description, and he had...but he'd only say you'd been left off in some field to make your way to Paris. We've heard that so many agents have been caught there. I honestly thought I'd never see you again."

He covered her hands with his own. "Peter Churchill didn't trust me," Henri stated flatly.

"I don't think he trusts anyone with former ties to Vichy," she replied, and they both allowed their arms to fall by their sides. Henri could tell she was keeping her tone light. "Come on," she said, her worried look returning, "we've got to get off this hill."

Catherine picked her bike off the ground, and they walked a few minutes more without speaking. Then Henri said, "I think the only reason Buckmaster was willing to assign me this mission was when I told him that I've known this region since I was a child, coming here with my parents from our home in Perpignan."

"Isn't that also on this coast, near the border with Spain?"

"Practically on it," he said, feeling a tinge of melancholy for a life that now seemed as if it had barely ever been real. Springing instantly to memory was his family's villa, nestled against the base of a medieval fortress that towered above the home's red-tile roof and smooth plaster walls. Thinking how Catherine would love it, he said, "We've never really had the time for me to describe my wonderful family place there. At any rate," he continued as they came to the end of a narrowing in the dirt track, "I persuaded Buckmaster that as a supposed traveling printing rep, I was the perfect choice to survey the coastline from Cannes to Marseille and report whatever I found."

By this time, Catherine had led them the final yards to a path that came out on a road Henri assumed would lead into town. "We'll enter Villefranche this way," she said, pointing to another well-worn trail on the other side of a low stone wall.

Henri scanned an open slope that curved toward the first of the village's plaster-clad buildings whose rooflines were visible in the moonlit night. Below them was the bay he'd looked down on as he'd floated to earth. Catherine propped her bicycle against the wall.

"Henri," she said, her eyes searching his, "you know, don't you, that this reconnaissance mission you've taken on is horribly risky?"

"And yours hasn't been?" he replied, running the back of his fingers along her cheek.

"But the German presence here has been steadily building," she told him, sweeping her arm in an arc over the shadowy landscape.

"The Italians and the Germans have already surrendered in North Africa."

"We just heard about that," Catherine said. "Doesn't this mean our guys will be fighting their way up from Sicily soon? Little wonder our side needs to know what kind of defenses they'd confront during an invasion on the beaches here." She pointed to the harbor of Villefranche, the dim outlines of its crescent beach stretching around the coast eastward toward Monaco. "How terrible it'll be for this beautiful part of the world if the fighting comes here…"

Henri laced the fingers of one hand through the amber strands of her hair and gently brought her forehead to touch his. The world of war and danger retreated to the edge of his consciousness. It almost felt to him as if they were the last two humans on earth, standing on a moonlit cliff, with only the sea and the sky for company.

Before he could say another word or be tempted to kiss her again, he warned, "Tomorrow I have to start my survey in Nice and work my way along the coast to Cannes, St. Tropez, and then on to Toulon and Marseille. If I manage to survive all that, I'll make my way back to Paris." He brushed his lips lightly against hers. "We only have tonight, *chérie*," he whispered, smiling against her mouth. "And, by the way, jumping out of an airplane to get here was totally worth the risk."

A voice in the back of his head murmured, *"We should run for cover. Now!"*

But instead, he felt her reach up and wrap both her arms around his neck. For this night, at least, he refused to think about the future, or that he would leave her again and they'd both be risking their lives at every turn. He was certain that Catherine would arrange it so they would have tonight, and that was all that mattered.

———◇———

Catherine pulled an iron key from her pocket, opened the door, and pushed her bicycle across the threshold of the storage room piled with the fishing nets that had been doubling as mattresses for Sean and her. While Henri watched, she scribbled a note and weighted it down with a piece of thick rope.

"I've taken our visiting cousin to Nice by foot and then by coastal train as far as Cannes where he will travel onwards from there. I'll return by midafternoon. –C."

Henri peered over her shoulder. "We're walking to Nice tonight?"

"No, of course not," she answered with a smile she hoped was reassuring. "I just want to buy us time."

"It's good that no one beyond your network knows about my mission here, but it means I've just exposed you all to more danger."

"Part of our job," she replied with a shrug. "C'mon. Let's get you some food."

As quietly as she could, Catherine shut the heavy door to their most recent hideout and guided Henri down the narrow, shadowed, winding lane. At the bottom of the hill, she tapped lightly on a door at the back of Remy's restaurant. Not expecting anyone to respond at this late hour, she lifted the latch and led Henri into the pantry, where she found some bread, a hunk of cheese, and an opened bottle of wine.

Just as she was stashing them in her canvas sea bag, Remy appeared in a pair of undershorts at the threshold to his private apartments above the restaurant.

"Sorry for waking you. An emergency," she said by way of explanation, her easy smile belying the fact that her heart lurched with surprise at the sight of him. She inclined her head toward Henri. "We had an unexpected visitor fall from the sky tonight. He hasn't eaten since he departed from England."

"Ah, well, please, come in," Remy said. With the grace of the restaurateur he was, he urged Catherine, "Why don't you two sit down, and I'll make you an omelet."

"Oh, would you?" Catherine replied gratefully. "To tell you the truth, I'm faint with hunger, and so is Claude, here. Are you sure you can spare the eggs?"

Remy put a finger to his lips. "*Shhh.* My sister's contraband chickens do their part. But don't tell anyone, especially *Monsieur* Guy!" Remy inclined his head to look behind his visitors. "Where is that food hound, by the way?"

"Busy on the mountain," Catherine replied. She retrieved the hunk of bread and cheese out of the canvas bag and set it before Henri at a small table inside Remy's kitchen.

Meanwhile, their host poured each a half glass of wine. "Cheers, and welcome."

Catherine raised her glass to touch his and Henri's. "And thank you, Remy."

"It is nothing," he replied, cracking four precious eggs into a bowl and beating them briskly. He glanced at Henri curiously. "Landing in the moonlight this evening must be quite something. No wonder you're hungry. Where to next?"

Catherine intervened with a warning smile, "You know he can't tell you that."

Trust no one! Remy could always sell the knowledge of Henri's arrival to...

Catherine despised such thoughts about Remy Poché, but exhaustion from what had been required of her the past few days was pressing down on her. She was feeling absolutely dizzy from the lack of a decent meal.

And what if the SOE had screwed up supplying Henri with the right papers? What if he were stopped by the hordes of Germans now in Cannes? There were so many questions she wanted to ask Henri about the invasion of North Africa and what he'd heard in London about Hitler's next moves. They had so little time, even to kiss goodbye.

While they waited to be fed, she gazed across the table at the man she had to call Claude. For no reason she could fathom other than sheer fatigue, a morbid fear for Henri's next few days suddenly had her in its grip. He'd be in danger every second while he surveyed German defenses along the Côte d'Azur, and once he boarded the train from Cannes or Marseille to return to Paris, she would never know if he'd made it back safely.

Meanwhile, Remy divided the perfectly cooked eggs placed next to toasted bread and sat down to join them. Within minutes, she and Henri had cleaned their plates while she struggled to shake off her overarching sense of worry.

"Thank you again," she said to their chef, rising from her chair as Henri stood up from his. "I've got to let this poor man get some sleep."

With a look of apology, Remy said to Henri, "I'm so sorry all we can offer as a place to lay your head is a pile of rotting fishing nets."

Remy is a good man and totally loyal to Sean and me in our work here. What was I thinking just now?

Henri extended his hand to his host and shook it firmly.

"After the trip I had hurtling through the sky, a place with a roof and a flat surface sounds wonderful." Once outside the restaurant he said, "So, back up the hill we go? What about the note you left?"

Catherine shook her head. "No more climbing hills. Where we're going won't be the Ritz, but it'll be nicer than a pile of reeking fishing nets. Follow me, *mon amour*." She set off in the direction of the gravel path that skirted the water and the stone contours of the Citadel's tower and led to the boatyard.

Henri seized her hand. "You cannot imagine how much lovelier than the Ritz it is just to be with you."

———◇———

Remy Poché stepped outside his restaurant to light a cigarette. Tossing the match aside, he looked up and noticed with surprise that his departing visitors weren't scaling the hill in the direction of the safe house that he'd arranged at some risk to himself. Where was the redheaded young man that was his beautiful patron's constant companion? And why were Agent Colette and this stranger strolling hand in hand along the waterfront toward *La Citadelle* like lovers on a pre-war holiday?

CHAPTER 29

Henri stood near the bulkhead in the cramped captain's quarters atop the dry-docked fishing boat. He waited silently while Catherine tossed the contents of a suitcase onto a built-in bunk that had roped webbing but was minus its mattress. She had cracked open a porthole to freshen the air inside, and Henri felt calmed by the warm May breeze that wafted into the stateroom from the harbor. By this late hour, the moon had sunk lower on the horizon, its slanting beams casting a surprising amount of light into the vessel whose hull sat on its jack sticks that served as a cradle fifteen feet off the ground.

"At least these clothes will be softer than piled-up fishing nets," she commented, reaching for a pillow from on top of a pile of folded canvas nearby. "Now, this is a very special item," she said with a droll expression.

Henri looked at the pillow she held, wondering at her ingenuity finding a decent place to lay their heads where they both hoped no one would think to look for them.

"I call this my pregnancy pillow," she explained. "When I first got here, Sean—I mean, Guy—and I pretended we were a couple expecting our first child while he recovered from eye surgery."

"I wondered about those thick glasses he was wearing."

So, Agent Guy's real first name is Sean.

Henri chastised himself for wondering how close to reality the pair had lived their cover story. After all, he and Catherine at first had pretended to be lovers, and then...

We're at war, Leblanc! And admit it. There were times this year when any man in this business would have loved to find a woman to warm his bed, so why not her?

But Henri had never made any effort to fulfill those occasional masculine yearnings for someone other than Catherine to lie by his side. He realized with a start that his wife, Alice, hadn't even entered his thoughts for months. It was only dreams of Catherine that had persisted since the day he first encountered her in a forest-green suit that matched her eyes. He knew he had to stop speculating whether there had been other men in her life since they'd last been together in the Scottish Highlands. As he watched her now making up the bed, the rush of memories from that memorable night only heightened his anticipation of spending this one with her.

Meanwhile, Catherine stretched a wool shawl over the makeshift mattress she'd created. She looked up. "My poor partner in crime actually needs those Coke-bottle specs to see anything. His rotten eyesight kept him out of the regular military."

"If he ever lost those glasses, it could be a hazard for you both," Henri frowned.

Catherine merely shrugged and tucked a corner of the shawl to finish building her tidy nest. He decided then and there to let the matter of Guy, a.k.a., Sean drop and pointed to the pillow that would support both their heads this night.

"Don't the locals wonder what happened to the baby when you suddenly stopped looking pregnant?"

"Our story was the baby was born too early and died," she replied without elaboration. And then her guarded gaze changed into a look signaling he was the lover she wanted this night as much as he wanted her. She walked to his side and extended a hand to touch the metal fastener on his flight suit's zipper. "May I?" she asked softly.

Henri's breath caught as she seized the tiny piece of metal and pulled on it until soon, the entire suit gapped open from shoulder to crotch. With the upper half dangling at his waist, she smiled faintly as she reached with one hand to cup him through his trousers and then gently stroked the swelling object of her desire.

"Nice?" she whispered.

The warmth and sheer presence of her touch on his groin sent bolts of sensation throughout his body.

"Oh, dear God, Catherine," he groaned, pushing the suit to the floor and reaching for the belt buckle of his trousers. "You cannot know how often I—"

She interrupted him by moving closer to press her lips to his. He curled one arm around her back and, with his other, reached up to cradle her head while he met her tongue in a dance that was unspoken proof of how much he wanted her.

There were so many words he wished to say, so much he yearned to tell her, but the thought that there were only a few hours before he had to leave drove him to express his passion and sadness and frustration with a strangled demand.

"Catherine!" he said, fumbling for the button at the waist of her trousers, "If you don't take these damn things off, I'll go berserk. I want to make love to you properly."

"Properly?" she teased in the low, throaty way she had that made him go rigid with longing to be inside her. In the next moment, she turned and walked away from him, saying, "Hold that thought."

Henri stood motionless next to the captain's bunk. He'd been startled by Catherine's abrupt move and unsure what she was doing as she plunged her hand into a canvas bag nearby. She lifted out what looked to be a kind of clamshell, opened it, and triumphantly held up a small rubber object specifically designed to prevent pregnancy.

"Remember this old friend? she said, a hint of uncertainty creeping into her tone. "Given our current occupations, we can't afford to have any delayed surprises."

"No surprises," he repeated. "Especially not for you. Only pleasure and love, *chérie*."

In unison, they began to disrobe, his shirt to her blouse, her slacks to his trousers. When they both stood naked in the moonlight, Henri murmured, "Thank God it's the month of May or we'd freeze to death in here. Come. Lie down." He reached out and gently took the diaphragm from her hand. "Please, let me do the honors."

Henri was a mature man, neither embarrassed nor repulsed by her honesty about the need to protect herself. He understood such things as birth control as only a man of his age and experience would. Catherine's smile seemed almost beatific in response to his wholehearted endorsement of safeguarding her from a pregnancy that could put her life and that of any child at risk.

"Thank you," she said simply. He lay down on the side of the bunk near the bulkhead and beckoned her to join him. "You know, *Monsieur* Leblanc," she said, stretching out beside him, "I have told you before that I was drawn to you from the first moment I met you."

"And, certainly, I to you."

Catherine's low voice was almost a purr.

"And just now," she said with a nod toward the object he held poised in his hand, "your gallantry proves how right I was right about you. In fact," she said, her smile widening and her jade eyes crinkling at the corners, "your selflessness places you as number one in my Pantheon of Worthy Men, including FDR and Winston Churchill."

As she leaned nearer, he was finding it the height of intimacy to gently place the diaphragm between her thighs and carefully insert it to block her womb. Catherine stared at his face during his tender ministrations. Her expression seemed on the brink of tears.

"You managed that little operation almost better than I could."

He bent over her, cupped her breast, strafing his thumb lightly around her nipple before suckling it, pleased beyond reason at the low moan his actions elicited.

So often, Catherine had taken the lead in their lovemaking, but this night, Henri took command, pinning her to the lumpy bedcovering she had devised. He lovingly held each of her wrists above her head and stared into her eyes, his glance unwavering, so that she could not miss how much he urgently needed to meld his body with hers.

When he entered her, she wrapped her legs around his waist, the proof he craved that she truly wanted him as much as he desired her. With his every move, with each muscle in his exhausted body, he summoned his last ounce of strength to stamp her with his scent, to mark her as *his* this night. She met the slow, deliberate motion of his hips with a perfect rhythm of her own that maddened them both until she sobbed her release at the same moment he cried out his own.

His last thought before drifting off to sleep in a tangle of street clothing and the woolen shawl was the otherworldly sensation of floating through the night sky and landing by moonlight at Catherine Thornton's feet.

———◇———

The first rays of morning sun crept beyond the arch of the Roman aqueduct whose shadow had shielded the dry-docked craft from view of the boatyard itself. In the shifting light, two sleeping forms stirred on the makeshift mattress inside the cabin.

"*Bonjour, chérie,*" Henri whispered in Catherine's ear.

She reached above her head and stretched like a cat, wondering if he were only half awake as she felt.

"I'm guessing the first local train to Nice leaves around eight," she warned him.

Our time is almost at an end.

Abruptly, Henri leaned toward her, grasping her chin between his fingers.

"Don't picture me leaving," he insisted, perfectly reading her thoughts. "Just picture me as I am, right here. Right now. Still beside you. Loving you."

And without saying another word, he pulled her close, and she was lost again, enveloped by the intensity of his desire to show her his need for her and hers for him.

Ironically, she thought later, it was Henri who was the first to come to his senses. When their breathing became regular, he rose up on his elbow, casting a glance out the porthole.

"My staying here any longer is dangerous for you. We must get up now and go to Nice. Agent...Guy, is it? He may wander down here looking for you, as I assume he knows about this boat."

Catherine swung her legs over the bunk and stood naked before him on the worn teak floorboards. "He does," she agreed. "You were sleeping on some of his clothing. And, yes, we should definitely be on our way. I kept a little of the bread and cheese I liberated from Remy's last night, so we can have that before you leave."

*Before he leaves...*she thought. *Will I ever see this man again?*

She studied Henri's face to memorize how he looked after a night in which each revealed to the other who they truly were and how miraculously they'd found love among the ruins of war. Then he rose to his feet, leaning in to give her a feathery kiss.

"Bread and cheese," he murmured. "You think of everything."

As she reflected on the night they'd spent together, she realized that, for the first time in her life, she'd been solely conscious, not of thoughts but of sensations. She would never forget the feel, taste, and sight of the man now gazing intently at her across the small space that separated them.

And now another day of war had dawned.

They dressed in silence and exchanged few words as they

returned the interior of the boat's cabin to exactly as it had been when they arrived. She knew they were both thinking back to the French embassy in D.C. when they'd performed similar chores to restore the code room so that no one would ever suspect they'd cracked the safe.

"See?" Catherine said, holding up the clamshell-like container. "Back it goes."

She made a deliberate show of storing the diaphragm in the deepest recesses of her canvas bag. Her reward was Henri casting her a heartfelt smile that rimmed his eyes with tears. The next instant, he enfolded her in his arms and held her without moving, standing like a Rodin statue, their two bodies pressed together, frozen in time.

"Remember this. Remember how we fit together so perfectly," he murmured.

For Catherine, their newly donned clothing became the barrier that gave her the strength, finally, to pull away. They were dressed, ready to go, and dared not tarry.

"We'll eat our bread and cheese on the train," she said with the demeanor of an agent in charge. "I'll go down the ladder first and then signal for you to follow."

———◇———

The local trains on the short run from Villefranche to Nice still operated on a reasonable schedule. To Henri and Catherine's relief, both sets of their documents passed muster with soldiers at the platform where their coach was about to depart.

They had taken a few steps beyond the checkpoint when one of the soldiers barked, "Halt, there! You! Lady!"

Catherine felt a rough tap on her shoulder. She turned around and, to her consternation, recognized the young Italian soldier that had checked her papers the day she'd stashed the hand grenades into the farmer's beehives on the road to Villefranche. She'd been on her bicycle that day in her pregnancy disguise.

"I remember you," he said, flicking a glance at her amber hair. "You had the baby?" He stared at her breasts as if she should be nursing the child in front of him.

For a second, Catherine's mind went totally blank. Then she

twisted her features into a look of sorrow mixed with the indignation she actually felt that this man should feel it his right to undress her with his eyes.

"My baby *died*!" she spat in perfect Italian. "He was born too soon because you soldiers take our food so a pregnant mother starves the child growing in her body!"

For a second, her words appeared to bring the soldier up sharp. He scrutinized her documents. "Your papers say you're French, yet you speak to me in Italian," he said, meeting her angry stare, his own eyes narrowing.

"My mother was Italian. Dead, now," she lied, "thanks to no medicines anymore."

Shrugging, he shifted his glance to Henri and then back to her. "This man is not your husband. The names on your documents are different. Why are you together?"

Catherine sensed Henri stiffen with caution, but she refused to avert her eyes from the soldier's accusing stare.

"My brother here came to help me with the baby's funeral. You saw by his documents that he's a printer," she said, pointing to the papers the solder continued to hold in his grasp. "Now he's on his way back north to his business in Paris," she informed their inquisitor. Her mind whirling, Catherine judged that Sean's brief and separate encounter with this soldier the day she hid the grenades in the beehives wasn't likely to jog the Italian's memory if they should meet on a future day. She jutted her chin out and said, "And if you *must* know, my husband was sent to Germany to work in a munitions factory. He wasn't even here when I lost the baby!"

Catherine felt genuine outrage underscore her words, as she'd known of local women facing similar dire circumstances when their husbands were conscripted to work for free for the Third Reich. She wiped her eyes with the back of her hand as if the conversation had summoned tears, which it nearly had due to the sheer terror they'd been detained by this swaggering punk.

Henri said quietly to the soldier. "May we go now, sir? We'll miss our train…"

With a mild look of chagrin, the uniformed guard turned on his heel and marched back to his post at the head of the platform as a steady stream of passengers hurried toward their respective coaches.

Henri took hold of Catherine's arm, murmuring, "A brilliant bluff, but you've aged me ten years. Let's get on this train."

———◇———

The Nice train station was relatively deserted when they arrived. A round kiosk displaying newspapers and sweets featured mostly bare shelves. Its proprietor leaned against one wall, asleep on his stool.

Catherine led the way toward a café she knew on a back street where she proposed they spend the time until the train returning her to Villefranche was due to leave. As they walked along the narrow passageways, Henri swiftly summarized his concerns about Agent Gilbert, a.k.a. Lucien Barteau.

"I'm sure he tipped off the Germans the night your Jockey circuit leader, Roger, landed in France." he told her. "I just had that mission feel, you know? Like a fox catching the scent it recalls as danger."

Catherine nodded. "I would have thought this Gilbert character's choice of a landing field positioned so close to the camps run by Germans was suspect."

"Exactly!" Henri agreed. "And the moment I saw that distant string of headlights coming up the mountain, I knew instantly we were in deep trouble. Instead of following the weapons canisters to the farmer's barn, we headed straight back to Paris."

Catherine nodded, silently confirming to herself that Roger had in fact related a similar story as to his own impressions of that night, a validation that Henri must be telling her the truth. Lucien-Gilbert undoubtedly was the double dealer. The fear she always pushed to the back of her mind—that Henri had become a double agent—had to be baseless.

Wasn't last night proof enough he would never betray me or France?

Still, hadn't both Roger and Peter Churchill warned her to be wary of this Frenchman despite whatever her heart might say? She wondered if some sliver of doubt about him would ever be completely vanquished.

She saw Henri glance at his watch as they turned another corner in the twisting path to the out-of-the-way cafe.

"We don't have much time," he said. "I won't be able to contact you while I do my survey of the coastal defenses the Axis has put in place. I'll have to find my own way to Cannes, St. Tropez, and Toulon to report on the state of the potential landing beaches there. Hopefully, there's a Marseille-Paris train I can take, with no one the wiser."

"How do you justify your long absence to your network in Paris?"

Henri looked at her and deadpanned, "As it turned out, I was troubled by a kidney stone, not my appendix. Luckily, as far as Agent Gilbert or anyone else in my local circuit were concerned," he added with a droll expression, "I somehow passed the pesky thing in a London hospital after days of pure agony."

"Well done!"

The two of them had reached the door to the café Catherine had selected. She paused and turned to him, saying in a low voice, "I suppose it's crucial for General Eisenhower's invasion forces to know what they'll be up against if they ever assault the beaches here, but please, *please* be careful," she urged. "You could see in the train station that there are a lot more of those dark green SS uniforms here now."

"I'll be as careful as I can, *chérie*."

She found herself quietly struggling with the feeling that the odds against a German defeat were well-nigh overwhelming. Henri would have to make his way on this mission, city to city, facing danger every second. She feared that the brutal SS would see him poking his nose into places along the Riviera that were absolutely *verboten*.

She began to fret that any invasion of the Côte d'Azur was bound to inflict horrendous civilian casualties. *No wonder Winston Churchill and the SOE bigwigs had doubts about the wisdom of such a dicey move,* she thought.

———◇———

The café was nearly empty, and they were forced to be patient until someone came from out of the kitchen to take their order. Henri asked for two coffees that turned out to be more chicory than beans. With another glance at his watch, he reached into his pocket.

"Before we have to leave," he said, his expression almost boyish, "I'd like you to have this." Between his fingers he held a ring studded with one large diamond surrounded by dozens of tiny ones.

"Henri? What—"

"It was my mother's. She gave it to me when I first became a pilot to carry with me for luck." He cast her a sheepish grin. "It always worked, because I even survived that air crash during the last war."

She pushed his hand holding the ring toward his side of the table.

"You must keep it! To keep you safe!" she insisted, with a feeling of almost dread that he should want her to have it.

"No, but that's just it, don't you see?" he said, smiling at her with the same tender look he'd had when they first had lain in bed on the boat. "She told me to keep it only until I found my own true love, as she had found my father."

"But...well...what about Alice?" Catherine almost felt as if it were bad luck even to speak the name of Henri's estranged wife.

"I never gave Alice this ring," Henri said, placing the jewel on the small, round table and pushing it toward her, "and that should tell us both something."

"But you and I are already married—to other people!"

"Please, no *buts*," he countered fiercely. "To me, the luck of this ring will continue if you'll accept it and keep it close, even if you feel you dare not wear it." He reached for her hand. "Keep it on today, though, until we must leave here, will you?" He slipped it on the fourth finger of her right hand. "One day, we'll sort all this out, and I'll place it on your left hand as you do in America. I will take you to my home in Perpignan, where my parents lived in the only truly happy marriage I've ever witnessed. I give you my solemn promise on this, Catherine, so stay alive for me, will you darling?"

"You always say that." Catherine stared down at the sparking gems and inhaled a deep breath. Then she sought his gaze. "I love the ring. I will cherish it always."

Henri would never know what the deeper meaning of the ring he'd just put on her finger was to her. *He was no double agent.* He was, in fact, her own true love—a revelation that almost astounded her. Her heart had been encased in arctic ice since she was fourteen years old, and now she felt, as dangerous as their world was, that for the first time in her life she'd reached a safe harbor.

Henri covered the ring and her hand with his own.

"Stay alive," he repeated.

"And will you promise to do the same for me?" she whispered. "Use your wits, your gun, your wile...whatever it takes, but stay alive!"

"I'll do my best. Whatever happens, know you were my last conscious thought."

She raised her hand and pressed the ring against his cheek.

"The same, *mon amour*. The same."

CHAPTER 30

Catherine insisted Henri not accompany her back to the station but instead took him to a safe house she knew on a back street behind the broad *Promenade des Anglais*.

"They're a family of French Jews Peter Churchill introduced me to. They've taken in a bunch of refugees who've fled from the Nazis in the northern half of France. One more guest won't be noticed, but don't stay more than a night or two here." Before she knocked on the door, she added, "The Klajmans are good people, and they'll know someone you can stay with in Cannes. In fact," she cautioned, "each safe house can often recommend the next one on your route, so avoid all hotels as you travel. The Germans and the *milice* are everywhere down here now, and that's the first place they look."

When the door opened and they were bid to come inside, Catherine quickly explained Henri's need for temporary shelter. Once the invitation was extended to him, she shook hands all around, and then she swiftly departed without looking back.

Her throat tight, she resolutely walked away from the Klajmans home, tucking her right hand into her pocket to hold Henri's diamond ring, which she had reluctantly taken off when they left from the café. The edge of the largest stone protruding from a circlet of smaller gems felt sharp against her palm. It served as a reminder of Henri's love and a warning she mustn't give in to the flood of tears she'd never before shed.

———◇———

Approaching noon, the Nice station was jammed with a large crowd of people weighted down with bulging cardboard suitcases and layers of clothing. All their jacket fronts had yellow cloth Jewish stars stitched onto their garments as a mark of public identity, and Catherine's heart sank at the sight as she waited for her afternoon train to return to Villefranche.

She stared at another large cluster of people shuffling into the station from the street. The parade of men, women, and children formed a sidewalk cavalry of the damned. Silent and tearful, the crowd was surrounded by the vicious *milice*, French hooligans recruited by the Vichy as an ersatz SS now reigning terror in the country.

Catherine's attention was caught by a young man loudly protesting that he wasn't Jewish. He was roughly pushed away from the crowd and slammed up against the kiosk only a few feet from where Catherine stood.

"Your trousers!" growled the paramilitary policeman. "Pull them down! I want to see." The man reluctantly unbuckled his belt, but before he could comply any further, his tormentor stripped his pants down his legs, along with his underclothes. "Circumcised!" the guard declared triumphantly. He pointed to the man's naked groin. "You lie! You're a filthy kike! Get back in line."

"But I'm not," sobbed the young man. "My father is a doctor! He believes circumcision is better for health! He—"

The policeman jammed the butt of his rifle into the ribs of his victim. Crying out in pain, the man struggled to pull up his trousers and hastened to limp back to the crowd of hapless onlookers who stared at him with dead eyes.

Catherine leaned against the kiosk to inhale a few deep breaths. Before she could calm her racing heart, another altercation broke out on her right, just as a family of six entered the train station. The late arrivals were immediately accosted by the same member of the *milice* who had just harassed the unfortunate young man.

"Papers!" he demanded.

The father dug into his breast pocket marked by the ubiquitous yellow star and pulled out a fat stack of documents. They were examined one by one while the mother, her three young daughters, and a babe in arms waited, the faces of the adults white with fear. The smallest girl of the three held a stuffed rabbit by the ear and wandered toward Catherine, adrift in an imaginary world of make-believe that she and her rabbit were going on a trip to see *la grand-mère.*

"Miette, it's lovely in Monaco," she crooned. "You'll see. Our *grand-mère* gives us sweets, and I'm sure she'll have a carrot in her garden for you."

Harsh instructions from the uniformed members of the round-up brigade mingled with the shrill whistles proclaiming imminent departures of various trains, including Catherine's. The guard appropriated the family's travel documents under his arm while poking the barrel of his gun into the father's shoulder.

"You! Jews, all of you. Move!"

Other shouts from the police rang out. "Move on. Go, go, go, you dirty swine!" could be heard echoing around the crowd that stooped now to collect baggage and grasp the hands of their loved ones.

A chorus of isolated protests erupted, and a few in the group made a run for the door that led back to the street. Shots rang out, women screamed, and a few bodies fell to the ground. The brutal gang of soldiers pushed the milling crowd with shouts and curses toward a waiting train that Catherine was sure would ultimately take them to Drancy, the prison for incarcerated Jews outside Paris. From there, as she had learned, the prisoners would be deported to German slave labor camps—or worse.

Catherine heard a child's muted crying and looked behind the rounded edge of the kiosk. All she could see was a toy rabbit's ear and a small hand clutching it. In the melee, the little girl had bolted away from the gunshots. By this time, Catherine had lost sight of the child's family, whose papers had just been confiscated. In fact, all she could see fifty yards from where she stood was a mass of humanity being herded down a far platform and onto trains that appeared to be mere boxcars designed for cattle and other animals regularly transported to the slaughterhouse outside Marseille.

In the instant it took to make a decision, Catherine dashed to the kiosk's far side. Her fingers clawed at the little girl's cloth star, catching a fingernail on the piece of thread that had been used to sew it on her coat. The child looked at her, terrified.

"I won't hurt you, *petite,* but you must come with me!" Catherine whispered. She saw that the little girl's light brown hair and hazel eyes might even pass for Catherine's offspring, if her cover story was persuasive enough. "Your mama had to leave, but I'll keep you safe. If anyone asks, say I am your aunt and that I'm caring for you." She knelt down and held the frightened child by her shoulders. Staring into the little girl's eyes, Catherine willed her to pay close attention to her words. "You must trust me. It's important that if anyone asks, say that I'm your aunt, " she repeated urgently. "Will you?"

Wide eyed, the girl nodded.

"I promise you'll be alright if you come with me now."

Catherine could tell the youngster walking beside her was in a state of shock as she allowed herself to be led down the platform, her stuffed toy dragging by her side. Once on board, Catherine lifted her into her lap, and they both sat silently as the train pulled out of the station and headed east along the shoreline with the bay sparkling outside the grimy window.

Oh God. What have I done? I've just risked our entire mission!

But something burrowed in Catherine's gut for a decade made it impossible for her to abandon this child so cruelly ripped from her family, just as Jeremy had snatched her own baby from her arms when their ship docked in Caracas.

I couldn't just leave her in that train station. Perhaps the olive farmer's wife…

Catherine sat still as a stone holding tight to the little girl in her lap. As happened occasionally on the short trip from Nice to Villefranche, there'd been no checking of documents when the passengers boarded. Catherine assumed this laxity was most likely due to the hubbub and confusion of the latest deportations that had demanded the attention of an army of officials at the train station. She handed the child her last, tiny scrap of bread, which the girl quickly consumed.

"What's your name, sweetheart?" Catherine whispered, taking in the child's thin, pinched face, framed by light brown, lackluster hair. The child's extreme pallor and cracked lips gave evidence of the deprivations she and her family had suffered.

"Tamara," she whispered back. "I'm five," she added with a surprising show of pride. She held up her rabbit by its ear. "This is Miette, who is just a baby. Where is *Maman*?" she demanded again.

"She had to take another train, but we will try to find her when we can." Catherine tightened her arms around the little girl's frail shoulders. "You and Miette both must be very tired. Why don't you take a nap for now?"

And, to Catherine's relief, Tamara's light-brown eyes eventually fluttered closed. As the train rocked its way toward its next stop, the child fell fast asleep. Catherine, as tired as she was, remained tense and alert. She had no ticket for the child, nor a scrap of identification for her. She thought of Peter Churchill and her new leader, Roger. Wouldn't her superiors be absolutely furious with her for taking such a risk?

But, then, what are we fighting for? Why are we doing this work at all?

Catherine inhaled a deep breath, the weight of five-year-old Tamara pressing against her chest. She thought of Henri, perhaps gone from her life forever. A strange sense of the rightness of her recent actions began to take hold.

Even so, what in the world would happen once the train pulled into Villefranche?

———◇———

Catherine nearly groaned aloud when she saw that the same Italian guard, to whom she'd silently given the name Guido, was still on duty. He was checking papers as passengers exited the platform at the depot, only a stone's throw from the curving bay. Holding tight to Tamara's hand, she edged to the left through the crowd, hoping to make it to the other soldier working the same shift. Fortunately, they were surrounded by scores of travelers, and little Tamara practically disappeared from sight.

"You there! You're back already?"

This time, the soldier who had recognized her earlier exhibited a friendly demeanor and waved her over. Catherine glanced to her right and nodded, but before she could hand her documents to the other official, Italian began to flow from the lips of this now familiar face. He looked down, noticing Catherine holding Tamara's hand.

"You have another child?" he asked.

Catherine handed him her documents. "This is my brother's daughter," she answered with the story she'd concocted on the journey from Nice to Villefranche. "The man who was traveling with me this morning," she reminded him.

He gave a cursory glance to Catherine's papers and the evidence she'd paid for the train ride from Nice.

"And the papers for the little one?"

"Sir," Catherine lowered her voice as if sharing a confidence, "her mother died last year. My brother thought it best she be with me during this turbulent time. Sadly, her father had to immediately return to his post in Paris printing broadsides for the Vichy. He couldn't provide the care needed by one so young. Since I recently lost *my* child, my brother thought..." She allowed her voice to trail off, as if tears were about to flow.

"Yes, yes...but where are her papers?" he demanded.

Catherine dug into her canvas satchel and rooted around with her hand. Feigning that she was greatly flustered, she blurted, "We picked up the child from her other aunt in Nice. We were in such a hurry to make arrangements for her care, and to get my brother off on his train on time to return to his duties for the Vichy..." She sought the soldier's gaze. "I can't believe we were so stupid! When we said good-bye in such a rush, my brother must have forgotten to give me Tamara's documents—and I forgot to ask!"

The soldier looked at her with renewed skepticism. Catherine summoned her most imploring expression.

"Please, sir. She's only five and already misses her father. I must get her home and feed her. I promise I will go to the authorities later. They'll confirm her identity and obtain the proper documents right away." She made a show of swallowing hard and swaying on her feet. "I'm afraid I'm feeling a little faint," she said. "I lost a lot of blood during the, uh...birth of the child that just died. Please," she pleaded again, "could you just let me pass this time? I promise, I will have everything in order as soon as I can."

The Italian guard glanced over at his colleague who was busily examining individual documents and granting permission for passengers to proceed out of the depot. He returned his gaze to Catherine and hesitated.

Then with a shrug, he said, "Your husband is away in Germany, you said earlier? Then I hope one of these evenings you will share a glass of wine with me here in Villefranche." He glanced at her documents. "I know your name. How can I find you?"

This Guido's meaning was clear.

Catherine summoned a friendly smile, silently grateful for the safe house on the hill above the harbor chock full of fishing nets. "How kind you are, sir," she replied. "I live above an engine repair shop in the boatyard. Anyone there can direct you."

She tightened her grip on Tamara's little hand and passed onto the street, fighting an urge to run.

—◇—

Catherine sat Tamara on a bench within view of Remy's kitchen and filched more bread and some cheese while the restaurant owner was out front serving his customers. Thankful that no one she knew had spotted her, she took the youngster by the hand once more and strode up the hill to the storeroom, where she fed the little girl and made a bed for her on top of the fishing nets. The exhausted child had fallen asleep once more by the time Catherine heard the door creak and turned to see Sean standing at the threshold.

"God, Catherine, I've been looking everywhere—" He stopped, midsentence, staring at the child curled up on the nets with Catherine's coat covering her. "What the hell?"

Catherine gave a vehement shake of her head and rushed to the door, where she pushed him back into the narrow lane and closed it behind her.

"I'll explain, I'll explain, but shush! Quiet!"

She pulled him by the sleeve and signaled he should follow her higher up the hill. They didn't speak until they reached the spot where the cobbled lane ended and the grassy hill that led up to the road to Nice began. She motioned they should stand in a deserted doorway of one of the last houses at the top of the village.

"You didn't sleep in the safe house, did you?" Sean said, his tone accusatory. "I know because I snuck back here at five this morning, worried how you were going to safeguard yourself and our unexpected visitor who fell from the sky last night."

"No, I didn't. Sleep up here, I mean. Like I said in my note, I took the agent to Nice," She continued to look at him steadily. "Let us hope he'll safely get a train from there to Cannes and on to Paris."

As protocol demanded, she didn't tell Sean about Henri's mission to survey German defenses for the SOE brass.

Sean said, "When I went down to Remy's, he said that after he gave you something to eat, you and *Monsieur* Claude-Whoever walked off hand in hand toward the citadel. Don't tell me you two risked staying in the sailmaker's loft?"

"No, we didn't. I got him to a safe house in Nice. Don't you want to know the reason there's a five-year-old Jewish child asleep in *our* safe house?"

Sean remained silent a moment and appeared to collect himself. Catherine prayed she wouldn't have to tell him about staying on the dry-docked boat. That place harbored private, sacred moments; still, she wouldn't lie about that to Sean.

Finally, he spoke. "Who is she?"

"Thank goodness she could tell me her full name: Tamara Polakov. She got separated from her parents at the Nice train station just as several deportees were shot by the guards. A melee ensued, and hundreds of poor Jews were herded at gunpoint onto a train headed for Drancy prison outside Paris."

"And you ended up with a five-year-old because…"

He allowed his question to trail off. Catherine could see he was furious with her, a reaction that she understood, but still, did he feel no compassion for the child?

"Look, Sean, I know this complicates things—"

"I think *jeopardizes* is a more apt word," he retorted, his tone icy.

Catherine put her hands on her hips, feeling her own anger rising.

"Well, I couldn't just leave that little girl there to be thrown willy-nilly into some railcar and sent off to die."

"You didn't know that's what was going to happen," Sean snapped.

"Oh, for God's sake!" she retorted. Suddenly, she was furious. "You've heard what the Nazis are doing! They're not rounding up Jews and gypsies and downed Allied airmen to send them to a nice German spa!"

"So, you were willing to risk our entire operation playing rescuing angel when you were in Nice seeing off Agent Claude? And, by the way," he demanded, "between the time you sent me off to Eze for the night and now, did you and Claude *walk* to Nice?" Spend the night in a café?" He turned away slightly, muttering, "I highly doubt that, since Remy says he saw that you both appeared very well acquainted."

Catherine reached out to lay her hand lightly on his sleeve. Her anger gone now, she knew what was provoking Sean.

"Actually, Claude and I are very well acquainted."

Sean turned around to stare at her, his eyes behind his thick glasses shot with pain. She could practically see the wheels revolving in his head.

With a bitter edge to his voice, he said, "Claude is the French diplomat you knew in Washington, right? He's the same one that Roger warned you about when he came to see us after he'd parachuted back into France and Claude was on his reception committee in Compiègne. You also saw this guy, again, during training. You said so to Roger." As if putting together pieces of a puzzle, he blurted, "So, you put yourself and all of us here in peril for one night with that guy?"

"I did," she admitted. "Just as you and I threw caution to the wind, once upon a time, because there's a war going on, and there are moments when we think *that* moment may be our last. But—and I hope you will try to understand me, Sean—I owe it to tell you that Claude is…a very important person in my life. More important than I realized." She hesitated and then plunged ahead. "And I wish I could convince you what a brave patriot he is."

"You just think that because you love the guy."

Sean's ragged words were a statement, not a question. Catherine inhaled a deep breath before replying.

"I guess I do."

"And you slept with him last night, even though he's someone Roger and Peter Churchill both think could be a double agent."

"He's not a double agent!"

Catherine put her hand in her pocket and wrapped her fingers around the diamond ring that once belonged to Henri's mother. "Believe me, I realize that what I did last night was foolish as well as foolhardy, but that's how it was with Claude and me. But beyond that, you'll just have to accept my word: Claude is no double agent," she repeated.

"Or so you believe." Sean turned to stare at the hill that lay behind the last cluster of houses where they were standing. Over his shoulder he said in a low voice threaded with anger and pain, "You know, don't you, that you've completely broken the trust between us?"

"Not on my side," she replied to his back. "I still trust you with my life, and you would do well to get over this jealousy and realize that you can totally trust me with yours."

"Not with a five-year-old Jew sleeping in our safe house."

Another blaze of temper coursed through her, but all she said, as calmly as she could, was, "Don't tell me at this late date that you're an anti-Semite?"

Sean turned back toward her. After a long moment he replied, "No, I'm not. It's just you and I have a mission to do, and you have to admit, she complicates what is already a very precarious position for us."

"If you'd witnessed what I did in Nice, Sean, you'd have done the same. At least I hope you would have."

The two of them remained silent. Sheer fatigue had dulled Catherine's will to battle with him anymore. Dismissing Sean with a shake of her head, Catherine turned to start walking down the hill.

CHAPTER 31

"Wait!" Sean called out, his voice and footsteps on the cobbled path louder than was prudent. He reached out and caught hold of Catherine's sleeve. "You're right."

"About what?" she asked, fatigued, not looking at him.

"I *was* jealous." She turned and stared at him. "I mean," he confessed, "I *am* jealous."

He pointed uphill where they could remain out of earshot. Retracing their steps to stand beyond the last house on the lane, Catherine waited for Sean to speak first.

"It's all so crazy!" he said, with some vehemence. "All three of us are married to people whose faces we can hardly recall. And now there's a little girl you and I must look after and—" He pushed his glasses down and pinched the bridge of his nose as if his head was throbbing. After several moments, he spoke in a tone that no longer made Catherine feel defensive.

"But what about the practical stuff, Catherine? We have to find someone to steal or forge some documents for her. She's only five and needs food and continuous care." Now that his anger had dissipated, his expression had become more empathetic "You and I still have a job to do—planes to meet, downed airman to hand off to the underground, and some serious weapons to hide."

"I know. All this is hard, but I have a plan," Catherine replied. She silently prayed he would agree it was a good one or at least would consider it plausible. "Tamara is light-haired with hazel eyes. She could pass for a cousin of almost anyone in Villefranche. We'll find her a safe place to live with a *résistant* and get on with our work. As a matter of fact, I think you and I must leave this immediate area right away," she said, briefly describing the encounter she'd had with the Italian soldier who would doubtless come looking for her and ask a lot of questions. "And besides, I think I made that moment's decision because I'd just said goodbye to Claude and I couldn't bear another loss, watching Tamara's parents being dragged away like that."

She had never told Sean about her baby son whom Jeremy had given away to virtual strangers. She realized, now, that trauma had also played a part in her snap decision. But the mere thought of relating that personal history aloud was overwhelming.

She closed her eyes and heard Sean say, "You look about to drop."

He reached out, pulled her into his arms like the brother she'd always wanted, and pushed her head against his shoulder.

"Oh, for God's sake, Catherine." He kissed the top of her head. "I forgive you. Sort of. When I opened the door early this morning and you weren't asleep on top of the fishing nets, I-I sort of panicked. I thought you two had been arrested. Then I saw your note, waited a bit, and then went down to Remy's, figuring you'd gone there to grab something to eat before you got an early start escorting Claude to Nice. When Remy told me he'd seen you walking toward the boatyard and—"

Catherine raised her head. "I do understand how you'd feel." Sean gave her a look of mild disbelief, but Catherine held her hand aloft as if to ward it off. "And I hope you can understand about the history I share with Claude and my...well, my feelings for him. I know I keep saying it, but he's no double agent, Sean!" She was surprised to hear the vehemence in her own voice. "But he and I think we know who is." She met her fellow agent's gaze with a penetrating look of her own and briefly told him about the agent known as Gilbert. "As for you and me, I need you as my friend and comrade. We need each other if we're to stay alive in this nightmare."

Sean pressed her head against his shoulder again.

"Damn it. You're right. But do *not* think I like the way this has turned out." She felt him sigh, and again he kissed her, this time on the forehead as if she were the child who had just been rescued. "Oh, hell!" He shot her one of his cock-eyed smiles, though this one was tinged with palpable sadness. "I definitely need you in my life, at least as my friend and comrade in arms."

Their spat was over, Catherine realized with relief. Their relationship would never quite be the same, but there'd be no permanent breach between them.

Sean stared into the distance. "My twins turn five this year. I can't imagine what it would be like if someone just grabbed them and sent them off to..." His voice trailed away. Then he turned to Catherine, behaving as if he'd just dreamed up the plan she had already outlined. "We'll beg Jules Menton and his wife, up on the olive farm, to take in Tamara, with the promise we'll provide a convincing birth certificate, ration cards, and so forth. We can get that guy in Cannes we know to phony up something. She'll just stay there for the duration. A new 'cousin' among Jules's kids won't even be noticed."

Filling Catherine's chest was a renewed sense of affection. "Sean Eisenhower, you are definitely a sterling chip off your distinguished family's block."

They were back to fighting on the same team.

Catherine leaned toward him and brushed her lips against his cheek in benediction. Then she took his hand, and the pair started walking down the hill, back to the storeroom brimming with fishing

nets that sheltered a little Jewish girl who had tragically been
orphaned that day.

———◇———

Jules Menton stood at the entrance to the building that housed the
olive press, its stone wheel the size of a small fishpond. This
October day, piles of empty wooden boxes and nets that would be
hung to catch the olives were stacked on the back of a flatbed, ready
to be hauled into the groves, where the pickers would use them to
corral their harvested bounty. The stored olives would be pressed
into oil in a few weeks; it was a precious commodity in this season
of having nothing. Several of Menton's children, nieces, and
nephews, along with the fair-haired Tamara, were taking turns
hopping on one foot toward the center of an outline of a snail drawn
in the dirt.

"It's like our hopscotch," Catherine explained as she and Sean
approached Jules. "I'm so relieved to see that Tamara seems to be
fitting right in."

"But will Jules keep her for the duration?" Sean muttered. "Just
more risky business on his part, but at least we got her some
convincing documents."

Just then, Tamara looked in their direction and recognized
Catherine. Not tall enough to reach her waist, within seconds she
was throwing her arms around Catherine's upper thighs. "Have you
heard from Maman or Papa? Will they come back on the train?"

Catherine knelt in the dirt to bring her eyes level with Tamara's.

"It is very hard to get messages to them, sweetheart, but I'll do
everything I can to let you know more when I do. I know they miss
you a lot." She smiled with what she hoped was reassurance. "I see
you've made friends. That game looks like fun."

Tamara glanced over her shoulder at her playmates.

"It's called *escargot*. It is fun, and I can hop all the way into the
center of the snail without stepping on even *one* line in the dirt."

"Good girl!" Catherine enthused. She looked up, waved to Jules,
and rose to her feet as he nodded in acknowledgement. To Tamara
she said, "We have to talk to *M'sieur* Menton now, but I'll be sure to
watch when it's your turn to hop, hop, hop."

Tamara smiled shyly and skipped back to the other children.

When she was out of earshot, Sean said under his breath, "Let's pray Jules will let her stay on his farm once he hears our latest news."

Areas of southern France east of the Rhone had been in Italian hands since the start of the war, but wireless messages that Catherine had deciphered with Sean's help that morning had warned of a big change coming. The Allies' conquest of North Africa, followed by a successful invasion of Sicily and southern Italy in July, had resulted in Italy's capitulation and Mussolini being deposed. For Catherine's part, the message she'd just decoded was the fruit of her hard work improving some of the telegraphing skills she'd learned at Bletchley Park. Even so, as she declared earlier that day, "I hated this stuff then, and I hate it now!"

She'd been thrilled, however, by the steady unspooling of news being tapped to them from London over the wireless. Perhaps the secret French naval codes she and Henri spirited out of the French embassy in D.C. had actually been one of the reasons that Hitler's forces had finally suffered a defeat in the Mediterranean. Thanks to the copied codebooks, the Allies had been able to pinpoint the location of French and German ships off North Africa and had access to their communications. How wonderful it would be if she and Henri could raise a glass together to salute this feat.

Sean broke into her reverie, calling out for Jules to walk with them past the tractor standing ready to pull the wooden boxes to the groves that marched up the hills behind them. The summer's warmth had lasted into early autumn, and the olives had matured to a rich green shade. Catherine swiftly brought the most important member of their Trenches network up to date on the latest developments.

"Italy has quit the Axis and declared war on Germany."

Jules reared back with surprise. "When?" he demanded.

"Two days ago, October thirteenth," Sean confided, and the Americans have begun air raids over Germany itself."

Catherine chimed in, "We've been told to expect tons of German troops storming into Marseille any day now, then they'll move on to occupy Cannes and Nice. The Free Zone is totally a thing of the past. It's going to get even uglier when the Krauts toss out all the Italians. The Guidos will likely try to escape along our coast in order to cross the border back into Italy."

"*Merde!*" was Jules's only comment.

Catherine was well aware the Italian border was a bare ten miles from where they stood gazing toward the broad field. Their mission had totally depended upon the olive farmer allowing at least a dozen RAF planes thus far to take off and land on moonlit nights without detection.

But with more German troops coming into the area... Catherine worried silently.

"What this latest development means for Catherine and me," Sean explained to Jules, "is that the two of us have to make ourselves scarce for a while."

He cast a glance in the direction of Tamara, whose turn it was to hop from square to square toward the center of the snail. Catherine waved at her, indicating that she'd be watching the little girl show off her prowess at the game.

Meanwhile, Sean lowered his voice. "Jules, the pressure will be worse than ever to get some leading Jews out of Nice, along with some downed fliers who've been hiding in safe houses along the Riviera. Can we still bring them to you? London tells us they'll send two planes in one night on the next moon."

Catherine's gaze drifted over to the knot of children whose happy shouts seemed in such contrast to the life-and-death discussion the three adults were having.

"That's two weeks from now," Jules murmured. "Right in the middle of the harvest." He glanced down at his callused hands, toughened from years of picking olives and heaving heavy wooden boxes to and from his fields.

Catherine blurted, "And can you keep Tamara here with you for a while longer? Now that we're going to have to stay at a different place every day for a while, I see no way I can—"

"*D'accord,*" Jules said with an impatient wave of his hand. "My wife has taken to the child, and she fits in well with the others. Tamara is the least of our worries." For a long moment, Catherine felt Jules Menton's speculative gaze shift from her face to Sean's. Then he said, "We'll do the flights. And my cousin has a small basement flat attached to his house at the top of the village of Menton."

"The hill town named after your family?" Catherine asked.

Jules Menton allowed himself a faint smile denoting his pride at being a member of one of the oldest families on the Côte d'Azur.

"You both can stay there if you like. It's so remote, you won't have to move about every day, and your wireless should have a fairly clear signal from up there."

Sean grasped Jules's hand and gave it a hearty shake. "As always, Jules, you're literally a lifesaver. Tell us how to find your cousin's place and we'll be off."

Sean was halfway down the hill by the time Catherine caught up with him.

Out of breath, she said, "Tamara won the game!"

Sean briefly glanced at Catherine and kept walking. "You know, despite your sultry ways, you might make a parent, yet."

Catherine summoned a smile in return but felt Sean's quip like a punch in her gut.

I am a parent, and once this war is over—if it ever is—I'll make Jeremy tell me...tell me what? she wondered. That was a problem for another day.

———◇———

Henri looked up as his deputy, Alain Chapelle, walked into his small inner office at the Paris printing shop and closed the door.

"Well, did London respond to my report on the Riviera's coast defenses?"

Alain nodded and sat down opposite Henri's desk. "Our wireless man said you got the usual one-word answer. Two words in English."

"*Merci,* as in only 'thank you,'" was Henri's sardonic reply, attempting to hide the frustration he often felt in his dealings with SOE top brass. He had spent from May to September doing the ordered reconnaissance along the Riviera, while subsequently dodging arrest at almost every step of his journey back to Paris.

I barely escaped the SS two different times, and that's all they can say?

Outside, the clank of the printing press under Alphonse's direction could be heard pushing out a new set of threatening broadsides calling for an even earlier curfew that *Kommandant* Heinrich planned to post in the neighborhood. Henri sometimes marveled that the Nazi appeared to be clueless about how often the German's printing orders were stacked cheek-by-jowl with a clandestine Resistance newspaper or a pile of menus for a local bistro. Life, death, and the mundane, all in one place.

He opened a drawer and handed Alain one of his precious rationed cigarettes and offered him a light. "Any word on London's thoughts about our Air Operations agent, Gilbert?" he asked. "Does anybody there but us think he's a double agent and that we can't trust him?"

"No news on that score either," Alain replied with a shrug, "except word that they're sending over someone from their MI6 soon to check it out. Their opinion alternates between 'he might be a German collaborator' and 'he might not.'"

Henri leaned back in his wooden chair and lit up a cigarette of his own. Obviously, his reports about the dodgy situation with Gilbert had forced SOE's French Section leader, Maurice Buckmaster, to go to higher authority. And from what Henri had heard since joining the Allies' side, British MI6 despised Churchill's creation of his "amateur brigade of so-called secret agents"—the Special Operations Executive under the Prime Minister's control. Instinctively, Henri felt that whomever was being sent to look into the matter, the visitor would be arriving by plane, courtesy of Gilbert himself. Would some flunky from MI6 be more likely to believe the Air Operations officer who guided him here or the word of a former Vichy diplomat like Henri Leblanc?

"Here's a bit of news though," Alain said, inhaling his cigarette smoke. "Now that North Africa is in the Allies' hands, the Yanks and Brits are battling their way up from Sicily. It seems the Germans are now seriously worrying about an invasion in the South of France. They're kicking out the Italians who surrendered to the Allies a few days ago."

"Well, well," chuckled Henri, hearing this intelligence for the first time, "our side finally got a win in North Africa." He wondered if the codebooks he and Catherine had temporarily liberated from the Vichy embassy were ever cited by top brass in the war rooms at Whitehall and the White House as part of the reason for this success. But all he said to Alain was, "At least this is turning out to be a much better year than forty-two was."

"Not so fast," cautioned Alain. "A Panzer division, along with a lot of German troops and SS, have been sent to guard the major cities along the Riviera. Word is there'll be a big push to arrest thousands of Jews who have fled down there."

Henri, mid-puff, began to cough and fought to regain his breath.

Agent Colette and her team will now be constantly on the run…

———◇———

Catherine and Sean spent the rest of the autumn and early winter of 1943 lying low in a basement inside the small stucco house that Jules had provided, courtesy of his cousin. As in Villefranche, their safe house in Menton was nearly the last dwelling in the furthest reaches of the town, tucked away at the top of a winding cobblestoned lane. The place was heatless and offered only a latrine in the tiny back garden and well water via an outdoor pump. Fortunately, the weather had been mild, and the wireless reception had proved decent, as predicted by the olive farmer.

Keeping out of sight most days, Sean and Catherine had undertaken numerous perilous nighttime missions during those months to guide downed airmen and prominent Jewish leaders from Cannes and Nice to the upper field at Jules's olive farm. On two successive moonlight evenings, a Hudson—the amazing short-takeoff-and-landing plane—had proven how efficient it was for rescuing passengers as they waited on the makeshift airfield. Both flights had successfully picked up these groups and flown them to Britain, although dodging flak fired from many new German outposts along the way.

Over this same period, there were also the numerous weapons and supplies air drops that required the services of the Trenches reception committee. The team recruited by Jules each time retrieved the metal canisters floating down on silken parachutes and spirited them to suitable hiding places. All these clandestine activities were becoming increasingly fraught for the *résistants* as additional German troops continued to pour into the cities along the Riviera. More troops meant more ears for listening in white vans for telltale wireless signals and the droning of Allied planes conducting their missions over France.

"You realize, don't you, Sean," Catherine groused one morning when she hadn't left their basement quarters during daylight hours for two weeks, "when we're not organizing operations at two in the morning at the olive farm, we're creeping like moles into Nice, literally throwing sand and explosives into the gears of locomotives to cripple them. We haven't felt the sun on our faces in days. I'm getting a serious case of cabin fever!"

"Sorry, dearie, but nighttime industrial sabotage is now a big part of our job—preventing German war material being shipped where it could do a lot of harm."

"I know that!" she snapped. "But we're heading toward Christmas with no sign of an Allied invasion north *or* south. How long can we keep up telling the *résistants* 'soon, soon' and keep asking them to risk their lives?"

To say nothing of putting their families in constant jeopardy.

A vision of Tamara playing *escargot* flitted through her mind.

"Hey, it's the Frogs' country," Sean replied with a shrug that annoyed Catherine no end. "We're living like this. Why shouldn't they?"

"Don't call them Frogs!" Catherine retorted, curbing a strong desire to throw the wireless at his head.

By middle December, the weather abruptly changed, and to Catherine's way of thinking, their safe house at the pinnacle of Menton was now a frigid refuge akin to an Eskimo igloo. The olive harvest had long passed, many trees were leafless, and the stucco walls trapped the cold air and prevented any warmth from the house itself from seeping into the structure's lower confines.

One bleak, gray day near Christmas, Catherine sat hunched over the wireless, housed in its battered suitcase. The antenna stretched seventy feet from its leather side across the room, looped out a tiny window near the basement's ceiling, and extended across the back yard like a deserted clothesline and up the hillside, its tentacle ending in a bare branch of an apricot tree.

The door behind her opened suddenly, and a waft of icy wind blew in, scattering Catherine's papers to the floor. She turned to see a figure in silhouette, his face obscured by a muffler wrapped around his neck and a cap pulled down to his eyebrows.

Catherine's heart lurched with icy fear that her transmission spot had been discovered. Then the figure advanced inside the basement room, clapping his frozen hands together and stamping his feet.

"Have anything hot to drink? I'm frozen solid."

She saw at once, of course, it was Sean, stripping off his woolen scarf, his demeanor grim. Speechless with both relief and irritation, she managed to say, "For pity's sake, close the door, will you?"

Sean slammed it shut, clumped over to their small oil stove, and rattled the tin pot in which they boiled water.

"Ever heard of Alois Brunner?" he asked over his shoulder.

Before the interruption, Catherine had just finished her latest transmission and turned the dials that shut off the wireless.

"Brunner? No, I haven't. Is he SS?"

"Yup. He's SS *Hauptsturmführer* Alois Brunner, fresh from rounding up Jews in Austria and Greece. The bastard has now been sent here, charged with overseeing what Brunner has called the 'final solution to the Jewish problem' in the Maritime Alps."

"Oh, wonderful," Catherine replied, her sarcasm biting as she stood up and stretched out the kinks in her shoulders. She began hauling the long length of antenna in through the window as she mulled over the fact that the number of Jewish refugees in Nice alone had now swollen to some twenty thousand. Rooting them out in hotels and boarding houses would be easy pickings for Brunner's storm troopers.

"And get this," Sean said. "Brunner has just taken over the Hotel Excelsior in Nice. One of our men told me that Brunner's minions are arresting Jews everywhere this week, seizing their possessions and then stuffing the poor souls into barren former hotel guest rooms until he's ready to march them to the train station for deportation."

"Where they'll be herded into rail cars for the trip to Paris" Catherine added with a rush of anger, "and then sent on to slave labor camps God knows where in Germany." The memory of Tamara's family being force-marched onto cattle cars was all too fresh in her mind. "So, what do we do now?" she demanded. "With SS everywhere, you and I are as likely as Jews to be nabbed by the SS one of these days, given how many hours we sit here, keying the wireless." She pointed to the set whose cover she was just closing. "I'm probably as safe riding my bike out and about as I am sitting here and transmitting all these messages that half the time London doesn't answer or even acknowledge."

"Whether we're in the field or here in the safe house," Sean said with an uncharacteristic baleful expression, "it's all one big risk for the likes of you and me. We might as well pick our poison."

"Then, I'd rather be in the field."

"And I'd rather be here with you," Sean said. Catherine realized he was as frustrated as she was. "It's been months since you tangled with that guard at the train station," he added. "No one has come after you, thanks to our move out of Villefranche. How about, together, we split our time between the duties of wireless versus field operations?"

She grinned, holding out her right hand to shake. "You got a deal, buster!"

CHAPTER 32

January 1944

Sean's prediction of increasing peril for non-Germans as well as Jews in the South of France turned out to be all too true. By the end of 1943, some three thousand refugees and enemy aliens who'd fled other war-torn areas had been rounded up and processed at the Hotel Excelsior by the newly arrived Alois Brunner.

A few weeks into the new year, Catherine stood beside Sean on a cold, second-story balcony of an apartment in Nice belonging to one of their *résistants*. The winter winds were blowing down from the hills and toward the sea. The outlook offered an unobstructed view of the Excelsior and the spectacle of Brunner's latest unfortunate captives disembarking from trucks lined up on the street.

"Oh God, look what they're doing to those poor people," Catherine murmured, shivering in spite of her thick woolen coat. Every time she saw one of the SS or the hated French *milice* rough up innocent civilians, her stomach roiled. She wanted to pull out her service revolver and shoot the uniformed goons as if she were in a penny arcade.

With a brief glance at Sean, she peered over the railing onto the street directly below. Soldiers were methodically stripping their prey of their money and jewelry and then herding them upstairs into one-time guestrooms, now devoid of decor except for a few filthy pallets on the floors. Catherine had on good authority that, before the inmates were deported, they were tortured to gain information as to the whereabouts of relatives not yet caught in Brunner's net.

Sean pointed to another of the hotel's entrances. Just as with Tamara's family members, people with yellow Jewish stars stuck to their clothing were being prodded at gunpoint toward the train station, walking the first steps of a journey that would send them north and then on to camps with names like Auschwitz or Ravensbrück.

Movement near a window on an upper floor caught Catherine's eye. She gripped the balcony's banister and pointed.

"Oh, God…Sean!" she cried softly. "Please, no!"

A young man had been pursued to the window ledge by a uniformed officer brandishing a gun who clearly was about to march him downstairs. The prisoner swung his leg over the sill and, from the fifth floor, opposite them, hurled himself to the ground.

Catherine turned and burrowed her head into Sean's shoulder, feeling his swift intake of breath at the moment the man struck the pavement below.

"We've got to get out of here," declared Sean. "There's nothing to be done for that poor soul or any of those people down there. My contact at the hospital says that the staff there has been hiding a downed RAF pilot brought in last night. Thank God, the guy apparently spoke excellent French and claimed to passersby who found him on a road that he'd had a farming accident. By some miracle, they actually took him to the Nice hospital to get the wound on his head looked after. Let's go rescue him and get the hell out of here."

Catherine raised her head. "But these poor people! We can't just stand here and watch—"

"No, we can't just watch," agreed Sean. "All we can do is save the ones we can. Let's go!"

The pair managed to ride their bicycles to the hospital above Nice harbor without incident, entering through a basement door according to the plan Sean had previously worked out with sympathetic medical personnel there. A slender young nurse who introduced herself as Yvonne met them and, without even offering a greeting, led them down a corridor to a room on the right.

"He's ready," the nurse whispered, nodding in the direction of a haggard-looking young man with a bandaged head. "We've dressed him in a white coat and given him a doctor's bag and a bogus physician's pass, but you all must leave immediately."

"Sean, give him your hat to cover up the bandage," urged Catherine, "and if he can, let him ride my bike. It'll be quicker to get him up to the olive farm. If you're stopped, say he's going to Villefranche on a house call to see your dying mother or something. Jules will hide him until the next airlift."

"But what about you?" Sean asked. "How will you get back to the Menton safe house?"

"I'll figure out something or walk, if I have to. Now go. Go!"

With Catherine bringing up the rear, the two men followed the nurse out of the surgeon's lounge. Catherine got as far as the end of the corridor when she stopped at a doorway and peered into a basement ward full of women lying still as corpses under sheets pulled up to their chins. The hospital worker who had escorted Sean and his charge out of the hospital's back door returned and stood by her side.

"Our TB ward," Nurse Yvonne whispered. Then she winked. "At least a few of them here have tuberculosis. The others are Jews. The Germans are deathly afraid of catching the disease, and so far, we've had virtually no one apprehended and removed."

Catherine fought to keep from breaking into a grin.

"Genius." She leaned closer to the nurse. "So, you're saying that there are one or two that are actually in good health or at least strong enough to follow me on foot to a safe house? With any luck, we might be able to courier them to Switzerland or fly them out on our next transport."

With a pleased look, the nurse said confidentially, "We have a mathematician and a Resistance leader who would continue the fight if they could get out of here safely."

"Are they Jewish?" Catherine asked, *sotte voce.*

The nurse halted and looked at her intently. "Does that matter?"

"Yes. They're the ones I want today. To make up for something I witnessed at the Hotel Excelsior right before we came here."

———◇———

"I taught statistics at the Sorbonne," disclosed Rachel Rozanski, a Polish Jew who'd lived in France since her days as a university student. She glanced over her shoulder at a small, olive-skinned woman with dark, curly hair of about her same age. Liv Abel had remained virtually silent since they'd left the hospital and skirted the main road in favor of the smaller thoroughfares that headed east toward Villefranche. "Liv here hid me for weeks after the damned SS arrested our husbands when they went out to look for food. It was Liv's idea to seek asylum at the hospital and be put in the TB ward."

For the next few blocks, the trio trudged along without speaking. Catherine looked over at Rachel's silent companion.

"How clever to know about the Germans being terrified of contracting TB."

"Yes," was all Liv said, her coffee-colored eyes staring straight ahead.

Rachel looked over at Catherine and shrugged as if to say "She's moody and depressed. Who wouldn't be?"

Without warning, they heard the *putt-putt-putt* of a motorcycle, and before they could dash into an alleyway, around the corner it came, equipped with a sidecar painted the color of ripe olives. The pair of occupants in dark green SS uniforms appeared instantly alert to the fact that three women were walking down a street with no shopping baskets or any apparent reason for being out and about so late in the day. The motorcycle came to a halt, and the next minute, the two men strode toward them.

Catherine inhaled deeply, fighting to remain calm, her mind racing.

"Papers, please, ladies!" demanded the motorcycle driver.

Catherine assumed a bored expression, although her heart was pounding wildly. This was precisely the kind of dire situation that lurked in the thoughts of every secret agent working in the field. What could a pair of Jewish women and a supposed wife of a man recuperating from eye surgery do against two broad-chested men with pistols strapped to their waists and sporting swastika armbands?

Catherine pulled her documents from her jacket and prayed that her charges possessed some sort of identification, however bogus it might be. In a gesture of defiance, chin jutting in the air, she put her hands on her hips while she waited for the soldier's verdict on her papers. As she stood in the street staring at him steadily, she was conscious of the lump created by Henri's diamond ring that she'd recently sewn into the waistband lining of her wool trousers. Feeling it press against her palm through the fabric gave her a strange sense of courage.

But what if the women don't have convincing documents...

Slowly, Rachel retrieved papers tucked inside her winter coat. Liv did likewise, and the three of them held their collective breaths as the motorcycle driver first flipped through Catherine's and handed them back to her. Rachel, the attractive professor of mathematics with deep, claret-colored hair, appeared composed, as if she'd endured such scrutiny countless times. All Catherine could think of while they waited for the soldier's examination of their documents was the harrowing sight she'd seen earlier that day. How could she ever forget the moment when the young Jewish man hurled himself from the fifth-floor balcony to escape the horrors of what the Gestapo planned for him?

"Here!" said the soldier, shoving one batch of documents into Rachel's hands. When he began examining Liv's ration card, his eyes narrowed. "This is a forgery!" he declared to his companion. "See the stamp on the photo? The ink is blue! It should be red for this part of the Riviera."

Catherine froze. The smallest mistake—in this case, the wrong shade of ink on a mundane card enabling one to buy food—could spell disaster when it came to counterfeited documents. Catherine's hands were curled into tight fists as she waited for what would come next.

With a sharp nod at Liv's curly, dark hair, the soldier spat, "And she looks Jewish to me. I heard there was a ruckus at the Excelsior today. Maybe she's one of those who got away, helped by these two," he added shifting his imperious gaze in Catherine and Rachel's direction.

Catherine protested, "None of us has set foot in the Hotel Excelsior!" She waved her residence document in the air. "I live in Villefranche! These women were only—"

"Shut up!" barked the soldier who'd examined the documents. His hard look swept from one woman to the other. To his companion he said, "I think we'd better let Josef Gumbel have a little chat with all three of you."

———◇———

Unluckily for Catherine and her charges, one of the local jails in Nice stood directly beside the SS headquarters. Both buildings were only blocks away from where the group had been apprehended, the local structures having been requisitioned when the German army took over Southern France.

Chief jailor Josef Gumbel was not in his office when the latest prisoners arrived. Even so, within minutes, Catherine and the two Jewish women were under arrest, their identity papers confiscated. They were marched without further ceremony down a dingy corridor that led to the back of the building. Catherine's mind was whirling as she scanned the hallway, searching for a means of escape. All that lay ahead were jail cells.

The chief guard pulled out a large metal key from a pocket in his uniform and opened a barred gate that creaked on rusted hinges. The other two guards herded Catherine, Rachel, and Liv into an eight-by-ten-space, with nudges from their pistols.

Another trio of unfortunate females with thin, drawn faces and vacant eyes were already in residence and appeared to Catherine literally on the verge of death. One was sprawled in a corner on the floor, and the other two perched on their haunches, hovering over her. Catherine glanced over her shoulder as the door clanged shut behind her. Once it had, she knew they were trapped.

In spy school there had been simulated arrests in the middle of the night with SOE recruits rousted out of bed for mock interrogations.

This is the real thing, with a brutal enemy. What if they torture us? What if they know about the résistants *in Villefranche and the olive farm and try to get me to—*

Before Catherine could formulate any believable cover story for why she was with two Jewish women heading east on foot, a cacophony of deep, hacking coughs ricocheted off the cement walls. When the unsettling noise subsided, Catherine took in the disturbing sight of a pale, emaciated fellow prisoner who was obviously the sickest of the inmates. "How long have you all been held here?" she asked quietly.

Propped up in a corner, her caramel-colored hair plastered with sweat to her forehead, the prisoner gazed up at the newcomer, her brow furrowed in pain.

"Just a few days," she rasped.

One of her two companions hastened to relieve her of the burden of trying to talk.

"They caught us heading east," she explained. "We'd fled Nice when the lower floors of our hotel were being raided by Herr Brunner's men."

"You must stay away from us," warned the woman in the corner, the lids on her dull eyes fluttering closed.

The third woman who hadn't uttered a word thus far said softly, "We all have TB." She indicated the woman collapsed in the corner. "But she's...well, she's..." She fell silent and raised both hands as a sign of their mutual helplessness.

Catherine couldn't believe she'd just left a hospital ward where only half the patients actually had the disease, yet here she was, locked up in a small cell with three women who were obviously suffering from full-blown tuberculosis.

"Have you all been ill long?" she asked sympathetically. Meanwhile, she had an immediate concern for the safety of everyone else in the cell, including herself.

After another coughing fit subsided, the woman who introduced herself as Sarah Levy struggled to answer the question.

"My sisters and I came to the Côte d'Azur a few years ago to recuperate in the sun. The war started, and now, in the cold, without medicine and cooped up in—"

Before she could finish her sentence, another paroxysm of coughing choked off her words, leaving her gasping for breath and spewing phlegm into the crook of her arm. Catherine stiffened as she saw the smear of blood left on the woman's coat sleeve. Her two sisters merely stared and fell silent. They, too, looked as if they were as feverish and listless as the woman who could not repress her terrible cough. She nodded with compassion but backed away, quietly warning Liv and Rachel to keep their distance.

"They'll take us back to Nice, won't they?" Rachel whispered under her breath.

"To the Excelsior, I bet," Liv said, a bitter edge to her voice. She gazed accusingly at Catherine. "We were safe staying at the hospital, and then *you* came."

"Liv, be fair!" hissed Rachel, trying to keep her voice down. "They warned us we'd have to leave at some point. This was as good a chance as any to try to escape."

Catherine looked from one woman to the other, fighting a wave of remorse mixed with fury that her actions and plain bad luck running directly into a motorcycle patrol had landed the three of them in such serious jeopardy.

"I'm so sorry," she began, but her apology was cut short when the door opened at the end of the corridor. A pair of soldiers assigned guard duty at the jail stomped down the length of the hallway, heading straight for their cell. The door clanked open once more, and Catherine's two Jewish charges were roughly hustled out of their confinement at gunpoint.

"Wait!" Catherine called after them as Liv and Rachel were marched away from the cell where she and the three sick women remained. "You can't just—"

"We'll deal with you later," snarled one of the guards, turning around. "These companions of yours are obviously dirty Jews, just like the other women with you in there. These two," he said with a sharp nod in Liv and Rachel's direction, "were carrying documents any fool could tell were forged."

"Well, my papers aren't!" Catherine yelled, realizing her amber hair color, green eyes, and fair skin, along with the expert quality of the documents the SOE had issued, had classified her into a more favorable category. If she could just escape these goons, maybe she could save Liv and Rachel before they were—

The guard harshly interrupted her spinning thoughts.

"Being caught with these Jews has put you in serious jeopardy, you know that? We think you must be a courier or something!"

"We were all just walking along the road!" Catherine called after the retreating men, feigning insult.

The word *courier* sent bolts of alarm down her spine. Secret agents, despite their officer status, were declared terrorists and were shot by the Germans without any compunction or consideration of international law.

Another guard shouted from the far end of the corridor, "The officer in charge here will be back from lunch in an hour. He'll want to know exactly what you were doing helping these swine!"

Catherine stared through the bars in their cell as the guards disappeared into the front office with their captives. She sat down on the bench, leaned against the cement wall, and closed her eyes, trying to still tremors that threatened to turn her limbs to jelly.

Breathe. Just breathe.

In her mind's eye, she could practically see the women she'd tried to rescue being pushed into a black Citroën at that very moment. She dreaded the idea the two would be driven to the Hotel Excelsior, where a fate that Catherine knew all too well awaited them.

For the first time since she'd become a secret agent, she felt a crushing sense of failure.

Liv and Rachel would *have been better off if they'd taken their chances to remain at the hospital.*

Catherine kept her eyes closed for several long minutes, wishing she could fall asleep and blot out the entire day. Then, the woman named Sarah who had remained slumped on the floor in the corner began to cough again. The deep, wracking noise ended in a gurgle that sounded as if a sink pipe had broken.

"Oh, no!" cried out one of her sisters at her side. "Sarah? Oh, Sarah!

Catherine's eyes flew open in time to see that the woman had completely collapsed onto her right side on the filthy cement floor. Her mouth gaped open, blood gushing down her chin. Her eyes stared straight ahead, glazed and motionless. It was as if she'd been startled by something the rest of them hadn't seen and now gazed wide-eyed, as if looking beyond the crushing life she'd endured for so many months.

Her two sisters looked around imploringly at Catherine as if she somehow had the power to reverse what had just happened. Then one of the young women leaned over her sister, placing a finger under one ear to feel for a pulse.

"Oh, please God, no!" she cried, her index finger still pressed to her sister's neck. "Sarah. Sar-aaaah!" she sobbed, sinking to the floor beside the prone figure, the pitch of her voice ending in a screech. "She's dead! My sister has died!"

Catherine could only stare at the three siblings huddled in a tangled human knot of misery.

War is all about dying, she thought, *one way or another*.

Her training had supposedly prepared her to witness scenes of death but observing someone who was alive one second and lifeless the next sent bolts of both sorrow and revulsion down her spine.

The keening of the two sisters began as low moans and soon rose to a pitch that grew deafening. One of the guards who'd just left came running toward their cell. His face red with annoyance, he pulled up short, five feet from their cell, casting only a brief glance at the dead women before looking away, physically repulsed.

"*Mein Gott!*" he muttered, putting a hand over his mouth and nostrils.

His horror at taking in the death scene suddenly gave Catherine an idea. Her mind whirling, she impulsively shouted in her best schoolgirl German, "One of these women has just died of *TB*! Stay back, sir, or you're bound to catch it. For your own sake, the rest of us should be taken to the hospital immediately!"

Without response, he turned on his heel, charging down the hallway from whence he'd come.

Catherine turned to the two remaining women and whispered hoarsely. "I'm so sorry this has happened to your sister, but there may be a way to get us out of here. Will you do exactly as I say?"

The two women, absorbed in their grief, appeared not to have taken in a word she'd just uttered. Catherine began shedding her clothing as she approached the dead woman. "Where are her papers?" she demanded.

"With the guards," one replied distractedly. Then the other was seized by the same hacking cough as the dead woman.

"*Merde,* so are mine," murmured Catherine as she hurriedly removed her trousers. She pointed to the woman's jacket and blouse and reached to remove the outer garment. "Help me!" she demanded of the sister who seemed healthier than her remaining sibling.

"What?" she replied in confusion.

Catherine explained in a rush, "We'll dress Sarah in my clothing and try to persuade them to take us all to an infirmary or something."

"What are you doing?" the sister exclaimed angrily, watching in horror as Catherine pulled down Sarah's skirt.

"I'll explain later! Just put my trousers on her!"

"But—"

"Do as I say!" Catherine ordered harshly. "Just dress her in my clothes, and I'll put on hers. Trust me, it's our only chance."

CHAPTER 33

Catherine's hands were shaking as she struggled to exchange Sarah's clothing for her own. She thanked the fates that at least the deceased woman had caramel-colored hair, unlike her sisters. But, like them, Sarah also had a Semitic cast to her features. By the time the guard and his two comrades had entered the hallway, trudging toward them with a stretcher to remove the body, Sarah's still form was clad in Catherine's wool outfit designed in London by the SOE for her to wear during long hours on her bicycle.

When the guards drew near their cell, she conjured up a hacking cough while biting down hard on her tongue until she produced the metallic taste of blood in her mouth. Just as the first guard passed by, she spit through the bars onto the floor at his feet. The man stared first with dismay at the puddle of saliva and blood spattered on the cement and then, eyes widening, gaped at Catherine, who now clung to the bars as if she, too, were about to expire.

Pretending to gasp for air, she cried out in French, "Look, please! We all have TB!" She pointed to the blood-spattered blouse she was wearing. "For your own safety, you must send us to the hospital, or you'll contract it yourselves if you keep breathing the same air!"

The two guards holding each end of the stretcher let go of it with a clatter. All three jailors exchanged worried looks. In the next moment, the one in charge in the absence of their commanding officer pulled out his revolver. For a split second, Catherine wondered if he was going to execute them all on the spot.

"*Mein Gott. Mein Gott.*" He mumbled to the others how much he hated the duties he'd been assigned in this war—a remark Catherine could translate.

With the hand not holding his gun, he began to fumble in his pocket. Retrieving a large iron key, he opened the cell door and quickly moved back as if the furies of hell were about to asphyxiate him. All three guards now had their service revolvers drawn. With a frantic gesture, their leader motioned for the women to exit the cell and march on ahead, while their captors remained at a distance.

Catherine knew enough German to determine that they were debating anxiously among themselves if they dared ship their prisoners to a hospital without their leader's direct permission.

"Enoch, can't we just shoot them?" inquired one.

"Not without orders, you idiot!" his comrade barked.

"If we send them away to hospital, won't he thank us for acting so quickly?" suggested the third.

Catherine could tell all three guards were practically holding their breath to avoid inhaling the miasma they feared might be swirling around them.

As the women were herded into the jail's front reception area, Enoch, the head guard screamed at their prisoners, "Stand in the corner, and don't touch anything!"

Catherine spotted a pile of identification documents resting on a desk. Still at gunpoint, they ordered all the women to remain silent. One guard dialed the phone attached to the wall, while the others clustered near and strained to hear whether the hospital would admit three more patients.

Catherine stealthily reached across the desk and snatched as many identification papers as she could in one grab. She turned toward the window to stuff them down her bloodied blouse. Just then, the jailor returned the phone receiver to its cradle and pointed to the door.

"Johan," ordered the main guard to his younger comrade, "you wait outside with them until the ambulance arrives. I'll call the morgue to come get the body." To the women he ordered hoarsely,

"Now go. Go outside! And if you make a move, you'll be shot where you stand!"

———◇———

Within a half-hour, Catherine and the two women ill with TB arrived at the hospital Catherine had so recently left. She could tell that Nurse Yvonne, who'd been so helpful with the downed airman and Jewish escapees earlier in the day, was shocked to see her again, this time accompanied by two strangers genuinely infected with tuberculosis. The German guards signed the necessary admittance forms and hurriedly departed.

"And the other women you took from here?" asked the nurse.

Catherine inhaled a breath and replied. "Liv and Rachel? They were arrested before we got two miles away." She pointed to her head. "My fair hair apparently saved me. That, and my pretending to be as ill as the two women now in the TB ward."

"I see. Well, let's get you cleaned up, and we'll talk later," said Yvonne.

Catherine handed the nurse the documents she'd stashed inside her blouse before Yvonne led her to the shower room. There, a nurse orderly asked her to strip off the dead woman's clothing and then thoroughly hosed her down with disinfectant, followed by repeated sluicings of cold water. Next, she handed Catherine a hospital gown, led her to the basement TB ward, and tucked her in a bed far removed from the genuine patients.

The stack of documents Catherine had pilfered off the jailor's desk was now piled beside her on a small bedside table. After a brief look at each, she handed the first she'd examined to Nurse Yvonne.

"Only one of these is truly mine," Catherine, pointing to her picture. "Thank God I managed to retrieve my main identification. I'll need that photo on it to transfer to the dead woman's ID." She pointed to Sarah's documents that bore the obviously false name *Jacqueline Bise* to disguise the deceased's Semitic origins. "I barely had time to be sure that at least I had Bise's identification card and that I left my own ration cards and local residence document laying on the desk at the jail so they'd assume the dead woman was me. Hopefully, those papers of mine will convince the SS that it was Colette Durand who died and that Jacqueline Bise may soon succumb to TB."

"*Mon Dieu*, that was pretty quick thinking to scoop up any documents at all," observed Nurse Yvonne.

For her part, Catherine began to think she hadn't been so clever after all. She fretted silently that the resident card now in the Gestapo's hands meant they could trace her to Villefranche and jeopardize the safety of anyone who knew of her there. She had to get back to warn Sean.

And what if Remy gets caught up in this or is tortured for information about Sean and me? Or if the trail leads the SS to Jules Menton and the olive farm...

Feeling the walls were closing in, Catherine handed over several more papers to Nurse Yvonne. She nodded in the direction of the beds on the other side of the ward.

"Some of the documents belong to the women with me who actually have TB."

The nurse put them all in a drawer in the small table beside Catherine's bed.

"Yes, they're very sick," she replied, her voice barely above a whisper. "But who knows? We'll just keep these papers in the drawer here, for now. I hope they survive, but if not, their documents can always be altered for others, if it comes to that."

"Liv Abel's has the wrong colored ink...the stamp should be red."

Yvonne nodded. "I'll remember that. Thanks."

Catherine gazed at the empathetic woman who was busy tucking in the rough linen sheets pulled up to Catherine's chin.

"Do you think I'll get TB, having worn the clothes of—"

"Unlikely," Yvonne interrupted reassuringly. "You were only with the women a short time, and we've scrubbed you down head to toe. You should be fine."

"But Liv and Rachel, the women I took from this ward. The SS whisked them away right after they arrested us." Catherine felt her throat tighten. "They're probably already on one of those cattle cars, headed for God knows where." She looked at the nurse who had been so brave and kind. She could hear her own voice was cracking with emotion. "I-I shouldn't have played the almighty rescuer. I should have just left them here."

"Shh..." soothed Yvonne. "We couldn't have kept them here forever. You did what you thought was best, and I agreed with your decision, remember? That's all any of us can do. We're not gods, and we can't control the fates. You saved yourself and these two," she added with a nod across the ward.

"But they're so sick. What real chance do they have?"

"Whatever the odds, you've given them that chance," Yvonne replied. "And now you're free from that horrible jail and can continue your work. What you've done was daring and brave. Now, get some rest before you leave. I'll find you something to wear."

The nurse had barely reached the door exiting the ward when Catherine sat bolt upright in bed.

"Oh no! No, no, *no-o-o.*" Her protests ended in a wail.

Yvonne turned and ran to her side. "What? What is it?"

"My ring!"

Catherine covered her face with her two hands, her mind spinning with the vision of her frantic exchange of clothing with the dead woman. The goal had been to make the jailors think that, because of her tweed suit and the food ration and residence cards she'd deliberately left behind, it was Colette Durand—a suspected *résistant*—who had died. Clad in Jacqueline Bise's garb, Catherine had, indeed, convinced the guards that she was one of the three women ill with TB and had escaped jail. But sewn into the waistband lining of her woolen trousers now worn by the dead woman was the beautiful diamond ring Henri had given her.

Catherine's fists repeatedly clutched and released the bedclothes. Her throat clogged with tears, she felt as if a rock was sitting in the pit of her stomach. Henri had asked her to keep his mother's precious ring until they might meet again. Losing it now made her almost certain they never would.

————◇————

What a complete cockup, thought Josef Gumbel, the commanding officer of the Nice jail, just back from what had been a leisurely lunch.

Elbows on his desk, he leaned forward and listened closely to the complicated tale the guards laid out in the wake of the cell that was now empty of all prisoners. He needed to get the facts straight before he filed a report about these events to *Kommandant* Wintermuden at Gestapo headquarters in the next building.

"So," said Gumbel, trying to understand the sequence of events that had transpired in his absence, "you sent two of the captives the SS arrested today—Jews picked up on the street—down to Herr Brunner at the Hotel Excelsior, correct?"

"Yes, sir. As is your standing order, sir," reminded the burly guard left in charge when their leader had departed for his lunch with fellow officers from next door.

"And the dead woman was sent to the morgue?"

"Correct, sir. To be immediately cremated, due to her having TB. Johan here stripped off her clothes, which are bundled in that bag over there."

The officer raised an eyebrow at Johan as if he might have the plague.

"I wore gloves, sir, and put on my old gas mask. I didn't want the others—or you, sir—to be in any danger."

Good man," he replied. "And the other three women with tuberculosis, they were sent by ambulance to hospital, do I have that right?"

"Yes sir," all the guards replied in a chorus.

Young Johan volunteered, "They were the prisoners that were here before you left for lunch. They were very sick and very contagious, coughing all over the place. In fact, the woman who died expired in the cell soon after you left. One of the three arrested while you were at lunch was also sick, as it turned out, and was spitting blood on the floor. We thought you'd want us to get them all out of here right away, sir, given—"

Cutting him off, Herr Gumbel gave a sharp nod of agreement. He shared his underlings' horror at the thought of catching TB. "And which woman, again, was it that died?" he pressed. He wanted to be certain he clearly had a grasp of the situation. Pointing to the small pile of identification documents stacked on the desk, he tried to sort through the confusing sequence of women captives who'd come and gone from his jail this day. He knew the paperwork would be a nightmare.

The three guards exchanged looks. The most senior of them held up a rations card and a document identifying a residence in a sail-maker's loft in Villefranche.

"From the papers there on your desk, we determined that Colette

Durand is the dead woman's name, sir. One of the two women out of the six that had lighter hair," he added helpfully.

"I wouldn't know. I never saw the three brought in while I was at lunch," their commanding officer reminded them tersely.

"Of course, sir," the guard hastened to reply. "Well, these were the documents she had on her when she was arrested."

"Durand...not a Jewish name. Did she look Jewish?" Gumbel asked.

"So many we arrest have false names on their documents, don't they, sir? Hard to keep it all straight."

"It's our job to know who's who," Gumbel snapped.

"To be honest, sir, it all happened so quickly, and there were so many sick women in there, I-I never got a good look at any of them after they started screaming." With the expression of a man assigned to an onerous task he asked, "Should I have the dead woman's clothing burned, sir?" pointing to the laundry bag that he'd grabbed in haste when dealing with the corpse.

The *Kommandant* gestured in the direction of the papers stacked on his desk and heaved a shrug.

"No. It's all evidence. We've long suspected there've been people around Villefranche working in the Resistance, trying to escort Jews and airmen along escape routes out of France. Maybe this Colette creature was one of them." He gestured toward the linen bag on the floor. "Send the Durand woman's clothes and her papers to the counter-intelligence department at Eighty-Four Avenue Foch in Paris for the master file." He pointed to the identity documents on his desk. "Enoch," he said to a senior guard, "I want you to check out the address in Villefranche that's on her residence card. If she wasn't Jewish but was with two Jews, she could well have been helping them escape despite being sick herself. Maybe she's an enemy agent who'll lead us to others."

"The three we sent to hospital appeared ill for sure, sir," the head guard said, his tone a touch defensive. "My guess is they're all going to die soon."

"Yes, we'll let the hospital deal with all that for now," Gumbel said, thanking his lucky stars he hadn't been exposed to the contagion.

The commanding officer slowly shook his head, wishing that the memory of his delicious lunch of *fois gras* and a bottle of *Veuve*

Clicquot had not been replaced by such unpleasant business as a jail cell that must now be completely disinfected.

He turned back to the paperwork resting his desk and considered his options. He'd order the next Jew they arrested to thoroughly scour the contaminated cell with a solution of diluted carbolic acid they had in the storeroom. After that, he'd have his men hunt down everything that could be found about the deceased, fair-haired woman named Colette Durand whose residence card said she lived in the boatyard in Villefranche.

Who knew what she'd been up to when alive?

Josef Gumbel leaned back in his chair, pleased with his decisions in the wake of today's odd events. The death of Mademoiselle Colette Durand just might be one of those threads that led to unraveling an entire ball of yarn.

————◇————

Henri left the windblown streets of a cold February afternoon in Paris and slid into a seat at a small table in the back of the café around the corner from the print shop. He was sipping from a glass of what purported to be cognac, when Alain Chapelle came through the door, looking over his shoulder even before he scanned the room for Henri.

At length, he crossed to Henri's table and sat down, saying under his breath, "I was being followed, but I managed to shake off whoever it was a few blocks before I arrived here." He signaled to a waiter to bring him a glass of whatever his companion was drinking.

Henri asked quietly, "Is it true that the last two agents arriving in France were immediately picked up by the SS within an hour of landing on one of the flights arranged by *Monsieur* Gilbert?"

Alain nodded. "And so were three others here in Paris who had somehow survived the blown Prosper network. If it isn't Gilbert, it's someone he knows that's telling the *Bosches* our every move."

"And no word about this from Buckmaster?" Henri asked.

"From the latest wireless transmissions, I get the feeling that he's at the mercy of decisions made higher up. Major Bodington has come and gone after supposedly looking into the issues around Gilbert. Maybe MI6 finds those contacts that you and I suspect our Air Operations office is having with the Germans are in fact useful to the agency in some double-triple-dealing master plan of theirs." Alain's cynicism revealed how depressed he was about the recent deadly Nazi sweeps throughout Paris.

"Buckmaster can't be willing just to sit around and let the cover of agent after agent be blown as soon as they parachute to the ground on landings organized by Gilbert!" Henri protested.

Alain looked downcast. Henri could see his deputy was feeling as discouraged and bitter as he was.

"All I know," Alain replied, staring hard at Henri across the table, "is that an invasion better come soon, or we won't know who we're working for—or why."

"We're working for France," Henri reminded him quietly, "although, believe me, I am just as sick and tired of this war as you are."

CHAPTER 34

April 1944

Hints of Spring wafted in the air above the village of Menton. Rows of lavender had begun to sprout sage green stalks. Soon there would be buds an inch long that would turn fat, purple, and redolent with a distinctively pungent scent.

In her basement lair, Catherine stared at the notes she'd just dispatched by wireless to London. Her skill as a wireless operator was markedly improving, she thought, although progress on the blasted machine had been slow and painful. For the next scheduled transmission, she'd planned to haul the equipment even higher up the mountain to continue to avoid the SS troops roaming the main roads with their triangulation gear, bent on homing in on Allied signals.

She heard the door open behind her and turned to find Sean

standing at the threshold waving a *carte identité* above his head in triumph.

"*Bonjour, Mademoiselle* Jacqueline Bise," he said, advancing into the room. "*M'sieur* Forger in Cannes has done one of his most brilliant jobs to date. Look!"

He handed her an improved version of falsified identification for Jacqueline Bise, now made to look much more authentic, with the proper colored ink on the stamp placed across the corner of Catherine's original Colette Durand photograph.

"I guess our new cover story here in Menton is that we're sister and brother," Catherine mused, fingering the card's corner, "not husband and wife anymore. And apparently I'm helping you recover from your recent eye surgery."

Sean shot her a mischievous look. "Actually," he said, "I liked our other cover story better, but given these new papers and the fact you've barely left this room in Menton, it'll have to do. We can thank the fates that poor Jacqueline Bise, a.k.a. Sarah, was posing as an Aryan of about your age and size. It made the forger's job much easier." He smiled. "Your good luck held yet again."

Catherine offered a shrug of agreement but silently contemplated that Liv and Rachel's luck had certainly run out, thanks to her. And every day she wondered about the fate of Sarah's two surviving sisters currently battling TB at the Nice hospital. That is, if they hadn't died by now, like poor Sarah.

Staring sightlessly down at her desk, she fought a feeling of foreboding that invaded her thoughts ever since the day she'd sneaked back to Menton dressed in a pair of Nurse Yvonne's trousers, blouse, and jacket with sleeves slightly shorter than they should be. Yes, she'd devised a way to escape from a Nazi jail and saved two of the five women also incarcerated there. Even so, now that she would be assuming the persona of the invented Jacqueline Bise, she was at an even greater risk of slipping up in a way that put herself and everyone in their network in danger.

She murmured her thanks to Sean and gazed at her new identity card for a long moment. It appeared a reasonable match with her old one, but Catherine knew that she couldn't afford a single misstep.

"Did you hear if the authorities have been nosing around Villefranche?" she asked. "Did Remy have any news?"

Sean's expression grew somber. "He told me that two goons have been showing your Colette Durand residence card all over town, especially at the boatyard. Apparently, a couple of *milice* were sent to ransack our sail-maker's loft, finding nothing, of course."

"And what about the dry-docked boat?" she asked, seething at the thought of those dirty dogs sniffing around the place where she and Henri had made love during their last night together.

"If they went there, they wouldn't have found evidence we'd been there. After all, we carted everything up here ages ago." He put a hand on her shoulder. "Look, Catherine, I know what happened in Nice was plenty unnerving, but Remy said the *Bosches* only had your old residence card but no photo of you. The few tradespeople who knew you as Colette said you'd suddenly disappeared, which, as far as they're concerned, corresponds with your reported death. The bastards will probably soon give up trying to nail the identity of the woman they think died in their jail cell."

"What else did you hear?" she asked, staring at the papers she'd been working on.

Sean walked toward a narrow table pushed to the side of their tiny basement quarters and pulled off a hunk of stale bread and began talking while he chewed.

"Not so good on that score. In Cannes, one of our agents told me he'd heard that Paris is in functional lock-down as far as our people are concerned. Many arrests there."

Catherine bit the inside of her lip but remained silent. Neither of them ever spoke of Henri, a.k.a. Agent Claude Foret. As for her, she hadn't had a single scrap of information whether Henri had made it back to Paris unscathed.

Sean gnawed on a second hunk of week-old bread that they had conserved, since food was growing scarcer by the week. Finally, he swallowed hard and continued describing his reconnaissance mission into the towns west of Menton.

"The other thing I heard in Cannes was that several Jockey circuit agents north of Avignon have been nabbed. Roger and his group, thank God, managed to avoid getting caught in the sweep and have moved on, though exactly where is top secret."

Catherine pointed to a pile of her recent transmissions that she was about to burn.

"Well, here's a clue," she observed, picking up one of her notes. "We were just notified that Roger has been put in overall charge of operations executed by those of us in his surviving networks. One group is to derail every train leaving Marseille for Lyon on a single day if given the signal—but nobody says when that signal will come."

Sean shook his head. "Do you think it means an invasion is finally in the works?"

Catherine lit a match and soon her small pile of messages caught fire. Before her fingers burnt, she dropped the paper scraps into a large metal bucket next to her table.

"Who the heck knows? But guess what our next assignment is," she said, her spirits lifting a notch. Without waiting for Sean's reply, she went on. "We're to expect more men and material at the olive farm and..."

Sean's eyes were alight.

"And what?"

"We've been ordered to locate a small craft and practice rowing two miles offshore."

"Offshore?" he repeated, his voice hinting at his excitement.

"At some point in the next month or two—or three," she said with a Cheshire Cat smile, "we'll be arranging a rendezvous with a submarine, ferrying downed airmen out and guiding forward observers back to shore, where they'll do what forward observers do."

"Like calling in artillery fire power from hulking Allied battleships in the Med?" he asked, a big grin lighting up his face.

"You got it, partner!"

———◇———

"How the hell do we know the submarine's even *out* there?" demanded the RAF pilot, one of two they were ferrying to the pick-up spot.

"Pipe down, will you?" Sean croaked. "Voices carry over the water."

The coastal seas were as dark as the moonless sky above. Fortunately, the lack of breeze this night made rowing out two miles from shore somewhat easier than Catherine worried it might be.

"Were you even given the right coordinates to know where the sub is supposed to come up?" demanded the impatient flyer, his tone just as insistent as before.

"Don't you imagine that we'll see whether the information transmitted to us is accurate when the sub surfaces?" Catherine retorted.

She couldn't keep the sarcasm out of her answer, her patience as worn thin as Sean's. The arrogant attitude of the two RAF pilots toward their American couriers had been apparent from the moment they'd climbed aboard the dinghy, especially vis-à-vis Catherine personally.

All evening, she'd sat in the bow of the small wooden craft being rowed by Sean off Cap Martin, east of Monaco. Her job was to peer into the misty April night for any signs of the sub. By the look and sound of their cranky passengers, she guessed that the airmen were feeling somewhat green around the gills by now. For more than a half hour, their rowboat had been tossed by swells as they waited for the vessel to show itself two miles offshore. Fortunately for both Sean and her, years of plying the waters of the Potomac and the Chesapeake Bay had made hardy sailors of them both.

"It's only a quarter past two," Catherine said over her shoulder, adding in a tone she hoped sounded condescending, "it shouldn't be long now."

No sooner had Catherine spoken than the waters around them began to boil five hundred feet off their position. Within moments, a conning tower and then a long black hull rose from the Mediterranean like a menacing whale, streams of water pouring back down to the sea.

Catherine turned on her pocket torch and blinked the coded signal, soon receiving the answer she expected.

"That's them!" she hissed. "Row, Sean, row!"

Given the challenging logistics, the transfer of airmen up the ladder and onto the sub, and the delivery of the forward observers climbing down into the dinghy went smoothly. As a quartet of men in American Army uniforms settled themselves and their packs into the small boat, one of them noted cheerily with a grin directed at Catherine, "Swell water taxi service they have here in France."

Catherine smiled back and said in English, "Well, boys, welcome to the Riviera, but it'll be no holiday for you, I'm afraid. Be mighty careful. Most of the beautiful beaches are mined."

One of the GIs offered a low wolf whistle. "Hey, guys, forget the beautiful beaches. Just get a load of our beautiful escort—and she's a Yank!"

Their passengers' looks of surprise at seeing a woman speaking to them in their native language and with an American accent was matched by their hearing Sean's urgent caution, "Quiet, everyone! We're going to try landing you guys without getting blown out of the water by the gun batteries the Krauts have positioned along the coast."

Catherine returned to her job as lookout, praying they could make it back to shore and then row out once more to the sub and pick up a second group of special operations troops to ferry them safely onto the Côte d'Azur's dry land as well.

Within twenty minutes, the small craft nosed onto a secluded part of the beach on near a point of land that they'd made certain ahead of time was free of mines. Catherine jumped ashore first, followed by the four men. One by one, they disembarked, staggering on shaky sea legs with their unwieldy backpacks weighing them down.

"Just rest against that seawall over there and get some sleep," Catherine directed. "We'll row back to get the others in your unit. Then we'll point you toward Nice."

"We've got maps, lady. We know where we're supposed to go," grumbled one.

"First, we find us some food," groused another. "We don't need no dame telling us what to do."

"Look, gorgeous," chimed in the soldier who'd spoken aboard the boat, "it's not our first time at the rodeo. How 'bout you let us decide—"

Before any of them could say another word, Catherine interrupted coldly. "You've just landed in a country whose language you don't speak and which is infested with a hornet's nest of SS. I strongly suggest you gentlemen do as I say. Sit over there and wait. We'll be back within the hour."

Catherine turned and waded into the water. Within seconds, she'd pushed the boat off the sand and vaulted aboard in one smooth motion.

Once out of earshot of shore, Sean joked, "Nothing like a ride in a sub and a bout of seasickness followed by hunger to erode a guy's good manners."

In the gloom, she could just make out that three of the four soldiers she'd ordered to sit down and wait for them were instead leaving the beach, apparently making their way inland on their own.

"*Merde!*" she said, mumbling more to herself than Sean. "I forgot how stupid some men are."

———◇———

Several days later, in Catherine's next transmission to a receiving station in the south of Italy she forwarded a report that Remy had brought to her: Within two hours of landing, three of the eight American soldiers they'd transferred from the submarine had been captured by the SS.

She told Sean, "I tried to be tactful in what I coded about those idiots in case they've been executed." She reached for a watery drink barely resembling coffee that she'd made on a small burner in their Menton basement hideout. "We might as well have their families thinking they were heroes."

Her disgust at learning of the foolhardiness shown by the three who had set off to find their own way toward Nice was equal to her sadness they'd gotten caught.

Sean sat quietly. "They behaved like the hot-shot forward observers they figured they were, daring to go into enemy territory to call in firepower."

"In a place they'd never been?" she shot back. "They were here to get the lay of the land, not start an invasion yet. So, what did they do? Take off in the wrong direction and saunter into the outskirts of Monaco where they decided to try their hand at the roulette wheels? What fools!"

"They probably figured since Monaco is a separate principality, they'd be fine."

"Yeah?" Catherine replied, her patience with Sean's excuses growing thin. "In a place where the Nazis have free rein to arrest Jews and that's notorious for storing German money in their neutral banks? Admit it, Sean. Those three that took off from the landing spot were arrogant pricks. They were probably arrested at a checkpoint by Germans occupying the place, and no one will ever hear from those G.I.'s again."

"Very dumb," agreed Sean.

"Oh, and here, look at this," she said, abruptly handing him a transmission she was about to burn. "You've been named Roger's official deputy, in charge of all operations from the Italian border, east of here, to the west as far as Cannes. Congratulations."

Sean stared at the paper and then looked at Catherine.

"They should have named us both."

"Yup, they should have, but haven't you heard? It's a man's world." She stretched out her hand for Sean to give her back the message. She then lit a match at the corner of the transmission and watched flames curl the paper before tossing it into the bucket.

Sean said in a cheerful tone she knew was intended to soothe her ruffled feathers, "What do you say we head up to the olive farm? We can have a decent dinner with the Mentons and Tamara before the next load of supplies falls from the sky."

———◇———

May 1944 flew by in a blur of landing parties, air drops of weapons and supplies, and other covert operations coordinated with various Riviera *résistant* units. Their targets included manufacturing facilities, power stations, railway tracks, and trains planted with explosives that could cripple the enemy.

By the first of June, Catherine and Sean were joined in their next clandestine operation by Remy, who'd pleaded to be part of the augmented sabotage missions that all those working underground in the Resistance steadfastly believed was a prelude to some invasion—either north of Paris or in the South of France.

For Catherine's part, rather than feeling exhilarated that, finally, the Allies were gaining the upper hand, she had begun experiencing a kind of war-weariness and perpetual apprehension she'd never felt before.

Cycling toward the night's destination at a rail yard outside Nice, she said quietly to Sean, "What is this, our seventh sabotage mission in a month? I can't stop thinking that our number is bound to come up, and not in a good way."

"Don't say things like that!" he shot back as they pedaled along.

"This next job's gonna be a piece of cake compared to all the crazy stuff we've done these last months."

The three rode another mile in silence, parking their bikes on the outskirts of Nice. As the trio trudged along the railroad track that led to an outer side yard at the station, Catherine thought of all her close calls and wondered if tonight was when her luck would run out. Word everywhere was the Germans were panicked about rumored Allied invasions launched from who-knew-where. Locally, the Gestapo had redoubled their efforts to stamp out Resistance networks wherever they were suspected.

Sean poked a gentle fist into her arm. "When we get done here tonight, we'll get Remy to sacrifice some eggs from his sister's hens. He'll make us the best omelet outside Paris, right Remy?"

"*Oui, d'accord*," Remy replied, but Catherine sensed their friend was jittery too.

Sean reassured Catherine, "It's all going to go fine, kiddo."

Catherine tried to breath in some of Sean's positive outlook. Instead of their normal heavy cache of explosives, she carried large printed shipping labels in her canvas pack. Each large label, with adhesive on the back and written in German, had been delivered as part of the most recent parachute drop. The agents' instructions were to plaster them in appropriate spots on freight cars destined to send important German war material to incorrect destinations.

"Tonight's little operation feels like the Allies want us to play one big practical joke on the Krauts," Sean said in English with a laugh for Catherine's benefit.

"I just hope the joke isn't on us," she replied, hearing the sour note in her voice.

The hour approached 3:00 a.m. Catherine knelt, opened her pack, and divided the labels into three groups, handing a stack each to Sean and Remy. Then she gave them each a sponge.

"Use the bottles of water in your packs to rewet the sponges as you go along so the adhesive on the back of the labels will stick firmly to the cars." To Sean she directed, "You put all your labels on the sides of each car on that train over there. Stick one on the front end, one on the back, okay?" She turned and said, "Remy?" pointing towards the two tracks between which they were standing. "You plaster that train, and I'll do this one. Start at the last car and work forward. We'll all meet at the locomotives at the front and then beat feet out of here before dawn breaks. Sound like a plan?"

Sean nodded, holding up a whistle on a lanyard around his neck. "And if either of you sees anyone or anything that poses a risk, blow one long sound and run the opposite direction, agreed?"

With a brisk nod and holding her own whistle aloft for a second, Catherine donned her canvas pack and headed for the rear of her assigned train, the labels stacked in the crook of her arm. She worked steadily, getting into the rhythm of affixing a label on the side rear of a freight car, dashing forward, and then repeating the process on the front of each flatbed or coach. Every third car or so, she had to rewet the sponge. She had no idea what was actually being transported in the trains they were mislabeling, but she hoped it was war material that would end up far from where it was needed.

The locomotive attached to the front of the train she was plastering with false directives was in her sights when she spotted a two-man patrol rounding the corner of a building at the end of the rail yard.

"Oh, double *merde!*" she muttered under her breath.

She could barely believe her eyes. Not a hundred yards from where she was shrouded by shadows stood the burly guard who had called the hospital from the Nice jail to see if it would accept three women prisoners with TB. Was he inspecting the trains due to carry more captives to prisons north and east of the Riviera? Whatever the reason for him and his companion to be in the rail yard before sunup, Catherine's only thought was how to hide from their view.

Clutching her remaining labels to her chest, she dropped to her knees and swiftly slipped between cars hooked together in a long row, making a dash for the fence that encircled the perimeter. In their canvas bags she and Sean always carried small pairs of wire cutters that they'd used during numerous operations where barbed-wire fencing was often an obstacle. She fell to her knees and, with shaking fingers, clawed her way into the pack, stowing her leftover labels inside. She pushed aside the hard steel of her service revolver and retrieved the cutters. Frantically snipping a hole large enough for her to slip through, she stumbled down an embankment into a field strewn with years of debris hurled from passing trains. She gave one long blast from the emergency whistle that hung around her neck. Her only hope was that the guards would think it a normal sound in a rail yard and prayed that Sean and Remy would hear its piercing sound and understand her warning.

Heart pounding, she set out along the line of the embankment, heading in the direction of Villefranche, on tenterhooks to learn if Sean and Remy had done the same. She'd barely taken ten steps when shouts rang out in German.

"You there! Halt! Halt where you are, or I'll shoot!"

With a gasp, she turned around. The long line of train cars that ran parallel to the rail yard fence prevented her from even guessing where the commands came from. Looking right and left, she saw no one. Cautiously, she climbed back through the opening she'd made in the fence and scrambled part way up the embankment. Just before reaching the top, her gaze drew level with the few feet of space between the train tracks themselves and the bottom rim of the train that ran parallel to the fence. Through that strip of open air, she made out two pairs of storm trooper knee-high boots facing, toe to toe, Sean and Remy's ragged trousers and scuffed shoes. It was as if the top three-fourths of a screen at the cinema had been blacked out and the only action was to be in the bottom quarter.

One of the boots stomped hard in the dirt, and Catherine heard the shrill command, "Both of you! I said, hands up. Higher!"

A prickling sensation she identified as terror washed over her. This time, it was her fellow agents who'd been stopped by the same Nazi soldier who'd locked her in the cell. Her mind raced ahead, cataloguing the dire consequences doubtless in store.

Before she had time to consider what she was doing, she plunged her hand into her pack and pulled out her service revolver. She squinted down its sight at the boot-clad leg nearest her and pulled the trigger. Her victim fell backward with a scream. She watched for one instant as the entire length of his body writhed on the dirt.

His keeling over onto the ground revealed a second set of boots at which she aimed and shot. In the next instant, she saw a jumble of hands scrambling in the dust to retrieve the soldiers' guns that had dropped when the bullets had found their mark, shattering the shin bones of the pair of Nazi soldiers.

Catherine's own right hand was trembling, the pistol heavy in her palm as she allowed it to fall by her side. She had absolutely no idea which of the four men on the other side of the train had seized the wounded soldiers' service revolvers.

All she could do was strain her ears to listen for what would happen next.

CHAPTER 35

On a sun-filled Paris afternoon, *Kommandant* Erik Heinrich, the same Nazi officer who had given Henri Leblanc permission to reopen the family printing business, arrived without warning at the basement operation.

Henri had been deeply absorbed in editing the weekly clandestine *Résistance* news sheet dated June 3, 1944, due to go to press. Alphonse had left at his usual time, but one of his helpers, Gaston Peppard, had remained behind to do the run. He was in the production area, applying a solvent to clean a hard-to-reach area of the large printing press. A stack of menacing broadsides Heinrich had recently commissioned were piled high on a table pushed against the wall, awaiting delivery the following day.

"Leblanc!"

Startled, Henri looked up. Heinrich, imposing in his gray-green uniform with medals plastered across his chest, filled the threshold at the entrance to Henri's small office. At attention behind him was a double row of his henchmen, guns drawn.

The *Kommandant*'s scowling demeanor was devoid of the mild cordiality the two men had once displayed, having reached an accommodation with each other when Henri first arrived back in Paris.

"Stand up, hands in the air!"

Henri swiftly glanced down at the papers on his desk.

So, this is how it ends.

In point of fact, some part of him had always thought it was almost inevitable from the moment he invented his cover story of resurrecting his family's printing business. It had only been a matter of time before his playing the good Vichy semi-collaborator would eventually go wrong.

"*Kommandant*," Henri said, rising slowly from his chair, deliberately keeping his pen in one hand and the steepled fingers of his other on the sheet he'd been editing. He kept his voice steady despite his heart racing in his chest. "Please be assured that the new broadsides you ordered are finished and will be delivered to you tomorrow. I'm afraid we got behind a bit this week, but you could take them with you now, if you prefer."

"That's not why I'm here, and you know it!"

"I'm afraid I don't know why you are here," he said with all the *politesse* and bravado he could muster. Meanwhile, he eased open the middle drawer in his desk an inch, hoping for a chance to slide the contraband news sheet into it.

Henri knew—or strongly suspected—what had brought the *Kommandant* to his door. Either Air Officer Gilbert had finally turned him over to his Nazi handlers, or perhaps someone as lowly as the printer's assistant, who'd been busily preparing the machinery right outside his office, had betrayed him. Over Heinrich's shoulder, young Peppard had just thrown his cleaning rag on the floor beside the mammoth press and sidled out the door with nary a Gestapo henchman calling halt. It was even possible Peppard had been paid by Gilbert to gather proof turned over to the *Kommandant*.

The Germans were frantically aware of the many signs that they were losing the war. Despite Nazi dragnets, *résistants* all over France had continued their sabotage, blowing up bridges and disrupting electrical grids. Henri had even heard of sand literally being tossed into the gears of factory machinery in every province. The very newsletter he'd been editing when Heinrich stormed into the printing shop called for more such acts of rebellion, large and small, to be launched when word came that the Allies had finally made their move—somewhere.

"I said, put your hands in the air!" Heinrich repeated, his full-throated anger darkening his features.

Henri obeyed. Heinrich stepped aside to allow two of his men to roughly search him for weapons. Satisfied he had none, they then grabbed him by the shoulders while the *Kommandant* seized the papers on his desk.

Heinrich would have all the evidence he needed to keep his captive in custody as long as he pleased—or have him killed. In fact, Henri knew he'd just been caught with evidence so incriminating the Nazi officer could easily have him executed within hours or, even worse, torture him first to reveal the names of others in his Resistance network. He cursed the fact he'd left the lethal cyanide pill in his desk and not in his pocket. There it sat in his middle drawer, just out of reach.

In the next moment, Henri was dragged past the silent printing machines. A black Citroën of the make and model the Vichy embassy had used in Washington D.C. was parked outside the door. *The damn Germans have confiscated every solitary thing the French government possessed*, he thought. Fury at the impotence of the entire nation, as well as his own frailty, ricocheted through him like a tracer bullet.

The cool air of spring chilled his cheeks as he was thrown into the car's back seat, the door nearly slamming on his foot. The *Kommandant* slid into the front passenger seat and sat stiffly as the car pulled away from the curb.

As familiar neighborhood landmarks glided by his passenger window, a million thoughts whirled through Henri's mind, focusing first on concern for Catherine in the South of France. What he feared most was if Gilbert knew about Henri's sole trip to the Riviera to scout enemy installations along the coast. Even worse would be if Gilbert could name the other agents and *résistants* there who had assisted him. There wasn't a person alive who knew—until they were tested—how long they could hold out to the kinds of torture the Nazis employed. No human being could guarantee they had the strength not to give up what they knew, even about those they loved the most. If he could just keep silent for two or three days, at least Alphonse and the others would have time to go into hiding.

There was one good thing, Henri considered, turning to look out the vehicle's back window as the building housing Leblanc Printing grew smaller each second. Thanks to never receiving a response from Buckmaster in London about possible duplicity on the part of SOE's Air Operations officer, Henri had been cut out of the loop on virtually everything having to do with infiltrating new agents into the field. He hadn't been informed where recent recruits had been sent to bolster any forthcoming Allied invasions. The SOE's thinly veiled distrust of him had resulted in his knowing virtually nothing about when troop landings might be launched, or even where exactly that might be.

If *Kommandant* Heinrich thought Henri had specific information, he'd eventually discover that his captive couldn't tell much more than was generally known.

Even so, Henri was under no illusions. Heinrich had enough on him regarding the printing he'd done for the Resistance to prompt this sudden arrest. After they tried to pry all the information possible out of him, they'd either shoot him or, at the very least, dispatch him to one of the slave labor camps in Germany.

Henri slumped against the Citroën's luxurious leather seats and closed his eyes. Tears welled beneath his lids at the thought that he was more than likely never to see Catherine again. He could almost feel her smooth, slender fingers that morning at the café in Nice when he'd slipped his mother's ring on her hand as a symbol of his love.

All I ask is that these bastards don't find out that I once parachuted into the hills above Villefranche.

———◇———

The journey that changed everything in Henri's life took mere minutes. The passenger in the back of the Citroën was dismayed to see that the car had stopped at Heinrich's SS outpost in the 2nd Arrondissement, where he got out. Without a word, the uniformed driver continued to an even more infamous address: Number 84 Avenue Foch. Everyone in Paris knew that the elegant, *Beaux-Arts* building in the fashionable 16th Arrondissement neighborhood was the headquarters of SS counterintelligence and the dreaded location where captured SOE agents were brought to be interrogated.

Henri was immediately escorted into a luxurious dining room. There, a tall, imposing figure who politely introduced himself as SS Major Hans Josef Kieffer of the *Sturmbannführer*—representing the German Security Service—was clearly in charge.

The commander bid him to sit down in front of a long, polished oak table set for a meal beneath a crystal chandelier. "We will talk later," he announced in a pleasant, unruffled tone. Then he departed, leaving Henri to eat alone.

A few minutes later, a white-coated waiter brought in a large, rich meal of *fois gras en croûte*, followed by a plate of *boeuf bourguignon*, accompanied by a glass of excellent red wine.

The food was delicious, the best Henri had eaten in over a year, in fact. As he wiped his lips with a starched linen napkin, he deliberately avoided draining his wine glass, recalling the warnings he'd been given in training. He'd been told his interrogators would attempt to lull him into a false sense of security and even sleepiness in hopes he'd be prone to lapses in his cover story. If his answers weren't satisfactorily forthcoming, there would likely be physical torture to get him to divulge even small details that would lead to his revealing more important information.

Kieffer wants to know everything about my missions and the whereabouts of all the agents I've ever worked with.

Henri knew very well that the Germans wanted to destroy the surviving SOE networks that had been sabotaging the war effort, coordinating with de Gaulle's Free French fighters and then feeding information back to the Allied High Command. With all the rumors of invasions swirling about as spring was turning to summer, Henri was certain that those types of questions would soon be put to him— perhaps with a lighted cigarette pressed into his back, or pulling out his fingernails, or nearly drowning him with Nazi waterboarding techniques—as forms of persuasion.

If Gilbert, as SOE's Air Operations officer, was in fact a double agent for the Nazis, Henri had to assume he'd told his German bosses about having been parachuted into France, along with his travels back to London for consultations. Fortunately, his flight to survey German defenses along the Riviera had been an assignment that Buckmaster himself had organized from a secret airbase outside London.

Whatever Major Kieffer already knew about one Henri Leblanc, the Nazi officer ruling 84 Avenue Foch was bound to feel angry that officers like Heinrich had unwittingly allowed Henri to operate as an enemy agent right under their noses.

A door to the large dining room opened, and two tall soldiers marched in to stand on either side of him.

"You will come with us now," announced one in guttural French.

Henri pushed back his Louis XIV satin upholstered chair and was prodded with the barrel of a gun in his back up a carpeted, curving stairway to an equally well-appointed sitting room he speculated was likely to be its own kind of torture chamber.

Hans Kieffer sat behind an ornate desk of inlaid marquetry. To his right stood a tall, handsome man with dark hair Henri recognized immediately as Lucien Barteau—code name Gilbert.

Well, there you have it...

Off to one side was another strapping figure clad in well-cut civilian clothes. With his slicked-back blond hair, rosy complexion, and even features, except for a broad, misshapen nose, the man appeared well muscled enough to be a professional pugilist, dressed by a top-quality French haberdasher.

Henri turned to stare steadily at Gilbert until the despised creature averted his eyes, bent down, and whispered something into Kieffer's ear. Henri had been trained about German interrogators enough to know that they were always clever enough to find someone of the prisoner's own nationality to confirm the identity of the prisoner. It appeared to Henri they'd assigned a strapping example of Aryan superiority to serve as torturer to make clear he was now utterly alone in his opposition to German domination.

Disjointed thoughts began to revolve in his mind like a roulette wheel. Then he recalled the mantra he'd been taught during his SOE training to repeat as often as necessary these next hours.

For these first minutes, I can endure. And for one more minute, I can endure. And so, minute by minute, I can endure.

Henri knew full well that all human beings had a breaking point, but if he could just keep convincing himself that he was able to hold out for one minute more, the torturers would never own him. In the end, they might have a dead body, but they would never have him or, through him, the one person he held most dear.

For Catherine and the others, I can endure...

———◇———

Three cyclists sped through the pink glow of dawn as if in a final sprint of the legendary *Tour de France*. Their legs a blur of furious pedaling on the deserted road from Nice, they finally reached the crossroads above Villefranche where they halted at the fork in the road, collectively gasping to catch their breaths.

"When the Germans find those bodies in the rail yard, they'll rain down reprisals everywhere," said Catherine between gulps for air.

"The immediate environs of Nice will bear the brunt, I'm afraid," Sean agreed. He looked over at Remy, whose normally cheerful demeanor had become a mixture of fear and fatigue. "Can you open your restaurant on time this morning? Your best cover is to go about your business as usual."

Still breathing hard, Remy merely nodded his assent.

Catherine prepared to remount her bicycle, announcing, "Sean and I will be making ourselves scarce for a while. No bragging about this little adventure to anyone, right Remy?" As much as she adored the man, he could be loquacious after a few too many glasses of wine. She patted him on the shoulder. "And good job grabbing those two guns. You absolutely saved us." She turned toward Sean. "And bravo to you, too."

Sean's quick thinking had also helped save the day. The instant that the SS officers were hit in the shins by Catherine's gunfire, he'd appropriated one of the weapons from Remy and shot the soldiers in a part of their bodies that guaranteed neither of them would live to see the day they could produce any progeny. Now that all three resisters had safely fled the scene, Sean flung an arm around his two comrades.

"Let's be honest, here," he said, his voice hoarse with emotion. "Shooting those bastards from *under* the railcars, Catherine, was the thing that saved us from disaster."

"Uh...*d'accord*," said Remy with a slow shake of his head, as if he didn't quite believe what the triumvirate had just experienced. "*Au revoir, mes amis.*"

The restaurateur climbed back on his bicycle and headed down the steep road that led to Villefranche and his harbor-side bistro.

Meanwhile, Catherine and Sean continued on their bikes through the dawn's early light, toward Menton, musing to each other along the way about the miracle of surviving yet another day.

CHAPTER 36

Henri didn't care that he was sitting alone on a wooden chair, naked from the waist up. He didn't even acknowledge to himself that his entire body was covered with welts and black-and-blue marks, proof of the steady hours of beatings and interrogations. He only cared that he had survived three days of such treatment and had not told Kieffer or his henchmen anything of value. Most crucially, he had not given up any agents' names. The mantra, thus far, had worked.

I can endure one more minute. Just one more is all I must ask of myself.

The brutal treatment had started gradually. Kieffer's man in the well-cut suit had initially met him in this torture room for a "chat" over a glass of schnapps. When that didn't produce anything of value, the methods swiftly became harsher. Yet, over several days, Karl, the big blond, had only gotten out of him what Kieffer already knew: that Henri Leblanc had been the author and publisher of the ubiquitous *La Résistance* newsletter, in charge of plastering the sheets on walls throughout Paris when no one was looking. Henri never revealed that he had a team of clandestine couriers that delivered hundreds of copies wherever *résistants* met in every arrondissement in the city. Nor did he reveal he'd been in charge of finding safe hiding places for weapons that had been dropped from the sky. Gilbert had already told Hans Kieffer all about that.

Henri knew full well that the SS chief of counterintelligence was growing frustrated and would no doubt order his minions to step up his methods of inflicting pain. As a former diplomat understanding rudimentary German, Henri also sensed a new kind of desperation among the whispers he'd overheard in the halls of 84 Avenue Foch. Something big was expected somewhere north and west of Paris. The guards seemed on edge, and the officers had become increasingly punitive in their demands for information.

Over and over, Henri had been able to say to his interrogators that he had no knowledge when any invasion might be launched. For all he knew, it could come from the north or the south or not at all.

Interrupting these thoughts, the door to his interrogation room banged open, and Major Kieffer walked in, accompanied by a soldier Henri didn't recognize. He was carrying a linen bag that he put on a table in front of Henri, who was strapped in a chair.

Kieffer said to his captive, "I have some unfortunate news to share with you, but I think I'll let an old friend of yours tell you instead of me."

He ordered the soldier who had deposited the bag to fetch someone just outside the room. Marched in by two SS, a haggard Alain Chapelle appeared in the doorway. Henri's deputy also had bruises on his face and most likely other ones beneath his clothing in the same tender areas of his body as Henri.

"Tell him, Chapelle," Kieffer commanded. "Tell Leblanc here how the terrorists you two have been plotting with all this time are faring." When Alain remained silent, Kieffer yelled, "Tell him!"

Alain shrugged and rasped through his cracked lips, "Nearly everyone we knew has been rounded up, mostly those betrayed by Gilbert, of course," he said, shooting a look of hate at Major Kieffer.

"And speaking of another of your comrades in arms," Kieffer said, his mouth forming an even line, "an RAF pilot whom Air Operations Officer Gilbert knows let it slip that, not too long ago, that same pilot flew a man of Leblanc's description to a drop point in the South of France." Kieffer nodded in the direction of the towering blond with the misshapen nose who had again entered the room. "Gilbert was kind enough to tell us what he'd heard about this trip of yours, Henri." He smiled at the muscle-bound blond giant who'd been standing silently to one side. "Karl here," Kieffer noted pleasantly, "would also be fascinated to know more of that particular adventure, wouldn't you, Karl? Just where did Henri land with that parachute of his? What was the purpose of the trip? Who was on the reception committee? And what other agents helped him work his way back to Paris?"

Kieffer waved his hand at the two SS flanking Alain who then roughly escorted him out of the room and back to his cell. Meanwhile, the major donned a pair of his military-issue leather gloves and pried open the linen bag, dumping the contents onto the table in front of Henri and then standing back as if he feared contamination.

There was a crumbled blouse of palest cream silk, a woman's tweed jacket, and a pair of women's cycling trousers piled in a heap. Henri could only stare at them, wondering what clothing Catherine could now be wearing.

What have they done with her? What have they done to her?

The fury and fear that shot through him was unlike anything Henri had ever experienced, but he knew his response in the next few moments would determine whether he would live or die this day. And perhaps it would determine Catherine's fate as well. He composed his features into a look of studied nonchalance.

"And you've brought these…garments to my attention because?"

"You don't recognize the clothing?" Skepticism laced Kieffer's every word.

Henri made a show of leaning forward, despite hands tied at his wrists, and awkwardly fingered the wrinkled silk blouse. He shifted his attention to the inside of the waistband of Catherine's trousers to study the label. As he did so, he noticed a small lump protruding from the fabric, as if a pebble had been sewn inside. He settled back in his chair and met Kieffer's piercing gaze.

"They're French-made, certainly," Henri commented, keeping his voice steady. He paused for effect. "Am I missing something here?"

Kieffer smiled faintly.

"They belong to a dead woman, cremated in Nice."

Henri struggled to remain calm. This kind of announcement was often a method the Germans used to make their captives feel hopeless and bereft.

"So?" he said. "You Nazis have caused the deaths of many innocent civilians. One more is no surprise."

"Well, maybe this will jog your memory." He pulled an envelope out of his uniform's breast pocket. To Karl, standing by Henri's side, he ordered, "Untie his hands. We will allow our friend here a moment alone to look over the documents that accompanied these clothes to see if they help him recall anything about the person who once wore them."

"*Ya, Herr Kommandant,*" Karl replied, bending to do as Kieffer ordered.

"Because, you see, Karl," said the Major with a chill that Henri knew was a warning to prepare for the worst, "Agent Gilbert distinctly remembers seeing the woman whose clothes these are sitting cozily beside our friend here in London's Special Operations Executive headquarters. Given Leblanc's probable flight to the South of France, my guess is that he and the dead woman most likely met up, which, if true, would make both of them spies against the Fatherland."

Kieffer's menacing words hung in the air. Henri rubbed his raw wrists to avoid looking at Kieffer or showing the intense emotions that were impacting his body like an airplane plummeting toward earth, nose down.

"Be sure to open the envelope," Kieffer urged in the same strangely pleasant tone he'd used when bidding Henri to enjoy his first meal at Avenue Foch. "Karl and I will be back in a few moments."

As soon as Henri heard the door close, he slipped a trembling finger under the envelope's paper flap and ripped it open. Inside were two cards, both with the name Colette Durand typed on them. One was a ration card for food allocations, the other a residence card listing an address.

> *Sailmaker's loft, the boatyard*
> *Villefranche-sur-Mer.*

Henri fought to suppress a sob. He fell forward, his cheek resting on the crumpled silk blouse that smelled musty and without even a whiff of Catherine's Chanel Number 5 scent. His hand grasped the fabric of her woolen jacket, rubbing it back and forth against the right side of his face.

Catherine. Oh, God, no...

He twisted his head, cushioned by Catherine's crumpled trousers, and stuffed the knuckles of his left hand into his open mouth to keep crying out. Pressing against that hand, he was dimly aware of a small lump next to the French label in the waistband. *There's something in there*, he thought, battling his desire to curse and scream.

Sitting bolt upright again, he pulled the waistband to his lips, baring his teeth so he could tear a hole in the fabric. Frantically, he worked the object over to the jagged opening he'd made until it appeared in the hole he'd made—and winked at him. Slowly, and with trembling fingers, he withdrew his mother's ring from its hiding place.

Catherine would never have abandoned her clothes voluntarily with the diamond sewn inside the waistband. A million possibilities revolved in his mind, all of them seeking a way to believe that Kieffer's possession of Catherine's clothing and her documents did not necessarily prove she was dead.

Perhaps she's only been arrested and is being held in a prison somewhere. They might have stripped her of her clothes as they did my shirt. She can't be—

He heard a hand on the doorknob behind him and plunged the ring into the left pocket of his trousers before anyone entered. Major Kieffer strode in as Henri placed one of Catherine's identity cards over the hole he'd made in her clothing's waistband.

"Ah, so you've seen the documents Agent Colette Durand had on her when she died in her cell."

Henri steeled himself to behave as if she were merely someone he had met briefly in his travels. "Poor woman," he murmured. "What did she die of?" He held up her food ration card. "Malnutrition?"

Henri felt a momentary lift when Kieffer's look of triumph shifted to uncertainty.

"I told you!" he snapped. "Gilbert confirmed to us that you two knew each other in London. Our information is that Durand was sent to work with Peter Churchill's SOE networks in the South of France. You were sent there too at some point, weren't you? I think you'd better tell me all you know of that operation down there if you want to avoid further discomfort."

"Gilbert is correct," Henri said coldly. "But I met Durand only once in London, and I never saw her again."

"You're lying!"

"That's all I can tell you. Like Lucien Barteau—your pet double agent, Gilbert—said, the three of us briefly met in London."

"At SOE headquarters!"

"If you say so," Henri said.

His mind was spinning. He prayed neither Gilbert, Kieffer, or even *Kommandant* Heinrich—who'd given him permission to reopen his printing business—were aware that Catherine and he had known each other in Washington D.C. when Henri was a press attaché there.

Henri gazed at the pile of Catherine's clothing and repeated, "As I said, after meeting her in London, I never saw her again."

"Liar!" Kieffer screamed, slapping Henri hard across the face with his gloved hand. He grabbed Catherine's jacket and shook it in his face. "You two met up somewhere in the South of France! You had to have. Gilbert told us he's sure it must have been you who was transported there and parachuted somewhere along the coast."

"*Gilbert* is the liar," Henri countered, a strange calmness taking hold of his numbed emotions. "He tells people like you what you want to hear. For money. Before the war, he was just a stunt pilot in circuses and carnivals, reckless and ambitious. You must know that. He's a double dealer, Major. How can you trust a man like that?"

Henri knew he shouldn't goad his captor, but he couldn't help himself. Kieffer took a step closer, towering over Henri's chair.

"Rest assured, Leblanc," he threatened, "I know exactly who Lucien Barteau really is, but as SOE Agent Gilbert, he's helped us catch and kill scores of agents all over France, especially now, on the Côte d'Azur. We'll find out about your work there soon enough." His eyes narrowed. "And in case you doubt that Colette Durand was unfortunate enough to die of TB, here's her death certificate."

He pulled another document out of his breast pocket and slapped it into Henri's hands. As he took hold of the paper Kieffer force upon him, it took all the strength Henri still possessed to keep his hands steady.

"Karl!" Kieffer shouted, summoning his muscleman while Henri stared mutely at the official death certificate, signed by the Nice coroner, testifying to the truth of Kieffer's assertions. "Henri here is being very stubborn about what he knows. I'll leave it to you to see if you can't make him more forthcoming about the late Colette

Durand and the other scum still alive in the South of France. Gilbert's guess is that *M'sieur* Leblanc was sent to report on our defense installations in that area. If true, it would warrant immediate execution," he added with a murderous look in Henri's direction. To Karl he added, "He's all yours. Find out who else he knew on the Riviera."

———◇———

Hans Kieffer was relieved to quit the confines of Room 302, a former bedroom-turned-interrogation chamber. As he headed down the corridor, he had far more on his mind than the fact that Henri Leblanc was failing to crack despite seventy-two hours of sleep deprivation and a severe dose of physical abuse. Even if the SOE agent had reported to London on the placement of German defenses in the South, it was far too late for German forces to do much to counteract the damage.

Reaching the head of the stairs that led to the lower floors, Kieffer barely took notice of Henri's tortured screams echoing down the corridor. A few minutes later, the Major entered his office only to be informed that the Allies had landed that very morning along the coast of Normandy. The calendar on his desk noted it was the sixth of June 1944—a date that probably marked the end of any reasonable hope for a German victory in this war. All that spring, Kieffer had been privy to other coded messages confirming that Allied enemies were outfoxing them and winning battles. For the second time in a century, the Fatherland was going down to defeat.

Gazing out his office window, his thoughts turned to his own survival. Perhaps it was time to face facts. Hitler's megalomania had led to utter disaster, and Major Kieffer could already see that the dictator's subordinates were bound to take the brunt of the victors' reprisals. It might very well be time to plot a way to return home to Bavaria before the Allies, with their guns, tanks, and a lust for revenge, marched down the Champs-Élysees.

———◇———

A week later, to Henri's amazement, he remained alive and Alain Chapelle was put in the room next to him in the former servants' quarters at the top of the building. Both men were too weakened by the treatment they'd received at the hands of the brutish Karl to tap out messages on the wall separating them. Even when all but two of their guards left the hallway to go down to dinner, the two *résistants* could barely summon the energy to communicate softly by voice.

So far, Henri had been subjected to seven sessions with his designated torturer, and seven times he'd managed to whisper his standard refrain through swollen lips, "That's all I can tell you."

Each day, thanks to his grasp of a French diplomat's German, he'd understood additional snatches of conversations between the guards. In hushed tones, they anxiously spoke of Allied troops having landed on the beaches of Normandy and were reportedly making their way toward Paris. They also whispered about rumors of an Allied pincer movement, with several additional landings suspected along the Riviera.

But will the Brits and Americans arrive in time to save us? wondered Henri. He was sure Alain felt the same.

———◇———

As June turned into July, and after each brutal session with his captors, Henri was amazed to see that, to date, his master printer, Alphonse Moreau, had not been brought in for questioning by Karl the persuader, nor had Gaston Peppard, the printer's assistant. This either meant the pair had miraculously escaped the Nazi sweep or were themselves Nazi collaborators.

By early August, SS Major Kieffer didn't even bother to attend Henri's interrogations anymore. During the time Henri had been held by the SS, he'd lost nearly twenty pounds, and his teeth had begun to loosen from a diet of thin soups and stale bread. Several of his ribs had been cracked, and skin sores all over his body were slow to heal. After Karl had torn several toenails off both Henri's feet during one particularly vicious interrogation session, his worry had been that the stalemate between his torturer and himself could ultimately result in his being marched downstairs to the basement and shot—the fate rumored to have been that of a few fellow prisoners on his floor.

One afternoon on a hot Wednesday in mid-August, Henri was informed by one of the guards that, in two days' time, he was to be transferred to the notorious Fresnes prison outside Paris. Both feet were now painfully swollen due to his infected toenail pads. Then, a few hours later, he was alarmed at hearing a key being inserted in the door to his makeshift cell.

Have plans changed? he wondered, his heart pounding. Was he about to be put on a cattle car departing for a slave labor camp in Germany?

To his utter shock, when the door opened, the guard merely stepped aside. A moment later, in walked the tall, dark-haired SOE Air Operations officer once again wearing civilian clothes. Henri recoiled at the presence of the double agent who was clearly curious as to how badly he'd been beaten to date.

The guard said to Henri's unwelcome visitor, "Just give a shout, Gilbert, when you want me to come back for you." At that, he exited and locked the door.

CHAPTER 37

The SOE agents stared at each other for a long moment. Henri could hardly breathe for the hatred that filled his chest.

"What are you doing here?" he demanded.

"Major Kieffer sent me, of course," Gilbert replied, leaning his well-fed frame against the wall nearest the door. "He thinks you know whether or when the Allies are going to invade the Riviera as they have already in Normandy."

"He's been asking about that since the moment they brought me here," Henri replied dismissively. "I know nothing more to tell him—or you."

Gilbert pulled out a pack of cigarettes and offered one to Henri. When he gave an angry shake of his head, Gilbert shrugged and lit one for himself.

"You do understand, don't you, why they keep drilling you about this? Kieffer is certain that's why you were dropped somewhere in the South of France—to survey German defenses there. Today I came by Avenue Foch to show him a flight manifest I located with your code name on it."

"Did you have it forged?" Henri asked. "To earn some points with the Major? Or maybe you're just short of francs."

"He was delighted with my evidence," Gilbert retorted. "If you'll just tell me where you went and what you were doing in Nice—and with whom—I'll make another tidy sum, and perhaps I'll get them to let you go without killing you. Or maiming you for life," he added, with a downward glance at Henri's feet, swaddled in dirty rags.

"If that goon, Karl, beat nothing out of me at this stage," Henri said in a low voice, "it's because I can't tell you anything more. I was a propagandist printer. I wrote and published *La Résistance* newsletters and distributed them where they could be most effective. That's the extent of my efforts. You're wasting your time."

"That's bullshit," Gilbert retorted with a long draw on his cigarette. "The flight manifest is genuine, and you know it. And you know as well as I do that Buckmaster would never risk one of his RAF planes on a secret flight all the way from Britain to the hills above Nice, through hails of tracer fire, just to drop a printer of leaflets into the area." He offered Henri a crocodile grin, acknowledging they both had once been pilots. "We both flew in the Great War. You and I know they'll make things a lot easier on you as an officer if you just tell me exactly where you landed and what you did afterwards."

"I can't tell you anything more," Henri repeated wearily.

"Oh, do stop that nonsense!" Gilbert exclaimed, irritation bubbling through his studied coolness. He gazed at Henri for a long moment and then said, "Too bad that Agent Colette Durand ended up dead in a jail cell in Nice."

Henri's breath caught, but he simply stared in silence at the double agent.

"Kieffer told me all about it," Gilbert continued with a chuckle. "Showed me her name on some documents that I recognized. Pity, her dying. She was one gorgeous woman, wasn't she? That day I met you both at SOE headquarters, I honestly figured by the looks of it that you two knew each other pretty damn well."

Henri's fight for control over his emotions was becoming more difficult by the second. Gilbert kept goading him.

"You mean to say you never actually saw her again in the South of France or ever got to fuck her?" Gilbert asked. "Too bad," he said, removing a speck of tobacco from his tongue. Henri would have sold his soul to hear the crunch of bone and cartilage if he swung his fist into the bastard's jaw. Gilbert cocked his head to one side. "I kept hoping she'd be flown into France on one of my flights, but no such luck."

Henri thrust his hand into his pants pocket and felt for his mother's diamond ring, grinding its sharp edges into his palm to keep from leaping at the man's throat.

Finally, he said, "One of these days your luck will run out permanently, Gilbert. Or should I call you by your true French name, Lucien Barteau? You obviously will work for anyone and do anything for money. But don't you find this double chess game tiresome? It requires you to betray your own country when, in the end, the Germans will be driven out by the Allies and you will likely be hung by your neck from a lamppost. I hear that sort of thing is happening a lot since the invasion of Normandy."

Gilbert pushed away from the wall and took a menacing step toward Henri. "I'll be on the side that wins, whichever one that turns out to be."

"With the help of MI6?" spat Henri, his ire at last getting the best of him. He knew of the suspicions that Britain's professional intelligence services had been undermining the rival SOE.

Gilbert raised an eyebrow and answered with an amused expression, "Does it bother you so much that there are certain elements in MI6 that want to be rid of Churchill's amateurs in the spy department? If the Allies win, whatever MI6 has done to agents like you will be papered over in the flush of victory. And if Germany wins, nothing you or *Mademoiselle* Durand or any of the other SOE agents have done for your sacred cause will matter one whit. All your noble sacrifices will have been in vain."

Gilbert dropped the remainder of his cigarette on the bare floor and ground it out with his flight boot.

"All your noble sacrifices will have been in vain…"

Henri pictured Catherine's many acts of bravery on behalf of her country and his. He could almost feel the smooth flesh of her beautiful, slender hand nestled in his own, his mother's ring winking at him from her fourth finger the last day he'd seen her.

Rage as hot as the iron Karl had applied to one of Henri's own shoulders gave him a strength he didn't know he possessed. His muscles and the toes on his feet screamed in agony, but he lunged for Gilbert, digging his fingers into the man's shoulders as he raised his bent leg and viciously brought the full force of his knee into Gilbert's groin. Before the traitor to France could even let out a howl of pain, Henri clapped a hand over his mouth and, in a rush of fury, shoved him into the wall, deliberately slamming his upper body into a metal light fixture.

Gilbert slid down the wall, leaving a wide trail of blood from the deep gash in his head on the dingy, white paint. His large form landed on the floor in a seated position, where Henri pummeled him into unconsciousness in the name of Catherine and the other agents who had lost their lives because of his treachery.

Henri hovered over him, gasping for breath, his injured ribs feeling as if they'd been hit by a battering ram. He thought briefly of the German soldier he'd killed silently in the storeroom months before. Today was different, he knew, rage still burning in his gut as Gilbert began to stir. This was for Colette Durand, an act done in Catherine's honor, purely in the name of revenge.

Gilbert's eyes fluttered open, focusing on Henri with a look of fear and hatred that matched his own.

Henri knelt beside him and made a swift grab for Gilbert's throat. His thumbs sought the spot on the man's neck that he'd been taught would choke whatever life was left from the bastard. Henri's own body was near collapse, but he exerted as much pressure as he had left on Gilbert's flesh. His gaze focused on Gilbert's face, the man's bulging eyes now framed by skin the color of slate.

Henri's own strength drained dry, he finally relaxed his grip, allowing the body to slump sideways onto the floor. He stumbled back a few steps, sucking in gulps of air, and stared at his motionless victim, a tall, good-looking man who had daringly flown airplanes in his youth, just as he had. Henri had once considered himself a civilized man, but no longer. Not when he felt exhilarated to have exerted such brutality on a mortal enemy. His uncivilized truth was that it was worth any price—including his own ultimate execution—to rid the world of this rabid dog before he could hurt anyone else.

An eerie silence filled the room on the top floor at Number 84 Avenue Foch. Given the noise of the life-and-death struggle between himself and Lucien Barteau, Henri waited for the guards to arrive. He cocked his head, but no sounds came from the hallway outside his door. A few moments later, Alain's muffled voice penetrated his daze.

"Henri? Are you there? What's going on in there?"

"Nothing."

"Look out your window! They're leaving!"

Henri staggered to the other side of the chamber and peered through dusty panes. His first reaction was disbelief. Then amazement. A line of SS soldiers, carrying file boxes and suitcases, were streaming toward four canvas-covered flatbed trucks parked along Avenue Foch. Directly in front of the building, Major Kieffer stood beside a sleek, black Citroën. An aide opened the rear passenger door, and the officer climbed inside.

Alain called out once more, "What is going on in there, Henri? I think some of the guards are coming back."

Hearing this, Henri ran back to roll Gilbert's prone body across the small room. He pushed him under the straw sleeping pallet lying on the floor, piling his one blanket in a jumble on top of the lump to disguise the body as best he could. A moment later, he heard doors being unlocked all along the hallway and German guards uttering frantic commands in garbled French.

A different guard than the one that had admitted Gilbert into Henri's cell waved his pistol distractedly, ordering the prisoner out of the room. Only too happy to obey, Henri limped into the hallway and closed the door behind him. Alain emerged from his room, and soon some two dozen other captives on the same floor were being hustled by their armed guards with MKb 42 assault rifles down the four flights of back stairs.

"This isn't good," murmured Alain.

"No," replied Henri under his breath, only too aware that the basement was a destination to which no SS prisoner would want to be sent.

Men and women from several other floors, in various stages of injury and disability, funneled down to a subterranean corridor, marching past the building's boiler and laundry rooms. At length, the group was herded into what appeared to be a large storeroom with shelves of cleaning products and handyman tools lining the walls. As soon as all were inside, a guard turned off the overhead lights with the only remaining illumination coming from the open door.

Henri instinctively pushed through the milling throng to the far corner, grabbing Alain by the sleeve.

"Get *down!*" he yelled. "*They're going to shoot!*"

He elbowed his friend and deputy to the ground and dove for cover. In the next second, a hail of bullets sprayed into the room, the bodies falling on top of each other as screams rent the air. Henri had landed flat on the concrete floor on his broken ribs. Piles of strangers crushed him from above. The door slammed shut and the world went black.

Yet another mass grave in this war, he thought, searing pain reverberating throughout his entire body. Before he lost consciousness, he whispered, "Catherine…"

After that, the only sounds in the bowels of Avenue Foch were the agonized moans of the dying.

———◇———

The summer sun beat down on Catherine's back, and sweat trickled between her shoulder blades beneath her blouse. Thankful for the slight breeze wafting over the harbor, she pedaled her bike down the hill from the olive farm, where she had just deposited a dozen grenades in their new hiding place. Things had gotten so dicey with German reprisals since she escaped from the Nice jail and shot the soldiers patrolling the railroad station, she'd taken to wearing a dirty cotton scarf on her head and no make-up on her face to disguise her Colette Durand identity now pasted to her Jacqueline Bise documents. She feared people in the area could recognize Colette's face and amber hair.

On several occasions during the first week of August, Catherine had managed to outfox the swarms of German soldiers and the hated French *milice* combing the Riviera for secret agents. Sean's and her urgent goal was to further arm the populace in the aftermath of the invasion of Normandy. Catherine understood that Hitler's finest in the South of France were wildly disturbed by the bad news coming from all over France. Talk was everywhere that the Allies were steadily pushing toward Paris with the aim of liberating the capital. German occupiers in the South of France feared the French underground were now preparing for what everyone assumed would be a second D-Day along the Côte d'Azur.

So far, so good, Catherine thought, coasting faster down the hill, refreshed by the breeze on her face. The use of the Jacqueline Bise identity card with her picture applied by the Cannes forger had passed muster at all the checkpoints. Even so, she felt a pang of remorse each time she pulled the card from her pocket, thinking of the tragic, light-haired Jewish woman named Sarah, posing as Jacqueline.

Catherine was nearing the spot where the farm road on which she was traveling met the main thoroughfare. She turned left and guided her bicycle along the upper road past Villefranche. Four miles beyond Monaco, the route brought her to the outskirts of lower Menton. Her heart skipped a beat at the sight of a checkpoint established a hundred yards ahead that had not been there hours earlier when she passed the same spot. Two travelers ahead of her stopped and presented their documents. Catherine dismounted her bicycle and dug into her jacket pocket for her own identification.

"Next!" droned one of two German soldiers on duty.

The man inspecting Catherine's identity card was balding, and his uniform strained over his substantial paunch. He was middle aged, and she speculated that he'd probably been assigned to this post as someone no longer suited for combat. Catherine stared at her bike's handlebars, waiting for him to hand back her card.

"Look at me!" he demanded, scrutinizing the photo on the identity document and then staring at Catherine swathed in her ragged scarf. "Take that off!" he commanded, gesturing toward her head. "You don't look like this picture."

"It's me, all right," she snapped, sick to death of putting up with the incessant bullying of these occupiers. She stuffed the scarf in her bike's wicker basket next to a jar of olives Jules had given her. "It's just that I'm thinner now. The picture was taken before you Germans invaded the Free Zone and left us with little to eat."

Instantly she realized that her sharp retort was a dreadful mistake. The portly guard pursed his lips. His roving gaze took in her light-colored hair and slender neck. His eyes, surrounded by puffy lids devoid of lashes, kindled with interest.

"*Fräulein,* why do you hide such lovely hair, I wonder?" he murmured in his guttural French, a sound that grated against her taut nerves.

His gaze returned to her face, and he appeared to be studying her with growing concentration. He glanced at her bicycle basket and rifled past her scarf, his eyes zeroing in on the glass jar of pickled olives.

"Ah...you have some of these lovely olives that are so prized around here," he said. His expression narrowed. "You've just come from the olive groves above us, have you? I suppose you planned to trade them on the black market, eh?"

"I planned to eat them," Catherine replied. In attempt to gain some sympathy after her expression of overt hostility, she added, "It's all I have to feed myself and my disabled husband."

"A married woman, are you? Quite accustomed to doing a husband's bidding, I imagine? Well, madam, I have an idea." The soldier looked over at his comrade. "I need to check something," he announced. To Catherine he declared, "You. Come with me."

Catherine anxiously walked her bicycle behind the guard who had kept the jar of olives in his hands. He led her around to the back of a building and turned to face her.

"Lean your bicycle against the wall. Now!"

Catherine sensed the point of his forcing her to follow him to this secluded spot had little to do with olives. Even so, she pointed to the jar and said, "Keep them, sir. Please let me go home. My husband is blind and will be worrying where I am."

To her surprise, the soldier placed the jar back into her basket. For an instant, Catherine thought that her words had had a good effect.

"There, see? I've returned your olives," he said, unbuttoning his jacket. His stomach oozed over his leather belt. "Now, I would like you to do something for me."

Catherine wasn't surprised in the slightest when he began to slide down the zipper on his trousers and took a step closer, backing her into the wall next to her bicycle.

His voice slightly hoarse, he said, "I'll let you go in a bit if you can show me your appreciation for such a kindness. You understand?"

Catherine met his glance. "I said, you can have the olives. Please let me go."

"Not when I see what a pretty *fräulein* you are without that scarf."

Another step closer and his belly brushed against hers, his palms flattened on either side of her shoulders. He thrust out his pelvis and began rubbing it against her skirt, mumbling his body's desires, his breath sour in her face. He fumbled for her hand and thrust it against the fabric of his trousers, moaning that she should rub him. "In there. Ya! Fast, *fräulein!*"

Catherine felt as if she were suddenly thrown back into her role setting a honeytrap for middle-aged men with secrets she'd been ordered to pry from them. While she considered her options, she obeyed his command as if her hand belonged to a stranger.

"Ah, *fräulein*. Jacqueline, isn't it?" he groaned, surprising Catherine that he remembered the name on her fake identity card. Beneath her hand he held pressed against his cock she could feel his swelling erection. "*Gut...ah...gut!*"

He looked down at the button at his waist and stepped back, his chin on his chest while he fumbled to unfasten it.

Catherine knew exactly what he would do next. She would have been prepared to comply in the name of duty, except this repulsive German soldier would later demand to see her again and to demand to know where she lived. He would extract from her his pleasure, just as Admiral Moretti had once done, pressuring her and bullying her and threatening to ruin her life if she told anyone; as Lieutenant Farley had tricked her with his charm into believing he loved her; as Jeremy had verbally tortured her while she was lying in childbed and then giving away her baby to strangers. Only this German soldier, this man with his cock poking through his pants, had the power to order her death and the death of Sean and the Mentons if he ever learned who she really was.

Suddenly, a lifetime of fury aimed at men who had abused her sexually infused her with uncommon strength. As the distance between them widened slightly, Catherine turned to her right, reached into her bike basket with her free hand, and grabbed ahold of the olive jar. At the moment she turned to face him, the German was holding his member in his right hand, his mouth agape in supplication.

In a murderous arc, she smashed the glass as hard as she could over his bent head.

She would have thought his howl of pain should have summoned his comrade from around the front of the building, but miraculously, it didn't. Large shards of glass fell at their feet, her own hand nicked by a razor-like edge. The German's face was covered with blood pouring down his forehead and cheeks and onto the shoulders of his uniform. Bent over in pain, he peered up at her, a look of surprise turning to rage. Before he could retaliate, she used her shoulder as a battering ram as she'd been taught and threw him to the ground, stomping the sole of one shoe into his chest, knocking the wind out of him. Olive oil and red pimento, as well as brown olives themselves, oozed over his face, one lodging in the hollow of an eye.

While he groaned in the dust, immobilized, Catherine dove her hand into her jacket's left-hand pocket and pulled out the L-pill given all agents prior to their departure for France. The supply sergeant had solemnly described its fast-acting properties: *"A dose of cyanide guaranteed to bring about death in thirty seconds."*

Catherine flattened the palm of one hand on his forehead, forcing the back of his head into the dirt. With her other hand, she stuffed the capsule between his back molars and used the heel of her hand to push his chin upward so his teeth crushed the tablet. As she watched him begin to gasp for breath, she remembered the sergeant's words.

"Carry it with you wherever you go. You are to take it—if you choose—when you have no other choice than to commit suicide rather than submit to unbearable torture."

Catherine had lost her original dose, along with Henri's diamond ring, when she'd traded clothes with Sarah's body. For weeks, she and Sean shared his L-pill, switching it back and forth between them when they left on their missions. *Now, neither of us will have a merciful way out if we get into another jam*, she thought as she felt the soldier's body go limp. Quickly with her scarf, she wiped the oil and olives off the soldier's face, and threw them, along with the shards of broken glass, into her bicycle basket so the olives would not be traceable to the Mentons' farm.

Then, taking a few seconds to bind up her bleeding hand with the oily scarf, she yanked her bike from against the wall and, without looking back, mounted the seat. Pedaling furiously, she rode down the street that was parallel to the main road where the remaining soldier stood on guard at the checkpoint. Catherine knew it would only be a matter of minutes before he'd begin to search for the man who lay dead behind the building.

Her lungs were burning by the time she made her way up the hill to the safe house at the top of the village. Dropping her bike to the ground, she ran down the steps into their basement hideout, opened the door, and announced to Sean, "Time to move again."

He was wringing out a pair of his underwear and hanging it over the back of one of their two chairs.

"We'll be off as soon as these dry," he deadpanned. "Where to next?"

"The only place left," she said, pulling out their sole suitcase and gathering her few things. "The olive farm."

"What happened to your hand?" he demanded, pointing to her bloody scarf.

"Only a nick. I'll explain later." She pointed to his wet laundry. "I'm afraid you'll have to wear those even though they're a bit damp. We have to leave now."

CHAPTER 38

Jules Menton agreed to hide Catherine and Sean in a shed at the far end of his furthest olive grove, where the hills above Villefranche became too steep for planting. The farmer had removed the pruning tools and nets used in the harvesting of his crop and put two bales of hay on the floor they used to make straw pallets covered with the clothes they'd brought with them. The wireless transceiver was stored in a natural opening carved out of a nearby rock ledge. When sending messages back and forth to officials in London and North Africa, Sean or Catherine would take turns scaling the escarpment behind the shed to stretch the antenna as high as it would reach in order to get a signal.

Catherine had immediately gone to ground, as the SOE brass often ordered agents in jeopardy. She'd stayed hidden in the olive shed except when Sean signaled she could safely come to the farmhouse for a meal with Tamara and the Menton family.

Two days after she'd killed the soldier at the checkpoint, Jules returned from a trip to the weekly market to sell his olives, with news that Catherine dreaded and instinctively knew would come.

Her hand nearly healed, she crept down through the groves after dark to join the adults and Sean for a late dinner of a soup made from the scant vegetables Eve Menton had gathered from her garden behind the farmhouse.

"Are the children asleep?" Jules asked his wife, who nodded. He turned to Catherine and said somberly, "An entire village on the outskirts of Menton was lined up and shot yesterday in reprisal for the German soldier you killed."

"Oh, God, no…" she said, barely above a whisper. "Children, too?"

"The SS and their collaborators herded everyone into a field and ordered the adults to dig a big trench. Then they made them all stand on the edge…men, women, children, even a pregnant woman soon to give birth, and machine gunned all but two."

"Oh, *no*." Catherine could almost see in her mind's eye the Mentons' field where the Lysander and Hudson aircraft had landed and imagined members of the reception committee digging their own graves. She could practically hear the terrified screams floating past the olive trees as shots rang out, parents desperately trying to shield their children from the flying bullets. And Tamara…

She pushed her chair away from the table and stood, frozen on her feet, unable to move. Sean swiftly rose beside her and put his arms around her.

"No! Don't!" she rasped.

Catherine pushed him so hard he landed back in his chair. Jules and his wife stared down at their empty soup bowls.

"There was no easy way for me to tell you what's happened," Jules mumbled, "so I just had to say it. You mustn't leave the shed unless we say so, or all of us will be in even worse danger than we already are.

"How many people died?" Catherine asked, knowing that the Germans believed in far more than an eye for an eye.

"It was a tiny village, deep in the hills above Peille."

"How many *died*?" she repeated.

"Forty-two, they say."

"Forty-two innocent lives for one Nazi soldier," she whispered.

Catherine's heart felt as if it had congealed into lead. Sean rose from his chair a second time, swearing and cursing until Eve had to shush him not to wake the children. He turned and grabbed Catherine by the shoulders, digging in his fingers until she winced in pain.

"You killed the enemy!" he practically shouted. "You killed a bastard who would have raped you if he could have and probably *had* raped many other women before you. Yes, what's happened to those villagers is the absolute worst a war can produce, but that's why we're here, fighting these inhuman ghouls who commit such atrocities."

But forty-two people died because I killed one man, mostly for revenge.

Catherine could not find her voice even to tell Sean his grip on her shoulders was hurting her. Even if she, Henri, and Sean survived this nightmare, how could she ever claim any personal happiness after the darkness she had witnessed these past years and her part in it? The stealing of the naval codes, blowing up an electrical transformer to plunge a barracks full of Italian conscripts into darkness, and outfoxing the enemy time after time had been exciting—empowering, in fact. But, now the truth of war would be forever etched in her consciousness: blood, torture, and innocent deaths. All she felt now was soiled and broken, filled with the sense that, in this game, nobody wins.

Catherine pictured Tamara asleep with the Mentons' daughters in the back of the farmhouse. She could almost hear a door closing to her ever becoming a parent, to ever baring her soul to anyone who hadn't lived through the nightmare. She knew now that she would never live the life of a normal person. She would stifle these secrets of good and evil the rest of her days.

I'll always live with the truth that I killed another human being and his death caused dozens more. Even if I survive, this will never be over.

———◇———

In the long hours spent alone after Jules's announcement of the massacre in the hills ten miles to the west of the farm, Catherine found herself wondering how the Allies' landing in Normandy and their agonizing push toward Paris had impacted Henri. She didn't doubt that the Nazis in France's capital were even more terrified than ever that they were losing the war. She imagined that they were as brutal to their enemies there as the German troops now viciously striking out against their adversaries in the South of France. Sean had heard the rumors: Hitler had ordered the torching of Paris if his troops were forced to retreat.

At times, she felt that, in the months since Henri parachuted into Villefranche, he could hardly have escaped the ruthless net cast across Paris to snare SOE agents. The solitary times during the days and nights that followed left Catherine with literally nothing to do when Sean was on his assignments ordered from London on the wireless. She fought against mentally replaying the moments when she'd ended another human being's life. However disgusting a creature that groping, portly soldier at the checkpoint had been, she could not deny that having killed a fellow human in the way she had fundamentally changed her.

She felt this even more deeply the evening when Jules said it was safe to come down to the farmhouse to join Sean and the Menton family for supper. Little Tamara sat at the Mentons' kitchen table finishing her evening meal, chattering nonstop. The sweet, trusting child, with her light curls and girlish love of games, had shyly taken Catherine's hand and asked her if she had children of her own in America.

"No," Catherine replied slowly, pushing her memories of a baby boy into a deep corner of her heart, "no children in America."

She tried to smile at Tamara, but only felt a wellspring of hatred filling her chest for the man she had married in what seemed like another lifetime. Where was that child now, in this world of war?

Tamara squeezed her hand, bringing Catherine's thoughts back to the Mentons' kitchen. The little girl leaned close and whispered into her ear.

"My *maman* never came back on the train," she said, her eyes filling with tears. "Do you think you could pretend to be her, and I'll pretend to be your little girl?"

Catherine's entire body stiffened. Those village children had been killed in reprisal because of her action as an SOE agent. She felt like a fraud to serve as a stand-in for anyone's mother. She'd imagined, at times when she awoke in the middle of the night, that saving Tamara almost seemed to offer Catherine a chance to be a parent again.

But now, she would always stand apart, even if she guaranteed financially that the little girl could go to good schools growing up and be provided other advantages that Catherine could willingly offer.

She couldn't find the words to answer Tamara's request, so she just gave her hand a squeeze.

And despite the commonsense words Sean had spoken to her earlier, Catherine sensed that a blanket of depression had begun to engulf her. Having witnessed so much darkness, having been a part of the brutality and required by the Official Secrets Act never to reveal any specifics about her role in the fight made it so no child, no friend or family member back home, no man but Henri and Sean could ever truly know who she really was. Signing the Official Secrets Act meant that even if she wanted to or needed to, she could never one day tell Tamara or any child in her care what she did, good or bad, to try to keep her safe. The events of the past two weeks had prompted her to distance herself from everyone—including the child whose life she'd saved.

There will always be a barrier of silence between me and anyone who didn't take part in this battle.

And how could she not secretly feel tainted as a killer whose actions then caused the deaths of another forty-two souls, however noble the cause?

Can I ever truly open myself to love if I must forever lie to my nearest and dearest who don't know what ghastly, grisly things I've had to do?

Catherine had never shared these shadowy fears with Sean, although she sensed he was aware she'd become withdrawn ever since the incident at the Menton village checkpoint. Truth be told, Sean, too, had changed. Beneath all that charm there'd been an occasional look in his eyes that echoed the darkness that had begun to envelope her.

She imagined that, to others in her small circle, she merely appeared preoccupied and busy with her official duties with the wireless transmissions.

Catherine pulled her thoughts back to Jules, who reported that the coastal villages were being combed for the woman on a rusted bicycle wearing a headscarf. The poster declared the "terrorist" was suspected in the mysterious killing of a soldier found with white foam on his face, lying prone behind a building at the entrance to Menton.

———◇———

During her time exiled to the olive shed, Catherine tried to sleep during the day while Sean was away on assignments. She figured that the early hours after midnight were the safest times to unpack the wireless and transmit messages. At that hour it was less likely that the ominous, white SS vans with antennas on their roofs would be cruising along the coast seeking to lock onto rogue signals.

During these daylight hours of trying to rest, she'd suddenly awaken, her body drenched with sweat. Her racing thoughts conjured murky dreams that the Germans had somehow found this safe house and had killed the Mentons and Tamara in reprisal. For long minutes of deep breathing, she struggled to swim to full consciousness and focus on the fact that the only way to make sure the people she cared about were safe was to help win the war, to remain where she was and fight until the second Allied invasion came—if it ever were to.

The first week in August continued hot and humid in the hills above Villefranche. Sean continued to leave their newest safe house to guide Jewish leaders and downed airmen up to the olive farm for late-night pickups by Lysander or Hudson, the RAF's short-takeoff-and-landing aircraft. On occasion, messages via the wireless directed the leader of the Trenches network to row a boat with a prized escapee or two out into the Mediterranean a few miles to rendezvous with an Allied sub.

At the end of five straight days of such assignments, Sean's next task slated for August 9 was to take a mentally and physically exhausted agent—recalled to London by his concerned handlers—out beyond the harbor for yet another seaborne rendezvous.

At dawn's light the next morning, Catherine awoke on her straw pallet after barely an hour's sleep, instantly alarmed to find that that she was alone in the shed, the air stuffy, insects droning in the olive groves outside.

"Something has gone wrong. I know it," she said to Jules when she hailed him on his ancient tractor in the upper field. "He should have returned hours ago."

Jules's expression reflected her alarm; he nodded and promised to see what he could learn in Villefranche. Two hours later he returned from the harbor to the olive shed with the news Catherine had been dreading.

"Remy heard from one of his contacts that Sean and his passenger were caught by a German patrol boat as they were rowing out to the rendezvous spot. They were taken to the Nice jail at three o'clock in the morning."

Sean, captured?

"Oh, God no," Catherine moaned.

The memory of a putrid cell with three women dying of TB nearly made her retch. She and Jules exchanged glances, and she could only imagine his fears that any information tortured out of Sean by his captors could put every member of his family in danger of being shot or deported. Tamara, posing as an Aryan, and secret agents like Catherine herself could be caught in this net.

"Is Sean still alive?" she asked, a feeling that everything in her world was going wrong. "And the other agent?" That agent, Catherine recalled silently, was one being taken out of play because his colleagues had reported to London they thought he was ready to crack.

Anyone the Germans deemed a spy was regularly tortured for information then shot on the spot or immediately transported by railcar to slave labor camps in the Fatherland. Sean's emotionally shaky co-captive was just one more turn of the screw in the mess they were in.

Jules's obvious concern was etched on his brow. "What Remy heard last was that both Sean and the other fellow are being interrogated by the SS chief in the building across the street from the Nice jail."

"Do we know his name? The SS officer in charge, I mean?" Her mind was awhirl with all the implications and repercussions of Sean's arrest.

"Gunther Wintermuden. He was a regular army man, according to some contact Remy has. A captain, recruited into the SS when the war started."

Catherine breathed a small sigh of relief that Sean had been placed in the custody of an ordinary military man who would likely be less psychopathic than the average SS officer recruited from Hitler's brown shirts. An interrogator from the regular army might still retain some sense of the reasonable rules of war…

But Sean is captured!

Catherine thought back to his nonchalant wave as he pushed off on his bicycle to ride down the hill to the village. He was to meet up with a *résistant* from Cannes who would deliver the passenger to a boat in the harbor tied up in front of Remy's restaurant, and from there, they were to row out to meet the sub. It was the same craft that she and Sean had borrowed from a sympathetic fisherman for a few other previous dead-of-night missions. Had they somehow been set up by an SS stooge?

And now Tamara, too, is back in the worst sort of danger, despite having been accepted by the Mentons as one of their own.

With a thousand thoughts reverberating in her head, Catherine made the decision to trust Jules Menton with the secret she had been keeping even from Sean.

"As usual, I'm going to need your help, Jules," she began.

Jules merely gazed at her in silence. Catherine had just been struck by an idea for how to attempt to rescue Sean from the Nice jail. It was an outrageous, highly perilous plan, and it depended entirely upon Jules, a man already in great danger.

"It's so hot in here," Catherine said, pointing to the shed's open door. "Can we go outside?"

Jules nodded, and once a few yards beyond the small building, he asked in a weary voice, "And what is it you need from me this time?"

The summer's heat shimmered on the Mediterranean's waters in the distance. Dusty, sage-green olive trees surrounded them, radiating the warmth that would bring their buds to fruition in two months' time. Catherine pointed in the direction of the field just out of sight above the last olive grove.

"I want to request your permission for London to deliver one more small package by parachute."

Jules shook his head. "I thought we agreed last week it's just too risky for any more of those noisy, low flights with all the *Bosches* lurking everywhere?"

"I know, I know," Catherine said, raising her hands as if to ward off further protests, "but one last air drop involves my only chance of saving Sean from execution. At least the other agent knows nothing about our operation up here, but the SS will torture Sean, and no one can hold out more than a day or two not telling the SS about the rest of us. We have to get him out right now, or we'll all be arrested and killed."

Once again, Catherine felt she was balancing on the edge of a knife. Her plan very likely wouldn't work, but not to try meant Sean's certain death. She inhaled a deep breath, fully aware that what she was about to tell Jules seriously violated the Official Secrets Act and thereby warranted her own execution if her superiors at SOE ever found out she'd spoken her next words.

"London has informed me on the wireless that a second D-Day, on the Riviera, is coming soon."

Jules pursed his lips with disdain and turned to face the hill behind the shed, his chapped, hardened hands on his hips.

"Everyone up and down this coast has heard *that* before."

"But this time they've given a date."

Jules looked over his shoulder at her, the sudden eagerness on his face telling her this news might change his mind about permitting one more fly-over on his upper field. He turned around.

"When? What day?"

"*Very* soon. I'm not allowed to tell anyone the specifics at this point."

If Jules had any idea the landings were mere days away, he'd think her plan to secure Sean's release was clearly one invented by a woman gone completely berserk.

"You and your Secrets Act," he muttered.

"Ah, yes, the Official Secrets Act. But will you allow a landing?" she pressed. "One more drop? Something small. As soon as I can, I'll tell you about everything else."

After a long moment, Jules offered a reluctant nod, adding, "But what does another air drop of one small package have to do with an invasion on our coast or with getting Sean away from a building full of murderous SS?"

"All that is my concern," she said with far more assurance than she felt. "Yours is simply to alert our reception committee—but only when I tell you to—that we may be needing them to help guide the plane on your upper field after midnight, most probably in three days' time."

CHAPTER 39

Catherine took the risk of sending a wireless message to England during daylight hours. Dated August 10, 1944, she waited in the hot sun for a hoped-for response, but when it came, it merely said, "Message received."

A few hours later, discouragement had replaced her fledgling hope that she'd have a more detailed answer by the time she turned the dials to their off position and closed the lid of the leather suitcase that housed the equipment. No field hands were working in the upper olive grove, so she stored the wireless in its usual hiding place inside the natural cave a few yards from the olive shed and went inside to contemplate her next move.

London now knew about Sean's arrest, but not about her plan to rescue him from the SS imprisonment in Nice. She imagined that Buckmaster or one of his deputies would simply advise her to continue to go to ground until further orders.

By the time those bureaucrats make up their minds what to do next, my plan will have worked, or we'll all be dead.

She would have to execute the next step in her scheme on her own, she decided, pawing through her few clothes to choose something suitable to wear. The mere thought of what it would require of her to implement her plan made her wonder if these were indeed the last days of her life—and Sean's. It almost felt as if someone else was donning the one decent outfit she had left: a linen blouse and slim navy-blue skirt.

Her gloomy thoughts led, as they had so often lately, to wondering what had been happening in Paris in the two months since the invasion of Normandy on June 6. Already they were in the second week of August, and Allied troops had yet to liberate France's capital. Despite the presence of British and American troops on French soil, the Nazi noose had been steadily tightening on the civilian population all over the country. Word everywhere was that German reprisals had been as brutal in Henri's part of the world as they had been in hers.

Catherine ran a comb through her hair, now consistently minus her scarf made unwearable by the bloodstains. She picked up her canvas shoulder bag with her service revolver tucked inside. From the door, she scanned her surroundings before walking out of the olive shed and stowed her bag in her bicycle basket. Seizing the handlebars, she walked her two-wheeler toward the path behind the olive storehouse, mulling over the startling and very-specific message that had been transmitted over the wireless a few days earlier, a missive she'd quickly set alight as soon as she'd read the words.

"Confirming: Operation Dragoon scheduled for just after midnight, Monday, August 14, in the early morning hours of Tuesday, August 15. Area of attack: 45 miles of coastline east of Toulon to a few miles west of Nice. All SOE networks in this region are to proceed with previous sabotage instructions."

She began to wonder if her own urgent transmission today would immediately be put on Buckmaster's desk. She and Sean couldn't very well follow orders and execute the sabotage directives until she could somehow get him released from jail.

It was close to the noon hour when Catherine came to the dirt track that meandered down the hill to the main road. At the crossroads, she turned right, heading for the local train station at Nice. She had found an old lipstick at the bottom of her canvas pack and had carefully dabbed it on her lips, along with a bit of color on her cheeks to bring her gaunt appearance closer to a match of the picture on her identification card. As Jacqueline Bise, she would walk directly into the lion's den of the SS outpost near the Nice jail, praying that Josef Gumbel—the officer who thought Colette Durand had died in his cell—didn't see her entering the building across the street. There, she hoped to find and inform a certain high-ranking official that he'd soon be in the very path of a second invasion of France. But first, she required the skills of the forger in Cannes.

———◇———

Mid-norming the next day, Catherine stepped off the train, hot and sticky from sitting in the crowded car after a nerve-wracking trip from Nice to Cannes and back. She had paid a risky, unscheduled call on the forger who had performed so many favors in the past for Sean and her. She even had the nerve to beg him to allow her to sleep in his print shop in Cannes Thursday evening.

Back in Nice, she breathed a sigh of relief when she passed through the document checkpoint without incident as Jacqueline Bise. Her revolver, buried in a package of sanitary pads, passed inspection undetected. Her bicycle had remained where she'd hidden it in a bathing shed on an edge of Nice's *Beau Rivage*, a beach now completely covered with mines buried in the sand. In front of the shed, barbed-wire barriers marked the stark perimeter where, once, holiday bathers had scrambled down the slope with their towels and picnic baskets.

The closer she came to SS headquarters and the Nice jail across the street, the more her stomach clenched at the memory of her incarceration there. Perspiration dampened her blouse, and she began to wonder, with each turn of her bike's pedals, if this wouldn't be her last day alive—along with Sean's. Winding her way along Nice's narrow back streets, she pulled into an alley behind a café within a block of her destination and hid her bicycle out of sight behind a rubbish bin. She paused a moment and rearranged the contents of her canvas bag.

The moment she opened the door to the SS office, the men sitting at desks in the anteroom looked up simultaneously. Catherine felt their glances take in her linen blouse and smart skirt, along with her amber hair and her face displaying the last scraps of make-up she'd owned. Ignoring them, she marched through the entrance with what she hoped appeared to be a bold stride and confident air. An officer whose desk plate announced he was Corporal Wilhelm Scheff sat closest to a door to the inner offices.

Catherine addressed him in German. "I wish to see Captain Wintermuden."

"And just who are you?" said the officer with more curiosity than rudeness.

"I am Mrs. Sean Eisenhower."

Eyes widening with surprise he repeated, "Eisenhower?"

"Yes. As in American General Dwight D. Eisenhower, whose troops will be arriving here before you know it." Scheff arched an eyebrow but remained silent. "The general is my husband's *uncle*," she added with deliberate emphasis.

Catherine had determined that merely making Dwight Eisenhower Sean's cousin wouldn't be persuasive enough, so she'd decided to declare the family connection more immediate. It was risky on both ends of the equation, but she figured step one was to impress and secure an agreement with the SS chief. She was certain that if she obtained terms to get Sean released, the SOE would likely approve her scheme. She prayed that, without having to bother General Eisenhower himself, the SOE brass would then supply the necessary bribe money and phony documents the *Kommandant* would undoubtedly demand.

"I must speak to Captain Wintermuden immediately," she insisted to Corporal Scheff. "I have a message of vital importance."

She tossed a glance over her shoulder at the other officers sitting at their desks, obviously straining at her every word.

The corporal leaned back in his chair, his growing astonishment at her words turning quickly into a mixture of skepticism and perhaps fear. Catherine could only assume that the corporal's superiors in Berlin had decoded enough Allied communications to anticipate that another invasion was coming and that it would be somewhere in the South of France. Scheff and his comrades just didn't know precisely where or when—and that was the dangerous card she was about to play.

"And what proof do you have of anything you're saying? I can't just go to the *Haputstrumführer* with a fantastical tale like this."

Officer Scheff waited while Catherine dug into her canvas bag and pulled out several documents, including a French civil marriage license with the names Jacqueline Bise and Sean Patrick Eisenhower scrolled on the page. Next, also thanks to the forger in Cannes, she waved a handsome document featuring the Seal of America stamped at the top, along with a photograph of a distinguished and familiar-looking man in a military uniform identified in print as *"General Dwight D. Eisenhower, Supreme Allied Commander,"* and auto-graphed in a black scrawl, *"All best to my favorite nephew, Sean, from your admiring uncle."*

The soldier on desk duty snatched both documents from Catherine's hand, stuttering his shock and amazement, "I-I will need to show these to Captain Wintermuden."

To an officer sitting at one of the desks close by, Scheff barked, "Guard this woman." When the man merely nodded, Scheff screamed, "With your *gun!*" and in the next instant, he'd disappeared through the door into the *Kommandant*'s inner office.

Less than two minutes later, Corporal Scheff ushered her into Captain Gunther Wintermuden's inner sanctum, then departed closing the door behind him.

Captain Wintermuden, head of the SS office in the district, offered no word of greeting but merely indicated with a nod that she should take a seat in the chair opposite his desk. Of medium height, he appeared to be in his early thirties, a trim figure, displaying short, blond hair and a high forehead that, without his military cap, indicated that he would soon be losing the straw fringe that remained to inherited baldness.

"I understand what Corporal Scheff said to me just now, but I want to hear from you exactly why you are here today, Mrs....Eisenhower, you say?"

His last words, sardonic and almost pronounced with amusement, hung in the air.

In response, Catherine allowed a silence to grow between them to indicate the gravity of her next words.

"What I have to tell you today, Captain, will determine whether any of you in this office survive a second Allied invasion—right on the beach, less than fifteen miles from where you are currently sitting."

Catherine took satisfaction in the startled look that crossed Wintermuden's face. She could almost hear his thoughts: *How would this woman know the enemy armada is currently poised in Corsica for an invasion of the South of France?*"

Keeping her tone even, she continued, "I think you should know that General Eisenhower is already aware his nephew is in your custody."

Wintermuden narrowed his pale-blue eyes and stared at her across his desk.

"How would General Eisenhower possibly know we had captured his nephew? Or perhaps you are in possession of your very own wireless transceiver?" he scoffed. "I think you're bluffing."

"The General knows, all right," she assured him, amazed by the sound of her boldfaced falsehoods. "And those documents on your desk there don't lie," she said, pointing to the skilled forgeries spread out before him. "I should warn you, even if you are so foolish as to kill Sean and me," she continued, pointing to the desk between them, "the Allies will be here in three or four days, regardless—as I'm sure you know from the recent interceptions that undoubtedly have landed on your desk. I have been told that a squadron will be dispatched to this exact address and you, Captain Gunther Wintermuden, will *personally* be hunted down and either shot or hanged from the nearest lamppost."

Wintermuden's eyes had become slits of blue ice.

"Told by whom?" He seized the Bise-Eisenhower marriage certificate between his well-manicured fingers. "Perhaps you, not our prisoner with the thick glasses, are the spy?"

Ignoring his spot on accusation, she pointed a finger. "If you are sensible and release Sean Eisenhower and the other man you have in your custody, I will guarantee that your life, specifically, will be spared."

"And how in the world would you be able to do that?" he demanded scornfully.

Wintermuden seemed unaware that he had started to drum his finger nervously on top of the documents. Catherine could tell that the captain had heard the rumors running wildly along the Côte d'Azur that the Allies were already on the island of Corsica and that perhaps upwards of two hundred thousand troops were soon to cross some 233 kilometers via the Mediterranean and invade a forty-mile stretch of the Riviera.

Catherine offered a shrug and said, "I can keep the noose around your neck from tightening by supplying you with a letter of safe passage authorized by the Allied Command. If you run into enemy troops when the Allies storm the beaches just miles from Nice, you can show it to an officer and save your life. Unlike you Germans, we honor such agreements between our commanders and line officers such as yourself."

Catherine was betting that Wintermuden was aware that the news after June 6 had been disastrous for the German troops in the north. Hitler had ordered all but one of his precious Panzer divisions to try to block the troops heading south and east toward Paris. In the two months since the Normandy invasion, French partisans had risen up from Brittany to the Loire Valley and sabotaged railway crossings, bridges, electrical transformers—anything and everything to clear the way for the Allied advance.

Wintermuden pursed his lips in thought, and then he said, "You claim you can obtain a letter signed by General Eisenhower himself?" The captain had shown his hand. He was plainly interested in her proposal—but still incredulous.

"Yes, I can get such a letter," Catherine answered calmly, although her heart beat so rapidly, she found herself gripping the arms of her chair.

The Cannes forger had already made up a safe passage document that looked vaguely authentic from "Headquarters, Allied Command." She'd stashed it in the bottom of her shoulder bag, but now Wintermuden was demanding a letter that looked genuine *and* was purportedly signed by General Dwight Eisenhower himself. The mind boggled.

The captain leaned back in his chair and tilted his head. He glanced toward the door, as if he didn't want anyone within earshot to hear his next words. His body language set off the smallest kernel of hope in Catherine.

He's willing to negotiate.

Wintermuden murmured under his breath, "And I would also

need three hundred thousand francs, should I consider releasing your husband."

Three hundred thousand?

Catherine used every ounce of willpower not to look dismayed. She and Sean were living on the few francs they had left that she'd stuffed in the leather suitcase under the wireless equipment. With fifty francs to the dollar, Catherine swiftly calculated that three hundred thousand was about sixty thousand U.S. dollars—a lot of money by anyone's calculation, especially since the regular airdrops had been halted.

She drew in a long breath as if considering his demand.

"Three hundred thousand?" she repeated. "I can certainly try…"

"Three hundred thousand, or your husband and the other terrorist die on Monday at noon—General Eisenhower's nephew or not." To emphasize his demands, Wintermuden brought down his clenched fist on the desk. His glance was glacial as he stared at her across the narrow space separating them. "I presume my stated requirements will soon prove what a charlatan you are, *Mrs.* Eisenhower."

The captain rose from his chair, and Catherine sensed she was about to be dismissed. If not arrested on the spot.

Before Wintermuden could bark any orders through the closed door, she said, "I will get both for you, the money and the letter of safe passage—*if,* and only if, you agree to release Sean and the other man the minute I've met your demands."

"And when is that?" he shot back. "You claim the invasion is about to happen three or four days from now? I want the money and the letter in two days."

"I can get the money and the letter in three. By noon Monday."

He scowled. "But how could you possibly do what you say?"

"You will just have to wait and see if I can, won't you, Captain? Isn't saving your own life worth a bit of a gamble? Meanwhile, will you take me to my husband? I want to confirm that you haven't shot him."

"Yes, he's alive, and no, I will not allow you to see him."

"How do I know you haven't already killed him?"

"Ah…" he replied with a thin smile. "It will be *your* turn to just wait and see."

Catherine had kept her right hand inside her open purse that rested in her lap. As she rose from her chair, she withdrew her service pistol.

"Since you are not showing very good faith, Captain, let me just say one more thing."

His eyes blinked rapidly at the sight of her gun as she leveled it at his chest.

Keeping her voice even and emotionless, she informed him, "You will not get the money on the day I return *until* I first see that my husband and the other man you are holding are alive." She took a first step toward the closed door. "You might be able to kill me when I leave here or before I can provide you your only chance for surviving this war—which would be stupid of you—but General Eisenhower and his troops know exactly who you are and what you've done to Sean Eisenhower, along with the exact location of this office. Trust me, they will hunt you down."

Catherine noted the pallor that had drained Wintermuden's complexion of its rosy tint. She kept her steady glance glued to his and her gun pointed directly at his heart.

"You are an officer," she said in her distinctive, soothing tone. "So was my husband, before his eye surgery. And, of course, so is General Eisenhower. Let us obey the normal rules of war. I would hope a military gentleman of your rank would conduct himself according to a code of honor, but we shall see, won't we?"

Wintermuden's eyes remained on her revolver as she slowly began to back toward the door. She took solace that the captain's own pistol was securely embedded in his holster strapped around his waist. She knew that she had risked infuriating him by brandishing her weapon. Even so, she was gambling that by proving she was far from defenseless, he might be less likely to send his thugs immediately after her the moment she made her exit.

"Your husband is alive," Wintermuden acknowledged without further elaboration.

She beamed a broad smile, saying, "Excellent and sensible of you to say so. If you'll allow me time to obtain for you the items you'll need this coming week, I can assure you that all will be well, and you may survive this mutual nightmare."

Once again, silence filled the room. At length, Wintermuden shrugged, which she interpreted to mean he would allow her to leave his headquarters in order to execute their tentative agreement—and *that* seemed to indicate that Sean indeed was still alive.

"So, are we clear on each other's term and objectives?" she asked from the doorway, her left hand behind her resting on the knob. Would he keep their bargain?

Wintermuden made no reply. Catherine spoke more sharply.

"Should I just shoot you, if you deem it's a hopeless situation for both of us?"

Her adversary kept his eyes glued on the barrel of Catherine's gun. She could see him making a last mental review of the various choices he had before him.

Catherine counted the seconds of silence—eight in all—until he said, "Today is Friday, August eleventh. I'll give you until Monday, the fourteenth, between noon and one o'clock, to deliver the money and the letter. Otherwise, all our prisoners locked up across the street, including your Sean Eisenhower, will be shot at dusk that day prior to our retreat—that is, *if* the invasion is actually next week as you claim."

Catherine's last wireless transmission said the invasion would start at first light Tuesday, August fifteenth. She had to get word to the powers that be to requisition the money and, she fervently hoped, create a better Allied Command letterhead in London laboratories than the Cannes forger had produced. Then, within the next day, her superiors had to order a plane be sent Sunday evening to the over-used drop spot above the olive farm to deliver the goods by parachute.

Catherine's heart began to pound at the sheer audacity of the scheme she had so haphazardly devised.

We'll probably all die.

Ignoring her own silent prediction of doomsday, Catherine managed to offer Wintermuden a sharp nod signaling that they understood each other.

"Monday, between noon and one," he insisted, repeating the deadline he'd set.

"What you've asked will be difficult," she acknowledged, "but at least you've provided me an opportunity to save you from an Allied firing squad *and* save my husband at the same time." She kept her gaze trained on the man standing five feet away. With the hand behind her back, she turned the doorknob, saying by way of farewell, "When I return, Captain, please have one of your Citroëns waiting at the back of the jail next door. I also request that small Nazi flags be attached to the fenders. Agreed?"

"*If* you return," he said, his voice showing the strain of their encounter, "I will make a vehicle available."

"With the flags, full of petrol, and a letter of safe passage for us, signed by you."

Catherine thought she detected the trace of a smile, as if he were complimenting her on her thoroughness.

"*Ya*. Flags, a letter, and a full tank of petrol."

"And you will allow us to drive away, won't you? Because even if you kill us as we leave here, a squadron from the landing troops will have already been directed to come to this building as soon as they hit the beach, understood? But, with three hundred thousand francs in your uniform and a letter of free passage signed by General Eisenhower, we both know that you will have a far greater chance than your comrades to depart immediately after we leave and make it back to Germany alive."

"*Ya, ya!* That will be our bargain," Wintermuden snapped.

She flashed him her most dazzling smile. "Then, I thank you. And now, please remain where you are while I leave through the doors I entered. If you keep your part of the bargain and don't have me followed," she added waving her gun, "I'll keep mine."

Wintermuden was beginning to look a bit dazed but gave a brief dip of his chin in apparent agreement. Catherine swiftly concealed her gun in her open shoulder bag, although she kept her hand on the trigger. She opened the door wide enough to allow for her slim figure to step out of the room, closing the door gently behind her.

The next sixty seconds were the longest in her life. She briefly nodded to Corporal Scheff and the other men in the anteroom and strode out the entrance. Once outside the building, she kept a fast pace just shy of running, quickly ducking into a café she knew, situated a block away. She nodded at the barman, a partisan Sean and she had worked with in recent months, and dashed out the back door. Within seconds, she'd retrieved her bicycle from behind the rubbish bin where she'd stashed it and zig-zagged a frenzied course through the back streets of Nice.

CHAPTER 40

Catherine was three miles down the road toward Villefranche before she allowed herself to take a breather. It occurred to her that her safe exit had only been permitted by Wintermuden because he was playing the odds of an end game, just as she was.

If the Allies *were* coming, his life as an SS officer of the Third Reich would be in immediate jeopardy. A letter of protection, purportedly signed by Eisenhower, along with three hundred thousand francs might indeed save his skin.

If Wintermuden discovered she'd been lying, and there was no invasion confirmed by German aerial spotters in the next forty-eight hours, then all he had to do was execute his prisoners late Monday afternoon as he'd planned to all along. Either way, Captain Gunther Wintermuden certainly wouldn't give a fig about what happened to Sean Eisenhower's wife and would be, by then, too preoccupied by the invasion to launch a manhunt for her.

Or a woman-hunt, she thought, almost smiling.

Catherine realized, as she turned left off the main road to head up the dirt track to the olive farm, her odds for success in saving Sean were even longer than the SS officers' were for surviving the coming battle. Fatigue gnawed at her calves and thighs as she struggled to cycle up the hill. The gradient had never seemed steeper or longer. Her mind was awash with competing phrases of a short-but-convincing wireless message to Buckmaster in London. With all the demands currently pressing the RAF and American air powers preparing for what she thought of as 'D-Day II,' the leader of F Section would have to okay a risky emergency flight that would drop three hundred thousand francs from the sky.

And then there would be the task of Buckmaster's underlings creating a more believable "Safe Passage" letter than the one currently in her possession, addressed to Captain Gunther Wintermuden by name, with the forged letterhead of the Allied High Command, along with a credible signature of Sean's third cousin once removed. What could be a greater folly than her bandying about the name of the top commander of all Allied forces, who was preoccupied with keeping the northern onslaught roaring toward Paris and preparing a southern assault poised for immediate action?

By the time Catherine had scaled the final yards past the farm to the upper fields, her leg muscles were on fire. Gasping for breath, she tossed her bike to the ground and ran up the hill behind the olive shed to retrieve the leather suitcase from the cave and set it on a flat rock. Still panting from exertion, she quickly scaled the hill behind the safe house to stretch out the antenna to its full length, and then she scrambled back down to fire up the wireless radio transceiver.

Sitting cross-legged on dirt on the warm ground, she implored the SOE with a coded plea to follow her instructions to the letter. Two agents' lives depended on it. Equally crucial, her requisitions had to be delivered by late Sunday evening—forty-eight hours hence and twenty-four hours before the invasion of the Riviera was due to commence.

From the outset of this operation, she'd been betting that her extraordinary requests would not have to be approved personally by the Supreme Allied commander himself. She was hoping she'd been correct in her assumptions and the SOE brass would fake the signed documents and grant the funds she'd requested. Still, she had doubts.

All she could do was pray that Sean's having family and friends in high places just might pay off.

———◇———

For Catherine, waiting for a response from London had been excruciating. On Saturday, August 12, she kept herself busy filling two small canvas bags with the few possessions she and Sean had stored in the olive shed. Soon it would be relatively safe to fire up the wireless from a different location to see if anyone had replied to her earlier carefully worded requests to her superiors in London. All she could do in the meantime was prepare for the next meeting with Captain Wintermuden—if there was to be such a dangerous encounter—and then plan for what would happen after that. At various intervals, Catherine sporadically dared to turn on her equipment, but screeching static greeted her each time.

At two o'clock early Sunday morning, the 13th, she awoke from a fitful sleep, hearing rustling sounds outside the olive shed. She fumbled for her revolver and was barely able to grasp the handle when she heard Jules calling softly.

"It's me, and Tamara, too. We've brought you some coffee and bread that Eve sent up. She was sure you'd be hungry by now, since you never came down for supper."

Catherine, fully dressed when she'd fallen asleep after her last fruitless effort to summon London on the wireless, scrambled to her feet and opened the door. The night air had cooled the stuffy confines of the shed, but she motioned for her visitors to follow her up the hill to the spot where she'd left the wireless enclosed in its leather suitcase, sitting on a rock with a blanket draped over it.

Catherine gratefully took the thermos Jules offered and poured coffee into the cup held out to her in Tamara's small hands.

"What are you doing up at this hour?" she chided.

"I heard them talking in the kitchen," Tamara explained, sending a shy smile in Jules's direction. "I wanted to come with him to see if you were all right."

Catherine felt a stab of remorse. She could tell that Tamara didn't understand why, of late, the woman who had been her rescuer had avoided their usual playtimes together. She wondered whether her actions meant she was protecting the child—or herself? Catherine would be leaving Villefranche in the next few days...or she would be dead. She'd spent the last hours convincing herself that the shock of her inevitable departure would be diminished if there were some distance between Tamara and her.

She gazed down at the top of the little girl's curly hair and felt her throat close with emotion at the thought of their impending separation. Taking her first sip of coffee, she couldn't keep herself from reaching out to gently tousle the five-year-old's caramel-colored tresses.

"You were so sweet to come up here with Jules, Tamara," she said, finally. "I'm just fine, as you can see. Can you promise to tell no one if I use the wireless now, to try and rouse my friends in England for messages?"

Tamara gazed at her with a serious expression. "Jules is always telling me that everything I see at the olive farm is a secret."

Catherine glanced briefly at Jules and then sat down in front of the leather suitcase and began to twirl the transmitter's dials. For once, the wireless static had changed to sounds indicating that there was an operator on the other end of Catherine's attempted transmission. Soon, she was frantically writing down the code coming through loud and clear into her earphones. From her cross-legged position on the ground next to the leather suitcase, she cast a triumphant look at Jules standing close by.

"What are they saying?" he demanded.

"They're coming!" she announced, then lowered her voice, shaking the piece of paper she'd been writing on in front of their faces.

"What time?" Jules demanded.

"A flight to your field is scheduled for early Monday morning at their usual witching hour."

"Two a.m.?"

"Give or take. Tell the reception committee there'll be one fly over—coming to us straight from the Allied base in North Africa—and that's *it*!"

———◇———

From all appearances at the rear entrance to 84 Avenue Foch, the rumors spreading through the Free French underground were true. The Germans had left the building, carting with them as they left a stretcher with a prone body from the fifth floor.

Henri Leblanc's master printer, Alphonse Moreau, gazed at a door that led to the basement of the SS interrogation center. It had been left ajar, and all manner of debris, some of it burnt to ashes, was strewn around the small rear courtyard.

The August heat was intense, and even at fifty feet, a dreadful odor drifted toward Moreau's nostrils, causing his stomach to churn. He laced his fingers around a slat in the fence bordering the rear alley, unsure of his next move. A figure materialized in the doorway, stumbling into the sunshine of midday, appearing dazed and disoriented.

Moreau, suddenly alarmed, wondered if he was a Frenchman or a German. Then he saw that the man was clad in blood-spattered coat and trousers. When the shattered soul saw Moreau standing near the fence, he reached out in supplication.

"Help me. Please help me!" he cried.

Moreau rushed forward and took his arm.

"*Mon Dieu*, what has happened to you, *monsieur*?"

"Could I be the only one?" the man said barely above a whisper, the sound he made as ragged as the clothing he wore.

Moreau looked over in the direction of the door from which he'd emerged. "The only one? What do you mean?"

"In there," he blurted with a slight nod over his shoulder. "In that pit of death. Am I the only one to survive what those monsters did? The *only one*?"

His voice was raw, and he shook his head back and forth as if suddenly rendered mute with grief.

"You were a prisoner of the SS in there? With others in that basement?" Moreau asked, his guts churning at the mere thought of what the man obviously must have endured within the walls of Avenue Foch.

"Yes," he murmured. "My name is François Patou. I was held on the fifth floor, but yesterday…"

His voice faltered, and he merely shook his head. Moreau took a step closer, asking, "Did you see my nephew there, Alain Chapelle? He is a *résistant* who—"

"I heard the name," Patou intervened with a weary nod. "We were all herded downstairs yesterday…pushed into a basement storeroom."

"All the prisoners?" Alphonse asked with dread.

"Maybe thirty or forty of us." He began to sway on his feet, and Moreau held out a steadying hand.

"Ah, *m'sieur*, you must tell me what I can do for you. Who can I contact—"

But Patou kept speaking as if he hadn't heard Moreau's offer of help.

"The guards had long guns and dead eyes," he said, slowly shaking his head from side to side as if disbelieving his own words. "They kept slamming the butts of their weapons into our backs to hurry us along down those flights of stairs."

"To the basement floor there?" Moreau prompted when Patou fell silent again.

"Yes," he whispered. His voice growing stronger, he described how the prisoners were crowded, cheek-by-jowl, into a storeroom. "Then the *Bosches* turned out the light and opened fire."

"*Mais non...*" murmured Alphonse. "And they shot you...all of you crowded in that storeroom?"

"Machine-gunned within seconds. We toppled on top of each other, some killed by the bullets...others crushed to death."

"*Mon Dieu,*" Moreau muttered again.

"I must have been shielded by the man behind me," he said. "A big man, with broad shoulders. He fell on top of me, and I landed, face down, on the cement floor and heard the barrage of bullets ricocheting off the cement walls."

His voice trailed off, as if describing what had happened in the building behind them was too terrible to put into words any longer. He breathed heavily, fighting for the strength to speak again as if, despite the horror, he had a need to bear witness to what had happened in that cement room.

"I heard them dying, the ones on top of me who didn't perish instantly. I heard their cries...their agony...for hours, it seemed, as they left this terrible world, one by one."

Alphonse gripped the man's arm more tightly, as he feared he would soon pitch forward onto the ground. "You, too, are a *résistant*?" he asked him. "Is that why you were arrested and brought here?"

Patou nodded affirmatively.

"I was in the French diplomatic corps in North Africa. I resigned as soon as the Vichy took over. It turned out that my name was on a list of some two hundred members of the Resistance that was left on a train...who knows if by mistake or by a *traitor,*" he said with a bitterness that brought a touch of color to his emaciated cheeks. "One day in late May, I was picked up here in Paris for not having a proper ration card," he said with disgust, as if being caught for such a small infraction was an embarrassment that would tarnish him forever. "I have been in this hell ever since."

"My boss was taken here too," Moreau revealed. "I didn't know, at first, what had happened to him, until I finally beat it out of the stinking rat assistant of mine that betrayed him and my nephew Alain to the SS. That's why I've come today," he explained. "I heard the Germans left."

Patou replied, "They've abandoned Avenue Foch, all right, but the beasts are still all over Paris. Some say they intend to burn the city down when they finally do retreat."

"Then you don't know about the invasion in Normandy?" Moreau asked.

"Rumors," Patou replied. He scrutinized Moreau as if he would kill the next man who told him a lie. "It has finally happened, then?"

"Yes, on the sixth of June. We've heard that Allied troops are approaching Paris. Already, there are signs in the streets of an uprising, even before they arrive." Moreau paused and glanced at the building behind them. "You didn't actually know my nephew Alain Chapelle or Henri Leblanc? Leblanc was in the diplomatic service, too."

Patou's eyes blazed, and he spat on the ground.

"Leblanc was a swine! A Nazi collaborator! He worked for the Vichy for years at his post in Washington long after any decent men in the corps quit! Then I'd heard he joined the Brits. The SOE, they claimed. I shunned him here," he declared, his expression reflecting a deep antipathy at the mere mention of Leblanc's name. "Major Kieffer kept coming up to see him. I figured the traitor for a double agent all this time."

Moreau let go of Patou's arm, and the man nearly collapsed where he stood.

"He's no double agent and no traitor to France!" Alphonse Moreau said, glaring. "He was locked up here all this time, and he never gave *me* up to Kieffer. Henri Leblanc ran all sorts of dangerous missions that helped get our side to where it is today!"

Patou weakly pointed behind him. "Well, swine or hero, he's probably in there, just another corpse."

"Alain Chapelle, too…?" murmured Moreau.

"I would imagine so," Patou avowed, quieter now.

Moreau's hand covered his eyes, unable to speak. Finally, he choked out, "Alain was my sister's boy. I got him to join as a *résistant…*"

Patou seized Moreau's arm, the smell of death on him bearing witness to the horror Patou had so vividly described.

"When I sneaked out in the dark after the Germans left, I was too weak to walk, so I slept just inside the door. At least when I was awake, I saw no one else pass by." He stared at Moreau, hollow-eyed. "You mustn't go inside. It's beyond foul. Dangerous, by this time, with all the heat these last two days. And there's nothing you can do for your nephew now."

François Patou began to weep. Henri Leblanc's master printer and fellow *résistant* hesitated a long moment and then put an arm around the distraught man. Patou closed his eyes and sighed, "By now, they're certainly all dead in there. All dead…except for me…"

Alphonse Moreau's eyes filled, and he said, "I suppose you're right. Come with me. You can shower in Henri Leblanc's private bathroom at our printing office," he added with studied emphasis. "Then you must tell me how to find your family."

François Patou gazed past him with a thousand-yard stare. "My family?" he whispered. "I have absolutely no idea what's happened to any of them…or where in this world of carnage they might be."

Moreau could find no words of reply, so he turned toward the gate, guiding his charge into the alleyway. Turning left, and left again, the two men slowly walked down Avenue Foch, empty, at long last, of its German occupiers.

CHAPTER 41

The reception committee in the field above the Mentons' highest olive grove had taken positions in the standard *L* formation, even though the plane would only make a drop and not attempt a landing.

"*Merde!*" whispered Catherine to Jules, gazing through the late-night gloom at the low-lying clouds above their heads. "Fog! Of all the luck…"

"Even so, if your coordinates were good, you'll see a white mushroom land in the field," he reassured her.

"Our best pilots are pretty busy right now," Catherine fretted. Her thoughts fled briefly to Henri in Paris, wondering what assignments he might have had since news of the Normandy invasion—that is, if he was still alive.

She had finally been given permission to alert all those in the Trenches underground that Operation Dragoon was due to launch in less than twelve hours along the beaches of the Riviera. "Let's hope to hell that RAF has at least one hotshot flyboy left in Corsica who can find his way across the Med to anywhere *near* where we are."

Just then, Jules cocked his head and nodded. "Hear that? There he is!"

Catherine glanced at her watch and said, "Two a.m. Right on the money—literally."

In the space of a few minutes, the ghost plane had come and gone. In the silent predawn sky, an inflated, white silk canopy appeared through the billowing fog. Catherine strained to see the payload, which appeared as small as a footlocker but whose weight was pulling the parachute straight down to the middle of the field. The entire reception committee converged on a dirty green, cigar-shaped metal box with *"U.S. Army"* stamped in white letters on its lid.

"I'll pry it open," Jules volunteered, and in seconds Catherine peered at its contents.

"Long guns?" she said, her heart sinking.

"Stens," Jules responded, handing the weapons, one by one, to the men who encircled them. "No point wasting a chance to drop us some more weapons, bless 'em."

At the bottom of the canister was a small, rectangular metal container, also stamped with *"U.S. Army"* in white letters. Inside was a packet marked, *"SOE Only!"*

"Shine your light on me, will you?" Catherine ordered. She nervously opened the box, and inside was a linen pouch. "Thank God," she breathed, her thumb strafing along a thick packet of franc notes.

At the bottom of the stack was a file folder.

"Well, will you look at this?" she murmured, pulling out a sheet emblazoned with the Seal of the United States and the embossed letters, *"Allied Headquarters."*

Jules leaned closer, focusing his light on the document in Catherine's hand. "And just look at that signature." He glanced up and met her glance. "Do you think it's real?"

"Probably not, but who cares?" she said, pure joy broadening her smile.

Below the official letterhead was a typed message reading, *"Safe Passage Granted to Captain Gunther Wintermuden."* Scrawled below that, in fresh ink:

"General Dwight David Eisenhower, Supreme Allied Commander"

———◇———

Catherine figured she was officially running on pure adrenalin. She'd spent the hours after the plane flew off making sure that, for the sake of the Mentons, she left no trace in the olive shed that foreign agents had ever been there. She'd turned on the wireless one last time and had been startled to receive the last-minute message with further instructions that morning.

"Trenches agents ordered to evacuate by submarine off Villefranche at 02 hrs. prior to aerial bombardments commencing at dawn, Tuesday, 15 August."

Her chores done, she dreaded even glancing at her watch, for she had exactly forty-five minutes to walk into Captain Wintermuden's SS office in Nice before Sean and the other prisoners were scheduled to be transported in a canvas-covered truck, taken up into the hills, and executed.

She closed the leather suitcase one last time and tied its heavy weight onto a small metal platform above the back wheel of her bicycle. She stowed one small canvas bag in her front wicker basket, and the other satchel, she slung across her shoulders. It would be dangerous to travel with that much baggage, but SOE standing orders were never to leave a wireless for the enemy to find unless it was a choice between life and death.

We're not quite at that stage...but close.

Jules and Catherine had agreed hours before that, for safety's sake, she wouldn't stop at the farmhouse to say goodbye. She stored the wireless, the notorious blood-stained scarf, and Sean's canvas bag inside the tractor shed in a hollowed-out hay bale. She then pedaled past the Mentons' home, her throat constricting at the thought of the wonderful family that lived inside. The early morning August air was already starting to warm, but thankfully, the village lanes above the harbor were deserted as she made her way down to the Villefranche waterfront.

She left her bicycle in the storeroom behind Remy's restaurant and held her breath as her identity documents were inspected by guards she didn't recognize prior to boarding the train for the short ride to Nice. The pistol weighed heavily in the false bottom of her canvas bag, this time it's hard metal wrapped in a pair of knickers for easier access but to foil further inspection. Luckily, the platform was crowded. Attired in her linen blouse and blue skirt, she easily passed through the checkpoint like a matron minding her own business and then onto the coach. Once at the Nice station, it took less than ten minutes to enter the street where the looming jail and SS headquarters were housed in an old bank building. She paused on the corner, taking in the sight of a row of German army trucks lined up outside.

They've gotten word. They're preparing their retreat.

Catherine inhaled a deep breath and reached into her canvas bag's false bottom to place her gun where she could easily grab it. Squaring her shoulders, she strode inside the building. This time, the anteroom filled with desks of SS functionaries showed clear signs of an office in wild disarray. File cabinets stood open and half empty. Soldiers were tossing papers into boxes while others were handing the cartons, one by one, along a line of uniformed men that ended at the back of one of the trucks she had seen parked outside.

Much to Catherine's surprise, when she headed for the office inner sanctum, ignoring the soldiers she passed, the preoccupied functionaries barely looked up. She heard one say in German in a low voice to his companion, "Wintermuden got word they're pushing off from Corsica—tonight!'

"*Ya, ya*, keep packing!"

Corporal Scheff was not at his desk guarding the captain's office, so Catherine brazenly walked to the door, knocked, and peered inside.

The clock on the wall above his desk indicated it was twenty minutes after the noon hour. Captain Gunther Wintermuden looked up from stacks of files on his desk, an expression of surprise invading his features.

"You?" he said, placing both hands on his desk. "When the noon hour passed, I figured it was time to arrange for, well—"

"You've *shot* them?" Catherine cried in sudden fury. "You said between noon and one! I have the money and the letter and—"

The captain barked, "Close the door, damn you! The men you seek are still in their cells, for God's sake!" He shot her a harsh look. "You were right. We know, now, the invasion comes tomorrow or the next day. As you can see, we're making haste to withdraw before—"

"You've had orders to retreat, then?" Catherine confirmed, the blood that had been pounding through her veins slowly subsiding. She pointed to her canvas bag. "Then, you'll want what I have in here, so let's not delay. Please order the Citroën, give me *your* letter of safe passage, and we'll get out of your way."

Wintermuden shook his head. "Not so fast. Let me see what you have in there," he said, indicating that she should open her bag.

"I will be happy to, and while I do that, do not even think of pulling that revolver out of your holster. I took the precaution of placing my pistol on top of the letter and the three hundred thousand francs, see?"

She withdrew her gun in one hand and handed him the Eisenhower safe passage document in the other. Wintermuden reached across his desk and seized it from her, bringing it close to his face to scrutinize it within three inches of his pale blue eyes.

"It looks genuine enough," he said, and Catherine detected in his tone his grudging admiration.

"Friends in high places," she replied shortly while reaching inside her canvas bag to retrieve the small, metal ammunition box. With her thumb, she flicked open the top. Nestled inside was a two-inch wad of franc notes.

"I was able to get you small denominations that will be easier to use as you make your way back to Germany," she noted. Wintermuden raised an eyebrow that might have indicated a modicum of appreciation. Catherine continued, "The entire three hundred thousand is here, but you'll just have to trust me on that as I'm not handing this to you until my husband and the other SOE agent are sitting in the Citroën with a full tank and Nazi flags flying on the fenders."

"I haven't drawn up a letter of safe passage for you because, well, frankly, I never thought you'd return."

Catherine regarded him for a long moment. If Sean, the other agent, and she made it out of Nice alive, the three would be rowing directly toward the sub after midnight tonight and would have no need for such a document. Since Wintermuden wasn't demanding a full accounting of the money, she'd allow this omission to pass.

She smiled faintly. "Well, I can see you've been busy. Shall we say we're even? Our bargain still holds?"

"*Ya, ya!*" the captain exclaimed, apparently anxious to get the exchange over and done with. He'd seen the franc notes with his own eyes, and most especially, the document stamped *"Supreme Allied Commander"* with its impressive signature.

Catherine kept her pistol trained on the officer whose hand now rested on a shiny, black telephone. "Make the call to Josef Gumbel to release the prisoners next door," she directed, "and order the car sent to the back of the jail."

Wintermuden's brow furrowed and he said, "You know his name? Josef Gumbel?"

Catherine offered a thin smile. When she'd been locked up next door with the women suffering from TB, she remembered the guards wondering aloud when their commanding officer would be returning from lunch. "*Herr* Gumbel's name is well-known in Nice. Now make that call, and let's go!"

Five minutes later, Captain Wintermuden led the way down a long corridor toward the back of the building.

"You'll have to put that pistol away when we go outside," he advised over his shoulder. "My men are everywhere and so are Gumbel's at the jail."

"It's already in my bag," Catherine replied. "Of course, it can shoot through canvas," she added, "and it's still aimed at your back."

The captain made no reply as he opened the rear entrance door and led her across the street and into a back alley. A shining black Citroën, with small Nazi flags attached to each fender, was parked nearby, its motor running. Beside it, a uniformed driver was poised at rigid attention.

"*Heil,* Hitler!" the young man greeted them through stiff lips, arm raised.

Almost wearily, Wintermuden raised his arm in salute, replying, "*Heil,* Hitler. You will go inside now and escort the two prisoners in cell B out here."

For Catherine, the next few minutes felt as long and anxiety ridden as the first time she waited for her parachute to open. Her palm felt sweaty against the handle of her gun. At any second, she realized, something could go horribly wrong. She and the captain were both silent, both wondering how the next act in this drama would play out.

For once, Catherine didn't have long to wait. The door to the back of the jail opened, and the young soldier appeared, along with the scowling jailor Josef Gumbel himself. The soldier was prodding two haggard-looking men, who shuffled outside, squinting in the bright sunlight.

Catherine was almost amused by Sean's stunned expression, his mouth slightly ajar, as he stared at her across the short distance that separated them.

"Put my husband, Mr. Eisenhower, in the driver's seat, please," she ordered, casting a faint smile in Sean's direction. Meanwhile, the jailor Gumbel looked at her with a puzzled expression.

"Jacqueline Bise, are you, they tell me?"

Catherine held her breath. His confusion told Catherine the name seemed somehow familiar to him, if only from the rash of documents which perhaps his guards had told him months ago belonged to one of the ill women who'd been his prisoner.

Before the jailor had time to plumb his memory any further, she exclaimed to Sean in English, "Hello, darling. You have your Uncle Dwight to thank for this. Your devoted Jacqueline let him know your current plight, and he sends you and your companion here his very best. Do you feel well enough to drive?"

Sean's red hair was matted, his face stubbled with several days' growth of beard, and his ruddy complexion was marred by a black eye. One lens in his thick glasses was cracked, but his signature grin enveloped his face.

"I feel fine, *libeling*," he replied with a glance at Wintermuden, "—now."

But Catherine could tell the two men had received beatings at the hands of Gumbel's goons. She prayed Sean's reflexes were steady enough to drive at high speed.

With a wince, Sean eased his bruised body into the driver's seat, and the other agent, whom Catherine had never met, climbed haltingly into the backseat as if every muscle in his body was screaming in pain.

Wintermuden turned to address Gumbel and the other soldier, dismissing them.

Catherine waited until both men disappeared through the back door of the jail before she nodded at the captain and strode to the passenger side of the car, opening the door. She reached into her canvas bag and withdrew the small, metal ammunitions case and handed it to Wintermuden, who had followed her, standing two steps behind.

"I promise you, all three hundred thousand francs are there, but you better have a quick look."

Before she handed it over, she gave a brief nod in Sean's direction to confirm his hands were on the wheel and his foot on the gas pedal. In one swift movement, she thrust the box into the captain's hands, took her seat next to Sean, and slammed the door.

Just as if she were urging someone parachuting out of an airplane, she cried, "Go, go, go!"

The car lurched forward, picking up speed.

"Won't they be on our tails in minutes?" gasped the man in the backseat.

Fearing just that, Catherine swiveled around, straining to look out the rear window. In the few seconds that Sean had stomped on the gas, Josef Gumbel had bolted out the jail's back door, and the two men appeared to be in a death struggle over the metal box she had just handed over to Wintermuden.

"That son of a bitch Gumbel was listening at the door!" Catherine exclaimed as a shot rang out. "Oh my God, he fired on Captain Wintermuden! The commander has fallen to the ground, and Gumbel just scooped up the money!"

"That's dandy fine with me," Sean said, squinting through his cracked glasses as he wheeled at top speed through the back streets of Nice. "Frankly, though, I would have preferred our very nasty jailor had been the one with a bullet in his gut."

———◇———

With Nazi flags flapping jauntily on the Citroën's fenders, the black sedan streaked down the road between Nice and Villefranche with no attempt by any passing soldiers to stop its progress. Spitting dirt behind its rubber tires, Sean wheeled the vehicle up to the olive farm and into the large shed where Jules parked his rusted tractor.

"The wireless and your canvas bag are hidden in that stack of hay bales," she informed him. "Far right, second bale down from the top."

Catherine was in the act of yanking the despised Nazi flags off the fenders when Eve Menton and Tamara came rushing out of the farmhouse.

"We heard a car," Eve said, staring in shock at the sleek, black vehicle now sitting on Menton land. She turned to take in the sight of Sean as if a ghost had suddenly appeared before her.

"We've brought you a gift from the departing Nazis," Sean said, with a sweep of his arm toward the flashy sedan.

Eve threw her arms around him. "I can't believe it!" she cried. "I can't believe you're alive!"

By this time, Tamara had cast her arms around Sean's knees, hugging him fiercely. Catherine looked over at her other passenger and extended a hand to Sean's fellow prisoner, who was slowly emerging from the backseat.

"I go by Jacqueline Bise these days. And you are?"

"Code name Louis, but I'm Amory Hyde," he replied with a wan smile. "And, by the way, thank you, however you managed all this."

From his shaky voice and downcast eyes, he seemed a man almost at the breaking point. Catherine could understand, now, why this was the SOE agent that their London superiors had thought best to summon from the field and send back to Britain. His sojourn in the Nice jail with Josef Gumbel interrogating him must have been a horrific experience, along with other close calls and his recent capture by the German patrol boat.

Catherine placed her hand lightly on the filthy sleeve of the man who shared the same first name—Amory—as her father.

"Actually, I can't quite believe I pulled it off," she said with a smile. She could see the former prisoner's hand tremble, and he appeared exceedingly frail. "Only one more leg in our journey for the three of us," she said encouragingly. "and we'll be home free. We don't leave until after midnight tonight, so I'm sure the Mentons will let you rest in the children's back bedroom until then."

"Where are we going?" he asked, apprehension furrowing his brow.

"With any luck, we're being picked up by submarine."

"Oh God," groaned Hyde, "not rowing out of the harbor again. There are bound to be those German patrol boats around like last time!"

Catherine offered a smile of reassurance. "I know it's a hard thing to do, to head on out to sea again, but it's a risk all three of us have to take. And it'll be worth it to climb aboard an American sub, don't you think?"

Sean's fellow prisoner remained silent; fear and misery were written on his face. Catherine was beginning to be concerned that getting the agent to safety would possibly compromise their own chances of escape. She turned toward Jules, Eve, and Sean, who had heard their conversation. The trio were exchanging glances that telegraphed to Catherine that they, too, could see that the man was close to cracking.

Catherine urged, "What do you say we get you and your fellow escapee, Sean here, cleaned up and fed some decent food, courtesy of our hostess?" To Eve, Catherine asked, "Can these men have a wash in your kitchen?" She turned towards Sean and said, deadpan, "I'm afraid they both actually smell."

CHAPTER 42

Catherine and Sean left Amory in the Menton farmhouse, where he was finishing his first decent meal in weeks. They rescued the suitcase containing the wireless from its hiding-place in the haybale and lugged it back up the hill in hopes of sending a final transmission to London confirming the rendezvous with the sub. On a promontory behind their latest safe-house, Catherine typed with special care the news that Sean and the other SOE agent had been freed and that the three would row out of Villefranche harbor sometime after midnight to meet the ship.

The reply back was swift, congratulating Catherine on her coup and cryptically revealing that other SOE agents in Paris that week had not been so fortunate. Catherine stared at her scribbles on her notepad before crumpling the page and lighting it afire.

Oh, Henri, stay alive! It's almost over. Please stay alive!

"Come here, my rescuer," Sean said, pulling Catherine to her feet and into his arms. "This may be my last chance to tell you that—"

His voice wavered, and Catherine saw that he was suddenly overcome with emotion, as was she. They clung to each other for several long moments.

"I know you're worried that Henri was caught up in all that business in Paris, but all we can do now is stay as strong as we can till we get out of here." He gently kissed her on both cheeks, European style. "If you won't be my lover anymore, will you be my sister? You saved my life. So, whether you agree to it or not, you're family now. For life." Then he added with a laugh, "My own three sisters can be such bitches, sometimes. I'll definitely need a backup when we get home."

Catherine nodded, her eyes teary "I never had a brother, so you're it. And, just remember, I'm betting that nothing will be the same for some of us after this war, and we few—'we happy few,' to quote the Bard—will need to stick together."

Sean squeezed her hard. "You can say that again. A band of brothers...*and* sisters."

Sean buried his head in the crook of her shoulder. Mumbling against her skin, she could barely hear his words.

"I thought August fourteenth, nineteen forty-two would be the day inscribed on my tombstone. But it wasn't, thanks to you and you alone."

Catherine contemplated the dangerous hours that lay ahead.

"Let's just get through the rest of this day, and the next, before you say that."

Sean raised his head. "Man, you sure are a glass-half-empty gal! You pulled off a miracle today!" he chided her, his mischievous sense of humor returning. "Now all we have to do is row into the harbor a few miles and jump onto a sub. Piece of cake."

———◇———

"Tamara is asleep?" Catherine asked as soon as she sat down at the Menton's kitchen table. She gazed at its rough wood surface, where she'd shared so many meals with this family who had been incredibly generous and brave these last months.

These are the kinds of people that won this war...if, in fact, it is to be won.

Eve Menton smiled at the mention of Tamara. "She wanted to stay up, but I put all the girls to bed an hour ago."

Catherine asked, "May I just peek in their room?"

"Of course," Eve replied, pointing toward the back of the farmhouse.

Catherine tiptoed to the threshold, and in the dim light, she could just make out the shapes of three small children in one bed, under a quilt. She walked softly to the edge of the mattress, leaned down, and brushed her lips in a featherlight kiss on Tamara's forehead. She watched the child's even breathing, marveling at the fateful way their paths had crossed.

"Be well, little one," she whispered. "You are loved. Despite all the wickedness in this world, you are loved."

When Catherine reentered the kitchen, Sean looked up.

"She didn't wake." To Eve she said, "Tell Tamara that, if all goes well, I will be in touch with you when this is over, and it *will* be over soon," she added with more assurance than she felt. She turned toward Jules sitting at the head of the table. "Sean and I are urging everyone up here to remain where they are for the next week or so."

Sean chimed in, "There will be a lot of fireworks, Jules. It's going to be stuff that only the Allied troops can handle in the early days of the operation." He offered a grin in his host's direction. "But don't be surprised if you see a lot of white, silk mushrooms landing in your upper field this week. Better have your reception committee ready to welcome them." Then he added, "And may I suggest you bury those little Nazi flags that we took off the Citroën tonight and be ready to start waving French flags when the paratroopers are about fifty feet off the ground."

Catherine had a sudden thought, "And may I send Remy up to stay with you when the invasion comes? Villefranche harbor will be a pretty risky place to be."

Jules nodded. "I'll put him in the olive shed. Give him some fresh straw."

Sean put his hand over Catherine's on the table. "And will you please tell some of those French Resistance big wigs like de Gaulle that this woman deserves to be awarded the *Légion d'Honneur*? I heard in jail that your self-appointed leader intends to wipe out any traces of SOE's contribution to liberating France."

Eve said to her husband, "I never liked Charles de Gaulle. Such a blowhard!" To Catherine she declared, "You can be sure we will write whoever runs the *Légion* when this is over, won't we, Jules?"

Jules, in his usual taciturn way, responded, "*D'accord.*"

———◇———

"You can't use the boat," Remy said in a low voice as soon as Catherine and her two companions slipped into the back of his restaurant in the cover of night.

"Why the hell not?" Sean demanded.

"The owner was the guy who betrayed you the last time you rowed out in it."

"What?"

Remy nodded. "He figured he could make a few francs by letting the *Bosches* know you were agents heading out to make a rendezvous with whoever it was."

"Shit!" Sean exploded. He looked at Catherine. "Now what do we do?"

"To the guy?" Remy asked. He lit a cigarette and blew the smoke into the air. "Don't worry. We'll take care of him."

"Well, where's his boat?"

"The Germans hauled it into Nice after they nabbed you that time."

Catherine stepped out of the back of the restaurant and peered through the gloom of midnight at another small craft bobbing near the *quai*. She pointed to a wooden dinghy tied to the stern of a larger boat fifty feet further down the waterfront.

"How about that one?" she suggested.

Remy laughed. "That belongs to a guy from here serving in Nice in the *milice*."

Catherine gave a short laugh. "One of those French hooligans posing as police? Then it's the perfect boat to steal." She leaned forward and bussed him on the cheek. "Please make yourself scarce and go up to the olive farm when we push off tonight, okay?"

"Thanks, but I'm heading into Nice as soon as you leave," he responded. "We Free French have a few things we want to take care of when the party starts."

"How about you begin with the owner of the boat Sean used the last time?"

Remy offered a smirk. "First on my list. The louse divided the money with the guy in the *milice*. You steal that boat, and I'll go after him and steal the money back!"

Sean offered their first friend in Villefranche a bear hug and then, with a glance at his watch, said to Catherine and Amory Hyde, who'd stood silently by, "It's anchors away, folks."

Catherine stole a glance at Amory, who looked like he was about to be sick. His haunted eyes darted around the confined space at the back of Remy's restaurant kitchen. She reached over and patted his hand.

"We're on the last leg," she said encouragingly.

"We heard in jail that the harbor's been mined," he replied, avoiding her eyes.

"Not the way we're going," she assured him. "Sean and I have done this a few times before, remember?"

"But last time—"

"Amory!" Catherine said sharply. "We're going in that rowboat out there, and we'll need your help aboard, every single second."

Oblivious to this exchange, Sean concluded his conversation with Remy, joking, "If you don't kill the *milice* guy, tell him he'll probably find his dinghy bobbing on the Med about two miles out."

"I'll be sure to let him know—just before I slit his throat."

Catherine murmured, "*Au revoir, mon ami.*"

———◇———

Amory Hyde slumped in the stern of the boat while Sean and Catherine took turns rowing into the dark night at an angle that would theoretically bring them close to the coordinates where the submarine was plotted to surface. Catherine's heart went out to their passenger as he sat shaking, his knees pressed against the leather suitcase as if the wireless inside would help to keep him upright. He seemed a man on the jagged edge of collapse both from outright fear and the physical stress he'd been under for weeks.

"Amory was seasick the first time we tried this," Sean whispered to Catherine, who was perched in the bow after taking her turn rowing the dinghy out of Villefranche harbor. "I'm afraid it's just you and me powering this boat, babe."

"Sounds familiar."

Catherine's muscles still ached from her time at the oars, and she soothed them by rubbing her arms as she stared into the gloom. She could only wonder how Sean could row a boat after the physical abuse he'd endured in jail. All was silent except for the sound of water stirred by Sean's rhythmic pull on the oars.

Catherine peered back at Amory once more to gauge how he was faring. His upper body was arched over the side of the boat, and he was being miserably sick. The man was a liability, especially if the rendezvous with the sub never materialized due to circumstances beyond anyone's control; it was, after all, the eve of the scheduled Allied invasion of the South of France.

They were about a mile and a half offshore when they heard the sudden sound of a motor starting up. A second later, a bright light shone some two hundred yards from their position, heading out to sea.

"Oh, Jesus!" hissed Catherine. "A German patrol boat!"

Amory emitted a groan from the stern.

"We'd better swim for it," Sean whispered back.

"Are you strong enough?" Catherine asked, her heart racing.

"Got to be." To Amory, who still had the wireless clamped between his legs, he barked a sharp order, pointing to the heavy suitcase, "C'mon, pal, toss the thing overboard and you go in after it! We don't want the Krauts learning our cipher codes at this late date."

Catherine quickly removed her shoes and jacket, and the others followed suit.

"If we go overboard quietly," she urged, keeping her voice low, "we'll gain more time to swim toward the rendezvous spot before the Germans realize we've left the boat."

She slipped into the water without a splash, on the side of the dinghy facing away from the patrol boat whose flood light was strafing the waters to their right. A moment later, Sean slipped over the side. Both began to do the breaststroke as quickly and as quietly as they could to make room for Amory's entry. Behind them, Catherine heard a loud splash, which they took to be the wireless suitcase heaved over the side, and then another, which she surmised was the third agent himself.

Sean stopped and treaded water, nodding to the east. "Keep that point of land over there on your left side where the bay curves, and just swim straight ahead."

"Where are your glasses?" Catherine asked, horrified to see only Sean's black eye glistening with saltwater.

"In my pocket. I can see shapes, and I feel fine," he assured her. "Let's go!"

The trio ceased speaking then and swam as fast as they could, aware that, behind them, the patrol boat had started plowing its way through the water in the direction of their abandoned dinghy. Within five minutes, Catherine's arms were numb from exertion, and her feet felt like lead. Despite this, she forced herself to keep up with Sean, who certainly had terrible eyesight but was as strong a swimmer as she was despite the physical abuse he'd recently suffered. A few more minutes further on, she realized that Amory wasn't right behind her. She swiveled in the water and saw he was at least a hundred yards away. The patrol boat crew had come alongside their empty dinghy and boarded it, searching for anyone hiding there. As she and Sean swam on, she could hear the sound of the engine accelerating as it circled the rowboat and prepared to head into deeper water.

The three fugitives had come so far, she thought, glancing over her shoulder to try to catch a clearer glimpse of Amory's bobbing head. The sea was swelling up and down with the tide, and she imagined that it felt like a ruthless adversary to a man as weakened as their third companion.

"He's way behind us" Catherine cried.

"C'mon, Catherine!" Sean called to her. "The water's starting to boil straight ahead. It's the sub. We've gotta leave him. Keep swimming."

Obeying Sean's command, she broke into a full-bore Australian crawl, her arms flailing out of the water like a windmill in a hurricane. A hundred yards in front of them, the great black whale's conning tower rose up, and the waves it created pushed Sean and Catherine back thirty feet. The German patrol boat gunned its motor as if they, too, had spotted the huge ship.

Above their heads, the top of the sub's tower flipped open, and a sailor in a wet suit appeared. Sean and Catherine stroked all the faster, closing the gap between themselves and the sleek, black vessel. The figure on the deck deftly tossed a long line toward them with a circular life preserver attached to it.

"I've got it!" Sean shouted. To Catherine he ordered, "Grab hold of my waist and paddle for all you're worth!"

Catherine tried to match the rhythm of Sean's kicks with her own, receiving a mouthful of the Mediterranean for her trouble. Coughing and sputtering, she closed her eyes and lips and scissored her legs through the churning waves with all her might. By the time they reached the sub's slippery side, another frogman had climbed onto the deck with a second line and preserver that Catherine grabbed, and together, she and Sean were hauled up and over the side onto a shiny deck as the sound of a bullet ricocheted off the side of the ship.

"German patrol boat," Catherine gasped.

"Gee, really?" said her rescuer. "Welcome aboard."

The other frogman said, "Where's your third?"

Sean choked out, "Behind us. Seasick. Beaten in captivity. Couldn't keep up."

Just then the *rat-a-tat-tat* of machinegun fire rang out over the churning sea.

"Your buddy just got hit," announced one of the sailors, grabbing for Catherine as he peered over her shoulder. "I can't see him anymore."

She felt hands pushing and lifting her up and over the top of the sub's conning tower. Her body was limp with exhaustion, and she fought for consciousness.

"Wrap her in the blanket" ordered a deckhand as additional shots rang out, some pinging against the hull.

She was lowered onto a canvas stretcher in the narrow passageway just as the conning tower's hatch slammed shut. The edges of her vision had begun to gray out, except for a single bulb glowing over her head. The only thing she remembered after that was the sound of horns wailing to announce to all aboard that the ship was diving below the surface of the waters off Villefranche-sur-Mer, safe at last from an enemy fighting its final battle on the French Riviera.

———◇———

Catherine awoke when a naval ensign tapped her shoulder, extending a tin mug filled to the brim with steaming hot coffee.

"This should help you wake up," he said with a wry smile. "Not like the Frenchies make, I imagine. You can stand a spoon in ours."

Catherine attempted to pull herself up to a sitting position, but immediately bumped her head. Alarmed and disoriented, it quickly became clear that she had been sleeping in one of a stack of bunks—less than 24 inches separating each one from the deck to overhead—aboard a U.S. Navy submarine that smelled heavily of diesel fuel. Bent nearly double, she swung her legs to the side and struggled to stand. She was conscious of the sound of water swooshing along the side of the steel hull. She stared at the sailor holding out the coffee cup and seized it gingerly, the metal hot against her hand.

"Where are we?" she asked, her back braced against the edges of the tier of bunks.

"We'll be offloading you two in Corsica soon" he replied. "Then we'll turn around and follow the other eight hundred and eighty ships in Operation Dragoon back where we just were, only this time we'll be with more than a thousand landing craft."

The sailor reached up to the top bunk and gave Sean's shoulder a gentle shove.

"Wake up, sir."

"Don't try to sit up," Catherine warned, pointing to the low ceiling above Sean's head. "You'll have to get out of the rack sideways if you want any coffee."

Sean groaned faintly and rolled to one side in order to stand next to Catherine, arm outstretched to receive the other cup the sailor handed to him.

Catherine stood still as memories of the previous night roared back with a rush.

Amory hadn't made it.

He'd been so close to being rescued when the damn German patrol boat roared after them and shot him like a fish in a barrel. She had felt the terror herself that she wouldn't be able to stay afloat until the sub surfaced or strong enough to keep up with Sean. As always, Sean had made sure she was right there with him. In a very real sense, they had kept each other afloat throughout the entire time they'd worked together.

But they couldn't save Amory.

Poor broken soul, she thought, recalling the sight of the British agent huddled in the dinghy's stern, sick to his stomach from the churning waters of the bay and dreadfully weakened after the beating he'd had at the hands of jailor Josef Gumbel.

And all that trauma had happened to Amory *after* he'd been recalled from the field by the SOE brass for exhaustion and mental stress. Catherine felt her throat tighten with unshed tears, haunted by the memory of treading water, looking over her shoulder, and seeing nothing but roiling waves behind her. Had Amory Hyde been so afraid of capture again and the horrors of what he'd endured that he *chose* not to swim as hard as he could, allowing the Nazi bullets to find him? In the years to come, would there be others in this band of brothers and sisters *in extremis* who'd make the same decision? She pictured the L-pill every SOE agent had been given before departure for France.

Had Henri made such a lethal choice?

Catherine's gloomy reverie was interrupted by Sean, who began to pepper the coffee-bearing ensign with questions.

"How big a force is involved with Operation Dragoon? How many men will hit the beaches on the Riviera, do you suppose?"

"In the first wave? It's classified, but from the number of ships I saw, tens of thousands at least, including the airborne troops."

"There was a lot of fog early Monday morning," Catherine said worriedly. "I hope it lifted when those poor guys jumped out of their planes."

"Oh, they had fog, all right," agreed the sailor. "Even so, by now most of 'em have bailed out over the countryside. I heard that the American 517th Parachute Regiment, plus two more U.S. parachute battalions, were to drop over Le Muy." The sailor cracked a grin. "Our radioman said they captured the town!"

He headed out of the stateroom, advising them over his shoulder, "Better drink up, you two, and prepare to disembark in an hour." He pointed a finger at Sean. "I suppose, thanks to Agent Eisenhower's moniker," he said, pokerfaced, "both of you will be flown back to London today. The skipper said to let you know that your SOE bosses and our OSS guys are anxious for a complete report about your final days on the Riviera." He winked. "Nice assignments, if you can get 'em!"

When they were alone, Catherine said, "So, we're going to be having afternoon tea in Britain, even after we failed in our mission to get Amory out safely. I doubt we'll get any medals for that."

Sean stared at her and shook his head. "You are so hard on yourself, Agent Colette! Can't you see, Catherine, we did everything possible to save the guy? Who benefits if we'd gone back and then all three of us were shot out of the water by those Germans or we'd drowned on our own?" He pulled her against his chest and wrapped her in his arms. "I'd never let you drown, nor would you me. Amory had fallen so far behind, and the German patrol boat was bearing down on us, none of us would have made it if we'd tried to be heroes."

"And then the bullets started to fly," Catherine recalled with a shudder at the thought of how easily either of them or the frogmen who rescued them from the water could also have been shot.

"And it wouldn't have been so great if the Krauts had seriously punctured the hull of the sub with any more of that firepower they had on board their patrol boat," Sean added. "Look, it was a classic save-as-many-as-you-can situation. We'll tell the desk jockeys in London exactly what happened, and if they court-martial us…fuck 'em!"

"Still, we…" she said, letting her words die. She doubted she would ever feel totally absolved from leaving one of their own behind.

Sean bent down and kissed the top of her head. "You were a wonder, and I want you to start believing that."

Catherine only could offer him a shrug. If felt so strange just to be spectators now, she thought. The war zone they'd just left wouldn't be peaceful in a mere month or two. Exhausted men like Amory would continue to die, and she was sure that she and Sean would be facing an entirely new kind of battle from here on out.

CHAPTER 43

Neither Sean nor Catherine had ever set foot on Corsica, and once the submarine surfaced, they were rowed ashore amidst hundreds more warships heading in the opposite direction toward the southern French coastline. Before they'd left the sub, the captain handed them a report to give to their superiors.

"Since you're intelligence folks," he said genially, "I'm happy to let you two and your commanders know that, in the first hours of Operation Dragoon, the Allies have gained primacy over more than a fifty-mile front along the Côte d'Azur that stretches thirty miles deep—a total of some fifteen hundred square miles." The captain paused. "I'm guessing that it won't be long before General Eisenhower gets the Port of Marseille that he needs so badly to supply his troops coming south from Normandy." He shook hands with them both, bidding them, "Godspeed."

A car was waiting for them dockside to whisk them to a landing field nearby. From there, a small U.S. Army plane flew the short distance to Rome, only recently liberated by Allied troops. In that war-torn part of Italy, they boarded a larger plane for an eerily uneventful flight to an airfield at Tangmere, Sussex, near the coast of England.

The pair was ushered into a requisitioned stone cottage to have their first meal on British soil. Sitting across from them at a trestle table in the pint-sized officers' mess, a pilot from the Moon Squad that flew secret agents back and forth nodded hello. After learning they'd just been extracted from France, the flyer informed them, "You'll be pleased to know nine important towns on the Riviera are now in Allied hands."

Sean looked at Catherine somberly. "I'll bet every one of those SS bastards that held us at the Nice jail have had the tables turned on them by now. The place is probably swarming with GIs."

The RAF pilot nodded, his forkful of shepherd's pie suspended in the air. "Given that some three hundred and twenty-four thousand Allied military with vehicles disembarked onto French soil on the fifteenth, the entire operation went amazingly smoothly," he said. "My commander says our men are moving steadily north toward Grenoble and beyond, hoping to hook up with the troops fighting their way south from the Channel."

"And Paris?" Catherine asked, her thoughts, as always, hovering around her fears for Henri's fate during the past tumultuous few weeks.

"The troops are getting close," confirmed the pilot. "I'm flying out tonight, but I don't know exactly where yet."

The next morning, Catherine and Sean climbed out of the car that had been sent to Tangmere Field to bring them to Baker Street. They found themselves standing near Number 22, the address Sir Robert Conan Doyle had selected as his fictional setting for Sherlock Holmes. A few yards away was number 64: SOE Headquarters. Their route into the city had taken them through street after London street that had been shattered by incendiary bombs during the Blitz.

"Good God, the devastation is even worse than the last time we were here," Catherine said, stunned by how much of the city had been leveled.

"Well," Sean replied, "at least some landmarks like Big Ben and St. Paul's have been spared."

She glanced on either side of her surroundings. "Imagine, Churchill running a war from his underground labyrinth near here, with buildings getting bombed above him nearly every night." She gestured toward the other end of the block, where F Section was housed. "It's back to the Orchard Court lavatory waiting rooms for us!"

Sean halted on the sidewalk.

"You mean to tell me that you, too, cooled your heels before your first interview with Buckmaster in that weird little black-tiled bathroom?" he asked with amazement.

"Yup." She grabbed his sleeve, guiding him toward the entrance of the large building built around a courtyard where she and Henri had first entered as fledgling Special Operations Executive secret agents. "And I had two other agents squeezed in there for company," she said as they crossed the threshold.

A memory of Henri and the former stunt pilot, Lucien Barteau, a.k.a. Gilbert, rose in her mind's eye. She'd detested the swaggering French former flyer on sight in that cramped, dark bathroom-cum-waiting-room. She wondered about his fate, now that the war was winding down.

Sean held the door for her as they entered what was in reality an ordinary building full of residential flats. Catherine was amazed to see Mr. Park, the doorman who had greeted her that first day.

"So good to see you, miss and sir,' Mr. Park said, beaming. "I was told to expect you two. Welcome back."

This time, Park took them directly into Buckmaster's office where the slender, athletic figure Catherine remembered from nearly three years earlier rose from behind his desk and greeted them with hearty handshakes. Buckmaster's fair hair seemed a bit thinner to Catherine, his angular facial features gaunter and more drawn—both changes, she imagined, the product of his stressful job sending hundreds of agents into harm's way.

And so many of us didn't—or won't—come back…

For Catherine, seeing Buckmaster again only made her realize what a totally different person she was since she'd last been in this room. She knew at that moment that there would be no way to return to a normal life—whatever that was. Sean would be going back to a wife he barely knew, now, and twin sons who didn't know him. They'd both be strangers in their own land.

Catherine was startled to see that Buckmaster's deputy, Vera Atkins, was also in the room, sitting in a corner. The tall, attractive woman in her mid-thirties had experienced the war from behind a desk, acting as a sort of den mother to all the female agents who'd signed on for duty in France. Instead of the trim suit Catherine remembered her wearing when last they'd met, now Miss Atkins was in a WAAF squadron leader's uniform, a row of service ribbons decorating her left pocket. This woman, too, had lived a life of secrets. She'd fought the war from this office, never leaving London while keeping track, as best she could through wireless transmissions, where each one of her flock had been sent. Catherine imagined that it would be Vera Atkins's duty to chronicle for the War Office Archives the fate of each female secret agent who'd been sent on dangerous missions about which few outside this room would ever know.

Buckmaster gestured for the two returning agents to take their seats, urging Miss Atkins to move her chair closer to their group.

"It's our practice, of course, to debrief you separately," he said. Perched on the corner of his desk, his khaki uniform as neatly pressed as Catherine had remembered from their initial interview, he continued. "We've found that individuals remember different and often very useful things. But before we get started," he added, his smile generous and his manner sincere, "I want to congratulate you both for the outstanding jobs you've done. You two Americans joined us early, and fortunately for the SOE, the American Office of Special Services didn't have the benefit of your undivided attention, although they will receive copies of your excellent records fighting for the Allied cause."

Sean and Catherine remained silent, nodding their thanks. Catherine almost laughed out loud, recalling how her original assignment to steal, copy, and return the top secret French naval codes to the Vichy embassy's safe in Washington had been a joint U.S.-U.K. operation all along.

Buckmaster gazed somberly at Sean. "Frankly, son, when we heard you were captured by the SS a week ago, we didn't think it likely we'd see you again."

Sean pointed to Catherine. "If it weren't for Catherine Thornton—or should I say Colette Durand, a.k.a. Jaqueline Bise—you would not have seen me again. I'm just sorry that Agent Amory Hyde didn't make it. After everything he'd already been through, he just wasn't strong enough to swim that last stretch of the Mediterranean out to the sub before the German patrol boat got him."

"We know," Vera Atkins intervened gently, leaning forward from one of the wooden chairs arrayed in front of Buckmaster's desk. "The submarine captain's report described what happened.

We knew the agent was in bad shape long before he was in your hands. The poor fellow only made it as far as he did because of you two."

The difference between death and survival was nothing but luck, Catherine suddenly thought. Five-year-old Tamara, by wandering away from her parents at the train station, had escaped being sent to certain death. What would have happened if the little girl had been swept up into the Gestapo's net like her parents? What if Catherine, or some other sympathetic soul, hadn't been standing there to whisk her out of danger? Yet Tamara would remain in the thick of war until it was finally over. Would her luck continue to hold? Would the Menton olive farm and all who lived and worked there emerge unscathed after the onslaught of Operation Dragoon? Catherine could see now that luck and fate played the biggest roles in who survived in war and who was called upon to face the biggest test.

She turned to the colonel and asked, "Did word ever get to you that the Germans in Nice thought I had died in my jail cell?"

Both Buckmaster and Atkins registered surprise.

Sean jumped into the conversation, describing with obvious pride Catherine's outfoxing the jailors by feigning TB and convincing the frightened guards to avoid contagion by sending her to hospital. He looked from Buckmaster to Miss Atkins.

"We kept wondering if news of the death of Agent Colette Durand had ever filtered back to London."

Colonel Buckmaster glanced over at Vera Atkins for any confirmation of this tale.

"No, not that I'm aware," she said. "We should check with MI6 at some point to see if they heard of this." Then Miss Atkins turned to the recently arrived pair and smiled, bringing them all back to matters at hand. "Let's go to my office," she beckoned to Catherine, "and get started on your debriefing so you and Agent Eisenhower here will finish up about the same time and enjoy the celebratory dinner we've arranged for you at the Savoy."

———◇———

By the time Catherine had finished answering Vera Atkins's scores of detailed questions about the Trenches circuit's many missions in the South of France, she felt a crushing sense of mental fatigue.

Closing her notebook, Miss Atkins said quietly, "You've had an astounding time of it, haven't you? I want to underscore, as strongly as I can, that you have His Majesty's and the SOE's profound gratitude for your service and sacrifice. You were absolutely one of our stars."

Catherine inhaled a deep breath and offered a slight shrug of her shoulders. What words in response could she offer about a span of her life that had changed her forever?

The official debriefing concluded, Atkins reached into her drawer and withdrew a thin file folder, placing it on her desk. She gazed briefly at Catherine and then reached out and patted the file, her expression now somber.

"This is one of the hardest parts of my job when agents come in from the field," she said in a soft voice. Gesturing toward the file, she continued, "I am so very sorry to tell you that, while you were in service, your husband, Jeremy Thornton, passed away."

Catherine leaned back in her chair, fully aware of the stunned expression she was probably exhibiting, but Miss Atkins would never guess it was because the thought of her husband's whereabouts or wellbeing had scarcely crossed her mind in months.

"Jeremy's dead? When? How?"

Catherine could see that Miss Atkins was about to choose her next words carefully.

"He died while still at his post with the British diplomatic corps. In Buenos Aires."

"Ah…so he transferred from Caracas after I went to Europe."

Now I'll never be able to force him to tell me the names of the couple that took my baby at the foot of the ship's gangplank…

"Yes. Your husband passed away in March of 'forty-three. We make it a practice to withhold that kind of disturbing information from our agents in the field." She glanced down at the file. "It appears that he died by his own hand."

"What?"

"Our information is that he'd been given a diagnosis of cancer, and soon after…he shot himself." Vera leaned forward. "I am so very sorry to be the one to tell you this. You've been through so much yourself."

Catherine inhaled deeply again, trying to take in the news about

Jeremy and realizing she felt...nothing. Dry-eyed, she searched for words to ward off Miss Atkins's sympathy.

"We actually... Well, we'd had a...a difficult marriage, Jeremy and I. He was twenty-two years older than me. We hadn't lived together as man and wife for a long time. We'd been legally separated before I joined the SOE and—"

"I know," Miss Atkins interrupted quietly and, almost apologetically, added, "It's in your file. Even so, I imagine it's quite a shock. In the folder you will find a certified copy of his death certificate and his will, along with all the other details you might wish to know. Despite your legal separation, you will, of course, still be eligible for a widow's benefit from Britain's diplomatic service."

"Thank you," Catherine murmured, thinking that there was nothing connected to Jeremy Thornton that had any meaning for her now.

Miss Atkins paused and then said, "And I'm afraid I have some other sad news."

Catherine looked up, startled. Vera Atkins seemed to know about every nook and cranny of her life. Could this woman possibly realize how much *any* news of Agent Henri Leblanc's fate during the war would mean to her? Was that somehow in her file as well?

"Your mother also has died. Just four months ago, I'm afraid. In her sleep, we were told. There's a copy of her death certificate and will in the folder as well. Her solicitor—her lawyer, you would call him, I think—sent a letter that's been forwarded to us, assuring that everything is in order and that her entire estate and home in Washington D.C. were left to you."

Miss Atkins remained silent for several long moments, allowing Catherine time to absorb what her superior probably thought was a second heartbreaking blow.

For Catherine, news of her mother's death *was* a surprise. The social-climbing mining heiress from Minnesota had always seemed indomitable to her daughter. Gladys's barely disguised resentment of her offspring's superior looks, along with behavior the older woman often described to her friends as Catherine's "willful ways," had long condemned the two of them to a relationship of semi-estrangement.

But she was my mother! *Why do I feel so very little emotion?*

Catherine reached for the folder and placed it in her lap. As she did, a memory of her late father, when she was a little girl, appeared before her like a picture in a silver frame. He was clad in his full-dress uniform, smiling down at her and holding her hand just before departing on his latest assignment. The vision was quickly pushed out of her mind by a disquieting thought.

Like Tamara, I am an orphan in this world now...and a stranger in it too.

Miss Atkins waited and, when Catherine remained silent, finally asked, "Is there anything else I can do for you, my dear? Anything at all?"

Unbidden, she had an image of Henri sitting across from her at a small bistro table in a back-street café in Nice, handing her his mother's diamond ring.

At length, she looked up. "Yes, there is actually something you can do for me. Can you provide me any news of SOE Agent Henri Leblanc, code name Claude Foret? Have you heard whether he's alive or dead?"

There was a warning message in Vera Atkins' look of mild surprise as she gazed directly across her desk. To Catherine it seemed that her superior felt she had—despite her last offer of sympathy—provided as much practical and official assistance as was deemed appropriate to a secret agent recently returned from the field. Catherine placed a forefinger on top of Atkins's ringed binder containing the notes of their debriefing.

"As you undoubtedly know, Agent Leblanc and I have rather a long history together," she said with a meaningful look at Atkins's notebook. "We worked together as secret agents in Washington, even before the U.S. entered the war."

Miss Atkins nodded but remained silent.

Catherine paused for a moment before continuing. "We even trained together a bit here in the U.K. and saw each other briefly when he parachuted into the South of France on reconnaissance for Operation Dragoon. I have no idea what's happened to him, except that he was headed back to Paris the last day I saw him." She leaned forward, unable to keep the intensity from her voice. "It's very important that I know if he made it back to his printing operation and if he's still alive."

CHAPTER 44

Vera Atkins rose from her chair and walked to a file cabinet pushed against her office wall. A few minutes later, she placed one more folder on top of her desk. Black letters leapt out at Catherine as if they were incoming tracer fire: **MISSING S.O.E. AGENTS**.

"The last word we had about Agent Claude," Miss Atkins disclosed, flipping to a page Catherine was unable to read upside down, "was that he was arrested by the Gestapo at his family's printing establishment in the Second Arrondissement sometime in early June of this year and taken to SS counterintelligence headquarters at Number 84 Avenue Foch." She looked up, her glance full of concern, as if one more loss would be too hard for Catherine to bear. "Since then, I'm afraid we've heard nothing either way."

Henri, arrested by the Gestapo!

Catherine suppressed an audible gasp, her mind flying to the individual arrests of Sean and her and the terrible things that could be inflicted upon a captured secret agent in German custody. Henri was apprehended by the SS over *two and a half months* ago!

Meanwhile, Vera Akins glanced over at the calendar on her wall. Catherine's gaze focused on the date the older woman gestured to: August 26, 1944.

"It's just been officially released, this morning," she said quietly. "Paris fell to the Allies yesterday, on the twenty-fifth. The papers will be full of it by tonight."

Catherine's view of Vera Atkins sitting across the desk grew blurry before she realized that her eyes had completely filled with tears.

"Paris...liberated?" she whispered, brushing at her cheek with the back of her hand.

And no one has seen or heard from Henri?

"There is still fighting going on in many parts of the country, but yes," Miss Atkins replied, "Paris is a free city now. Allied troops marched down the Champs-Élysées this very morning." She hesitated a moment and then declared, "In fact, as of today, Colonel Buckmaster and I have been tasked with setting up an office there, immediately, to trace any missing agents. We want to be there to welcome and account for those who will soon be making their way to the capital from their final locales. We are also determined to find out as much as we can about the agents who haven't been accounted for." Miss Atkins's expression softened. "Catherine, dear, I want you to know that I, personally, will make a special effort regarding Henri Leblanc."

Catherine drew herself up with her shoulders pressed against the slats of the straight-backed chair. "I would like to volunteer to go with you," she declared, her gaze insistent. "I think that every last one of our agents should be tracked down and accounted for, no matter how long it takes or where the efforts lead."

"That's very kind of you," Atkins said, placing her hand again on Catherine's, "but I rather think you need a good long rest before you do anything else."

Catherine pulled her hand away and abruptly stood up.

"I don't want to rest!" she protested and heard the shrillness in her tone. Struggling to recover, she lowered her voice and sat down in her chair once more, making a case for the urgency she knew they both felt about any missing agents. "I know Paris well because my father was attached to the American Embassy there. I speak fluent French, German, and Italian. I could be of great service to you and the Colonel on a project like this. I have no family left at home now, as you've just informed me, and I—*we* owe it to the families of the agents who don't return to at least let their loved ones learn how and where these brave people died."

Alice Leblanc never behaved as if her husband, Henri, was beloved, but I swear to God I will do whatever it takes to discover what has happened to him.

Returning to Paris to look for Agent Claude meant discovering the fate of the one man, besides her father, that she had truly ever loved. It was about her own survival in a world in which she now felt utterly alone.

It was Miss Atkins's turn to inhale a deep breath. "My secretary, Shirley Newton-Elkington, has already agreed to accompany me," she began, but Catherine interrupted.

"I'm happy to help Miss Elkington, too, with whatever you need! I have the funds to pay my own way, if that would make a difference. Another set of experienced hands can only make the job easier for all of you," she implored, knowing that she was begging now to be allowed to search for Henri with the authority of the SOE behind her.

Vera Atkins nod was almost imperceptible.

"I'll see what I can do."

———◇———

Catherine and Sean arrived an hour apart at the Savoy dining room.

"Either Miss Atkins asked many more questions of you than Colonel Buckmaster did of me, or you went shopping for nylons in a bombed-out Marks and Spencer," Sean scolded Catherine as he held out a chair for her to sit down. "You're very late."

"The former," she said. "I need a stiff whiskey."

She swiftly recounted her long interview with Buckmaster's number two, including the intelligence that her mother and husband had both died and that Henri Leblanc was officially declared missing.

Sean reached across the linen-covered tablecloth and gently seized her hand.

"I'm so sorry, Catherine. And now I feel even worse leaving like this, but they have me on a plane flying home tomorrow. As of five o'clock today, I am officially discharged from the SOE."

"Pays to know a general in this war," Catherine groused, fighting the ridiculous feeling that she was being abandoned. She summoned a smile that silently asked Sean's forgiveness for her show of bad humor. "Your boys will be deliriously surprised when you walk through the door."

"To say nothing of my wife," Sean replied. The two exchanged rueful glances. "Well? What about you? What will you do next?" he asked.

"It's not clear. I'm still technically in the SOE—at least for now."

Sean studied her face for a moment and then threw his linen napkin on the table. "You're going back to France!" he exclaimed. "I knew it the second you said Henri was missing." He leaned forward. "Want me to come with you?"

Catherine shook her head with both a feeling of affection and exasperation. "You can't miss your flight tomorrow!" she protested. "And I don't even know yet if the powers that be will even let me join the team looking for missing agents."

"Well, I can always get another flight," he said, with the airy confidence of a man named Eisenhower. "Meanwhile, I'll wait to find out if you're go or no-go."

Catherine shook her head. "You, my *faux frère*, are way past due to go home."

"I am not your fake brother!" Sean retorted, casting her a reproachful look. "I'm the real deal."

Catherine squeezed his hand lightly. "Actually, you are both. And my guess is," she added, dreading the mere thought of facing her return to the States, "it won't be much longer before I might be back in Washington as well."

Sean's expression grew uncharacteristically somber. "And that's because…"

"It doesn't look good, Sean. Henri has been in SS hands since early June."

"Oh, Jesus! That's nearly three months."

They exchanged a glance that mirrored their shared memories of the brutality they'd both experienced in Nazi jails.

Just then, the meal arrived that Vera Atkins had arranged in celebration of their return from the war zone. For the first time in their relationship, they both fell silent while they ate the nondescript English food put before them. After drinking an entire bottle of indifferent champagne, erstwhile agents Guy de Bruyn and Colette Durand left the hotel restaurant and bid each other a chaste goodnight on the Hotel Savoy's second floor.

"Take care in Paris, will you, damn it?" Sean said, hugging her tightly. "The war might be over, but there are still plenty of desperate people who ended up on the losing side." He leaned back, a hand on each of her upper arms. "Write me once in a while, kiddo," he pleaded. He'd given her the address of his art studio above a coffee shop not far from her old townhouse on O Street in Georgetown.

"I will," she murmured.

He pulled her hard against his chest again, and the two of them clung to each other, each sensing their deepening apprehension about what the future might bring.

At length, Catherine took a step back, looked away to hide her emotions, and set off down the righthand corridor, while Sean turned to his left and slowly walked in the opposite direction.

———◇———

By the time Catherine awoke the next morning, Sean had left the hotel. Much to her relief, Colonel Buckmaster agreed that someone fluent in three languages and as knowledgeable about France as Catherine Thornton would be an important asset to help set up a base in Paris where agents could make contact when they began to come in from the field. A week later, the threesome, plus secretary Shirley Newton-Elkington, crossed the Channel to Honfleur in a British navy gunboat.

On the long drive into Paris, Colonel Buckmaster sat in the front seat of a U.S. Army jeep with Miss Atkins, Catherine, and Shirley Newton-Elkington squeezed into the back of the vehicle. Passing outside were virtually tons of equipment that had either broken down or been abandoned by both armies during the Allied forces' push toward Paris following the Normandy landings.

"I should warn you three before we arrive that newly-deputized French bureaucrats are likely to block our every move—or at least try," Buckmaster fumed. "Charles de Gaulle is bloody determined that everyone buy into the story that French troops and resisters *alone* liberated his country. He's already ordered scores of our people out of France. If de Gaulle had his way, he'd obliterate any trace of the SOE's contribution to driving out the Krauts!"

Catherine could barely disguise her shock at learning that Charles de Gaulle, the ostensible leader of a reconstituted French government, a man who'd sat safely in London during most of the war, was now exhibiting such a lack of gratitude for the sacrifices the Allies made in coming to the aid of his defeated nation.

"De Gaulle's attitude rather reminds me of SOE's interactions with MI6," Miss Atkins said dryly, her red lips pursed with a disgust that she made no effort to disguise.

Catherine was equally stunned to hear that Britain's own MI6 also wanted to obscure the work and accomplishments of the band of Churchill's amateurs that had parachuted into France to support all manner of Resistance efforts.

What in the world were we all fighting for?

When they finally arrived in the city, the Hotel Cecil on rue St. Didier was certainly not the impressive SOE headquarters that Catherine knew Buckmaster had in mind for chasing down the missing agents.

"Another reason to be cross with de Gaulle," Buckmaster murmured as the quartet exited the jeep, with their thanks to their skilled U.S. Army chauffeur. "He directed his staff to assign us this billet."

The foursome stood before a modest building pock-marked with bullet holes on the exterior walls, proof that the August 19th Parisian uprising against the German occupiers had done significant damage to the old hotel.

Staring at the shabby, battered facade, Catherine's breath caught with the realization she was back in Paris.

———◇———

Their makeshift SOE Headquarters was swiftly established in two no-frills upstairs bedrooms on the hotel's third floor. The modest surroundings served to welcome a spate of weary returning British, French, and American secret agents who managed to find their way to Paris and through the hotel's tarnished brass front door.

Just as Colonel Buckmaster had predicted, however, getting archival information was proving to be next to impossible. De Gaulle had already ordered that only limited access to French official records and abandoned German ones would be granted the SOE. This move resulted in short-circuiting the British agency's ability to identify French collaborators who might well know the fate of the missing Allied agents arrested by the German authorities.

More encouragingly, Catherine was present when her former circuit leader, Francis Cammaerts—code name Roger—strode into the hotel room to great accolades for his work as the head of the Jockey networks, including Catherine's own smaller Trenches circuit, in the southeastern territories of France. Cammaerts stopped in his tracks when he recognized his former courier and then enveloped her in a bear hug.

"I just came from the Hotel Bristol where we were told to also stop by here. I need two million francs to give to our French *résistants* partners who are in dire need of support. De Gaulle apparently doesn't have much concern about the groups that didn't necessarily support him."

"Dirty deals weren't snuffed out by the war, I see," noted Catherine dryly.

Cammaerts heaved a sigh. "Before we are all ordered to go home and mind our own business, I want to distribute SOE monies to the widows and families of those who had worked specifically for SOE units like your Trenches outfit."

Catherine glanced at Shirley Newton-Elkington, who had been deputized by Miss Atkins to hand out funds as authorized.

"We've allocated funds for that," Shirley said with a friendly nod to them both, disappearing into the other room where the money was stashed in a safe.

Catherine took a step closer to Roger, urging in a soft voice, "Please put Remy Poché on your list. He runs a restaurant on the waterfront at Villefranche, and he'll tell you who else deserves help, especially the local olive farmer, Jules Menton, and his family." Catherine gazed soberly at the brave leader of her former clandestine network. "They saved Sean's and my life countless times by their selfless acts of bravery."

Just then, Miss Newton-Elkington returned and handed Francis Cammaerts a fat envelope, which he tucked into the messenger bag slung over his shoulder. He nodded his thanks and gave Catherine his reassurance as he departed the room, "I'll be sure to connect with them all, if I can. And the best to you and that Sean fellow you worked with when you return to the U.S."

"He's already back in D.C."

Merely stating that fact made Catherine miss him all the more.

And Henri? Who is looking for him? Why hasn't he walked through our doors?

She glanced briefly at Miss Newton-Elkington, who had returned to her desk on the other side of the room, absorbed in filing the paperwork piled in front of her. Catherine lowered her voice as she asked Roger, "Remember my asking you about Henri Leblanc, Agent Guy Foret?" Before he could answer she continued, "We know he was arrested by the SS and taken to Avenue Foch. We haven't learned anything since."

Roger grimaced. "I guess that means our other agent was the double."

"Gilbert, a.k.a. Lucien Barteau?" Catherine struggled to keep her voice even. "Apparently so. If you hear anything about an Agent Claude Foret or Henri Leblanc in your travels, will you get in touch with me through Miss Atkins?"

Roger put a hand lightly on her shoulder. "I will...and I'm sorry."

CHAPTER 45

Autumn 1944

During the days that followed, more secret agents continued to trickle into the Hotel Cecil to be greeted by the SOE welcoming committee. Soon, however, the French security police took complete control of the few German records that had been found in the wake of the Nazis' retreat from Paris and other areas around the country.

One afternoon, the colonel and Miss Atkins left the hotel to wrangle with a group of French authorities over access to important files that had been under the authority of the Vichy regime. In their absence, Catherine quietly slipped out of the office to search for the building where Leblanc Printing had been housed.

Leaves along the Seine were turning yellow and beginning to drift onto the sidewalks and street when she emerged from the metro. Despite the fact the Germans had left Paris, war raged in other parts of France, and there were still dreadful shortages of food, as witnessed by the hungry faces of the people passing her by. Catherine entered the 2nd Arrondissement, sensing that the city had a kind of desperate feel with buildings everywhere riddled with bullet holes and a pervasive sense that one couldn't know who was telling the truth or whom to trust. Buckmaster had warned there were informers now attempting to claim their innocence, many even wanting the new authorities to believe they had been *résistants* all along. During several of Catherine's interviews regarding missing agents, fear of reprisals kept people silent despite the knowledge she knew they had. The Nazis had been driven out of Paris, but a different kind of war was being fought.

Catherine identified Leblanc Printing's nondescript exterior and walked down a set of cement stairs. There she found a bent, grizzled man sweeping the basement floor in a vast space that was otherwise deserted except for a large printing press and several smaller ones. Although Buckmaster had explained to Catherine that Henri's printing operation had been used as a cover for his clandestine activities as an SOE agent, she was unsettled to see Nazi posters alongside the restaurant menus littering the floor.

She showed the man—whose name she learned was Alphonse Moreau—her official badge confirming she was on assignment to try to locate missing SOE agents.

Pointing to the hulking machine in the middle of the room she said, "So, that was the press machine that the Leblanc newspaper was printed on?"

"Not for years," Moreau replied. "Since the war began, we just did small jobs to keep the place open—and pull the wool over *Kommandant* Heinrich's eyes while we recruited for the Resistance," he added with a vague approximation of a smile.

Turning her back on the enormous, silent press, Catherine approached a small office with a window overlooking the printing area. That room was abandoned too, except for a few pieces of wood from smashed-up furniture scattered about.

"And this is where Henri Leblanc worked every day?" she asked, walking inside and trying to imagine his life in the middle of a Paris crawling with SS everywhere. She ran her fingers along his desk, trying to picture him there while absently pulling open the center drawer. There, in its familiar packet, was an L-pill. Catherine closed her eyes for a second, then palmed it for safe disposal and closed the drawer.

Moreau said with a bleak nod, "Yes, this was *m'sieur's* office. Did you know him, or are you just charged with trying to find out what happened to him?"

"Yes, I knew him," she answered quietly. She was crossing a line to admit that to this stranger, but she sensed he felt as desolate as she did in this cold, abandoned basement. "I actually worked with Henri Leblanc in Washington, D.C. and in"—her voice broke. She forced herself to complete her sentence, "...in England and here in France."

"I wasn't here at work yet the day the SS came for him," he disclosed. "It was only a few days before the landings in Normandy."

Catherine searched the old man's face. "And did you ever see him again?" she asked, wondering if this fellow had any idea who might have betrayed Henri's underground operation to the German authorities.

"No, no one ever saw him after that. He and his deputy, Alain Chapelle—who was my nephew, actually—were both picked up and taken to Avenue Foch."

"And you had absolutely no word about either of them after that?"

Alphonse, a catch in his voice, replied, "A U.S. Army officer said he'd been told that that the bodies...scores of them...were carted away at some point or another and buried in a mass grave. The day I went there, a prisoner who somehow survived the massacre in the bowels of the building the previous day stumbled out of the back door. A *M'sieur* Patou." He paused, and Catherine could sense that his recounting the scene to her was prompting him to relive the horror of what he'd witnessed.

"I'm so sorry," she began.

But he waved his hand in the air, swallowing hard. Then he continued, his voice hoarse. "The man I saw that day was in a daze, barely able to talk or walk. He managed to tell me he'd heard Alain's name and that he was fairly sure my nephew had been shot in the basement with the rest of the prisoners."

Alphonse leaned against the open door to the office, his hand trembling slightly as he raised it to his eyes as if warding off a vision he couldn't bear to see. "As I said, I went there myself. Avenue Foch, I mean. As soon as I heard the Germans were retreating from Paris, I hoped I could find out something about my nephew and *M'sieur* Leblanc."

Catherine tensed. "And? You learned nothing about Henri Leblanc? Only news about your nephew?"

"Patou said a steady stream of prisoners had either been sent to Fresnes Prison outside Paris or deported by train to labor camps in Germany, Austria, or Poland. He told me he hadn't seen *M'sieur* Leblanc recently and didn't know if he was even there in that crowd of prisoners being herded downstairs at Avenue Foch. But, for those shot there when the Germans were leaving...well, it was bad, *mademoiselle*. Nothing a woman like you should ever see."

Her eyes swept the abandoned printing operation, committing every detail to memory for the report she would write for their files. To Alphonse Moreau she merely replied, tight-lipped, "Believe me, *monsieur*, I've seen quite a lot these last few years."

Her throat ached for wanting to cry to the heavens.

Oh God, Henri, were you shot with the others? Imprisoned somewhere? Deported? Where are *you?*

———◇———

Barely ten days after the team from London had installed themselves in the Hotel Cecil, Miss Atkins walked into the office and announced tersely, "The French appear to have cooperated with us as much as they intend to at the moment. The decision has been made to return to London and do our work from there."

Catherine pushed back her chair, pointing to the files on her desk.

"But that's absolutely criminal!" she protested "It's outrageous that de Gaulle has ordered his people not to help us try to find out what happened to our SOE agents. They risked their lives for France!" A wave of anger swept over her so potent she wanted to pound both fists on her desk. "Are they treating the American OSS the same way as the SOE?" she demanded, wondering if placing a call to Sean Eisenhower in Washington would do anything to help.

Miss Atkins curtly overrode her, their collective frustration at the situation all too obvious. "Please be assured that I've requested our colleagues in every intelligence service, British and American, along with the Red Cross, to pass all possible traces of missing agents directly to me in London."

"How many agents are unaccounted for?" Catherine challenged Vera, hearing that her own words sounded like a demand rather than a mere question.

Atkins glanced down at the *missing* file and replied quietly, "Nearly one hundred. F Section recruited some four hundred volunteers like yourself that we sent behind enemy lines, thirty-nine of whom were women." She paused. "Presently, sixteen—possibly eighteen—women are unaccounted for."

Catherine quickly calculated the number of men in Atkins's file. "So, Henri is among some eighty-four male agents still missing?"

Her tone softening, she added, "As I've said, I've put Agent Leblanc as a high priority, Catherine. If there's any news, I'll be the first to get word."

Catherine could only stare into space while attempting to stamp down her fear that the search for Henri was about to become even more difficult than it already was.

Finally, she managed to ask, "When must this office be closed?"

"By the end of the week," Miss Atkins replied, and then stalked out of the room.

———◇———

Vera Atkins's secretary had been packing the SOE files in boxes all morning for transport to London. Miss Atkins herself was sorting through a pile of folders and nodded assent when Shirley requested that she obtain more stamps at the post office.

As her assistant departed on her errand, Catherine sought Vera's gaze and plunged ahead to voice the decision she'd come to during her sleepless night.

"All things being equal, Miss Atkins, since you and Colonel Buckmaster are returning to London, I'd prefer to resign officially from the SOE and remain here in Paris. I need time to try to locate anyone who may have interacted with Henri's network or knows what happened after he was interrogated at Avenue Foch."

"I see." Miss Atkins glanced down at the files she'd been sorting and said, "One possibility we must consider, Catherine, is that all the relevant documents about Leblanc may already be destroyed by the departing Germans *or* that the French have secreted away whatever was left in their archives to ensure they won't see the light of day."

"But it's immoral to withhold that information," Catherine protested.

Akins nodded, "Of course it is, but it's all a very touchy subject as to which Parisians collaborated with the Nazis in the building where our captured secret agents were interrogated. De Gaulle's people want to be in charge of deciding who gets punished and who doesn't."

Catherine could no longer disguise her bitterness. "Isn't this stalemate about sharing records and documents all about de Gaulle *himself* wanting to consolidate power and punishing rivals who don't endorse his vision of the so-called New France?"

"One might say the General has rather clear views on the subject," Miss Atkins responded cryptically.

"Well, to me, it's still worth a try to see if I can gain access to any documents or other physical evidence that's still left," Catherine countered, knowing how stubborn her own actions must sound.

"You'll be on your own, you know, without official SOE sanction."

"I know." Catherine then decided to reveal a conversation she'd overheard the previous evening. "By the way, here's a scrap of information I did obtain in the bar downstairs from an American intelligence officer, who shall remain nameless, as he drank all my wine," she declared in an off-hand tone in an attempt to soften the seriousness of a charge she was about to level against one of SOE's standout agents. "My source claims he has evidence that the head of SOE's Flight Operations in France, Lucien Barteau, code name Gilbert, had been conspiring all along with the head of Avenue Foch, Hans Josef Kieffer, and was paid handsomely in the bargain."

Miss Atkins arched an eyebrow but remained silent. Did she already know this, Catherine wondered?

"My barstool friend insisted," continued Catherine, "that Barteau was seen frequently coming and going to Avenue Foch and having friendly dinners with Kieffer. If that's true, doesn't it follow that

Barteau might very well be the double agent who betrayed the Prosper network and perhaps Henri's Pinwheel circuit as well?"

Vera Atkins paused and then replied, "I'm sure in the fullness of time we will come to learn that not all the recruits enrolled in the SOE in those frantic first months were equally dedicated to the Allied cause."

This woman is the queen of understatements.

Catherine asked, "Do you think it's possible to arrange my official resignation from the SOE before you leave Paris?"

Miss Atkins pursed her bright-red lips in thought. After hesitating a moment, she said, "I'll see to it that you are mustered out with the excellent service report you so roundly deserve before I return to London next week."

"Thank you," Catherine said, grateful for Vera's sense of fairness and equity. "I can't tell you how much your support has meant to me."

By this time, she was well aware that Vera Atkins felt the same sense of fury and frustration she did. Here they had beaten the Germans, only to have Russia, led by Stalin—an ally—marching his troops into Eastern European countries like Poland, Hungary, and Czechoslovakia, one by one, subjugating entire populations with an iron fist, not unlike Hitler had done. And now, to also have to fight French bureaucrats for information about the ultimate fate of the SOE's British, American, *and* French secret agents that risked everything to free France was truly beyond the pale.

As Catherine tidied up her desk, a sinking feeling of exhaustion descended on her. The world, her life, seemed built on quicksand. Was there anyone who would tell her the truth or even know what Henri's fate had been? Or would she have to continue completely on her own until the clues ran dry or she no longer had the energy to fight those covering up the evil that had been done during this war?

Was her motto to forever be, "trust no one?"

———◇———

During October and November of 1944, war continued raging in several parts of France and elsewhere in Europe. On her own in liberated Paris, Catherine now faced food shortages and grim conditions as she continued her search for Henri.

From her new living quarters in a former maid's room on the top floor at the Hotel Cecil, she spent her daylight hours visiting the infamous Fresnes Prison, a hulking building on the outskirts of Paris, with a reputation for cruelty comparable to Avenue Foch. When that effort proved futile, she began searching every local hospital and convalescent home in the city and outlying regions, combing through lists of patients in a frantic attempt to determine if a Henri Leblanc or Claude Foret had been a patient.

Nothing.

The drumbeat of war news continued: Allied forces had now liberated Athens, and word had come that the legendary German general, Erwin Rommel, had committed suicide. Catherine, meanwhile, scrutinized pages of Red Cross records for any evidence that Henri had been put on board one of the cattle cars that had deported tens of thousands of French citizens and enemy aliens to the murderous concentration camps around Europe.

Zero turned up.

Then, as the Allies began moving eastward, liberating prisoners from the German death camps, Catherine kept busy scouring lists of detainees returning to France.

Again, nothing.

One evening, while nursing a glass of nouveau Bordeaux in the Hotel Cecil's gloomy bar and exhausted from another fruitless day of relentless search, a disturbing thought burrowed into her worried state of mind.

If Henri *was* alive, and cared as much about finding her as she did him, she mused, wouldn't he have somehow managed to contact the Red Cross or SOE authorities by now? Wouldn't he have been desperate to let them know he'd survived and that he was looking for Agent Colette Durand? Yet, despite several recent communications from Vera Atkins in London and her sources in Paris itself, not a scintilla of information about him had surfaced anywhere.

Catherine stared moodily at her half-consumed glass of wine when an obvious truth squeezed her heart in a vise. Wasn't Henri's death in the basement at Avenue Foch simply a cold, hard fact she'd been refusing to accept? The only information she'd corroborated was that master pressman, Alphonse Moreau, had confirmed that

Henri and his deputy, Alain, had been arrested and taken to Number 84. Alphonse had good reason to believe from the survivor, Monsieur Patou, that his nephew Alain had died in the massacre there. Patou had told Moreau he hadn't seen Henri that day, but an army officer told Moreau stacks of the unidentified bodies had been thrown into a mass grave.

And nowhere had Catherine found any written proof Henri Leblanc or Guy Foret had been transferred to other prisons or hospitals within France, nor any record he'd been returned from a German death camp.

He either died in that foul den only a few blocks from here or he was among the nameless who perished in a German prison camp somewhere...but I'll never know!

In the dark corner of the Hotel Cecil's rundown bar, Catherine stared into space until she was suddenly assaulted by grief as sharp as a bayonet run through her chest. She shot to her feet and ran for the elevator, whose doors stood open in the lobby.

"Top floor," she managed to blurt to the startled attendant.

The doors clanged shut. Catherine pressed her back against the elevator's leather-upholstered wall to keep herself from sinking onto the carpet and curling up in a ball in the corner. She tried to breathe and felt her throat closing as an unexpected wave of panic gripped her. She'd faced down Nazis. She'd long prided herself on her skill at masking her emotions. Yet, as the ancient conveyance rattled its way up the shaft, for the first time in her life, she felt herself losing her self-control.

The car halted with a jerk near her former maid's room tucked under the eaves. She couldn't seem, at first, to move her feet. Finally, she pushed herself away from the elevator's wall and struggled toward the hotel corridor, waving away the proffered assistance from the hotel's employee who, no doubt, thought she was dead drunk.

Stumbling down the corridor, her vision telescoped to the doorknob of her hotel room. She lunged for it, just as she had the life preserver thrown to her from the submarine the night she and Sean had fled the Riviera.

Catherine slammed the door behind her and threw herself onto the thin bedspread. She heard screams—her screams—that sounded like someone being mowed down by machinegun fire.

No, Henri! No, no, no!

With Henri alive, she could face a life without war, keep the secrets she must, and fight to hold at bay the memories of these last years in France that haunted her day and night.

But now...

Oh my God! He's lost! Lost...lost...lost...

PART III
CHAPTER 46

December 1947

Catherine stepped over the threshold of the brick house on Woodley Drive into a slushy soup of snow on the front step. How long had she endured her mother's 'mausoleum,' as she'd habitually described the impressive home in this fashionable neighborhood in Washington D.C.? Three winters like this? It seemed like forever.

From the moment Catherine had moved back into the late Gladys Farnsworth Cahill's domain, it had felt as if her mother's ghost haunted her. Gladys's presence permeated every square foot, thanks to each stick of formal furniture, each drapery of finest silk, even the magnificent, gilt-framed artwork that should have been donated to the National Gallery.

With a sigh, Catherine locked the front door and hitched one of her mother's fur coats more tightly around herself. Shoulders squared, she resolutely made her way down the snow-clad path to the cab waiting at the curb, its tailpipe trailing black exhaust.

Three dreadful winters along with four gruesome, swampy summers…

It had been early April 1945—barely four months after Catherine had returned to Washington—when FDR died. Soon after, the Germans agreed to unconditional surrender, and the war in Europe was finally over. She and Sean met occasionally, but she was aware she wasn't great company; besides, Sean was presiding over his family with another baby on the way. Their lives couldn't be more different now. Even so, she looked forward to her lunch with him and hearing whatever information he had been able to glean for her through his "mysterious sources" in the newly accessible American war archives.

On September 2nd of the same year as FDR's passing, the Japanese abruptly surrendered following President Truman's decision to drop the A-bomb on Hiroshima and Nagasaki. Death had visited so many throughout the world, and yet here she was, still breathing and practically sleep-walking through the days since she'd given up her search for Henri. The danger the two had endured together—and separately—had made her feel so alive, every cell in her body vibrating with awareness of her surroundings. Now she was just numb. There were times, as 1947 drew to a close, that Catherine wondered whose life she was living. Certainly not the one she had wished for.

Pushing aside such maudlin musings, she gingerly climbed into the taxi's back seat and gazed out of the window as the route to the Wardman Park Hotel took her down Wyoming Street, past the former Vichy embassy. Rumor had it that a private school would soon be in session there. Children would be stomping up the stairs onto the wrap-around porch where once she and Henri had stood, arms around each other, kissing as pretend lovers for the benefit of two FBI agents tailing them that night.

As the former Vichy embassy grew smaller in the taxi's rear window, it struck Catherine that war-torn Europe and the absolute wreckage there were as distant as the moon from life in the U.S. capital. For people here who hadn't lost loved ones in the conflict, she thought, staring down at her gloved hands folded in her lap, they could almost pretend the war didn't happen. A bad dream. But Catherine knew better.

The basement at 84 Avenue Foch, for instance…

Interrupting her melancholy recollections, the cab turned into a drive, and the tall, red-brick front façade of the Wardman Park Hotel loomed ahead, its white marble window frames gleaming in the wintery sun. There it stood, thought Catherine, rooted immutably in the snow, as if there had never been a World War II, or that Alice and Henri Leblanc had ever lived in an apartment on the fifth floor or Catherine on the second.

What a lot of blood has flowed under the bridge since then, she thought as the cab halted at the entrance.

She'd deliberately suggested the Wardman for today's luncheon meeting with Sean, just as each morning during these last years, she'd forced herself to confront the reality that no trace of Henri had been found among his former haunts in France's capital or anywhere else she and the SOE had searched.

As Catherine entered the hotel dining room, she spotted Sean Eisenhower before he looked up and saw her. His wine-red hair was clipped short, and he was clad in a smartly tailored cashmere sports coat. He even wore a tie, his stylish civilian attire jarring to Catherine somehow. Gazing across the restaurant at him now, it was almost inconceivable to her that he had ever posed as a vision-impaired professor, with a patch on the left lens of his horn-rimmed glasses, hiding his identity as a secret agent. Who could guess that this was a man with the singular ability to speak decent French, swim like a fish, and blow up electric transformers or railroad bridges at will?

The lunch reservation had been made in Sean's name, so Catherine wasn't at all surprised to see he had scored a prized table in a small alcove that overlooked a garden. The landscaping was now barren of all vegetation except dormant box hedges planted in a strict geometric pattern.

Catching sight of her, he pushed back his chair and held out his arms.

"Hey, *Mademoiselle* Colette. How's tricks?"

"Tricky," she murmured. While they embraced, the *maître d'* waited patiently for her to sit down in a chair he held out for her.

Without consultation, Sean resumed his seat and ordered her a glass of burgundy, waving away the hovering help. He handed her one of the two menus resting on the linen-covered table next to his frosted martini glass.

"I love it that you're a mining heiress now," he teased. "Lunch is on you?"

"Why not? It took longer than expected, but my mother's estate finally cleared probate just last week."

"Believe me, I was thrilled to hear this," he said with a wink. "I can use you for a reference, then, when I take out those student loans for the twins?"

"I see you read about my cash infusion in Annabelle Arlington's column."

"I sure did. Wanna buy one of my paintings and tell that cow how talented I am? I haven't sold even one this year. Guess I'll have to look for a real job art directing for *National Geographic* or something, now that I have so many hungry mouths to feed." He held up two fingers and added two more.

"No! Since I saw you at the OSS Honors? Your wife had—"

"Twins, again," he said, deadpan. "Girls, this time. As the Brits phrase it, it turns out that my wife is a 'double yolker.' Apparently, she ovulates two eggs every month. The doc warned us that we can expect a pair of kids, every single time."

"Whose family is responsible for this outrage?" Catherine demanded in mock horror.

"Not mine, for sure. The Eisenhowers tend primarily to have boys, one at a time."

"Actually, congratulations, Sean," she said, and she meant it. "But, while you're trolling for employment at *Nat Geo,* get me a journalist gig, will you? Seems like my late mother's close pal not only tells the world I inherited a pile of dough but hints in her gossip column that I spent the entire war flat on my back earning all those medals and ribbons they gave us last month."

"I read her innuendoes this week. That woman is a menace. Just ignore her." Sean smiled. "By the way, it's good to see you twice in one month."

"You've been busy having babies."

His eyes searched her face and briefly took in her black Chanel suit with its white trim and matching buttons that never lost its style.

"And you've been busy staying gorgeous."

Catherine wagged a finger at Sean. "Well…" she drawled, "I'm cruising toward the big four-o, so flattery will get you everywhere." She glanced around the dining room. "I wonder if Annabelle's spies are anywhere nearby. I've heard she eats lunch here pretty often. Before I know it, the dreaded Miss Arlington will be writing in her column that I'm stealing the spouse of another of her D.C. friends."

"Don't I wish," he said, straight-faced.

"Sean!" she exclaimed in exasperation, then quickly lowered her voice. "Look, before we order any food, I really need to know if you've found out anything through channels."

"Is the search for Henri the *only* reason you wanted to have lunch with me?" he demanded. "I'm hurt. I'm really hurt."

And despite his jocular tone, Catherine sensed he actually was.

"Not the only reason, but an important one."

He shook his head regretfully. "I'm truly sorry, *Mademoiselle* Colette," he said softly. "I've got a few friends working on it on two continents but, so far, not a trace."

Catherine wondered suddenly if Sean had enlisted in the newly constituted C.I.A. Until very recently, she had utterly given up hope of ever learning for certain what Henri's ultimate fate had been. But, now that the war had officially come to a close, it had occurred to her the old OSS files might contain some clues, and she'd asked for Sean's help. He'd responded immediately, promising to "talk to some people" he knows—whatever that might mean.

Sean, his expression serious now, leaned toward her and covered her hand in his. "I can only imagine how hard this has been for you, not knowing what happened to Henri," he said in a low voice. "And as for that viper, Annabelle Arlington, do just ignore her. I'm so sorry the bitchy scribe is being such a pain."

"Thanks, but—"

"I know, I know. You never indulge in feeling sorry for yourself. Still, everything that's happened in the time we were away has got to be a big adjustment for you, with your mother gone and even your husband's death, am I right? If it cheers you up any, life back here for me has been...well, continuously weird, not to put too fine a point on it. You and I are sort of like Mr. and Mrs. Rip Van Winkle; we wake up back in D.C. and nothing is as it was, although so much looks and feels just the same."

Catherine nodded. Driving down Wyoming or O Street in Georgetown had been torture the first year she'd returned to Washington. She pushed such memories away and leaned forward to tell Sean about writing to Jules and Eve Menton in Villefranche.

"I sent them a photo of you and me taken at the OSS Honors event," she disclosed.

"Well, it was kinda nice to be recognized for rowing all those Yank and RAF pilots out to the subs, wouldn't you say?" Sean said with a laugh.

"And a few other things we did for them," Catherine replied pointedly. "I also wanted the Mentons to know that I've set up a small trust fund for Tamara's future education."

"That's a damn decent thing of you to do."

"I might as well do something worthwhile with all this Farnsworth money."

"Your mother's side of your family?"

"Yes. The Minnesota Mesabi Mountain Range where they came from looks pretty awful as a result of my sainted family's strip-mining. Just like the Germans, I should probably make reparations one way or another, don't you think?"

"Well…" Sean said on a long breath, his expression droll, "you know what Balzac said—or was it Victor Hugo?—'Behind every fortune lies a crime.'"

"Ditto when it comes to wars," Catherine retorted, and she could hear the bitterness in her tone.

Sean cocked his head and cast her a thoughtful glance.

"I did find out one thing from my army contacts. Because Nice and Cannes took such a pounding during our assault on the Riviera, even *now* things there are dreadfully slow to recover. I'll bet the Mentons' olive business will probably be disrupted for quite a while. They could probably use an anonymous benefactor or two. I'll pony up a few pennies, if you will, to send them some funds. You can call it an investment."

"Buy the babies diapers with your pennies," Catherine replied, smiling, "but good idea about the Mentons. I'll arrange it," she added, and then felt her breath catch.

Out of the corner of her eye, she beheld the last person in the world she ever wanted to see again. Sean immediately noticed that her expression had frozen.

"What?" he demanded, turning to look where Catherine was staring.

For a moment, Catherine couldn't summon a reply. Surely, Henri's legal wife couldn't have rented another suite in the Wardman? But there, standing at the entrance to the hotel's restaurant, was Alice

Leblanc. She still favored bold slashes of bright red lipstick, a coiffeur featuring upswept swirls of dark hair the size of fat sausages perched above arched, black eyebrows that would—as Henri had always joked—make Joan Crawford green with envy.

Sean leaned across the table and whispered, "Get a load of those shoulder pads under that ladies-lunch tweed suit of hers! She looks like a Washington Redskins linebacker!"

"Behold Henri Leblanc's wife," she hissed.

Sean reared back in his seat, showing his surprise. Meanwhile, Catherine could see with silent satisfaction that Alice's face was noticeably plumper, along with her mid-section, then it had been a half decade ago. She wondered if Henri's estranged wife no longer played tennis or consorted with nubile young pros at the country club where they had both been members once upon a time.

The legal Mrs. Leblanc was escorted by a man, maybe in his late thirties, with slicked-back, thinning brown hair and clad in a three-piece, pinstriped suit. Joining the twosome was none other than the aforementioned gossip columnist, Annabelle Arlington, her own heavily made-up visage a close twin to that of her female luncheon companion.

"Good God, is the guy on the right Joseph McCarthy?" Sean exclaimed under his breath.

Catherine slowly nodded her head in the affirmative. "Yup. The new Commie-hunting senator from Alice Leblanc's home state of Wisconsin."

Sean scoffed, "Who's going to pay any attention to *that* cheese-head? He only just got elected last year, and he's the youngest guy in the Senate."

"They say McCarthy thinks he's the new sheriff in town," Catherine replied. "I have it on good authority that he intends to eventually run all the pinkos he can find straight outta Dodge." The *maître d'* was leading the odious threesome directly toward an empty table placed not ten feet from their alcove. "Oh no," Catherine groaned under her breath.

For some twisted reason, Catherine sought Annabelle Arlington's glance, feeling as if she had almost been spoiling for this fight.

"Catherine!" Sean warned under his breath. "Just ignore her!"

"Hey," she replied, "I figure if I could bluff my way out of a Nazi jail, I can face this harpy."

She must have said the word *harpy* loudly enough for the arriving party to hear. The gossip columnist rotated around with a glare that electrified the dining room.

"Why, Alice, just look who's having lunch within a stone's throw of us," Annabelle announced loudly, turning heads closest to the group.

Alice Leblanc put her hand to her throat as if she were suddenly having difficulty breathing. Senator McCarthy regarded Sean and Catherine with an expression of malevolent interest.

Annabelle turned toward the senator.

"That's the woman I wrote about in my column not too long ago," she declared. "Catherine Cahill Thornton, the widow of a British diplomat, Jeremy Thornton. He killed himself rather than return to his wife, I'm told." She leaned toward Alice Leblanc. "It was totally outrageous that the OSS pinned those medals on her last month. After all, she merely used her good looks to work the bedrooms of Europe, prying out secrets she claimed would help the war effort."

"Hello to you, too," Catherine retorted, forcing a thin smile to her lips. "And, Annabelle, do be prepared to hear from my lawyer about your slanderous comments about decorated American war veterans, while you and Mrs. Leblanc enjoyed four years' worth of three-martini luncheons."

During this exchange, Alice seized Joe McCarthy's arm for support. In the next instant, her eyes narrowed to slits spitting raw hatred.

"Joe, I agree with Annabelle. I really think you should ask Mr. Hoover at the FBI to look into the government handing out medals to people like *her*." She took a step toward Catherine. "You don't deserve honors of any kind, Mrs. Thornton, despite the things you claim you did in the war! I know what you were *really* up to at that embassy!"

Catherine's heart lurched in alarm, but she remained composed. Surely, Alice never learned about Henri and her stealing and copying the French naval codes? Everyone involved on both sides of the Atlantic had signed a version of the Official Secrets Act.

Alice turned to address the senator again.

"This woman is a disgrace to our country, Joe. An embassy guard named André told me some shocking things when the entire Vichy staff and I were interned in Hershey, Pennsylvania for all those weeks following Pearl Harbor. The guard swore that this woman and Henri used to sneak past him and his dog into the Ambassador's office for their—well you can imagine for what." Alice turned back to Catherine. "I guess you were just practicing your Mata Hari act even then, weren't you?"

Sean abruptly stood up from the table, but as Catherine rose to her feet, she put a restraining hand on his arm, forcing him to sit back down. She took a step toward Alice.

"Well, at least I fought the Nazis on the ground in France. All you did was play tennis at the Chevy Chase Country Club three days a week!" She turned toward the gossip columnist, feigning wide-eyed innocence. "And I learned from a very reliable source that Alice here was known to have indulged in a few other saucy games with the tennis pro. So, Annabelle, why don't you put *that* in your column tomorrow?"

"How dare you!" Alice sputtered.

Catherine rounded on her. "And how dare *you* disparage and cheat on a man who, for years, was just trying to do his job at the French embassy while his country was imploding." Catherine took another step within a foot of Alice, demanding, "The officials haven't even told you what happened to Henri, have they?" She no longer cared about anything other than the chance Alice might have information unavailable to anyone but next of kin. "He was last known to have been arrested in Paris by the Gestapo just before liberation in early June of forty-four. Haven't you tried to find out *anything* about what happened to him?" she demanded. "Have you heard anything at all?"

"No, I haven't, and I couldn't care less!" Alice screeched. "And if you must know, my senator here is helping me get that Frog officially declared *dead*—and good riddance!"

Catherine grabbed for the back of her chair to keep her balance. "You know, Alice, Henri was too much of a gentleman ever to say it, but you really are a contemptable bitch."

At this, Alice yelled even more shrilly, turning heads all over the room. "I hope someone rips those awards right off that C-cup chest of yours! You and Henri Leblanc deserve nothing but contempt for the way you've behaved before, during and—in your case—after the war, you…you…*honeypot!*"

"I think you mean honeytrap, right?" Catherine snapped. "And what would you know about that? What would you know about convincing powerful, sometimes evil men to share their secrets in order to save a democracy or two? I was following orders from the highest command. And am I ashamed for services rendered? Not in the least."

A strange calm had come over her. She gazed at Alice, feeling regretful she hadn't been given the years of marriage with Henri that this spiteful woman had squandered. "And those OSS medals you want to get your hands on, Alice, symbolize the work—yes, it was a job—that Henri and I did that saved thousands of British and American lives." She paused to catch her breath. "I realize that you can't possibly understand or appreciate this, but wars are not won using respectable methods, my dear. They're won with courage and grit, any way they can be. Any way they must be."

At this moment, Annabelle Arlington was regarding Sean with a steady stare.

"You're one of the Eisenhowers, aren't you?" asserted the gossip columnist. "I remember that *The Post* did a human-interest photo layout about you after you came back from overseas. Didn't your wife just have a second set of twins?"

Alice whirled to confront Sean, angrily gesturing toward Catherine, "Then, what in the world are you doing keeping company with *her*?" she demanded while forks throughout the dining room were suspended in the air. "I bet your wife doesn't know you're having lunch with a woman who's no better than a whore!"

Sean shot to his feet before Catherine could restrain him and bellowed, "My wife knows this woman saved my life more than once, even rescuing me from a Nazi jail hours before I was to be shot! *You're* the one who's acting like a harlot." He made a sweeping gesturing to the diners who were staring at the unfolding drama, mouths agape. "So, do us all a favor and remove your loathsome self from this venerable establishment right now and let us eat in peace. Haven't you heard? The war is over."

The *maître'd* was still hovering and wringing his hands as Alice Leblanc turned to address the companions with whom she'd planned to have lunch.

"C'mon!" Alice said, her angry tone punctuating the eerie silence. "I've completely lost my appetite, haven't you?" She pointed in the direction of the dining-room exit. "Let's take a cab to the Willard."

CHAPTER 47

Catherine barely recalled leaving the dining room of the Wardman Park Hotel. Sean had somehow secured a taxi in the wake of the one transporting Senator McCarthy and the two repellant women whose venom seemed, to Catherine, worse than a nest of poisonous snakes.

She and Sean rode in silence to her Woodley Drive address. Once there, Sean took her door key from her shaky hand and guided her inside the elegant foyer with its Louis XIV, icy-white satin upholstered chairs. The anteroom led into Gladys Cahill's all-white living room with a pair of snowy velvet loveseats flanking the Carrara marble fireplace, matching cream-colored velvet drapes that puddled on the floor, and a rolling, mirrored drinks cart next to a window toward which Catherine stalked.

"Scotch or whisky?" she said, pouring three fingers of an amber liquid into a tumbler. It suddenly occurred to her that she hadn't changed a thing about her mother's house because she had only been living half a life these past three years.

"I'll have what you're having," Sean said, "and add a little cyanide while you're at it. I'd rather kill myself than ever be in the same room with those harridans again. No wonder your Henri took the first plane to Europe when the Vichy embassy was shut down. Escaping from that creature must have been Mission Critical."

Catherine shot an appreciative glance over her shoulder as she poured out a second glass from the crystal decanter and replaced it back on the drinks trolley.

"Look, I was sleeping with her husband, so Alice has some claim to be pissed at me," Catherine said matter-of-factly. "It's Annabelle Arlington who's the certifiably nauseating one."

"But were Henri and Alice ever a happy couple?" Sean asked with genuine curiosity.

"Early in their marriage, he was occupied with coping with all the political upheaval going on at the embassy and back in France during the rise of Hitler. As you heard me say so very impolitely, she got bored and had a prolonged affair with a tennis pro early in the marriage, so I guess they weren't. A happy couple, I mean."

"Man, talk about a pot calling the kettle black."

"Here," she said, handing Sean his glass while pointing to one of the love seats. "Sit down and don't worry about getting dirt on those. I hate white velvet, and I hate this room. It looks and feels like an ice palace. I apologize for not having the energy nor the interest to do anything about this place." She took a large gulp of her whisky. "Doesn't it feel as if we just escaped from the Nazis again?"

"Well, from here on out, we both should make it a point to give that guy McCarthy a wide berth," Sean advised. "If he's palling around with that Arlington beast and Alice—Mrs. Malice-in-the-Palace—that band of furies could create some serious trouble for both of us."

———◇———

Unfortunately, Sean's predictions proved only too true, at least in Catherine's case. The following morning, Annabelle Arlington's newspaper column segued from reports on the latest D.C. party scene to a blatant personal attack disguised as gossip:

"Meanwhile, elsewhere in the city, erstwhile journalist Catherine Farnsworth Cahill Thornton (yes, that Farnsworth heiress of the Minnesota mining family)—recently was awarded a medal by the defunct OSS for her unorthodox wartime activities. One truly wonders why she was so honored, given that my sources say she was once found in flagrante delecto *by two FBI investigators raiding the former Vichy Embassy during a suspicious break-in. Before abruptly*

departing for Europe in 1942, Mrs. Thornton was rumored to be consorting with a known felon from the Atlanta penitentiary and playing the harlot with more than a few embassy staff in our fair city. Others in the know disclosed to me that she's now under suspicion for having collaborated with French Communists posing as Resistance fighters when living abroad on the Riviera. Other sources believe that she returned to America with "virulent Communist sympathies." All patriotic American citizens should be asking themselves: what in the world were the bureaucrats at the Intelligence agencies thinking?"

Catherine threw the newspaper on her dining room table and dialed Sean's home number, praying he'd be the one to answer. He was.

"Did you see that scumbag's column this morning?" she demanded.

"I did."

"You're just lucky she didn't mention you were having lunch with me."

"She's such a name-dropper, she's probably saving me for another column."

"Sean," Catherine said, fighting for calm, "do you think that rat Joe McCarthy would subpoena me as a witness in the Communist witch hunt he's supposedly planning to launch? Every one of us in the joint SOE and OSS operations signed some version of the Official Secrets Act. None of us would be able to clear our names by revealing the things we did to earn those damn medals!"

Sean's voice over the phone was somber. "Yeah, if you or I were ever hauled before a Senate committee, we'd be screwed if we told the whole truth to justify what we did in France, and equally screwed if we honor our oath and keep the classified stuff secret."

"Exactly," agreed Catherine. "And besides, I think Alice is launching a vendetta to do more than just get them to yank my OSS honors—which I honestly don't care about anymore. Senator McCarthy is a lawyer and a former judge. I think Alice is trying to use him and Annabelle Arlington to help put me in jail!"

Catherine had a flash of memory of being locked in a cell with women suffering from TB who'd been beaten in the course of their interrogations. What would inmates in an America prison do to a woman they considered a Commie?

"Welcome to the new post-war America," Sean said. "Look, Catherine, let me see if I can get someone to release the report I filed before I mustered out of the SOE. I related every detail about your absolute heroic mission springing me out of that jail in Nice. I'll try to get it slapped onto Hoover's desk and in front of a few other folks around town. It would be one way to let key people know about your service saving American flyers, to say nothing of blowing up those transformers and railroad tracks, and the amazing ploy you used to save Tamara from being deported to a Nazi prison camp. If I can actually get proof in front of J. Edgar, maybe he'll put a stop to all this nonsense instead of leaking pieces of your personnel file to McCarthy."

Catherine heard Sean chuckle into the phone. "One of these days, though, you'll have to 'fess up to me about 'consorting with a known felon from the Georgia Penitentiary.'"

"My lips are forever sealed about that little incident," she replied, "but ask William Donovan about it sometime." *Especially if Sean was in the C.I.A. now, with the unlikely cover as a fine arts painter*, she thought.

"You mean ol' Wild Bill?" Sean asked.

"The very one."

"And what about that crack you were '*in flagrante delecto* at the embassy?'" he teased. "How did that Annabelle vulture know about an FBI raid you were caught up in?"

"My guess? J. Edgar," she retorted.

"You're probably right," Sean agreed. "He knows where all the bodies are buried in this town, and if it suits him, he can leak just like the rest of Washington."

Catherine gripped the edge of the dining table to stop her hands from shaking.

"So, has Hoover become best buddies with McCarthy?" she wondered.

"The Senator from Wisconsin may think Hoover's his pal, but J. Edgar's got files on everybody. At some point, Catherine, the freshman senator has got to be worried about all the things Hoover probably has on him and his creepy sidekick, Roy Cohn. Especially if Hoover learns from powers higher up on the food chain that your wartime service was pretty damn amazing."

Catherine gripped the telephone receiver more tightly. "You are forever my *faux frère*, Sean Eisenhower. If anyone can get me out of this nightmare, it's a guy with your smarts and your last name. Meanwhile, guess where I'm going?"

"Now, Catherine," Sean said, his voice revealing concern, "is that such a good idea?"

He knows I'm going back.

"Believe me, I accept that after three years' silence, Henri very likely was one of the prisoners machine-gunned to death at Avenue Foch or was sent to the crematoriums at Dachau or Auschwitz or some other terrible place like that."

"Then why pick at that scab?" Sean asked gently. "Why go back where you'll just feel Henri's loss all the more?"

"I cannot stand Washington anymore!" she exclaimed. "The back biting. The power plays. I miss France. I want to go to see where Henri was from," she said, her voice catching. "I want to know about the place he spent his earliest childhood...and where he grew up before learning to fly for France in the First World War. I want to visit the part of France that he called home and that you and I never saw."

"Where is Henri from, exactly?" Sean asked. "I thought you rode that bike of yours along the entire Côte d'Azur."

"Only ever as far as Marseille," she replied. "I remember Henri telling me about Perpignan, where his family had their main residence. He said it was a town much further west of Marseille, right near the border with Spain. He loved it as a boy. I want...I just want to honor him by going where he was happy." She fell silent.

"Catherine?" Sean asked over the phone. "Are you still there?"

"Yes," she answered barely above a whisper. "And I want to give any surviving family members my medals, so they'll know what a hero he was. I think I just need to put a period at the end of the sentence."

"Want me to go with you?" he asked, his upbeat spirit roaring through the receiver.

Catherine felt like crying and laughing at the same time. How often had Sean volunteered to guard her back? "You never, ever give up, do you?"

"No, and I probably never will, Catherine, my love." After a long pause he added, "Yes, you should go. Go back to France and see what you find."

"Hopefully, some peace?" she ventured with a numbing sense of sadness that she couldn't seem ever to shake.

"Maybe saying goodbye to him where you know he had been happy will make a difference?"

Catherine heard in Sean's voice the kind of steadfast affection she'd always yearned for from members of her own family. Sean *was* her family now.

"You are the absolute best, *Monsieur* Eisenhower."

"Look, kiddo…I'll have you in my life in any way I can. Maybe it's a swell idea right now for you to blow this pop stand. It worries me, too, that McCarthy is nosing around, and Miss Arlington is such an out-of-control viper. I think the country's in for a bad time with this McCarthy character. But don't worry."

She could almost see him flashing his mischievous grin into the phone, a smile she had so depended upon when they were together in France. His voice, warm and reassuring, offered a scintilla of hope.

Sean said, "I'm going to keep working on my end to persuade a few folks I know in the Justice Department and elsewhere to convince *Herr* Hoover that, when it comes to the mysterious *Madame* Colette Durand, it's in his best interest to call off the dogs."

———◇———

At 6:00 a.m. after an all-night flight, Catherine stood wearily in Orly Airport's baggage claim area, waiting for her suitcase to appear with the rest of her fellow travelers' luggage. It had been a long, turbulent trip from wintery Washington to Paris, where the City of Light was cloaked in arctic temperatures similar to the place she'd just left. Sean had seen her to the airport on this quixotic adventure, and now that she'd landed, it suddenly hit her that she'd be utterly alone for Christmas. Alone and in Perpignan, a city she'd never been in, haunted by the memory of someone she hadn't seen in three years.

Just then, a group of men, all dressed in leather flight jackets and carrying helmets that air corps pilots had worn in the previous war, strode in from a side door marked with a sign and an arrow: TO PRIVATE PLANE TERMINAL.

They chatted for a moment, casually saluted each other, and then scattered in several directions, one shouting over his shoulder, "See you at the air show in April, Lucien, but try to avoid a collision next time, will you please? You came awfully close."

"Just stay out of my flight path," retorted a tall, handsome figure with dark wavy hair and broad shoulders.

Catherine, standing only a few yards away, felt her breath catch and could only stare. How could she forget the sight of former agent Gilbert, who had originally been introduced to her as Lucien Barteau in the black-tiled bathroom at SOE headquarters in the early summer of 1942?

This cold December day nearly five years later, the man almost seemed to sense her intense gaze and turned around. Like the other pilots who had apparently just returned from an air show in some region where the sun was warmer than northern France, he was clad in a well-worn leather flight jacket and knee-high leather boots. As their eyes met, Catherine could see that he looked for all the world like the daredevil stunt pilot Henri had said Barteau had been in his younger days. He hesitated a fraction and then strode to her side, addressing her in French.

"I know you," he stated flatly.

His dark eyes scanned her up and down from her shoes to the beret she was wearing for sentimental reasons. His inspection almost felt to her as if he were some Nazi functionary checking papers at a border crossing. A Nazi who'd like nothing better than to get into her knickers prior to executing her.

Barteau paused as if trying to decide if she were an apparition. "I *know* you," he repeated, "but how can that be? I was told on excellent authority that Colette Durand died at the hands of the SS in the Nice jail. Yet here you are." He pointed a finger at her. "And aren't you also the woman I met in that crazy bathroom-waiting-room at SOE headquarters at Orchard House in London?"

So, he remembered that odd introduction just as clearly as she did.

Shocked as he was that they should meet like this, Catherine remained silent, her mind turning as fast as Lucien Barteau's.

So, Monsieur Barteau heard I'd died in the Nice jail—which was the story I wanted the Germans to believe—but from whom?

Former SOE agent Gilbert was smiling now, but his expression exuded little warmth. He said unconvincingly, "How miraculous you're alive. And how wonderful!"

Catherine inhaled to steady her nerves and continued to meet his stare.

"And you are Lucien Barteau, also known as Agent Gilbert," she replied, deliberately revealing she knew his code name and putting him on notice that she was no shrinking violet. She remembered so clearly his being escorted into the strange waiting room where she and Henri were perched on the edge of the tub prior to their interviews with Buckmaster and Atkins. He had undressed her with his eyes then, just as he was doing now. Summoning a cool, appraising tone, she added, "You said that day we met in London that you'd flown for the *Air Bleu*. Am I right that you've now resumed your career as a stunt pilot in an air circus?"

She noted the look that flitted across Lucien's face was one not only of surprise but perhaps even fear. The question she really wanted to pose was, *"And aren't you the double agent so many SOE people suspected you were?"*

Barteau shifted his leather helmet from one hand to the other. "Ah, so you know my code name and about my earliest flying? You must have had some very high clearances at SOE."

"After the war, I scanned many a photo and file of our agents, the survivors…and those who never returned," she replied.

"And why was that?" he asked, his apprehension palpable.

She offered a faint smile, hoping to unnerve the man even more. "I'm afraid I can't really speak about that. The Secrets Act, you know."

Then, the thought struck her that perhaps she could learn something about Henri's last days from him. She summoned a more friendly expression and said with a note of apology, "I guess now it's all right to say to a fellow SOE agent that Francis Cammaerts was my circuit leader who was dropped near Paris during one of your operations. He sang your praises for the efficient way you moved aircraft on and off those farmers' fields."

Oddly enough, Cammaerts, code name Roger, *had* spoken about Agent Gilbert as a highly skilled air operations manager. Yet, Henri had told her the night he'd dropped into Villefranche that Roger, too, had instinctively thought something was fishy about Lucien's arranging a landing zone practically next door to a camp run by Nazis.

Catherine's mind was ticking over, and the puzzle pieces were beginning to click into place. Lucien Barteau had been introduced to Catherine Thornton at London's SOE headquarters, but how had Agent Gilbert learned that Colette Durand, whose code name he wouldn't have known, had reportedly died unless some SS person had told him? Even more damning, no one in the SOE, post war, would have informed Lucien differently, because they wouldn't trust him with that information. Vera Atkins had written Catherine that there had been a hearing about Lucien's physically assaulting certain people and acting as a double agent for the Germans, but that there hadn't been sufficient witnesses or enough damaging documents to carry the inquiry further.

Barteau could be a very dangerous man if he thought someone had proof he'd been a double agent…

"Ah, yes. Francis Cammaerts," Lucien murmured. "Agent Roger, as you called him. A good operative. I've been told he made it through the war."

No thanks to you, she thought. But Catherine merely nodded. She found it astounding that she should run into a person suspected by some in SOE to have been sporadically reporting to Hans Kieffer at 84 Avenue Foch—for money. Here she was with barely one foot in France and she'd encountered one of the last people still alive who had been in the same Paris interrogation center as Henri. Chances were excellent, though, the arrogant Lucien Barteau had most likely been a Nazi informant. A snitch. A traitor and a Judas to his own country for his thirty pieces of silver.

Lucien set a duffle bag onto the floor near other pieces of baggage awaiting their owners just as Catherine spotted her own luggage arriving. He said, "You must tell me the story of your escape from German clutches. I was told there was even a death certificate with your name on it, along with your clothing."

"Sadly, my purported heroics are hidden in some file stamped *classified*," she replied with what she hoped was a wry but genial answer.

Her next thought struck her like lightening. If this ominous but dashing figure—whatever his loyalties had been—knew what the Germans thought had happened to her, did he also know what had ultimately happened to Henri?

"That day I met you in London," she ventured, "I thought for sure you'd end up in the RAF, but you choose the SOE. Why was that?"

"You have an excellent memory," he said, dodging her question. Instead he asked a question of his own. "And what brings you to back France?" he asked, continuing their game of cat and mouse. "Or did you never leave at all and you're in Paris for the holidays?"

She offered her most ingratiating smile, gazing up at him through her lashes. "I returned home to Washington in forty-four. I'm just here for Christmas."

"Ah, a sentimental journey."

"I guess you could call it that. And you?"

The corners of Lucien's eyes crinkled with amusement that struck her as false. "Well, that is quite a long story too," he replied, "but one that should be told over a coffee. I'm curious to hear how you got yourself into France during those perilous days since you weren't ferried in on any of the flights I oversaw." He glanced at his watch. "It's nearly noon. Do you have time for me to buy you lunch and a glass of wine instead of coffee in the terminal?" His eyes sought hers with a message that assumed she was as instantly attracted to him as he pretended to be to her. "Are you catching another flight, or could I take you to a charming place I know in the city? Our meeting like this is really rather remarkable, don't you agree?"

Two can play this game.

Catherine tilted her head to one side and said in her most beguiling fashion, "I have a flight in two hours," she said, taking a hold of her single piece of luggage. "But if you're sure you have the time, I'd love at least to have a coffee with you."

As the two walked through the passageway with Lucien carrying her bag, Catherine was experiencing a well-remembered feeling of danger being just around the corner. Surely, meeting with the man in a public space full of people was a safe way for her to speak with someone who might know more than she did about Henri's fate at Avenue Foch. Despite the queasy feeling she got in Barteau's presence, this might be the only chance she had to quiz him about what he knew of those last days of the war before the liberation of Paris.

Like so many others who had betrayed the trust of their comrades, Barteau's treacheries hadn't been proved in a court of law. Even so, Catherine strongly suspected that Henri had been right: that he was a man who might have been responsible for the deaths of numerous fellow agents. One more life—her own—wouldn't matter to someone like him if he thought she might jeopardize his own safety.

Catherine made a show of casting her eyes down as if hiding great sadness, a grief that she actually felt deeply.

"You know, Lucien," she said as they walked side by side, "I left France with so many unanswered questions about the agents I worked with, and it's haunted me ever since." She gave him a beseeching look, as if somehow she considered him a knight in shining armor and not the consummate liar she now knew him to be. "One of my hopes on this trip is to track down those colleagues who are still alive. Perhaps they'll be able to fill in some blanks."

"Ah, *oui,* it is at least a beginning," he replied, nodding as if he heartily agreed with her sentiment. "I've been troubled by many of those same questions." He squeezed her arm. "What a lucky man I am to have run into you like this."

Catherine silently replied, *Oh, no Monsieur Barteau, I am the lucky one…*

CHAPTER 48

Catherine kept an eye on the clock from her perch among the small collection of tables in the airport, where coffee and an odd assortment of cold cuts were served. She was conscious of every precious minute she had to learn as much as she could from the former agent Gilbert, whose very presence made her skin crawl.

As they waited for their order, Lucien volunteered, "I own my own plane now. A single engine vintage Sopwith Snipe from the Great War. I'm competing in airshows until I can sign on with a commercial airline. Perhaps I can fly to meet you somewhere during your visit and we can compare more notes on finding old friends?"

"Well, my plans are fairly fluid, as you can imagine," she replied, avoiding giving him a direct response, "but what an amazing life you must have now performing in those airshows."

Lucien described the recent air circus in Spain where he'd flown the WWI-era Sopwith. "Everyone there said I did the most dangerous tricks of any of the pilots."

"You can do those barrel rolls and loop-the-loops in such an old plane?" she said, hoping her expression was full of flattery.

"It's a rotary engine with nine cylinders. Thanks to that, I specialize in flying upside down, but the swine running the show paid me the same as all the others." Lucien bemoaned the fact that the commercial airlines were still struggling to get up and running and few French citizens had the funds to fly. "There aren't jobs even for veteran pilots like me, so I do what I can to get by."

Catherine nodded to convey sympathy and then tried to steer the conversation to the subject of Avenue Foch.

"I'm surprised you recognized me after all this time. We only met that once."

Lucien looked as if he were about to reach for her hand across the table, so Catherine took a sip of her coffee, keeping her other hand in her lap.

"Ah, but we also met at the Ringway Airfield, don't you remember? It was the day you earned your parachute wings." Catherine had hoped he hadn't recalled that occasion. "How could I ever forget that crown of amber hair and those amazing green eyes of yours, *chérie?* And your voice, well..." His glance of appreciation was either sincere, Catherine thought, or very practiced when it came to women. "I still can't get over the miracle that the reports of your death were untrue."

"If only that were the case for our comrades," she said.

Oddly enough, it was Lucien who brought up the subject of Henri Leblanc, which set Catherine's nerves on edge again.

"Whatever finally happened to that man who was with you that day when we met in the ridiculous waiting room at SOE? You seemed to know each other rather well."

Catherine pursed her lips and offered a small mew of acknowledgement.

"Henri Leblanc? He was a press attaché in Washington when I was a reporter for an American newspaper. We knew each other from that circle, although I must confess I was amazed to learn he was being recruited by the SOE."

"They were pretty desperate for French speakers back then," said Lucien dismissively. "He'd worked for the Vichy, I'm told."

"That day you and I met," she said, "*Monsieur* Leblanc was whisked away from Orchard House by the time my interview with Vera Atkins was over. I never knew where in the world the SOE sent him," she lied.

"Paris," Lucien said abruptly, and she could tell he instantly regretted revealing he knew that fact. He paused and regarded her silently. She could practically hear him formulating a way to probe her for what *she* knew, if anything, about Henri's final days. Confirming her suspicion that Barteau knew more about Agent Claude's clandestine life than he would if he wasn't a double agent collaborating with the Nazis, he said, "I heard Leblanc ran some bogus printing operation in Paris and was later caught turning out an underground news sheet that, predictably, got him arrested by the SS."

"Really?" Catherine continued, deciding to play out her fishing lure a little more. "When I was on the SOE team after liberation, searching for missing agents, his name turned up on a list of SS-captured prisoners. All that was known was that he was taken to Avenue Foch." She watched Barteau closely, curious as to his reaction.

Lucien shrugged a shoulder. "I imagine he was. Avenue Foch was the ultimate address when Allied secret agents got caught."

He knows! He knows, at least, that Henri was arrested and brought to Avenue Foch because he frequented that address too—having cozy dinners with Hans Kieffer!

Catherine was eager to ask more direct questions but feared that would tip him off that she knew he had been under suspicion by both the Americans and the SOE.

Changing the subject to catch the pilot off guard, she asked, "Speaking of the SOE interviews in London, did you ever meet Miss Atkins?"

She knew full well he had, and that Vera had a poor opinion of Lucien Barteau.

The good-looking man wrinkled his prominent nose and scowled. "Oh, her? That glorified secretary of Buckmaster's? Did you know that she was actually a Polish Jew? Lucky for her she only saw duty in England."

And you would have probably been the one to turn her over to SS criminals like Hans Kieffer.

Catherine pulled out her plane ticket and glanced at the time stamped on it. "Oh, glory! I only have a few more minutes. But I'm curious. I'm amazed you never personally ran into Henri Leblanc in all the time you were working with the SOE in and out of Paris? I never heard a word how he even got into the country after he left England," she lied again, "although I expect he arrived by parachute or landed by Lysander, like so many others."

"I never knew," Lucien demurred, and Catherine once again confirmed for herself what a perjurer he was. Henri had told her all about his emergency trip to London, due to his faked illness, that

Lucien had supervised. And then there was that near-fatal day when Henri and his deputy whisked Roger Cammaerts and another newly arrived agent into Paris, barely avoiding arrest at a landing field—personally selected by the former agent Gilbert—positioned next to a Nazi camp.

Catherine summoned a puzzled look. "After the liberation of Paris, it was so tragic that no trace of Leblanc was ever found, even though it was known, as I said, he was taken directly to Avenue Foch when the SS arrested him." She waited, and when Barteau remained silent, she said, "We did hear unsubstantiated reports that many of our people were shot there just before the Germans abandoned the city."

"Well, you know how it was. Rumors flew everywhere after liberation. Like nearly every surviving agent in Paris, I had heard that a bunch of SOE men died at Avenue Foch right at the end, but I never knew for sure."

"And women agents, too," Catherine added, regretting the tart note in her voice. Every fiber in her body told her Barteau knew more than just rumors, but she had no more time to poke and prod. For the first time, she noticed an angry scar on his neck.

Tilting her head to one side, she noted, "That's a pretty serious wound you received there on your neck." She hoped her sympathy sounded sincere. "A badge of honor from the war?"

Lucien gave a harsh laugh. "I suppose you could call it that, along with the one on the back of my head when I was slammed against a metal sconce attached to a wall." He stared at her steadily. "I was attacked by an enemy who tried to choke me to death."

"Good heavens! But you survived, thank goodness. Was it a long recovery?"

He nodded soberly. "I was taken in a coma to hospital in Paris right after D-Day. They cut open my neck and stuck a tube in my larynx to get me breathing again. I completely missed the liberation of the city."

"Your SOE assignments must have been pretty intense to have exposed you to hand-to-hand combat like that."

Lucien sat up straighter in his chair and pointed to the puckered skin on his disfigured neck. "That fight was just one of those moments in a war." His eyes narrowed. "You know, pretty much everyone knew back then that I was the SOE's Air Operations Officer and coordinated flights in and out of France. Yet, you didn't?"

Catherine felt she was tip-toing across a tightrope stretched over a wide chasm and that any moment she might fall into the abyss.

She affected a shrug. "In the end, I never parachuted into France, nor flew out, so I suppose that's why you and I never met again." She decided to give him a bit more information to see where it might lead. She smiled up at him as if trusting him with a confidence. "I guess now it doesn't matter anymore if I tell you that I was inserted into the South of France from a *felucca*, a Portuguese fishing boat, out of Gibraltar. And believe it or not, I left France by swimming out to a waiting American submarine! All that parachute training was for naught," she said with a depreciative laugh.

"You were taken out before D-Day?"

Not the one you think.

When she nodded, Lucien gave her an odd look. "Did your fellow American that I also met at Ringway—Viv I think her name was—survive the war? I scheduled her flight to France. Bad weather kept the Lysander from landing, so in the end, she parachuted."

Catherine's mind raced to protect Viv from ever seeing this creature again. She shook her head as if full of regret, flashing on one of the most important lessons she'd learned in her SOE spy craft training. "I never saw her after parachute school."

Lies that are close to the truth are the most plausible.

She and Vivier Clarke had spoken several times on the phone recently but had yet to meet up, so truthfully, she hadn't *seen* Viv.

Lucien said, "Well, the fact you infiltrated France on a fishing boat explains why our paths never crossed." He paused, then volunteered, "Leblanc, I was told, was sent down to the Riviera to survey German emplacements prior to the invasion down there. And you say you never ran into him even then?"

It was obvious to her now that the freak happenstance of Lucien Barteau recognizing her at Orly Airport had prompted him to speak to her for one reason only: to know what she might know of his connections to Henri, who warned Catherine of Lucien's double dealing with the Nazis during the war. She could plainly see that, because of the link he'd sensed had existed between Henri and her when they'd all met in London, she might have later learned something of Lucien's betrayal of either Henri or the dozens of other Joes that had been arrested soon after they landed on flights organized by the SOE Air Operations chief.

He wants to be sure no ghosts will rise that could land him in a war crimes trial.

A chill crept down her spine. A former Nazi collaborator would murder anyone who might possess information that would destroy him. Catherine suddenly wanted to get as far away from Lucien Barteau as she could.

"Well, I'm afraid I must head on out," she said pleasantly. "What a lovely coincidence that we should meet like this."

Lucien reached across the table and pointed to her airplane ticket as Catherine slid her train ticket to Perpignan that lay beneath it into her purse. "You're going to Marseille?" he said with glance that demanded she not look away, "Look, Catherine…I'd like so much to see you again. Please do take me up on my offer to fly my plane to meet you sometime during your visit here. You can telegraph me care of the private plane hangar here at Orly."

"What a kind offer," she murmured. "I'll keep that in mind if the timing could work out," she replied, summoning her most coquettish smile.

Lucien studied her plane ticket before handing it back to her. "Gate Seven. Let me walk you to your flight."

———◇———

Catherine's Paris-to-Marseille flight had been in plenty of time to catch her train to Perpignan. She stepped off the first-class coach at the station into bright blue skies and winter sunshine. Her first thought was how glad she was to be rid of the chilling presence of Lucien Barteau. She felt relieved that he seemed to accept her sentimental journey excuse for being back in France, and she'd managed to get away from him without betraying her ultimate destination or that she knew about his activities as a double agent. She'd even evaded making a specific date to rendezvous with him, so perhaps she hadn't lost her touch.

Because if he even suspects I can corroborate any of his crimes, he'll kill me, even though the war is over.

Despite the sun's bright rays, the nip in the air in Perpignan thrust her back to earlier December days when she and Sean had ridden their bikes in and out of Nice and Cannes on various missions. Upon her arrival, the stationmaster gave her directions to the nearest post office, where she hoped to find an address for the Leblanc family's villa.

Even though she'd been told that the post office was an easy stroll from the train, Catherine was glad she'd only brought a small suitcase, as the steep cobbled streets made for difficult walking. She headed up a narrow lane lined with stone houses that were a distinctive orange-red brick color, each structure topped by red tiled roofs more reminiscent of nearby Spain than of the buildings typical of the French Riviera.

It was the day of Christmas Eve, and she knew she should probably locate a hotel to stay in before attempting to find the Leblanc villa. Even so, she felt that a force greater than mere logic pushed her through the doors of the post office crowded with locals picking up holiday mail or belatedly sending it off.

"The Villa Leblanc?" repeated the harried postmaster. "Ah, it's in a very sad state, I'm told, madam. The castle above it is much neglected, too, but probably of more interest to a visitor like you. Built in the nine-hundreds A.D." He pulled a map from behind his desk and spread it out, pointing. "Walk out of our door, turn right, and just keep climbing the hill. The villa will be on your left, just before you reach the high walls of the fortress. The path will continue to take you up to the castle above it."

Catherine thanked him and took her time following his directions, stopping for a coffee at a little café halfway up the hill. She asked the waiter if he'd known anyone in the Leblanc family that owned the villa further up the road. The man paused, as if sizing up Catherine's odd request for information about a family that had clearly been one of Perpignan's leading dynasties.

"Everyone here knew the Leblancs. They were rich, and their sons carried on the proud tradition of defending France and freedom of the press." He regarded her carefully. "Why do you ask?"

"I knew one of the sons…during the war."

"Which one?"

"I only knew Henri. Henri Leblanc."

The waiter gazed at her somberly.

"You'll find him very changed, I'm afraid, if he'll see you at all."

Catherine's nearly empty coffee cup fell into its saucer with a clang.

"What?" she managed to say with a strangled cry. "Henri Leblanc? A man in his late forties? Tall? Salt-and-pepper hair? He's *alive?* Here in Perpignan?"

"I thought you said you knew him?" the waiter declared accusingly, as if he were a protector of an ailing member of the respected Leblancs. "He came here a broken man, *mademoiselle.* Shattered, some say. He's still not well. A recluse, I guess you'd have to call him."

"When did he come here?" she demanded, a rush of anger and anguish making her want to scream. She'd been looking for him all this time, and Henri had made absolutely no effort to find *her?*

"He arrived in a sorry state right after the liberation of Paris," the waiter said. "Refused to speak to anyone. Never came down to the village. Some old lady who knew his mother brought him food for years." The man who'd served her coffee halted his narrative and demanded, "Who are you?"

"Someone who worked in the Resistance with him," she managed, her voice sounding fraught to her own ears. "I came to honor his memory," she blurted, her throat feeling like a vise about to close off all her air, "because I thought he was dead."

"*Mon Dieu,* what a shock this must be to learn..." his voice trailed off.

"You say he's not w-well," Catherine stammered, still trying to take in the waiter's assertion Henri was alive. "Was he wounded? Physically disabled? What will I find if I go up that hill?"

"No one has seen him except the old lady, and she will only say he was tortured by the Nazis and to leave him alone." The waiter looked at her sympathetically, warning, "It's Christmas, remember. A difficult time for many around here. You may not get the reception you expected, even as a former comrade in arms."

Catherine ignored his gentler tone. The reaction that had grabbed her by the throat was one of feeling like a complete fool. She'd mourned for Henri for nearly three years. And, yes, he may have emerged from the war a shattered remnant of his former self, but so was she in some ways. Yet he'd made no attempt whatsoever to find her, and in all that time, she'd been suffering like a lovesick idiot. Like a woman who had never learned a thing from the series of betrayals at the hands of every single man she'd cared about from her distant father to Lieutenant Peter Farley, to...to....

She jumped from her spindly wire seat, knocking the chair to the stone pavers. Throwing some money on the table, Catherine made a lunge for her suitcase and set off at dead run, her heart nearly exploding. The lane grew steeper and increasingly more twisting every fifty yards or so until, finally, she caught sight of a large house. This one also had a red tiled roof but with walls made of smooth, ochre-colored plaster and a tiled plaque embedded in the wall near a wrought-iron gate stating, "*Villa Leblanc.*" Part of the rusted gate was hanging off its hinges, and one end of the house was caved in, as if it had taken a direct hit from a falling bomb.

Catherine came to a halt just inside the gate, gasping for breath as she let go of her suitcase and heard it drop with a thud. She slowly circled the large, walled-in property with the castle looming above, casting shadows on sections of the grounds. She listened for any sign of life but heard nothing except absolute stillness in the tall, overgrown weeds choking what must have once been a formal garden.

As she came around the far side of the yard, she spied what probably had been the groundskeeper's quarters or an outlying cottage for the Leblanc's chauffeur or some other servant. In contrast to the grand villa, it was made of Perpignan's indigenous reddish stone boulders, like the small houses throughout the town, and was capped by another of the area's distinctive red-tiled roofs. Deep-set windows with wide stone ledges framed paned glass squares. Each one was dark, except for a solitary light weakly shining inside. More weeds pressed against the base of the cottage walls, and the path to the thick wooden door was likewise strewn with tall grass, except for a thin trail where someone occasionally tramped in and out of the forlorn structure.

Catherine's breath caught as she raised her hands to the cold glass and framed her face, peering through the window. A man with an unkempt beard sat in a battered brown leather chair that clearly had rested in the impressive villa during better days. His shoulders and upper body were swathed in a blanket against the obviously chilly interior. His feet were minus shoes or slippers but were instead swathed in white cloth, as if he'd just come in from walking in snowdrifts. Catherine squinted to try to get a clearer view. Was it a disheveled family retainer? A former chauffeur or gardener living in this hovel?

On a small wooden table by the man's side sat a bottle of some sort of spirits, along with a glass half full of amber liquid. A black and white cat was curled in a ball on an unmade bed. Beyond that chamber, everything else was shrouded in darkness.

The man turned and looked in her direction, as if hearing something. Enough light from the window revealed his salt-and-pepper hair.

Yes. Henri Leblanc was alive and in a very sorry state indeed.

Catherine marched over to the front door and yanked it open.

"Merry Christmas, *M'sieur* Leblanc!" she shouted. "Remember me?"

CHAPTER 49

Henri started in his chair, grabbed for a pistol that lay on a table beside him, and stared at the open door.

"Yes, it's Catherine," she exclaimed, taking a step beyond the threshold. "For God's sake, put down that gun. It's me! The woman you never intended to see again, but here I am."

Henri's hand fluttered to cover his eyes and then dropped it into his lap. "They told me you were dead!" he said, barely above a whisper. "That you died of TB in a jail cell in Nice."

"Y-you heard that?" Catherine stammered and took a step back, leaning against the threshold for support. She felt her anger collapsing like an unopened parachute into the chilled air inside the stone cottage.

Henri pulled himself up to stand, swaying slightly. "At Avenue Foch, they showed me your silk blouse. Your tweed jacket. Your death certificate!" He was the one shouting now. He dug into his pants pocket and thrust his hand toward Catherine. "I found my mother's diamond ring sewn in the waist band of your trousers! They said you were dead!" he repeated, anguished.

He fell backwards into the chair once more while, at the same instant, Catherine bolted across the floor and fell to her knees, burying her head in his lap.

"And I thought you were dead!" She had begun to cry. "I searched for you in France for months after liberation," she sobbed. "And in Washington, I pulled every string I could to try to find out what happened to you! And when I finally gave up...when I finally accepted you had died at Avenue Foch or Fresnes Prison or in some oven in a Nazi concentration camp, I remembered you speaking about your home in Perpignan. I-I wanted to come to where you grew up and where your life was once good." She raised her head, seeking his gaze. "When they told me at the café here that you were alive, that you'd been here since the liberation of Paris, I thought...I thought that you hadn't even bothered to—"

"Search for you?" he said, his own voice hoarse as if he hadn't spoken in a long time. "Hans Kieffer used the proof of your death to try to break me and get me to give up the names of your Trenches group and my own Pinwheel network. Lucien Barteau had seen us together in London and showed Kieffer the flight manifest proving I'd parachuted into Villefranche where you'd been. They both thought you were dead! Why should I have looked for you when Hans Kieffer had physical proof you'd died in the Nice jail?"

Catherine could only stare at Henri, thinking that earlier, Lucien had indeed said he'd been told she'd died.

Henri waved the diamond ring he still held in his hand. "Once I found my mother's ring in your clothing, I didn't care what happened to me anymore. In fact, there were times I wanted them to just shoot me." Henri's shoulders began to shudder. He pulled her off the floor and into his lap, wrapping his arms around her while they both were shaken by sobs for several long minutes.

Catherine sat up and wiped her eyes with the back of her hand. "I went to Paris right after liberation. You were on a list of prisoners at

Avenue Foch where there'd been a horrible massacre, but neither of your names, Henri Leblanc or Claude Foret, were to be found anywhere else. I scoured all the information about survivors of the death camps and Red Cross patients for months! Where the hell were you?"

Henri confirmed the harrowing description of how the remaining prisoners on the eve of liberation were herded down to the basement by the Germans and gunned to death in the storeroom.

"I saw those guards with their long guns prodding us into that room, so I dove to the floor before the other bodies fell on top of me, which, as it turned out, shielded me from the deadly spray of bullets."

"Oh God, Henri," Catherine whispered, closing her eyes.

"When I escaped from that hell a few hours later, I could hardly walk because of the beatings I'd gotten at Avenue Foch...and especially because of what they'd done to my toes," he said, pointing to the bandages on his feet.

"What did they do to you?" she asked, her tone anguished.

Henri waved his hand, as if it was of no consequence. "I vaguely remember limping down back alley streets behind Avenue Foch, unable to speak. I was in total shock, I suppose. I don't even remember much of how I got back to Perpignan. I recall somehow making my way to *Gare de Lyon*, boarding the last train allowed to leave for Marseille before the Americans stormed into Paris. Everything was chaos, and the Nazi guards had just melted away. I didn't even have a ticket, but no one seemed to care. It must have taken several more days to find my way to Perpignan."

"Oh my God, Henri."

"And then, when I saw the villa completely uninhabitable and learned my mother had died just the previous month, I crawled into this place and prepared to die myself."

"And when the Allied invasion of the Riviera happened that August?" she wondered aloud, thinking of the villa's shattered wing outside Henri's window.

"I'm sure you noticed the destroyed section of the house. The villa was mistaken for a Nazi regional headquarters nearby built to imprison Allied escapees headed over our Pyrenees mountains for Spain. I wished I'd been sleeping inside when the bomb hit, but here

I was in the old stone groundskeeper's cottage. Alive again, despite it all. An old friend of my mother's brought me food and kept me alive. She died, too, last year."

Catherine rested her cheek against Henri's chest, where she felt comforted by the steady beat of his heart. "For such a long time, I didn't see much point in living either," she admitted. "I kept putting one foot in front of the other these three years. All I really wanted to do was fall asleep and wake up with you beside me in the shepherd's hut."

"The one in the Scottish Highlands?" he asked softly. She nodded, staring up into eyes that held such sadness she wondered if either of them would ever again feel like normal human beings living a normal life. Henri's gaze slid away from hers. "I'm not the man anymore that you loved in Scotland," he said. "I doubt I ever will be again."

She glanced down his legs and took note again that his feet had only soiled bandages wrapped around them. She gently slipped off his lap and knelt once again, placing a hand gently on top of his left ankle.

"What's wrong with your feet? Why are they wrapped up like this?"

"Don't look!" he growled, his voice projecting a dangerous tone that she'd never before heard him use.

"Stop it, Henri! It's me. What happened to your goddamned feet?"

Ignoring his protests, she carefully unwound the strips of cloth until a swollen foot emerged revealing several of his toes that were mere black stubs where Henri's nails had once been.

"Avenue Foch," she whispered. "They did this to you there?"

"And the nails won't grow back because of all the scar tissue from the…from the damage caused by the instruments they used."

"*Merde, merde, merde*! What else did they do?" she demanded.

"This," he said, his tone now matter-of-fact as he laid bare his right shoulder, where the skin puckered in a line that looked to Catherine to be seven or eight inches long and where, clearly, a hot poker had pressed against his flesh.

"I want to kill Lucien Barteau!" she screeched. "Because of him, this happened to you!" And out tumbled the story of her chance encounter at Orly airport only hours before. "That bastard played innocent when I asked what he knew about the fate of prisoners at Avenue Foch just before the Germans retreated from Paris."

"Impossible!" Henri replied with vehemence. "It couldn't have been Barteau."

"Of course it was! I saw him at Orly six hours ago." Henri just stared at her as she continued her tale. "Can you believe that, since the end of the war, that son of a bitch has gotten off scot-free? Miss Atkins wrote to me a year ago that there'd been a hearing about his suspected double dealing, but there wasn't enough evidence to—"

"That could not have been Lucien Barteau you saw," Henri repeated. "I killed him. He came to my cell to tell me he had the flight manifest proving I'd been dropped above Villefranche and had shown it to Hans Kieffer. I went crazy when I thought it might lead them to you. I smashed Barteau against the wall and crushed his windpipe. He didn't make a sound afterward. Two minutes later, the guards were herding us downstairs to the basement. But I *killed* him!"

Catherine rose to her feet and stared down at Henri.

"I asked him about a big scar on his neck," she murmured, stunned by Henri's story. "He told me he was attacked by some enemy soldier and was found in a coma. Apparently, he was taken to the hospital just before the liberation of Paris."

"It can't be," Henri whispered, shaking his head in disbelief. "I left him for dead."

"The Germans must have saved his life, I'm sorry to say."

Henri seemed dazed. "I crushed his windpipe, just as we we'd been taught."

Catherine placed her hand lightly on his shoulder. "He's still very much with us, I'm afraid, and flying in airshows as a stunt pilot now because he can't get work with a commercial airline." She paused for a moment, thinking back on her entire exchange with Barteau. "He accosted me at Orly because he recognized me, not only from that time you and I met him at SOE headquarters," she said slowly. "I had also briefly run into him at Ringway during one of my practice parachute jumps. From his shocked reaction when he first recognized me today, I realize, now, he couldn't believe *I* was still alive."

"No wonder," said Henri. "At some point I'm sure Kieffer must have shown him your death certificate. The SS was after all of us because Barteau had supplied Kieffer the names of every SOE agent he'd ever heard about, you included."

"I could tell by Barteau's questions that he was very anxious to know how much I was aware of the rumors he was a double agent. Whether I had any evidence or knowledge that could reopen the case against him. He seemed extremely eager to learn if you and I had ever communicated about what a Judas he was. I played dumb, of course."

Henri turned his head away.

After a long silence he said, "Barteau knows that I could get him hung as a traitor, and now you know the same about him." He raised his hand once again to cradle his head, muttering, "This war will never be over. There will never be peace or a safe place for people like us." He gazed at Catherine, standing beside his chair. "Look at me," he said, anger lacing his words. "Look at where I am, *who* I am now." He slowly shook his head and repeated, "It will never be over! I am grateful to know you are on this earth, Catherine, but it's no good. I can't—"

"Oh, do shut up!" she shouted, her own nerves at the breaking point. "I'm here. I'm staying here, Henri, and you'll just have to pull your socks—or your *bandages*—up," she amended, knowing how cruel that sounded. She hadn't come this far to be turned away. "No martyrs are allowed in this stone hut, do you hear me? No dramatics that we're not fit to be with each other. We are with each other, which is a total miracle, for God's sake!" She gazed around the hovel that had been Henri's home for three years. "We're both definitely two wrecks, but we'll manage somehow. And here's some news," she said, her hands on her hips. "I long ago deep-sixed the name of Thornton because Jeremy died in forty-three in Buenos Aires. Found out he had cancer and shot himself. My mother died, too. I am now *the* Catherine Farnsworth Cahill, a very wealthy Minnesota Mining heiress, and I intend to use that money to clean up this dump!"

———◇———

For all her bravado urging Henri not to lose heart, Catherine could see that he was a radically changed man. In the short time since she'd shown up at his door, it had become more obvious by the minute how physically and mentally tortured he'd been. Depression, too, had clearly taken its toll, and while she could see he was trying to rally for her sake, she had no illusions that the road ahead would be easy.

The Villa Leblanc itself was in complete shambles. After Catherine made tea and a simple lunch for the two of them inside the stone outbuilding, she determined the first order of business was to make Henri's cottage more habitable. She scoured the big house for anything serviceable or attractive that could cheer up his environment. Several expeditions in and out of the crumbling villa's rooms resulted in useful cooking pots, some lovely pieces of linen from the upstairs rooms, and two pairs of curtains with thick, silk ties that brightened the place immeasurably.

By early afternoon, she settled Henri for a nap, with the cat making room for him on the bed. Grabbing her purse and a basket from the kitchen table, she prepared to walk back down the hill to find the shops near the café where she'd had coffee. The waiter there could tell her where to find the supplies they needed to make life more comfortable. As she was about to leave, Henri stretched out his hand, which she took and then knelt beside the bed that was tucked into a corner of the small room.

"You swear I'm not dreaming?" he said, his eyes searching hers as his head lay on the pillow clad in its newly discovered embroidered linen covering.

"No, it's really me." She smiled down at him and pointed at the pillow. "Do you always keep your service pistol under there?" she asked, noticing the tip of the gun barrel peeking out.

"Now, more than ever. After all, Barteau is still alive," he replied.

"Well, thank heavens he has no idea where you hail from, and anyway, he assumes you died in the basement massacre. I wouldn't spend any energy worrying about his coming here. Besides, it's almost Christmas!"

Henri propped himself up on one elbow. "I'll keep this under my pillow until I feel that what has happened today is real. That you're here to stay despite the chaos you find me in. I'll keep it close by until it feels as if the war we fought so many miles apart from each other is truly over—which I doubt it ever will be—or until I feel I'm not such a hollow wreck."

Catherine offered a small shrug of understanding. "My two and a half years in Washington made me realize how much the war has changed me, too. Sean Eisenhower—"

"Guy de Bruyn?" Henri interrupted, arching a dark eyebrow.

Catherine looked at him sternly. "Yes, my *faux frère*, as I call him. He was the only person I could stand to be around in D.C. because he understood what all of us had been through. He can't tell his wife a thing about his experiences, nor can any of the agents who had personal relationships before they joined the SOE. The nondisclosure documents we all signed have condemned us to perpetual silence, except with each other, which is one of the million reasons I am so happy to be here, no matter what." She bent down to kiss his forehead, thinking of the OSS medals she'd stowed in her luggage. "And now that I am here, you can't imagine what a relief it is to just speak the truth. I love you, Henri. I'm filled with such gratitude for the miracle to have come to Perpignan to pay honor to your memory and, instead, to find you alive!"

"*C'est vrai*," he answered soberly. "Perhaps gratitude is the only path out of this darkness."

"*A bientôt,* my love," she said as she, too, easily slipped into their old habit of speaking a combination of French and English. "See you soon. And that's a promise."

CHAPTER 50

Lucien Barteau stood outside Perpignan's Hotel de France, an impressive nineteenth century building untouched by the war's destruction. The landmark was adjacent to a lush, walled pocket park near the banks of the River Basse. Confidently aware that he cut an arresting figure in his leather flight jacket and boots, Barteau strode toward the desk clerk and offered a perfunctory nod.

"Is a Catherine Thornton registered here?" asked the visitor. "A friend of ours who served in the war with us said she might be staying locally."

He flashed an engaging smile, wondering just how much the stunning American truly knew about his past. Her train ticket he'd glimpsed at the airport coffeeshop before she'd tucked it in her handbag had given away her final destination. Ever since the recent hearing in London where he'd barely avoided arrest for treason, a man with his history couldn't be too careful. She said she'd been on an SOE team searching for missing agents, a fact that had made him realize instantly he needed to learn more about her intentions coming back to France.

To the desk clerk he added, "I'd love to surprise Mrs. Thornton, if I can. We haven't seen each other since forty-four."

The clerk's demeanor brightened in response to the smile of the dashing, distinguished-looking gent Barteau knew himself to be. He watched as the clerk bent over to consult the open guest book, his index finger skimming down a list of recent arrivals.

After a minute of searching the previous page, he looked up and shook his head. "I'm afraid I don't see the name registered, sir. Perhaps she's booked at another hotel, although I must say, we are among the oldest and most prestigious, and one of the few open for full service these days."

"That's why I inquired here first."

"Perhaps you could ask at the post office if *Madame* has received mail since she's been here. That might tell you what hotel she's in or if she's even still in Perpignan."

"An excellent idea," Barteau replied, asking the clerk for directions and offering a jaunty salute as he departed as quickly as he arrived.

Accustomed to navigating his way in the skies, Barteau set off up a winding street past several lovely villas, turning this way and that as per the desk clerk's instructions for directions to the local post office.

After a climb up a steep hill, he was about to ask someone how close he was to his destination when, a few feet in front of him, embedded in a cracked plaster wall extending above him were several rows of ceramic tiles. The words *Villa Leblanc* were painted in colors now faded with age.

He stopped to stare before murmuring aloud, "So, that is why the lady in question came to Perpignan."

She came to this place to pay homage to her dead lover. How touching, he thought, his conclusion dripping with cynicism. But what Lucien feared was her possible knowledge of Gilbert's role in Leblanc's fate, knowledge that could turn out to be quite inconvenient for the man who'd betrayed him.

He pushed open the rusted gate, his sweeping glance taking in the derelict villa and its weed-strewn grounds. If she'd come all this way to Perpignan, he imagined she was bound to stop here as part of her pilgrimage. He'd have a look around and perhaps stake it out and see if she turned up.

To his right, a wing of the main residence had been completely destroyed by what could only have been an explosion or artillery fire during the war. As he advanced farther into the yard and rounded the larger section of the house that was still standing, he caught sight of a stone outbuilding that looked as if it might be the only habitable structure on the property.

Curious that the elegant Catherine Thornton—on a sentimental journey or not—might come to this ruin to pay her respects, he crept toward a window cracked open to catch the mild air of this Christmas Eve day. Cautiously, he peered inside.

"Incroyable!" he whispered under his breath. For the second time in as much as a single day, two people he'd thought were long dead had risen from their graves. Lucien stared through the window at Henri Leblanc, whom he'd sensibly assumed had been killed by the men under Hans Kieffer's command.

Lucien Barteau took a step back from the window. Now he needed worry not only about what Catherine Thornton might have against him but also the damning testimony of a living, breathing Henri Leblanc.

"Merde!" Barteau cursed under his breath. He felt behind to touch the bulge at his waist under his jacket. As was his usual practice, he'd taken his luger from on board his plane parked at a remote section of the Perpignan airport. Here was Henri Leblanc, stretched out on a bed, prone and vulnerable. Compared to a few other times during these post-war years when he had to silence

anyone who could accuse him of sending people to their deaths, snuffing out Henri's life would be easy.

Lucien advanced stealthily toward the door where destiny had so mysteriously brought him. This time, he thought, he had no need for his gun, as a familiar flow of adrenaline set his heart beating faster. He ran his forefinger down the puckered scar on his neck, the only blemish to his otherwise flawless physique. What an unexpected pleasure to deliver a death blow to the bastard's Adam's apple.

———◇———

Catherine's basket was heavy with the fruits of her search in town for household staples, along with something to make for their evening meal. The food offered in Perpignan's open-air market wasn't plentiful on the eve of Christmas, but it certainly was a grand sight better than what she remembered of shopping for food in Nice during the darkest times of the war. As she approached the door to Henri's cottage, she heard raised voices, startled that the reputed recluse had company. As she peered in the window, her heart turned over as she recognized both men standing inside.

She set the basket down on the ground in the villa's weed-choked yard to the left of the door that was slightly ajar. Just past the threshold, Lucien Barteau's leather-clad back filled the doorway, and beyond his shoulder, she could see that Henri was on his feet, his service pistol pointed directly at the chest of this unexpected visitor.

"Well, here's an interesting dilemma," said Barteau. "You're alive, and so am I. And you're still quick on the draw, I see," he added with hint of grudging admiration.

"My ears have long been attuned to hearing snakes in the grass," Henri snapped.

Looking at Lucien's back from an angle, Catherine could see a bulge beneath the former agent's leather jacket where she'd bet he had a pistol of his own tucked into the waistband. Henri must have heard him open the door and, in an instant, leapt to his wounded feet with his pistol drawn before his startled adversary could even react.

Focused on his adversary, Henri hadn't yet noticed Catherine standing just outside the doorway. At least he had known in advance that the double-dealing fellow agent had returned from the dead. And, in former agent Gilbert's case, not only had she risen from the grave, but so, in Lucien's eyes, had Henri Leblanc.

A trio of Lazaruses, are we.

Lucien's voice, low and menacing, seemed to amplify the danger of his next move to counter the threat of Henri's luger pointed at his heart. Catherine imagined their unwelcome visitor would soon seek a way to bring his own weapon into play.

"I must admit," he said, taking a step toward Henri, "my thinking you were among the massacred in that storeroom at Avenue Foch was compensation for the fact you left me for dead that day. Every moment of my recovery from the windpipe you'd crushed, I cursed you to hell."

"And I cursed you for every double-dealing act you committed against France and the Resistance. But you are no problem for me anymore, Lucien, as I can simply shoot you in the heart for the deaths of all the SOE agents your treachery caused."

"It's not war-time any longer," Lucien retorted. "You will be charged with murder."

"Justifiable homicide, when I prove what a traitor you were to France."

Lucien mocked, "Accusations brought against me in Britain went nowhere."

"Ah, but what if, rather than kill you here, I brought new charges to the War Crimes Tribunal?" Henri asked, taking a tighter grip on his pistol. "What if there were more witnesses to your betrayals than just me?"

Catherine watched Lucien take another step toward Henri and was suddenly panicked that the healthier man would simply try to knock away the gun and shoot his adversary with the one stuffed in his belt.

But Henri's words had hit home. "What do you mean *more* witnesses?"

Henri swept his other hand in an arc around the cottage interior. "As you can see, I'm alone here, except for my gun," he said, gesturing with his pistol. "But one of these days, there will be others who will step forward to prove you worked hand-in-glove with Hans Kieffer."

"You mean Catherine Thornton?" Lucien quickly glanced around the stone chamber as if expecting Catherine to jump from behind a curtain. "She's been here, hasn't she? She's told you we met at Orly?"

"Catherine's come and gone. I sent her on her way, as I am not the man she knew. Nor are you, I hope." Amazed to hear Henri's conciliatory tone, Catherine caught her breath at his next words, laced with the fatigue of battle. "You know, Barteau, I am weary of this endless war, aren't you? Why don't you simply leave me be, as I will you, and be on your way? There's no possible path to ever to settle accounts like ours. There never is."

Catherine could tell, by the fact Lucien had failed to act thus far, that he knew, for now, anyway, he couldn't do Henri harm without risking being shot at close range. But later? What could he do to either or both of them in the future if he feared they could one day present their evidence to the War Crimes Tribunal?

Catherine made a split-second decision. She bent at her waist and grabbed hold of a thick, orange carrot nestled in her shopping basket. Silently, she stepped a few feet into the cottage and, in a lightning-fast move, jammed her fake weapon like the barrel of a gun into the back of Lucien's leather jacket.

"Stay right where you are," she ordered. "If you move a muscle, Barteau, you could find yourself wearing a lace doily instead of a flight jacket." To Henri she said, "Sorry, darling, I was a bit late. Can you keep your gun aimed at our visitor's black heart while I relieve him of *this*?" Keeping the pressure on Barteau's back, she reached under his jacket and lifted the pistol from his waistband. She made a second request of Henri. "Hand me that bedsheet of yours, will you, my love?"

Catherine could tell both men were stunned hearing her command, but Henri did as he had been asked. She held tightly to Barteau's gun, pressing its very real barrel hard into his back while tossing the carrot in the corner. Then, with her other hand, she shoved the intruder into a straight-backed chair near the small kitchen table next to an ancient stove.

By this time, Henri had reached back and yanked a sheet off the bed and handed it to Catherine. With Henri keeping his gun trained on their captive at close range, she placed Lucien's gun out of his reach on a table near the door and quickly tied her prey tightly to the chair, wrapping the sheet snugly around his chest. She bound his hands behind him with two corners of the sheet, giving them a vicious yank. "Keep that gun on him a little longer, *mon amour*," she directed, "while I employ these curtain tiebacks to ensure we have *Monsieur* Barteau right where we want him."

Within minutes, she'd securely bound Lucien's ankles to the chair legs and gagged his mouth with a tea towel she'd spotted hanging next to Henri's tiny kitchen sink. Next, she thoroughly patted down their captive, chortling, "And just look what I found!" as her hand felt a lump on his calf. She pulled up Lucien's pants leg and retrieved a long hunting knife and scabbard strapped to his leg, handing both to Henri, who stored them beside Lucien's luger on the table.

"Okay, then, *Monsieur* Commando," she jested, a satisfied gleam in her eye. She spied her abandoned carrot near the sink and picked it up off the floor. With Barteau's gun once again in her right hand, she waved the carrot in front of her captive and noted with a mischievous air, "Here, would you like a snack? Meanwhile, I think those bindings should keep you in place for a while."

Lucien Barteau could only glare impotently at her, his dark brows bristling in fury. She turned to Henri and relieved him of the pistol that she could tell was weighing heavily on his weakened arm and aimed both weapons directly at Lucien.

With a broad smile she said to Henri, "I say we take these and the knife and go down the street for a coffee to decide what we're going to do next with this louse."

———◇———

"Coffee? Are you insane?" Henri protested as he and Catherine passed through the villa's rusty gate.

Catherine turned and smiled. "Getting coffee right now is like thinking that big, old carrot was a gun," she said with a grin. "I *lied*."

"We don't have any money with us and—"

Catherine waved her purse she'd grabbed from her wicker shopping basket that sat outside the cottage door. "You've got the canvas bag with the guns and tools, and I took my wallet when I went to the market, remember? We've got plenty of cash and we can—"

"But why don't we just kill the bastard?" Henri demanded.

"This is peacetime...supposedly," she reminded him. "What Lucien said in there was correct. We don't want to be tried for murder."

Henri leaned heavily against the villa's wall that faced the street, as if he didn't have an ounce of energy left. "Oh, God, Catherine. That bastard! I left him for dead, and even though you warned me he was alive, I nearly lost it when he walked through the door."

"Well, your reflexes are still damn good" she insisted. "You pulled your gun so fast he didn't have time to grab his. Look," she sympathized, "all three of us have had some major surprises today, and you were magnificent." She turned to face him, kissing him full on the mouth, willing him to accept her love and the electricity she felt at their having—together—foiled an enemy, at least temporarily, who was clearly intent on destroying them both.

"You were the magnificent one," he murmured. He stepped back. "Pulling a carrot on a brutal killer like that to trick him into not reaching for his gun. Brilliant!"

Catherine cracked a smile. "Didn't our SOE trainers always tell us to, in a pinch, make use of whatever is at hand?"

Henri's expression grew somber. "Our luck held this time." Before she could respond, his eyes bore into hers with a look of determination that was new. "Obviously the man is stalking you, but how did he know to come to Perpignan?"

Catherine shook her head in disgust. "I can't believe I led Lucien right to you! At Orly, he must have seen my train stub to Perpignan when I pulled out my plane ticket to Marseille. Totally stupid on my part. If you hadn't kept your gun under your pillow, you'd be dead now."

"Let's admit it, we're both a bit rusty," he said, with the first hint of a smile since she'd arrived. "But can't you see? You can't stay here. You must leave Perpignan right away. I can hide somewhere, but he'll work his way free at some point and go stay somewhere until he decides to strike back. I can't risk him coming in the middle of the night and murdering us in our bed."

Catherine gently poked her index finger in Henri's chest. "First of all, get this straight, Leblanc: I'm not leaving you, ever! Besides, I've thought of a way to end this war, and it's based on something you said earlier." She looked directly into Henri's eyes. "Are you willing to join me on one more mission? Because I'm going to do it whether you come with me or not."

Henri fell silent and then slowly nodded his assent. "Lafayette, I am here." Then, "Tell me your idea."

CHAPTER 51

A taxi stopped in front of the gate to the Villa Leblanc, and Henri and Catherine got out, each carrying a canvas bag. Henri relieved Catherine of hers, except for her pistol, and carried both in the direction of the family garage to see if he could get one of the cars to run.

Over his shoulder he said, "We can't very well lead our prisoner into a hired car with his hands tied behind his back. I know planes, but I'm no auto mechanic, so wish me luck."

Catherine held up crossed fingers and headed for the stone cottage, her gun drawn. She reentered the small dwelling with no fanfare and took a seat on the bed, facing Lucien. Still bound and gagged on the straight-backed chair, he had managed to free one of his legs and glared at the sight of her, his dark eyes alight with malice.

"Henri and I conferred over our coffee and a bit of lunch," she began conversationally, "and we've decided we won't kill you because, well, it's no longer wartime. And, besides, as you pointed out, we'd never get away with it. Nor would you, by the way, if you killed us."

Lucien's malevolent gaze gave Catherine chills, but she continued in a pleasant tone of voice, "So, we thought we'd strike a bargain with you. We will be leaving Perpignan to live in America.

You plan to remain in France, hopefully to work for a commercial airline soon, correct?"

Lucien merely continued to glare at her without answering.

"That being so," she continued as if he'd agreed with her, "why don't we both simply agree for Henri and I to keep mum about what we know about your double-dealing with the Nazis, and you will swear to allow us to live out our lives, undisturbed, far from France. There's been enough wartime death and tragedy, don't you agree?"

Catherine took a step forward and removed Lucien's gag. She could tell the former secret agent was surprised by her generous offer of a truce.

Now that his mouth was free, Lucien worked his jaw back and forth before he spoke. With a sullen glare he demanded, "What guarantee do I have you won't double cross me and file charges with the War Crimes Commission?"

Catherine shrugged. "What guarantee do we have you won't fly across the Atlantic some day and kill us in our beds? For there ever to be peace, we'll just have to trust one another one final time. It's the only path possible for any of us."

Lucien regarded her with an expression that was a mixture of incredulity and calculation. "How soon would you leave for America? Washington, isn't it? That's your home?"

"Yes." She nodded toward the window. "As you can see, the villa here would require far more money to restore than either of us possesses, so Henri agreed with me over our lunch that coming with me to the States is the only sensible alternative for him, as disabled as he is from—" She hesitated, finishing, "Well, let's just say that his stay at Avenue Foch did not turn out to be very advantageous to his health—or yours," she reminded him, gesturing to the scar on his neck from Henri's murderous attack.

Lucien swiveled his head to gaze stonily out the window and remained silent.

Catherine raised the pistol that had been resting in her lap and pointed it at Lucien's chest. "Or there's always this," she said casually. "There's a big, overgrown garden out there. No one ever comes around here. If I kill you now, my luck holds, *and* no one hears the shot, Henri and I will bury you before we can wish each other a merry Christmas, and then this discussion will be moot."

She took a step back and made a show of adjusting her aim. "So, what's it to be, Agent Gilbert?" she asked. "Peace, or a renewal of hostilities? Your choice."

Just then, they both heard the crunch of tires on the gravel outside the cottage.

"Ah, there's Henri with the car," she said. "By the way, if you do agree to this—*solution*, shall we call it?—we will be happy to escort you to the train or the airport, whichever you choose, just as long as you agree to leave us alone, and we will do likewise."

Silence hung in the air. His eyes cold and calculating the odds that this was the best offer he was likely to be made if he wished to live another day, Lucien nodded his acquiescence.

"Wonderful," she said quietly. "Just tell us where to take you. Airport? The train?" She paused, asking, "Or perhaps you have a car?"

There was another long pause. Catherine waited patiently until Lucien said, "The airport. You can take me to the airport."

"What airline?"

"None," he snapped. "I'm a pilot, remember?"

Catherine looked at him quizzically and then said, "Oh, how stupid of me! You flew down here in your own plane?"

"Of course," he replied, with a truculent tone.

"Well, then, we will definitely bid you a *bon voyage*—at gunpoint, you understand," adding, "just to be sure you take off and continue flying north."

———◇———

With drawn pistols, Catherine and Henri stood in the shadow of the tin hanger that sheltered Perpignan's private aircraft. Lucien Barteau stood with his hands still bound near a moss green biplane with wooden struts between the wings, an open-air cockpit with only room for one pilot, and a blue, white, and red bullseye painted on its side, denoting it had once been an RAF aircraft.

"A Sopwith Snipe," Henri murmured. "I actually flew one of those in 1918," he remarked as he began to untie the silk curtain cords that bound their captive's wrists.

Before Lucien could speak, Catherine waved their hostage's own luger in the direction of the cockpit and said, "Okay. Up you go."

The stunt pilot instead took a step toward the plane's nose, "I need to—"

Henri jammed the barrel of his gun firmly against the back of Barteau's leather jacket.

"No time for a walk-about inspection for this trip, Captain. Let's just hope you've done the proper maintenance on this old Snipe and have enough fuel to get to your next layover."

Lucien's sour look matched his retort. "If you ever flew one of these as you claim," he said icily to Henri, "you can see that this plane is in as perfect condition as the day it rolled out of the factory." As if having second thoughts about the bargain he'd agreed to, he turned toward Catherine. "How will I know you two have left France for good?"

"You'll just have to trust us, won't you?" Catherine retorted, her patience clearly at an end.

Henri intervened calmly, "I think it's best if we three just declare this a draw, shall we? At long last, let's end this chess game."

Lucien gazed at them both for a long moment and then offered a brief nod. Catherine kept her gun trained on their hostage while Henri untied his hands. Rubbing his wrists for several moments, Lucien gingerly placed a foot in one of the step holes on the side of the plane's fuselage and swung himself into the cockpit. Ignoring his onlookers, he donned his helmet and goggles and fiddled with some dials on the plane's console.

The only sound in the hanger was the faint noise of flicking switches. After a few seconds, Lucien yelled in Henri's direction, "You'll have to hand prop the propeller!"

Catherine held her breath as she watched Henri walk to the nose of the plane and, on Lucien's command, give a sharp tug on the wooden blade with both his hands, jumping out of the way of the propeller's first rotation as the Snipe sputtered to life.

Both their guns still pointing at the pilot's head, Henri joined Catherine's side as the plane rolled out of the hanger toward the narrow grass runway that was a hundred yards away and at right angles with the larger strip used by commercial aircraft.

It was only a matter of minutes until the Snipe began to roll down the secondary runway with a roar, its dark green wings lifting off the ground in the late afternoon sun. By the time Catherine and Henri got into the car to drive back to the villa, Lucien Barteau's plane was a tiny speck in the sky.

On their way back to the villa, they discussed the odds that Agent Gilbert could reappear in their lives. Nosing the vehicle into the Leblanc family garage, Henri urged, "We'd better stay in a safe house away from here for a few days in case the bastard double-crosses us and immediately circles back to the airport."

"As we discussed, that was always a possibility," she answered calmly. "So, I agree. Let's leave here immediately. If he goes back on his end of the agreement, at least he won't find us in Perpignan."

"And if he does?" Henri asked, his brow furrowed.

"How do you feel about living behind a gated mansion in Chevy Chase?" Catherine asked, her tone revealing she still harbored some serious concerns about the plan they'd gambled on. Then she summoned a smile and patted the canvas duffle bag that held her purse with all her traveling money on a day that seemed a thousand hours long. "What safe house do you have in mind?"

"Oh, one in a little village I know near Nice," Henri replied. "I think a room at that old Resistance refuge, the Welcome Hotel, might be nice."

Catherine smiled and said, "Well, I'm ready to go. May I help you pack?"

———◇———

The day after Christmas was filled with bright sun and mild temperatures along the harbor in Villefranche-sur-Mer. Catherine and Henri sat across from each other at a small table at Remy's seaside restaurant, sipping their morning coffee and sharing a croissant.

"I've invited the Mentons and Tamara to come down from the olive farm and join us for a lovely meal here this evening," Catherine said.

Henri nodded, looking pleased. "I've always wanted to thank them for providing the landing field the night I was parachute number thirteen, landing by moonlight at your feet." From across the table he seized her hand and brought it to his lips.

"Well, Henri," she replied, smiling back, "when you write your memoir, I'm sure that little adventure, among a few others, will help make it a bestseller. Let's hope it earns you lots of francs, *mon amour.*"

"You mean when *we* write *our* memoir, my love."

The café owner appeared at their sides and tossed the day's newspaper onto the table.

"Have you seen this?" Remy asked. "Was this man an SOE agent you knew, perhaps?" Just then, he was hailed by another patron. Apologizing to Henri and Catherine, he promised, "I'll just be a minute and bring you *les omelettes.*"

The headline read:

FIERY CRASH OF VINTAGE PLANE

Catherine grabbed the paper and read aloud.

"A 1918-era Sopwith Snipe, often used by airshow stunt pilots in modern times, plunged to earth sometime around December 24th or 25th in a remote area of the Pyrenees just over the border with Spain. Aerial photos of the wreckage show the plane to be a heap of ashes and the body of the pilot likely charred beyond recognition. Authorities are trying to establish the plane's owner, as no flight plans were apparently filed before takeoff.

A Sopwith Snipe of a similar description, owned by air-circus daredevil and former member of a wartime intelligence agency, Lucien Barteau, has not been seen since it departed Orly airport December 24th for an unknown destination. Investigators in Paris say no one has had contact with Barteau since that time. Spain's Transportation Minister, Ernesto Escobar, warns that making both a positive pilot identification and extracting the wreckage from such remote terrain are unlikely, given the steepness and treacherous—"

Catherine stopped reading and lowered the newspaper. Meeting Henri's steady gaze she murmured, "As you said, every aspect of the plan had to go perfectly. And miraculously, it did."

"Amazingly so," Henri agreed. "Perhaps there is justice in this world."

"Actually, not amazing," Catherine countered. "It was because of your knowledge of the Snipe and what would cause a catastrophic failure in flight while leaving no evidence of tampering."

"And your knowledge of Lucien Barteau's enduring belief that he was the smartest secret operative of us all." Henri's solemn expression morphed into a smile. "And here's another piece of luck. You can bet that the Spanish authorities won't bestir themselves for a dare-devil Frog like Lucien Barteau, a pilot foolish enough to crash during a holiday in such an inaccessible area."

"Sometimes I think what happens in this life is always just a matter of luck and fate," mused Catherine.

"Well, the fates were with us, and our luck held," Henri replied. "Yet again."

Without further comment, Catherine, smiling broadly, held out her hand. This time, Henri pumped it in a firm handshake just as their friend Remy approached their table with two plates and a puzzled expression.

"So, *do* you two know this Lucien Barteau?" Remy demanded. "Do you think that's his plane?"

Remy deposited an omelet at each place, and then pulled out a chair and sat down at their table. His patrons returned his gaze across the table, expressionless.

Their former comrade-in-arms declared with a note of exasperation, "But your almighty Secrets Act means you can't tell me why you just formally shook hands...or what, exactly, this is all about?" he declared.

"Only what you read here," Henri said, pointing to the newspaper. "Otherwise, I'm afraid our lips are sealed, *mon ami*," he apologized. "But here's a question: Do you happen to have a bottle of champagne on ice?"

"I have a 1934 *Veuve Clicquot* in the cellar, but, *mon Dieu*, Henri! It's only nine in the morning! Have you any idea how expensive that vintage is, with the shortages still so bad?"

"Never mind that," chimed in Catherine. "Time to celebrate. It's *my* treat."

Their wartime friend stood up from the table, shaking his head with resignation, and prepared to retrieve some champagne flutes and the bottle of bubbly.

In a matter of minutes, Remy popped the cork and filled three glasses. As the trio held them mid-air, Henri inhaled a deep breath and let it out slowly.

"*Finally...*" he said. "Liberation."

"If you say so," Remy sighed, as the three clinked the rims of their flutes.

"To liberation!" they chorused.

———◇———

Later that afternoon, Catherine waited until Henri settled down for a nap in their lovely room at the Welcome Hotel that overlooked the harbor of Villefranche. As soon as she saw he was asleep, she withdrew several pages of paper from the desk beside the window and began to write a report of the type she'd produced for SOE's Vera Atkins when the search was on for missing agents at the end of the war.

The previous twenty-four hours had underscored Catherine's firm resolve to establish a written record documenting Barteau's treachery as a means of honoring those who died in the Nice jail or Avenue Foch, and agents lost like Amory Hyde. It was time to chronicle the truth while there were people still alive to tell it, if only on pages of hotel stationery. As she had so often for Vera Atkins' archives at the SOE, she wrote:

MEMO TO FILE: I, the undersigned, Catherine Farnsworth Cahill (formerly Thornton; a.k.a. Colette Durand, BSC 1940-1942; SOE 1942-1944), swear that what follows is a true and accurate account of events that took place on December 24, 1947. A local newspaper clipping is enclosed."

In the first few paragraphs, Catherine described her chance meeting at Orly with SOE's former Air Operations Officer, followed by an unemotional account of her discovery that Henri Leblanc, a.k.a. Agent Claude Foret, was alive but in a dreadful condition due to his torture by the Nazis. Next, she related Lucien Barteau's following her to Perpignan with the clear intent to kill her and then eliminate Henri after he'd found out that his nemesis had survived the massacre in Paris.

Catherine then succinctly outlined the methods employed to subdue Barteau and the subsequent deal she had supposedly struck with the SOE's erstwhile air transportation specialist: Henri and she wouldn't turn him in to the War Crimes Court if he swore to leave them in peace to live in America. She continued to write:

"We knew, of course, that Barteau would never live up to the bargain and would soon begin to stalk us with intent to kill, along with anyone else he thought might one day produce evidence of his war crimes as a Nazi double agent.

On December 24, we left Barteau tied up on the Leblanc property and went by taxi to the Perpignan Airport, where we'd correctly surmised he'd landed his biplane. Henri Leblanc had also flown Sopwiths in the Great War. Therefore, he knew how to devise a catastrophic failure in flight that could provide the means to successfully dispatch a man who'd escaped prosecution, but who had caused the deaths of many brave members of the SOE and would continue to threaten the lives of other agents who'd survived.

Leblanc knew that three ingredients cause fire aboard aircraft: fuel, air, and an ignition source. The Snipe has a Bentley/2 rotary engine consisting of nine cylinders that spins around within the nose cowling—pistons inside pumping away—which then rotates the wooden propeller that's bolted to it.

With tools from the Villa Leblanc kitchen and garage, an ice pick was used to punch tiny holes in the backs of two of the copper fuel tubes feeding the nine cylinders that drive a Snipe's revolving engine. There would be time to get the plane airborne before the discreet holes would start to leak a combustible spray of fuel. Mixed with the air and adjacent to the hot cylinders, the fuel would then ignite the entire canvas-and-wood fuselage, turning everything on board into a blast furnace.

As added insurance, eight hexagonal bolts attaching the propeller directly to the engine were loosened with a socket wrench. In flight, the vibrations and centrifugal force of the propeller's rotation would shake loose the entire nose section in less than five minutes. Without its propeller, any plane would plummet to earth.

Fortunately, Barteau had no idea someone had been in the isolated hanger an hour earlier, sabotaging his plane. Once airborne, the Snipe's propeller soon sheared off, and the aircraft plunged earthward, catching fire.

The plane blew up just over Spain's side of the border, crashing onto a remote peak of the Pyrenees. We believe that the condition of the wreckage guarantees that no trace of tampering or foul play will ever be found.

As for Henri Leblanc and myself, we view what we have done to be an act of self-defense and justifiable homicide. However, we are weary of the political battles waged at Whitehall, 10 Downing, and 64 Orchard streets between factions within the bureaucrats who fought the late war from behind their desks. Indeed, we and other surviving SOE field agents saw this war in the air and on the ground. We wish the truth will be known one day, but as for now, all we seek is serenity and respite from a war that would never end for us, or for Lucien Barteau's other intended victims, until this murderous, immoral, and soulless man was no longer alive.

To us, justice was served when SOE's Air Operations Officer was incinerated in the crash, just as if he had been put into an oven at Auschwitz—the fate of many whom Lucien Barteau had betrayed. Even worse, he did his despicable deeds with the full knowledge of some factions within rival British and French intelligence agencies.

Further investigation is especially warranted into MI6 about those who were aware of, or sanctioned, the actions of double agent 'Gilbert.'

Whoever may be reading this memo is doing so at a time and circumstance of our choosing.

Yours sincerely,"

Catherine leaned back in her chair, regarded the sheet of paper with the hotel's name printed in raised, blue type at the top of the page, and then reread what she'd written. After a brief pause, she signed her name under the last line, leaving space for Henri to do likewise.

She glanced behind her chair at the man she loved so dearly who was dozing on their bed, his feet swathed in cool compresses to relieve the pain of his blackened toes. Picking up the document she'd created, Catherine folded it in half and stored it, along with the press clipping, at the bottom of her suitcase.

Closing the lid, she thought, *we'll decide what to do with this on another day.*

EPILOGUE

May 1953

The windows of the Villa Leblanc were wide open to the soft breezes of spring.

Catherine appeared on the newly completed terrace that overlooked the restored garden and announced, "Well, after five years of effort and with thanks to Farnsworth Minnesota Mining, the last workman has finally departed with his tools and trowels."

"And all the furniture has arrived?" Henri asked, with a smile of admiration.

"Most of it, and put in its proper place, I might add," she replied.

The renovation project had been a labor of love for the two of them. Henri was fond of showing visitors a corkboard attached to a wall in the brand-new kitchen. Pinned between shopping lists scribbled in two languages and a 1953 calendar was an enormous red, white, and blue "I Like Ike" metal button, a souvenir from the prior year's U.S. presidential campaign. Catherine, thanks also to her mother's estate, had been a major contributor to Dwight D. Eisenhower's bid for America's highest office. Much to her delight, Sean Eisenhower's third cousin once removed, the former Allied Commander, was now living at 1600 Pennsylvania Avenue. Catherine had never imagined that this would create some remarkable ripples in the lives of the villa's permanent residents.

"By the way," she informed Henri, handing him a glass of wine, "your new safe is now installed in your study, and you must remind me to teach you the combination."

"No safe cracker from the Georgia Penitentiary around to help?" he teased.

Beside medals granted by America's OSS, there were now four elegant jeweler's boxes secured in the home safe. Two contained the George Cross medals bestowed on Catherine and Henri by young Queen Elizabeth at a recent ceremony in London. The other two, nestled on velvet in red leather jeweler's boxes, held impressive, multi-colored lapel ribbons as well as a pair of green-and-gold enameled decorations attached to crimson ribbons denoting the *Légion d'Honneur*, tributes awarded to the former agents "who had served to liberate France." In 1946, De Gaulle had stepped down from France's provisional government, which Henri figured was the only reason he and Catherine were granted their due.

They had eventually learned that all this better-late-than-never recognition was courtesy of Sean Eisenhower's efforts. Catherine supposed she would never know what magic wand he had waved to have the powers that be on two continents become privy to several declassified files. The result was that the couple's service to the United States, Great Britain, and France, had been duly recognized with all appropriate public honors.

Also in the safe in Henri's study was a sheet of stationery from the Welcome Hotel in Villefranche and a news clipping about a plane crash, both tucked into a sealed envelope stamped, *"Send to UK/SOE archives after our deaths."* Beside it were the annulment papers signed by Alice Leblanc. Anxious to take a wealthy Wall Street tycoon as husband number two, Alice had willingly attested to documents swearing she had never been baptized in the Catholic Faith, "nor had issue" with one Henri Charles Leblanc. Soon after she'd put pen to paper, the French ecclesiastical authorities magically declared Henri an unmarried man.

Catherine would never forget the day, soon after the annulment decree had arrived, when she'd come to fetch him to walk with her to the open-air market. He rose from his chair on the villa's terrace where he'd been reading the newspaper and slowly bent a knee, putting weight on a foot that still pained him. He held up a gold band that had also been his mother's.

"My darling Catherine Farnsworth Cahill," he'd proposed formally in French, his dark eyes brimming with emotion, "will you please do me the honor of adding this wedding ring to my mother's engagement ring, the one that I gave you a second time when you walked back into my life that momentous Christmas Eve day?"

Catherine had fallen to her knees to face him and held on to both his hands for balance. "Yes. *Yes!*" she'd cried, presenting her finger with the diamond ring already in place. They had embraced, kissed, and struggled to their feet, laughing and crying all at once. The next day, they were married at Perpignan's City Hall.

Tucked into a desk drawer in their reconstructed villa was a tattered copy of a *Washington Post* article by a veteran foreign affairs correspondent. The large, front-page spread was based on the same declassified intelligence documents Sean had somehow managed to legally liberate. They exonerated Catherine of the charges of being a Communist by the now-discredited Senator Joe McCarthy. The lengthy story, written by the *Post* reporter who had been dispatched all the way to Perpignan, also put to lie the innuendoes perpetrated by the disgraced former gossip columnist Annabelle Arlington, who'd quietly been allowed to retire from print journalism. The article was complete with pictures of Henri and Catherine sitting in the Villa Leblanc's garden with two dogs, a black and white cat, and a castle looming in the background.

Sean had scrawled in the margins, *"And get a load of this part!"*

In the third graph from the lead, the story offered an assertion that Catherine might be "the greatest unsung heroine of the last war," according to a quote from now-*Sir* William Stephenson, who'd directed all British secret intelligence, and seconded by an additional quote from Wild Bill Donovan, former head of the OSS, a government department that had evolved into America's Central Intelligence Agency. The article strongly suggested that an operation she *"supervised in our very own city of Washington changed the course of the conflict in ways known only at the Allies' highest levels."*

"Damn it, Henri!" Catherine had complained. "That reporter didn't give you the credit you deserve!"

"That's what you get for marrying a Frog," he'd replied with amusement.

On this spring day, Catherine and Henri took their luncheon served on the terrace that overlooked the back of the house. The scent of lavender surrounded them, as did hedges of night-blooming jasmine. The villa's impressive variety of trees, planted a century before, had been returned to their former glory due to the gardener's strict attention to pruning and watering them these past five years.

Later that afternoon, the arrival of Catherine's ward, Tamara Polakov, was expected after her first year studying international relations at the Sorbonne in Paris. The maids upstairs were also readying rooms for tomorrow's appearance of the entire Menton family, scheduled to spend a holiday week at the villa as well.

Seated at the wrought-iron-and-glass table on the terrace, Catherine filled Henri's wine glass with sparkling rosé, and then her own, holding hers up in a toast.

"Here's to the anticipated disruption of our quiet, gentle life born, some would say, in fire and fury."

In response, Henri raised an eyebrow no longer dark black but now flecked with silver the same color as his hair. "I hope for your sake, *chérie,* it won't be *too* quiet, now that the workmen have finally left."

Catherine inhaled a long breath. "I don't know about you, but there are moments when silence descends that I still struggle to make peace with the past."

"As do I, my love," Henri agreed.

How often had she fought against her imagined vision of Lucien Barteau's biplane, its propeller careening off the nose, and then plummeting to earth with a full tank of fuel, incinerating the aircraft's canvas covering, wooden struts, and the pilot himself, screaming in the open cockpit? Then she'd think of his many victims who, because of his treachery, had met their deaths by firing squad or consumed in blazing ovens at Nazi concentration camps.

Catherine tried to free herself from such disturbing recollections by thinking about the good news that had filtered down to Perpignan. Their fellow agents Odette Samson, Peter Churchill, Virginia Hall, and Vivier Clarke, along with Roger—Catherine's leader, Francis Cammaerts—had miraculously survived harrowing years of service in the last war.

Barely, she thought, *and with no thanks to traitors like the notorious Lucien Barteau.* Only last week, Viv had written from New York saying she was busy penning a memoir about her adventures behind enemy lines in the French Alps, where she'd been assigned after she and Catherine parted ways in spy school. Her letter had roused reminiscences both sweet and sinister.

"My book can't be a tell-all since, like you, I signed the Secret Acts, but when I come to visit you next year, dear spy sister, you can be sure I'll tell you everything, including what I know about that rat, the late and unlamented Agent Gilbert, as well as the true story behind the amazing survival of Peter and Odette, who, as I'm sure you've heard by now, married after the war."

Viv's enduring friendship was merely one of the blessings Catherine counted regularly as a reminder that in her life now, the good far outweighed the bad.

Catherine reached for Henri's hand across the glass tabletop. "Whenever upsetting thoughts intrude from the past, I concentrate on the marvel that, for some of us, our love and friendship survived it all. I am so grateful for this quiet, gentle life we have."

"As am I," he murmured.

Settling back in one of the vintage bistro chairs she'd recently purchased, she pulled out a letter from the pocket of her skirt.

"But I give you fair warning," she announced with a grin. "Better gird yourself, Henri. Quiet won't immediately be restored around here, even after the Mentons return to Villefranche. Guess who's asked to come over?"

Henri closed his eyes and put an index finger on his forehead as if racking his brains. "Let me think. Could it be Sean Eisenhower, his wife, and two sets of twins?"

Sean and his boisterous family had visited a few years previously before the villa was completed. It had been utter chaos, plain and simple.

"Well, you're on the right track," Catherine hinted.

"What do you mean 'the right track?' Are they coming or not?"

Catherine repressed a sigh, sensing that, even now, Henri had difficulty dealing with the strange relationship between Sean and her, a rapport that clearly continued to baffle him. Even though she and Henri had no other secrets between them, Catherine would always keep to herself the brief sexual liaison she'd had with Sean during the war. Sean Eisenhower was and always would be her dearest *faux frère*—and nothing else. Even so, she could plainly see that Henri recognized the ardent admiration radiated by her former comrade in arms.

"*All* the Eisenhowers are coming to Perpignan," she announced, a bubble of pure joy animating her announcement.

Henri sat fully upright in his chair. "Surely not the President—"

"Oh, good Lord, no! I didn't give the campaign *that* much money."

"Then, who?" Henri asked warily.

"Sean and Marilyn just had a third set of twins!"

"A third set? Oh, *Mon Dieu*, that poor woman! What did they have this time?"

"A boy and a girl!" She waved Sean's letter. "They're asking us to be the babies' Godparents, and you'll never believe what they've named them."

Henri teased, "After your American gangsters, Bonnie and Clyde?"

"No, of course not!" she scolded, thrusting Sean's letter into his hands and pointing. "He says here he wants the children baptized in our local church, and he's naming them after two famous, heroic secret agents."

Henri's startled glance met Catherine's. "Who?"

"Claude Foret and Colette Durand!"

"Hmmm. American twins named Claude and Colette Eisenhower," Henri repeated softly. "Well, it's better than a marble marker, wouldn't you say?"

"Yes," answered Catherine, with memories of her baby son whose whereabouts she'd never know. She reached across the table for Henri's hand and pressed it against her cheek.

"It's much better than any stone memorial, my love."

AUTHOR'S NOTE & ACKNOWLEDGMENTS

A work of fiction set in a specific time period such as World War II is by necessity a hybrid. The story is an invention of the author's imagination, but it also must be grounded in historical fact to be convincing to the reader.

For this novel, I was first inspired by a photograph of a French woman, Odette Samson Churchill (married to one Peter Churchill who likely shared a smidgen of DNA with Winston). I saw her picture tacked on a wall in a very modest Resistance museum deep in a valley near Lake Annecy in the *Haute Savoie* in France. The museum is near a treasured spot in the Alps where my husband and I have visited nearly every June for some thirty years. In all that time, I knew little about the French Resistance in that area and had never gone to this pocket museum that looked more like a miniature ski chalet than a repository of true tales of heroism and tragedy.

My French friend, Claire Majola, insisted I would find the museum very interesting, given that much of my writing is based on the question, "What were the *women* doing?" at crucial points in the telling of human history. It was a big surprise to learn not only were there women secret agents who parachuted into France but, as I began to look deeper into the subject, a handful were *American* women recruited by the SOE (Britain's Special Operations Executive) intelligence agency, a pet project of the aforementioned Prime Minister Churchill. A few of these women even had enlisted in the organization *prior* to the United States joining the European war as one of the Allies in the wake of the Pearl Harbor attack in Hawaii.

The year 1995 marked the fiftieth anniversary of the end of

WWII, and many formerly classified archives were finally opened to scholars and researchers. This resulted in an avalanche of nonfiction books based on primary sources that delved into all aspects of that war and made details available to the public for the first time. These works of nonfiction inspired an equal number of novels, including one by my friend Kristin Hannah, author of the spectacular *The Nightingale,* about two French sisters caught up in the Resistance. These fictional works have entertained and enlightened millions of readers during the twenty-plus years since additional secret files have been opened. I was late to the party on this subject but among the first novelists, I believe, to focus on the lives of the few American women involved in the earliest days of British WWII espionage.

Landing by Moonlight's heroine, American Catherine Farnsworth Cahill Thornton, and hero, the Frenchman Henri Charles Leblanc, are *composite* characters. In other words, they are fictional figures based on the historical records of several real-life women and men who served their countries behind enemy lines on the Allied side. In the case of Catherine, many of her harrowing adventures can be claimed by Amy Elizabeth "Betty" Thorpe Pack (code name Cynthia), dubbed a femme fatale in the espionage business. No less than Sir William Stephenson, the director of all British secret intelligence activities, called her WW II's "greatest unsung heroine." Many authorities I consulted agree that Betty Pack's most successful coup—first stealing then copying the naval codes from the Vichy-controlled French embassy in Washington DC in 1942 and returning them undetected—"changed the course of the war" by making it possible for the Allies to track Vichy French and German ships in the Mediterranean and eventually gain control of North Africa. This military success enabled the Allies to launch campaigns up the boot of Italy and then, seventy-five years ago, on August 15, 1944, land by sea in the South of France in a forgotten invasion that rivaled the celebrated D-Day at Normandy.

It should be made clear that the character of Sean Eisenhower is a total creation of my imagination, though based on the power of a family name to alter events. The true-life Peter Churchill's moniker did indeed save two lives when SOE Secret Agent Odette Samson claimed to the SS she was married to a Churchill—an assertion that most likely foiled their death sentences during their Nazi imprisonment.

In my bibliography, I list nonfiction works that helped inform the novel's entire cast of characters—both fictional and historical—as well as the setting and time period, along with most of the missions and daring operations successfully accomplished by these silent warriors. And, yes, dead rats were used to hide explosives! To these scholars, I extend my gratitude and admiration for the enormous debt we civilians in this field owe for their hard work and perseverance in preserving this history.

I also found that my twenty-three years as a print and broadcast journalist equipped me with a very useful skillset to chase a story that occurred some eight decades ago. One of my first stops was the International Spy Museum in Washington, D.C. (www.spymuseum.org), a fantastic place for anyone fascinated by the clandestine arts, as well as James Bond fans who thrill seeing artifacts from Hollywood's version of the spy biz. At the exhibits (and the great gift shop) I gained a wonderful general background on spy and field craft and picked up some helpful books and pamphlets that have been by my computer for two years (plus a small, metal button that says "Trust No One"). The five-part Netflix series, "Churchill's Secret Agents: The New Recruits" proved to be an invaluable source of information about the SOE's various spy schools.

My husband, Tony Cook, a former financial journalist and magazine writer, and I spent an entire summer tracking down locations where many dramatic moments involving the French Resistance took place. We found the exact location where an American female secret agent inserted the pencil fuses linked to explosives that blew up a train storage shed in the town of Annecy at the mouth of the lake of the same name. We followed the trail of French Resistance hero Jean Moulin, the prototype for Henri Leblanc, near St. Remy and environs, and spent ten days tracing the hotbed of Resistance activity from Menton to Villefranche-sur-Mer (where there was indeed a large fishing craft on jacks in the local boatyard that became the safe house in the novel). We nosed around old Resistance haunts in Nice, Cannes, and westward along the Riviera toward Marseille. One memorable day, we visited a village where the Nazis executed all the inhabitants. We also had a private tour of Nazi-occupied Paris, paying close attention to Number 84 Avenue Foch, where Hans Josef Kieffer ruled over life and death in a beautiful *Beaux Arts* building that held terrible secrets behind its elegant walls.

None of these research activities would have been possible without the support and assistance of many friends and acquaintances. Our warmest thanks to Wenke Thoman and William Sterns for the generous use of their apartment in Villefranche-sur-Mer, along with the guidance on all things French from Sylvie Toinard, Claire Majola and Jacques Leblond, Jean-Marie and Pauline Hervé, Winship Cook, Leslie and Geoffrey de Galbert, Steve Barrager, and Sandraline Cederwall. We are grateful, too, for the hospitality of Stéphane and Carole Deloulme in our beloved village of Talloires on Lac d'Annecy in the French Alps that became our base of operations as we followed the trails of the American women secret agents battling to stay alive during a raging war.

Special kudos go to the production team at Lion's Paw Publishing. Peter O'Conner at BespokeBookCovers.com has my heartfelt appreciation for his stunning cover design. Huge thanks, also, to copy editor, Emilee Bowling, and interior book designer/formatter Amy Atwell for their excellent work, and to Paul Hirst, keeper of my cijiware.com. Travel writer Janet Chapman and I found monthly meetings at BAIPA.org (Bay Area Independent Publishers Association) a treasured resource for our projects.

In the U.S., I am indebted to my two "Plotholes" partners (Yes, that's our critique group), novelists Kimberly Cates and Cynthia Wright, who provided encouragement, editorial insights, and friendship during drafts of this work. Huge thanks, too, go to my beta readers Diane Barr, Naomi Fliflet, Donna Christie Kolkey, Maria Paterno, Cheryl Popp (co-owner of Sausalito Books by the Bay), Winship Cook, and my sister, Joy Ware. Members of the Sausalito Women's Club and my fellow hillside dog walkers have played supportive roles in every novel I've written since moving to Sausalito in 2002. My son, Jamie Ware Billett, a single-engine pilot, among several vocations, was my consultant in how to crash a Sopwith Snipe, although I take responsibility if I got any aspect wrong.

The late Cholly Knickerbocker—a stalwart Cavalier King Charles Spaniel of sterling character and impeccable sensibilities—lay loyally beneath my desk throughout the creation of my five most recent novels and, until May 25, 2019, saw me through *Landing by Moonlight* as well. This one's for you, too, Cholly boy.

And, as always, eternal gratitude to my beloved husband and partner in virtually everything, most especially in providing editorial advice and handholding for this novel. We had an absolutely magical time, didn't we, Tony?

I cannot conclude these Acknowledgements without a heartfelt expression of gratitude to doctors Jennifer Lucas and Joseph Poen and their teams at the Marin Cancer Institute for their amazing skill and care in my successful treatment for one of the declared "curable" forms of Non-Hodgkin's lymphoma during the writing of this book. I am well—thanks to them—and can't wait to start the next novel in this Spy Sisters Series!

Ciji Ware
Sausalito, California

Website: www.cijiware.com
Facebook: www.facebook.com/cijiwarenovelist

PARTIAL BIBLIOGRAPHY & RESEARCH PHOTOS LINK

For more information on WWII and the real lives that inspired the characters and settings of this novel, here is a partial bibliography of my research.

Mary S. Lovell, *Cast No Shadow* [Betty Pack a.k.a. "Cynthia"]

Howard Blum, *The Last Goodnight: A World War II Story of Espionage, Adventure, and Betrayal,* [Betty Pack a.k.a. "Cynthia"]

H. Montgomery Hyde, *Cynthia, The Amazing, True Story of the Seductive American Who Spied for the Allies in World War II* [Betty Pack a.k.a "Cynthia"]

Sarah Helm, *A Life in Secrets: The Story of Vera Atkins and the Lost Agents of SOE*

Madeleine Masson, *Christine, SOE Agent, & Churchill's Favourite Spy,* with Afterward by Francis Cammaerts a.k.a. "Roger"

Clare Mulley, *The Spy Who Loved, The Secrets and Lives of Christine Granville*

Jerrard Tickell, *Odette, The Story of a British Agent,* [Odette Samson Churchill a.k.a. "Lise"]

Larry Loftis, *Code Name: Lise, The True Story of the Woman Who Became WWII's Most Highly Decorated Spy* [Odette Samson Churchill]

Peter Churchill, *Duel of Wits*

Sonia Purnell, *A Woman of No Importance: The story of the American Spy Who Helped Win World War* II [Virginia Hall a.k.a. "Marie"]

Judith L. Pearson, *The Wolves at the Door, The True Story of America's Greatest Female Spy,* [Virginia Hall a.k.a. "Marie"]

Marcus Binney, *The Women Who Lived for Danger – Behind Enemy Lines During WW II*

Gordon Thomas & Greg Lewis, *Shadow Warriors of World War II: The Daring Women of the OSS and SOE*

Major Robert Bourne-Paterson, *SOE in France 1941-1945*

Giles Milton, *Churchill's Ministry of Ungentlemanly Warfare*

Bernard O'Conner, *Churchill's Angels*

Maurice Buckmaster, *The Fought Alone, The True Story of SOE Agents in Wartime France*

Jean Overton Fuller, *Déricourt: The Chequered Spy*

Ray Jenkins, *A Pacifist at War* [Francis Cammaerts, a.k.a. "Roger"]

George G. Kundahl, *Riviera at War: World War II on the Côte d'Azur*

Robert Kanigel, *High Season in Nice*

Andrew Stewart, Ed., *Operation Dragoon: The Invasion of the South of France, 15 August 1944*

Jean-Louis Perquin, *Clandestine Parachute and Pick-Up Operations, Vol. 1*

Sarah Kaminsky, *Aldolfo Kaminsky: A Forger's Life*

Cioma Schönhaus, *The Forger: An Extraordinary Story of Survival in Wartime Berlin*

Alan Riding, *And the Show Went On: Cultural Life in Nazi-Occupied Paris*

Landing by Moonlight Research photos:
www.pinterest.com/cijiware/landing-by-moonlight-research-photos/

ABOUT THE AUTHOR

Ciji Ware is a *New York Times* and *USA Today* bestselling author of twelve works of historical and contemporary fiction, two of nonfiction, and was short-listed for the Willa [Cather] Literary Award for Historical Fiction in 2012. A graduate of Harvard University in History, she is an Emmy-award winning television producer, a Dupont awardee for investigative journalism, and an American Bar Association winner of a Silver Gavel for her magazine work. For eighteen years, she was a broadcaster and commentator for KABC Radio/TV in Los Angeles. A recipient of Harvard's prestigious Alumni Award in 2004, Ware was the first woman graduate of the university to serve as President of the Harvard Alumni Association, Worldwide. Ware and her husband, Tony Cook, live in the San Francisco Bay Area.

Look for her popular Four Seasons Quartet books,
available in ebook and print at your favorite online retailer.

www.cijiware.com

Manufactured by Amazon.ca
Bolton, ON